Life Stories

original works by Russian writers[*]

[*] The writers and translators in this volume have donated their creative output
to this collective work, so that all proceeds from its sale
might go to benefit Russian hospice care.

stories for good

For more information about this and our other fine works of fiction,
please visit: **www.storiesforgood.org**

ISBN 1-880100-58-4

Published by **stories for good**
an imprint of
Russian Information Services, Inc.
PO Box 567
Montpelier, VT 05601-0567
www.storiesforgood.org
orders@russianlife.com
phone 802-223-4955
fax 802-223-6105

Пора, мой друг, пора! покоя сердце просит—
Летят за днями дни, и каждый час уносит
Частичку бытия, а мы с тобой вдвоем
Предполагаем жить, и глядь—как раз умрем.
На свете счастья нет, но есть покой и воля.
Давно завидная мечтается мне доля—
Давно, усталый раб, замыслил я побег
В обитель дальную трудов и чистых нег.

It's time, my friend, it's time! my heart begs for peace—
Days fly past, and each hour carries off
Another fragment of our life, but together we
Make our plans for life, and lo—in our time we die.
In the world there is no happiness, but there is peace and free will.
Long have I dreamed of that enviable fate—
Long have I, a weary slave, schemed to flee
To a distant abode of labor and pure delight.

Alexander Pushkin

Contents

Instead of an Introduction

Lyudmila Ulitskaya[1]

Dear Friends!

Today, you and I have no plans to die. Quite the opposite: we make our plans for the years ahead, and much of what we plan comes to pass. We value our energy and our time, enjoy the luxury of good health, take pleasure in being with loved ones, and occasionally even have the privilege to travel, taking in the nature and culture of other lands.

To enjoy life, to be grateful for its gifts is part of being human. But there are things—difficult, distressing, unbearable things like illness, suffering or death—that poison our joy of living. Yet even in this there is something good: it means that our souls are alive and can respond to the suffering of the others; the power of this response reveals to us our true place in the universe. As long as we are capable of empathy, we are morally alive.

---

[1] Author and member of the Board of Trustees of the Vera Hospice Charity Fund.

The natural progression of human life—from youth, strength, beauty and health to decay, illness, suffering and death, which none of us can escape—occurs in a social environment that can either aggravate our suffering or alleviate it. In this dimension, it is not the laws of nature that are at work, but the laws, rules and stereotypes created by our society. And Russian society today presents a dismal picture. Our state, which once assumed responsibility for the social wellbeing of its people, is failing to meet its obligations. Yet we as a community have other reserves—both material and spiritual.

Despite our society's deep inertia and pessimism, more and more of our people are willing to address great social ills. A few years ago, I was introduced to Vera Millionschikova's efforts to organize and manage the First Moscow Hospice, and this became a turning point for me: I realized that, even in our complex conditions, one could do this difficult work in a way that creates meaning and beauty, extracting dignity from the chaos that surrounds us. This is not only about helping people who are suffering and dying—this is about building a better society, about fostering people's respect for themselves. Vera Millionschikova's cause, the hospice center she created, gives us the opportunity to change our lives, to affect our world, to become more human.

Contributing to the work of the Vera Hospice Charitable Fund gives us an opportunity to nurture a noble and necessary cause, to subtract from the great sum of human suffering in our not-altogether-well state. It is also a conscious move to take responsibility for a sphere in which our government appears to invest little meaning or value. Yet, in fact, it is here, in the last hospital bed, that the miracle of human life, that greatest of values, is fully and ultimately present.

TRANSLATION BY NINA SHEVCHUK MURRAY

                                    LUDMILA ULITSKAYA

About Hospice Care

Hospice care is a free institution of social medicine that is completely new to Russia. Hospice care gives terminal cancer patients and their families not only relief from pain, but also other medical, social, psychological, spiritual and legal assistance; services are provided not only for the duration of the illness, but also in the aftermath of the loss of a loved one. Hospice accepts patients that other hospitals have rejected as "hopeless."

In the fifteen years of its activity, First Moscow Hospice, under the unwavering leadership of Vera Vasilievna Millionschikova, has earned an impeccable reputation and has helped thousands of people. When hospice workers care for the dying and educate their families about the basics of such care, they lift the immeasurable burden of guilt plaguing those who do not have time, confidence or knowledge to help a loved one when recovery is no longer possible.

In hospice care, more than in any other medical establishment, the staff work intimately with death, pain and the family's tears, 365 days a year, 24 hours a day.

Hospice cares for the dying, most of them elderly. But the more important thing is that the patients are still alive. What they need is not a speedy death but a dignified life. Like all living beings, they need love and care. There are many such patients; in Moscow alone 23,000 people succumb to cancer every year. And even though Moscow already has eight hospice care centers, the need for hospice care is far from being met. Hospice care is necessary for the handicapped, for coma patients, for those paralyzed as a result of a stroke, for AIDs patients and for disabled children.

Hospice does not abandon such patients. They are still alive, and this means that doctors must help them live for as long as life is given to them. Hospice is not the house of death; it is a home for hope and faith in human strength.

Contact information:
First Moscow Hospice
10 Dovatora Street, Moscow
Phone: 8-499-245-59-69, fax: 8-499-245-4322
E-mail: info@hospice.ru, website www.hospice.ru

Hospice Commandments

1. Hospice is comfortable conditions and decent life to the very end.

2. We work with living people. The only difference between us and our patients is that they are most likely to pass away before us.

3. We should not hurry death, nor artificially prolong life. Everyone lives one's own life. Nobody knows how long it will be. We merely accompany our patients in their last stage of life.

4. One must not take money from those who are leaving this world. Our work must be unselfish.

5. We cannot alleviate our patients' pain and sufferings on our own. Only together with patients, their relatives and friends, do we derive strength.

6. Patients and their relatives are a single whole. Be considerate when entering a family. Do not judge, but help.

7. If a patient cannot be healed, it does not mean that nothing can be done. What seems a trifle to a healthy person might be very significant for our patients.

8. Every person is unique. Do not impose your beliefs upon a patient. Patients give us more than we can give them.

9. Accept everything from a patient, up to aggression. Try to understand a person before doing anything. Accept a person in order to understand him/her.

10. Be always ready for truth and sincerity. Tell the truth if a patient wants and feels prepared for it... but do not rush.

11. An unplanned visit is no less valuable than a planned one. See a patient as frequently as possible. If you cannot visit—give a call; if you cannot call, think of a patient and call anyway.

12. Do not hurry when with a patient. Do not stand—sit beside him/her. However little time you have, it is still enough to do your best. If you think you have done less than you could, talking with the relatives of the deceased will comfort you.

13. Hospice is the patients' home. We are the hosts of the house. With this in mind, change your footwear and wash your face.

14. Your reputation is the reputation of the hospice.

15. The main thing you should know is that you know very little.

About Vera Hospice Charity Fund

Despite the renaissance in Russian traditions of charitable giving and patronage, some areas of life (for example, death and dying) remain taboos in our society, and as a result, terminally ill people—hospice patients—are left with little or no donor support, forgotten by the state and forced to struggle with their pain and fear alone.

The Vera Hospice Charity Fund undertakes such "unpopular" charity activity. We cannot appeal to our donors with the promise of producing a cure; all we do is help the dying live as long as they are meant to live, without pain, in comfort and with dignity. In Moscow alone, 50,000 people need such assistance every year. In addition, the Fund helps provide honorable compensation for the spiritually draining and physically demanding work of those who care for the terminally ill and who make hospice centers homes of mercy and humanism.

The Vera Fund was created to support the work of hospice centers and other medical establishments that practice palliative medicine in the Russian Federation. Our criteria for choosing beneficiaries are simple: the services must be provided for free, with the utmost openness and transparency; the establishment must have a good reputation and must work in accordance with the commandments of hospice care.

The current Board of Trustees includes Natalia Gutman, Eliso Virsaladze, Lyudmila Ulitskaya, Vladimir Voinovich, Ingeborga Dapkunaite, Tatiana Drubich, Andris Liepa, Marina Aleksandrova, Tatiana Arno, Avdotya Smirnova, Mikhail Alshibaya, Vera Millionschikova and Zoya Yeroshok.

Hospice establishments are in great need of charitable assistance, since the support they receive from state budgets is insufficient to ensure that patient services fully embody the hospice ideology: that the conditions of the patients' stay are as home-like as possible and that the staff receive appropriate compensation for their work. The state allocates 70 million rubles annually for hospice care, a sum that covers the cost of drugs and meals for the patients. Only with charitable support can we achieve dignity and comfort for our patients, with things like phones and TV sets in their rooms, flowers and gifts at holiday time, anti-sore mattresses and multifunctional hospital beds, and an unlimited supply of diapers and bed linens. Since all proceeds from the sale of this collection of stories are going to benefit the Vera Fund, your purchase of this book will result in a valuable cash donation to meet these important needs.

As part of its mission, the Fund not only assists medical establishments, their patients and staff financially, but also seeks to unite hospice centers into a team, hold professional development seminars for hospice staff, and educate the public about hospice care and the needs of the terminally ill people.

Contact information:
39, Proletarsky prospect, kv 27,
115477 Moscow, Russia
Phone/fax: 8-495-321-7685
E-mail: fund@hospicefund.ru
website: www.hospicefund.ru

TRANSLATION OF INTRODUCTORY NOTES BY NINA SHEVCHUK MURRAY

Joan

Andrei Gelasimov

He loved that little thing. Actually, he didn't like it much at first, because he was hot all over and was running a temperature, while that thing was cool, and he shuddered when it got pressed against him. He turned away and made a face. His head was all wet. But he didn't complain, because by then it was hard for him to cry. He could only groan hoarsely and shut his eyes. But then he started to reach for it anyway. Because it was shiny.

"You want me to listen to you again?" says the doctor and takes that thing off.

I completely forgot what it was called. That thing to listen to what goes on inside you. The one with green tubes. The disk that sticks to your back if they hold it there too long. Then, when it gets unstuck, it makes a funny sound. And it tickles a little, too. And your head spins.

Little Sergei grabs that thing and puts it in his mouth.

The doctor says: "Stop it. It's a caca. Give it back to me."

I say: "He'll let go of it in a moment. He just wants to lick it a bit. Let him hold it, because he cried the whole night."

She stares at me and says: "Are you all alone with him?"

I say: "All alone. There is nobody else."

She stares at me and says nothing. Then she says: "Tired?"

I say: "Not really. I'm used to it by now. Except my arms get tired. By morning, they feel like they're going to fall off."

She says: "Do you carry him like this all the time?"

I say: "He doesn't walk yet."

She stares at him and says: "How old is he?"

I say: "Two. Except he had trauma at birth."

She says: "I see. How old are you?"

I say: "I'm eighteen."

She said nothing and then began to pack her bag. Little Sergei gave her back that thing right away. Because he had no strength to resist.

At the door she turns and says: "There shouldn't be anything serious any more. But if something comes up, call us again. I'm on call till eight."

I said to her "Thank you," and she turned and shut the door behind her.

She's a good doctor. Little Sergei liked her. As to our regular district doctor, he doesn't like her at all. He always cries when she comes to see us. But the district doctor knows everything there is to know about us. That's why she's never surprised.

But this time I called the ambulance. I left him alone for ten minutes and ran to the all-night store that sells vodka. There is a guard there with a cell phone.

Because at four o'clock I got scared. He cried all night, but at four he stopped. I got scared that he was going to die.

"Your mother died because of you. It's all your fault." This is what the principal told me when I came to her to ask her if the school would hire me.

By then, I didn't need the diploma any more. I needed to feed little Sergei. The baby formula cost a lot. The imported stuff. In those pretty cans. The district doctor said I had to feed him those. They have good vitamins. That's why I came to the school to ask for work, not to go to classes. Especially since I had fallen way back, anyway. The money left over from Mom had run out. She used to say—what's the use of saving it? We'll go to France and earn a thousand times more. And she used to listen to her Edith Piaf tape all the time.

"You knew she had a bad heart," the principal told me. "And now you stand here shamelessly and stare at me. How could you even have come here again?"

I'm looking at her and thinking: "How could Mom spend so much time here?" Some calling in life. A French language teacher. They too had known that she had a bad heart. Still, they wagged their tongues about me in the teachers' room. Even in her presence. Because they were sure it was her fault, too. A teacher who didn't watch over her own daughter properly. She would then cry at home, but refused to take sick leave. She would put in her tape and sing along.

And then she died.

"You won't hire me?" I say to the principal.

"Sorry, my dear," she says. "It's too much responsibility. We have young girls here. We must think of them."

And what am I, a whore? Who can't even be shown to the kids?

"You know, this movie is not for kids," Mom used to say, sending me off to bed.

She would stay up and watch it on TV.

I would lie in bed and think—what's the point of watching all this heavy breathing? I could hear it even in my room.

When Tolik fell off the construction site, he too was breathing heavily. Except his eyes wouldn't open. He lay there with his head on the bricks and breathed very loudly. The construction site from which he fell was actually our school. It's where the principal now works.

Later we all went to that school. Except for Tolik. That's because after that he couldn't go anywhere at all. Even to the old wooden school—he never went there, not even once. He just sat at home. Sometimes they let him come down to the courtyard, and then I wouldn't play with anybody anymore. Just throw stones at boys, so they quit bothering him. Because he would start to yell when they bothered him. And his mother would come out of the house and cry on the steps. They were promised a new apartment in a big brick building, but they never got it. Some woman came from the Housing Management Department and said that it would be too much for a retard. That's why they stayed on in our neighborhood.

Mom always used to say that it's not a place fit for living.

"I'll die trying, but we have to get away from here. We have to run away from these projects."

I listened to her and wondered what "projects" were.[1] I thought they must be some kind of buildings with projections and chimneys, only nasty ones, unpleasant and coarse. And I was surprised, because there were no chimneys in our region. No one even used wood stoves. Although things were pretty awful where we lived.

Later I began to understand her.

That was when the police came and broke down our door. They were looking for someone. Someone who shot at them with a shotgun. Then they began going from house to house, breaking down doors. And when they left, Mom said for the first time that we should go to France.

"There is nothing here for us anymore. And who'll fix our door for us?"

She began writing all sorts of letters and buying expensive envelopes for them, but she never got any answers.

"We are going to Paris," Mom told the neighbors. "This is why I won't lend you any more money. Especially since you never pay it back, and waste it all on vodka."

For this reason it became difficult for me to go outside. Especially where they were building parking garages.

"Get lost," Vovka Spike-Eye would say, hitting me with a bicycle pump. "Stewardess Joan."

---

[1] In the original, Gelasimov uses the word *trushchyoby*, translated here as "projects," which sounds similar to the word *truby*—pipes or chimneys. The narrator also mentions how the word *trushchyoby* sounds unpleasant and coarse, like the letter *Shch*.

I would leave. It hurt and I was afraid of him. He was in second grade already. Although that was back in the wooden schoolhouse. His father was building those garages. Which was why if you wanted to jump off them into the pile of sand, you had to ask Vovka's permission first.

He wouldn't let me jump.

"Get lost, Stewardess. You can go jump off a garage in France, along with your mom. She's an idiot. You're both idiots. Get lost."

And he would hit me over the head with his pump.

He always walked around with that pump, even though he never rode a bike. He could never learn to ride and was constantly falling. And then he would beat up other boys who laughed at him.

Tolik never laughed at him. One day he came up to him and said: "Let her stay. What do you care?"

Then they started to fight, and after that they fought all the time. Until Tolik fell off the construction site. That was because we used to climb up to the third floor. We used to play school up there. When he fell, I looked up and saw Vovka Spike-Eye's face up there. Tolik's breath was loud and his eyes didn't open.

"Look how his eyes have opened," the nurse told me and showed me little Sergei. "You have a baby boy. See how big he is?"

I couldn't see anything because I was in pain. I thought I was going to die. I only saw that he was all covered with blood and couldn't tell whose blood it was, mine or his.

"Go on, hold him... Like this... Go on. You must start getting used to him now."

But I couldn't get used to him. Mom said she too had forgotten everything about little babies. She said: "My God, is it possible they're so small? Just look at his tiny hands. Look, look, he smiled at me."

I said: "He's just making a face. The doctor explained it to us in the class. It's reflexive contraction of facial muscles. He doesn't recognize anybody yet."

"Reflexive contraction my foot," she said. "Your doctor doesn't know anything about babies, either. He's happy because he's going to France soon. Have you seen where I put my Edith Piaf tape? For some reason it's not in the cassette player."

Our cassette player was very old. It rattled everywhere. I had hidden her tape on purpose. Because I just couldn't bear the joke anymore. Even our neighbors' kids called us Frenchies. And now little Sergei was born. It was time to put an end to it.

But she moped around the apartment all evening, not herself. She tried to check exams and then turned the television on. She was watching the news, but she was still not right. She just sat in front of the TV, and even her back seemed out of sorts. By then little Sergei had been screaming for maybe two hours.

"Here it is," I said, "your tape. Lying on the bookshelf. Except you won't hear a thing, what with all this screaming."

"I'll go to the kitchen," she said.

Then little Sergei stopped howling. Immediately.

I put him in his carriage and began listening to Edith Piaf singing in our kitchen. It's very good music.

My arms were stiff, and my back hurt a little. But I still thought he couldn't recognize anybody yet. He was too little.

Tolik recognized me when he turned eleven. Right on his birthday. Mom told me to go upstairs and take something to him. Otherwise they'd all get drunk up there again and forget about him.

She was worried that he would start eating potato peelings again and would end up in the hospital. Because he had just had surgery for appendicitis.

I had no idea what to give him, so I took our cat's ball and an old photograph up to him. It showed a few kids, Tolik and me. Uncle Petya, Mom's friend who owned a car, had taken it.

He took us for a car ride around the apartment block and then took that picture on the steps. The picture slid out of the camera right away. I had never seen anything like it before. But then mom said that I had to stop asking about him. "Stop it," she said. "I'm tired of your questions."

And covered her ears with her hands.

                                    ANDREI GELASIMOV

In the picture, we were six. That was before we began playing on the construction site.

"Wait," I said. "Don't stick it in your mouth. Look, this is you, see? Next to you is Mishka. See? He's sticking his tongue out. Next to him is Slavka and Zhenka. Remember how one time they hid in the attic the whole night and their dad chased them around the whole street with a belt? And this is me. Somebody put horns over my head from behind. Stupid Mishka most likely. He always used to do this. He doesn't live here anymore. His parents moved downtown. Mom and I may also go away one day. Wait. Wait. What are you doing? Don't bend it. It will break it and you won't see anything on it. Why are you pulling at it? What? I can't understand you. You're just grunting, nothing else. What? Are you trying to say something?"

He kept pulling the picture out of my hands and poking his finger at it. I looked at where he was poking and gave him the picture. Because he was pointing at me.

That's how he recognized me. On the day of his birthday.

"The birth of a child," said the doctor in the class, "is the most important event in every woman's life. From the moment he arrives, the child must be surrounded by care and love."

I sit there and look at the whole lot of us. It's as though we have swallowed air balloons. Here we are, sitting and listening about love. Wearing hospital coats. Except I didn't care about it anymore. I was thinking that I might die. And that it will be very painful. I didn't care about love at all, by then.

"You know," all the girls said when I got to the summer camp, "he's great. He's even cooler than Venya the P.E. counselor."

I say: "Who?"

And they say: "What are you, stupid?"

I say: "You're stupid yourselves. How am I supposed to know your Venyas? I just got here. I was helping Mom renovate her classroom."

They say: "Venya works as an airplane pilot. He has a car and he's 25 years old. On his vacations, he works here as a P.E. teacher. Because he needs to stay in shape. But he is not as cool as darling Vovka. Because Vovka—he's just out of this world."

I say: "Wait a minute. What darling Vovka?"

They say: "What are you, stupid? He's in the same school with you. He told us he knows you."

I say: "Do you mean Vovka Spike-Eye?"

They say: "We call him Darling Vovka."

That is when I tell them: "Vovka Spike-Eye is a creep. The worst creep of all the creeps in the world."

They laugh and say: "Well, we'll see. We'll see."

I worked at that camp to make some money. I wanted to buy myself a pair of new jeans for eleventh grade. I also needed a pair of sneakers. That's why I stayed.

Mom kept telling me love is cruel. But even she never suspected how cruel.

The first week the girls kept buzzing in my ears about him. Which one of them he looked at, who he danced with, which boy he socked in the eye.

I say to him when I finally ran into him: "You're a superstar here. A local Jackie Chan. A martial arts champion."

He looks me straight in the eye and says: "Come to the dance tonight. I'll teach you a funny little dance."

Then he smiles and says: "Stewardess Joan."

For some reason, I went.

"A normal baby," the district doctor told me, "should start walking at ten months. He's already two years old, but he's crawling like... Like a cockroach."

She didn't say right away how he crawls. She thought about it for a while and then said it. And pushed him away. Because he kept crawling to her. Usually he used to cry whenever she came, but now he was reaching for her boots and grabbing at the bottom of her coat.

"Look," she says, "He's drooled all over me. How am I supposed to go visit other kids?"

I say: "I'm sorry."

She says: "What of it, that you're sorry? You should've thought about it beforehand, whether to have this baby or not. Had you had an abortion, you wouldn't have been sitting here alone with him, without your mother. You would've graduated from high school, like you were supposed to. Who knows whether he'll develop normally. A trauma like this is no joke. You already have one retard upstairs."

I say: "He is not a retard. He fell from the construction site when he was six."

She says: "Who cares whether he fell or not. What I'm telling you is that traumas are no joking matter. Do you want to spend your whole life wiping his drool? You should be playing with dolls yourself, at your age. They make babies and somebody has to pick up after them. What were you thinking of? There is no reason to cry."

I say: "I'm not crying. I got something in my eye."

She says: "You got something in a different part of your body. I'll be back in a week. Same time. Please be home."

I say: "We're always home."

She stood up in her boots and left.

When she left, I picked up little Sergei, stood him on his feet and told him: "Come on, little one, please. Walk."

And I can't see anything because I'm crying, I want so much for him to walk.

But he doesn't walk, and every time he plops softly on his behind. I keep lifting him, and he smiles and sits down again.

Then I stand him one last time, push him in the back and yell: "It's all your fault, you stupid log. Why can't you walk normally for once?"

He falls face first and hits his face on the floor. Blood comes out of his mouth. He's crying because he's frightened of me. I grab him and squeeze him against me. I'm crying too. I can't stop. I keep wiping blood from his face and can't stop crying.

"Don't stop," I yell to Tolik. "Don't stop. Come forward. Don't stand still."

He doesn't understand me. He hears what I'm yelling but thinks we're still playing. But the ice is already cracking under him. He yells back to me and waves his arms, and I'm worried he'll start jumping. Because he is always jumping in place whenever he is happy. I yell to him: "Don't stop, please. I beg you."

Because the ice is very thin, and he is walking on the thin ice after the cat's ball I gave him for his birthday two days ago. He takes it everywhere now. He even eats holding it in his hand. Because it's my ball. Because I brought it.

When we came back, Mom looked at me and said: "Why do you bother with him? Your friends came by looking for you. You should play with normal kids."

I say: "Tolik is normal. He recognized me in the picture."

She says: "Still, they should have arranged for him to be sent to a special school. Except for you, nobody looks after him here. Those drunks will one day see him fall again and break his neck. Although maybe that is exactly what they're waiting for. And the construction pit near the school, it doesn't look like it's ever going to be filled in. Don't go there with him. He might run onto the ice and fall through. Do you know how deep it is?"

I say: "I do. We don't go there to play. We almost always play in the courtyard."

She says: "When I take you to France, who is going to look after him? See how it sometimes happens in life? Nobody cares about him."

Now nobody cares about me either. By winter, Mom's money ran out and I had to look for work. But nobody would ever hire me, not anywhere. Even the school principal turned me down. She said I'd set a bad example for girls.

I didn't want to set an example. All I needed was to feed little Sergei. And by then my boots completely fell apart. That's why I was running around looking for work in those sneakers I bought that summer. They were pretty scuffed, too, after almost three years. And your feet get really cold in them. Especially if you're waiting for the bus for so long. So you stand at the bus stop, stomp your feet like they're made of wood and worry

　　　　　　　　　　　　　　　　　　ANDREI GELASIMOV

yourself crazy whether or not little Sergei is already crying alone in the locked apartment.

It was horribly cold that winter. Everybody had just celebrated 2000. But I didn't celebrate anything. Because I had already sold the TV set. And the sewing machine. And the vacuum cleaner. But money ran out quickly anyway, and so I began selling Mom's things. Even though at first I didn't want to sell them. Except when I got to the cassette player, for some reason I couldn't. I sat in the empty apartment, watched little Sergei crawl on the floor and listened to Mom's Edith Piaf tape. Little Sergei liked her songs. I watched him and wondered where I could get a bit more money. Because, in general, by then it was nowhere.

And then the letter came. Some time in mid-March. My feet were no longer freezing in those sneakers by then. At first I couldn't figure out who it was from, but then when I opened it I was very surprised. Because I never really believed that this letter would ever come. Even though Mom waited for it probably every day of her life. I didn't believe in it. I thought she was probably a little nuts. I thought there would be no miracles.

The letter said that, in response to numerous requests from Mme. my Mom, the Embassy of France in Russia made the requisite inquiries with the proper sources and now apologizes for how long the procedure has taken. Because of legal and political reasons beyond its control, the Embassy of France had not been able to clarify the circumstances of this complex case until very recently. Nevertheless, it now hastens to report that, after lengthy research, they were indeed able to locate a Mme. Boche, who does not deny her family connection to my Mom through her grandfather, who during World War II was an internee in France and, at the end of the war, decided to take up permanent residency in France, having married a French citizen. The difficulty of the Embassy of France in this particular case was due to the fact that the progeny of the interned grandfather and the aforementioned citizen of France had moved to various other countries and assumed different citizenships. In particular, the parents of Mme. Boche are citizens of Canada. However, inasmuch as Mme. Boche has returned to France and married a French citizen, the Embassy of France in Russia no longer sees any reason why Mme. my Mom should not apply to them for permission to obtain a residency permit in France. The Embassy of France will be glad to provide all the required documents for this purpose at the following address.

After that there was a fax number. And some words. But I can't read French, and I had sold all of Mom's dictionaries. Because by then, Mom had been gone almost six months.

And I had no idea what "interned" meant.

But the envelope was very pretty and I gave it to little Sergei. He loves to rustle all sorts of papers.

He grabbed it and started to purr with pleasure. I looked at him and wondered: "Why haven't you started walking already?"

Because I had no intention of going to any France. Who's waiting for me over there? And I already knew that, as to Tolik, I couldn't just leave him. His parents by then had gone completely nuts. They got drunk almost every day and often beat him up. He couldn't understand why they were hurting him and screamed very loudly. The neighbors said that even people in the next building could hear him. I would then go upstairs and bring him down to my place. He would calm down right away. He would crawl around the rooms with little Sergei and whistle like a train. Little Sergei would turn on his back and laugh. A little, laughing boy, lying on his back. So I had no intention of going anywhere.

The only thing was, I felt sorry for Mom.

That was why next morning I went to look for work again. One of my old classmates had told me that her boss was looking to hire another salesgirl. For the night shift. It would be good for me. Because little Sergei had by then turned two and was sleeping through the night. He didn't even pee till morning.

And, she said, the pay wasn't bad.

But in the end, nothing came of it, as usual.

"You know," she said. "He doesn't want to hire a salesgirl with a baby. He says it'll be more trouble with you than it's worth."

"There will be no trouble with me," I said.

She only shrugged her shoulders.

I say again: "There will be no trouble with me."

And so we stand there and stare at each other, and she's waiting for me to leave, because she's already regretting that she asked me to come. The space is all crammed with Snicker bars and "Baltika No. 9" beer bottles. But I want to stay there all the same. Because I know that there is no other place for me to get money anymore.

And then I see a very small boy in the corner. He's just four years old or maybe a little more, and he's sweeping some dirt off the floor. Not really sweeping, actually, because the broom is taller than he is and he can't easily move with it from place to place.

I say: "What's he doing in here? Is it your nephew maybe? No one to leave him home with?"

She looks at him, laughs and says: "What nephew, are you kidding? They just got to me, that's all. They come here all the time and beg first for one thing, then for another. I've had it up to here with them. Now he comes in and says, 'Please, Lady, give me a yogurt.' I gave him the broom. Let him work for it. He has a sister, too."

I turned around and saw there was a girl at the door. Even smaller than he. And all covered with dirt, too. She stands there and stares at us. Her eyes are shining.

When I came in, I didn't notice them. Because I wanted very much to find out about the job.

I bent down to that kid and asked him: "You want yogurt?"

He stopped what he was doing and said to me very softly: "Yes."

I say: "Have you ever tried it?"

His cheeks are all filthy.

He says: "No."

He stands there and stares at me. He's shorter than the broomstick.

I straightened up and say: "Give them the yogurt, please. Here's the money."

And she looks at me and shakes her head. And smiles.

I say: "Give them yogurt. I've paid you."

Then I went outside, stood at the bus stop and began to cry. Because I felt sorry for those kids.

They're like slaves. Except very little.

Next day Vovka Spike-Eye came. I didn't even know he was in town. Somebody had told me he and his father had gone to Moscow. They had some business there.

I opened the door and he was standing there fancy-looking in a shearling coat and a mink hat. Even though everything was already melting outside. I was wearing Mom's old warm-ups. My shirt had a hole on the shoulder.

And little Sergei crawled out from behind me. Moving sideways, like a crab. First he swings one leg forward, and then pulls the other one up to it. But very quickly. Because he's already a big boy, and he wants to move around quickly.

I picked him up so that he wouldn't catch a cold from the open door, and we stood there for a while looking at each other.

At last he says: "I heard your mother died."

He came a few more times. He brought food, sweets and diapers. He also brought toys, but they were all very strange. He was also a little strange himself. He hardly even spoke. He only explained that they'd flown in for a week to sell his father's *dacha*, apartment and garage. And that there was nothing more for him to do in this town.

That's how he put it.

He said that and stared at me. And then at little Sergei.

Then he says: "Why doesn't he walk yet?"

I say: "A trauma at birth."

He says: "Really? What's that?"

I say: "I was too young when he was born. My pelvic bone was too small. When he was coming out, they applied the forceps. The head got a little deformed. And the vertebrae shifted a little in his neck."

He stares and says: "Maybe he needs surgery?"

I say: "They can't tell as yet. Doctors say we've got to wait. Time will tell."

After that he disappeared. He stopped coming, and I thought he must have sold his *dacha.*

And then I finally found a job. Actually, I wasn't even looking anymore. We were just sitting at home, finishing whatever Vovka had brought us over a few visits. Little Sergei was finishing the sweets.

At that point, the district doctor comes in and starts screaming at us.

She is screaming that I'm an idiot and that they should have whipped me more as a child, and that little Sergei needs a totally different diet and that I'm a terrible mother. We sit on the floor and stare at her screaming. Little Sergei is no longer afraid of her. Because he has gotten used to her and no longer starts at the sound of her voice. He just stares, his face upturned and his mouth open wide. His eyes are wide, but you can see that he's no longer scared. He just doesn't take his eyes off of her. I look at him, and I feel sorry for him, because he bends his head to his left shoulder all the time. It takes my breath away, to see that.

Then she asks whether she can sit down.

I say that we've got nothing to sit on.

Because I have sold all the chairs. First the armchair, then the chairs and finally the stools. In any case, little Sergei and I didn't need them. We hung out on the floor most of the time, anyway.

She says: "I'll sit down on the bed then."

I say: "Please, sit down."

She sat down and little Sergei started to crawl toward her boots. I wanted to pick him up, but she said don't. I was surprised, because before she never liked it when he crawled toward her.

"My husband found a job for you," she said. "You'll do the cleaning and wash the floors at his bank. They pay very well. In any case, more than your mother earned at her school. But you'll have to promise me that you won't let us down, because my husband vouched for you. They have a very strict employee selection policy. They have to trust you. Can you give me a promise?"

"What promise?" I said.

Because I really didn't understand her completely. Even though I wanted to. Very much.

"You're really an idiot. I'm asking you—can you promise me that you won't let my husband down. He asked them to do you a favor."

Then I said: "Sure. Sure I won't let your husband down. I'll do everything they tell me to do and I'll wash all the floors very thoroughly. And throw away all the papers."

She said: "Good girl. Finally you figured out what is required of you. The day after tomorrow go to this address at five o'clock. You'll work evenings. Do you have somebody to leave your boy with?"

She gave me the paper.

I say: "Yes, yes. Everything is alright. Don't worry about Sergei. He's a big boy now."

She says: "Very well then."

Then she got up and went to the door. At the door she turned back.

"By the way, how is he doing?"

"He is doing very well," I said. "Thank you very much."

When she left, I began to cry.

The next day toward evening Spike-Eye came again. I thought he had already flown off, so I was a little surprised. I was also caught off guard. Because they'd started drinking upstairs and I had to take Tolik. Otherwise he would have been screaming all over the street.

Little Sergei crawled to Vovka's bag right away. He'd already got used to expecting candies in there. But this time Vovka brought him nothing. He kept staring at little Sergei and Tolik crawling around the floor and said nothing.

Then he asked me: "Can he at least talk?"

I figured out he wasn't asking about little Sergei. Because about little Sergei he had asked everything there was to know already.

"He can't," I said. "He can only scream when he is afraid. But he recognizes me."

"What about others?" asked Vovka.

"I don't think so."

He stared at Tolik a while longer and then sat down on the bed. The same place where the district doctor sat the day before.

"You know," he said, "we need to talk."

"About what?" said I.

Because I saw that he was nervous. I was a little nervous myself, too.

He says: "Tomorrow I'm leaving for Moscow."

I say: "Moscow is cool."

I'm watching to make sure little Sergei and Tolik don't upset his bag. They got too close to it.

He says: "We must decide about something."

I turn to him and at that moment everything in his bag tumbles to the floor. I try to run over, but he grabs me by the hand and says: "Wait. It's not important. There is nothing important in it. We must talk."

Then I sit down on the bed. While little Sergei and Tolik laugh and toss his things about.

He says: "He can't stay here."

I understand that he is not talking about Tolik. Because he saw Tolik for the first time five minutes ago and maybe didn't even remember him at all.

But I did remember.

He says: "In short, I've figured it all out. This is what we're going to do."

I look at them, how they are playing over there by the door and worry they would cut themselves on something. He might have some sharp objects in there.

He says: "So, do you agree?"

I say: "To what?"

He stares at me and says: "I've just explained it all to you. Were you not listening?"

I say: "I was listening, but I'm a little tired. I have a bit of a headache today."

He says: "The most important thing is, you must sign this paper, which says that you make no claims that I'm little Sergei's father. I asked a local lawyer. He says we can draft a paper like that. Then I can take you with me. We'll rent you an apartment. One room, but it's okay. The most important thing is, I'll be helping little Sergei. Except there is no need to tell my father anything about it for the time being."

I turn to him and say: "You want us to come to Moscow with you?"

He says: "Yes, sure. Except you need to sign that paper first. So that later there won't be any mess in court."

I say: "What court?"

He says: "Well, what if you decide to sue me. Meaning that I'm little Sergei's father."

I stare at him and say: "But you are his father."

And he says: "I know. Except it's not important."

I say: "What do you mean, not important? He's your son."

He says: "I know."

Then he gets up, walks up and down in the room and says: "In short, you decide. Either you come with me to Moscow or not."

I look at little Sergei—how he crawls around Tolik, and then at Vovka, how he stands in our room in his shearling and hasn't even removed his mink hat—and say: "We're going to France. Pretty soon now. We'll probably take Tolik along."

Vovka keeps staring at me, and then laughs.

He says: "You're an idiot, just like your mother. You have gone nuts too. Wake up, she's gone."

Then I went to the kitchen and picked up a letter from the windowsill. I gave it to him and said: "There is no envelope any more. But all the official seals are in place. Look for yourself, if you don't believe me."

He read the letter and his face became very different. Like in childhood, when he used to fall from his bike and the kids used to laugh at him.

I even felt sorry for him.

He says: "When are you going?"

I say: "I don't know yet. I've got to sell the rest of the things. Also sort a few things out."

He says: "I see."

Finally, he removes his hat. His hair got all stuck together under it. And sweat is running down along his temples.

I say: "Thanks for the offer. Maybe we'll meet again someday."

Then he began picking up his things. Tolik and little Sergei crawled around him and bothered him a lot. Because they thought he had started playing with them.

Finally he put it all together, straightened up and pulled a small phone out of his shearling coat.

He says: "Take it. Press this button and you get connected to Moscow right away. I live separate from Father; you can call me at any time. I pay for the calls."

I say: "What for?"

He stares at me and says: "I don't know. Who knows what might come up."

Then he looked at little Sergei and Tolik, stepped over them and went out. I shut the door behind him.

I stood still for a little while and calmed down. But then they began to carry on. Because Vovka took away their toys, they liked to play with his things so much.

I crouched next to them and gave Tolik the phone. I also gave the letter to little Sergei. To keep them quiet.

They did get quiet. Because kids like to break everything. And little Sergei likes to tear paper.

I watched Tolik smash the phone against the floor and thought of nothing at all. I just liked watching him. I also liked watching little Sergei. How he shoved the paper into his mouth, spat it out and laughed.

Then he crawled to the bed, grabbed the headboard and got to his feet. He stood upright for a moment, then let go of the headboard, swayed and suddenly took a step toward me. I froze so as not to frighten him, and stretched out my arms. Then he took another step. I couldn't move; I just kept staring at him. He swayed again and took another step.

Then I said: "Come to me. Come to mama."

TRANSLATION BY ALEXEI BAYER

A Short History
of Amateur Performing Arts Groups
on the Ships of the Caribbean Pirate Fleet
in the First Half of the 17th Century

Boris Grebenshchikov

As Ludwig Mies van der Rohe said, "Interesting simplicity is a precious thing that is most difficult to achieve."

—⁓—

Captain Samuel Bellami was called "The Prince of Pirates." He was also called "Black Sam" because, unlike other pirate captains, he disdained the powdered wig, tying instead his long black hair into a ponytail. And even though his pirating career only lasted a bit under one year,

Bellami became famous both for his luck and for his unusual generosity to the crews of the ships he captured.

It was on one of his ships that the only attempt (known to history) to create an amateur theater in a pirate fleet occurred.

One of his crew members had an artistic vein. Once, in his former, land-treading life, this gentleman was a tramp in Yorkshire. But since, as he put it, "vagrancy did not reflect the grandeur of his soul," he became a Collector—that is, he borrowed from someone an excellent Horse, stuck his Pistols into the saddlebags, and set out in search of Adventures. When he met other travelers, he challenged them to a duel, and if they sought to avoid the combat, he lightened their purses and implored them to give themselves up to the mercy of his Dulcinea. This would have continued for a long time, but "a certain Enchanter, who had magically foreseen that one day he would have to surrender his dominance, made it so that our Hero found himself chained in Shackles and shipped to the famous island of Jamaica, where, after a few spins of the fortune's wheel, his destiny became entwined with that of the Sea Soldiers, Whips of Tyranny and fearless Defenders of Freedom" gathered under Captain Bellami's leadership.

As on any vessel, periods of frenzied activity were followed by long spells of idleness, when the ship was quietly carried by the winds, and the crew was left to its own devices.

During one of these quiet spells, the maestro whom we described above wrote a play that he called "The Royal Pirate." Among the characters in the play were Alexander the Great, probably some other historical figures, and, of course, pirates. Many crew members agreed to participate in the staging of this opus, and, after a proper period of rehearsals, they performed at quarter-deck, to a storm of applause addressed to the Author and the Actors.

An accident was to turn this make-believe drama into reality.

At the moment when Alexander, in the course of the play, was interrogating a pirate, the ship's gunner, who had avoided participating in the show, was drinking peacefully with three friends in the gunpowder storage room under the deck. When he came up on the deck to answer the call of nature, he suddenly saw a bound comrade of his being threatened by some unknown and strangely dressed individuals, and on top of that, one of the individuals, apparently the one in charge, was saying:

Thus you should know that death is the reward
For all your despicable deeds,
And, come morning, you will hang from the noose.

The befuddled gunner, not recognizing the thin line between Art and Life, decided that while he was engrossed in the conversation with his three friends, something terrible must have happened to the ship. Back in the orlop, he summoned his buddies to come immediately to the aid of their brethren.

"They threaten to hang the honest Jack Spinks; if we don't do something they'll hang all of us, one by one. I swear to God, I shall not let this happen!" was his fiery appeal. Taking a swig of his punch, he grabbed a grenade, lit the fuse, and rushed back to the top deck, his buddies with bared sabers on his heels.

Once on the deck, the gunner threw the grenade into the huddle of the actors; his friends slashed left and right with their sabers. The stunned audience, which had not expected this turn of events, dispersed at first, but then attacked the rescuers. The sailor who played Alexander had his left hand cut off, and the poor Jack Spinks, caught by the blast of the grenade, broke his leg. In the ensuing chaos, the crew caught and shackled its clueless rescuers, all but one, whom Alexander killed on the spot, avenging the violated art and the loss of his left hand.

The following morning, when passions subsided, the captain called the crew to court and questioned all parties intensely. Having heard the gunner's version of the story, the court unanimously found him and his friends to be not guilty; moreover, the court praised their vigilance. In the end, even Alexander, despite the loss of his hand, had to forgive his injurers. However, to avoid future misunderstandings, the Captain ordered no more plays to be staged aboard his ship.

Such is the short history of amateur performing arts groups on the ships of the Caribbean Sea pirate fleet.

TRANSLATION BY NINA SHEVCHUK-MURRAY

   BORIS GREBENSHCHIKOV

Serenity

YEVGENY GRISHKOVETS

It was the kind of weather where you couldn't be sure of anything. Summer had come to a close. Yet for some reason there was no real yellowing of the trees. Still, the wind was already driving dead, green leaves into corners and under fences. Outside the city, the grass was high and somehow unclean. Summer was ending, or more precisely, all indications were that it had already ended. Only a few more days of August to be endured, and...

Almost all his friends, buddies, comrades, acquaintances and colleagues had returned from somewhere tanned, and they wanted to get together, to share stories. But Dima had sat out the summer in the city. Of course, he had not sat all summer long, it's just that if a person spends the whole summer in the city, even if not without some pleasure or benefit, it is nonetheless said that he "sat it out." So this is what Dima told everyone: "Whaddya mean how was it?! I sat out the whole summer in the city!" After which Dima sighed, gave a brief, dismissive wave, and made a sad face.

Dima shipped his family off at the beginning of July. His son to an international camp, so the boy could practice his English; his wife and daughter first to her parents in the North, and then to the South, to the sea, where they'd gone together on many occasions. But he stayed in the city... on business.

There was in fact business to be done, and there was a significant and substantial reason for staying behind in the city and working, yet by the middle of July the city was melting from the heat, no one was making any decisions, and any business planned for the summer had come to a standstill. It had been stupid to plan so much business for summer. First, most of the people responsible for deciding various questions had taken off, and those who stayed behind were tired, or somehow ill-tempered... bleary-eyed... from the heat, from the sound of summer ringing in their ears, or from the buildup of static electricity. By the end of July, Dima fell into a state of lethargy. Into a strange sort of summer idleness where the days crawl by gruelingly slowly, and time flies incomprehensibly fast.

At first, Dima lay about for a few days on the couch, in front of the television. He flipped endlessly back and forth between channels, stopping for a while here and there... then flipping some more. When he stumbled upon an old movie, one he had known since he was a boy, he clapped, rubbed his hands, adjusted the nest he'd turned his divan into, and ran to the kitchen to put on some tea and throw together the unhealthiest—and therefore tastiest—snacks possible. Old movies, open-faced sandwiches, and sweet tea evoked serious and profound pleasure. There was something in this he had not felt for a long time: serenity!

On the third day of this serenity, he started to lose all sense of time. He went to sleep toward morning and woke late in the afternoon. He awoke to the sultry sounds of summer from the courtyard. When the refrigerator was empty, Dima fought back hunger for nearly an entire day. It seemed somehow impracticable to leave the building. Dima put off his departure for a long time. He had long since stopped shaving, but suddenly shaving brought great satisfaction. Then he spent a long time washing up, got dressed, and then went out to the store... with satisfaction. And selected a whole pile of stuff. Returning from the store, he didn't rush to eat, and didn't begin nervously snacking either, but with unexpected satisfaction straightened the apartment, washing all the dishes and carefully putting everything away in the refrigerator. Then he unhurriedly made himself lunch and dinner in one (meaning, Dima had not had lunch, but it was already evening). He prepared the meal while listening to the comforting sound of the radio... Dima opened a bottle of wine, and peaceful, disparate words flew around in his head: "not bad" or "that's it..." or "damn...." While the meal was finishing up in the oven, Dima drank down two glasses of wine. The wine hit the spot marvelously.... Dima picked up the phone. He called parents (his parents), then placed a call and got through to his wife in the South. Zhenya said that everything was very nice, just that the weather wasn't so good. Then his daughter took the phone, and she said she was resting fine, the food was fine, and in general everything was fine. When Dima asked if she missed her papa, his daughter quickly replied, "Yes." After this, Dima immediately called up an old friend, but couldn't get through to her and that finally calmed him down.

Things were good. Even very good. Periodically a thought would flare up: "Oy, there's stuff to do, I should..." But then responses arose like: "Just wait a bit, just wait..." or "But it's summer!"

The only thing that irritated him was the heat. And it wasn't because it was hot—in the sense that it was stifling, with sweat and all that. What was irritating was that the heat just hung around.... The previous year, Dima had spent the summer with his family on the Baltic coast. His friends had said, "Why there? The rain never stops and the sea is cold... beautiful, but cold." But they got lucky with the weather! And it was so wonderful to sun themselves on the beach or sit under umbrellas at a cafe and drink beer, to watch the news in the evening and learn there was nonstop rain at home, storms in the South, and hail in Greece.

How nice and proper it would have been if the summer had been grey and gloomy. Then on TV they wouldn't have said how the water was warmer in suburban reservoirs than at the Black Sea, and that they'd built public beaches at the nearest reservoir as good as anything any resort had to offer. Proposals arrived periodically from beyond his four walls ... proposals to visit someone or other at their *dacha,* or to go fishing with someone else. Dima came up with various excuses and never went anywhere. The serenity which had befallen him was deeper, more valuable, and more important than any summer blessing. Yet cold, grey rains would have made things more peaceful still—as peaceful as crystal!

How annoying the weather always was! For as long as Dima could remember, his relationship with weather had always been annoying. The last days of May, when it was particularly difficult to finish up studies and take exams, the weather would be splendid. It was always fresh and warm, but not hot... everything you could want. But as soon as vacation began—rain, wind and cold. As soon as they arrived at the sea, there would be a storm warning, rain, wind. That's how it always was. He recalled how he once spent half a summer in the village with his aunt and they didn't even once go fishing, even though he'd brought along an excellent rod. There was a lake right there, but his auntie's husband said he'd only go fishing if there was no wind. If there was wind, then there was no sense going fishing. Uncle Vova said, "Look, see that tree over there? If it's still in the morning and doesn't sway, then it means there's no wind. Grab your rod, wake me up, and the fish will be ours. But if it so much as quivers, don't even bother coming to get me. I'll sleep, and we won't be doing any fishing." Dima watched that tree for half the summer. Every day he would get out his rod just to look at it and then put it back in the shed. Practically every day he dug up worms and watched the tree. In the evening, the tree was almost always completely still. In the middle of the night, Dima got up to take a pee, went out onto the porch and saw, in the moonlight, the top of the motionless tree darkening against the summer stars. His heart skipped a beat from joy, he went back to his bed and fell asleep, deeply breathing in and

   YEVGENY GRISHKOVETS

noisily breathing out... In the morning, he woke before everyone else and ran to the porch... There, where the sunrise had begun to redden the sky, clouds were gathering, and the top of the tree was rocking, every leaf shivering. For some time Dima waited, looking at the tree, then his heart stopped pounding, and Dima froze, as a spitting rain began. Dima went back to his bed and quietly wept. After that, he would wake up late and endure each day, sometimes bored, sometimes enjoying himself. But to this day, if Dima went somewhere early in the morning and there were trees, he almost always would look at the tallest of them, watching... simply watching like he had back then.

The heat—that is, the fine summer—was the only thing that disturbed, or rather muddied, the serenity that had enveloped Dima. In the first days of August he nonetheless agreed one evening to get together with a woman he knew. They met around nine. There was an oppressive stuffiness that gave his friend a headache, so they went to the fountain, where there were tons of people. The city was out having a good time, going crazy. All the embankments and all the cafes on the embankments, and all the areas near the fountain—they were overflowing with people. Near the fountain, Dima and his friend ran into some friends of Dima and his wife. Dima introduced his friend as a colleague who had come to town on business. Her eyes widened in surprise. Unbelievable...

Then a downpour fell on the city, with lightning. It was the sort of downpour that didn't give you even half a minute to react. Everyone was soaked. And the storm was powerful. An operatic-cannonade kind of storm. In short, Dima became convinced that serenity shouldn't be tested and you can't deceive it. The next day he didn't go outside, and the weather was marvelous all day.

Serenity! It was such that Dima didn't even drink beer. He didn't feel like it. He was at peace. Amusing and strange thoughts came into his head. These thoughts arrived, were bandied about, and then left. After the downpour, Dima unhurriedly and sweetly thought, "If I were a weatherman, I'd always give the same weather forecast: scattered showers. That's the most universal and fitting way to put it. If you're hit by rain or snow, aha! It means you were in the right place. No snow or rain—wrong place. That's it. Very simple."

His son called periodically from camp and was, apparently, content. Dima's parents never left their *dacha*. From his wife and daughter, Dima—when he was able to reach them—heard only reassuring words. Serenity. Serenity.

Rain settled in for several days at the beginning of August. Dima rejoiced and spent his days in the greatest possible serenity. The rain was heavy and warm... Then it stopped and the mushrooms came out. His parents couldn't stop talking about this on the phone, and even the local TV station reported an unprecedented mushroom crop and recommended listeners not pick unfamiliar mushrooms or purchase preserved mushrooms of unknown origin.

Dima had not been in the forest for a long time. He loved to gather mushrooms. He loved to walk in the forest, treading cautiously, and suddenly, among the grasses, leaves and lacy shadows, to discover a mushroom. Just a second before, the mushrooms had blended in with everything that rustled and crackled underfoot, and then suddenly— whoop—a mushroom! You would slowly kneel down next to it and survey the ground nearby...

Dima loved that. But this time serenity won out. Arguments rained down such as: "And what would you do with these mushrooms?"; "Oh, I know all about that sea of mushrooms!"; and "Yeah, there are more people in the forests right now than at the market on market day." Dima stayed home and read a couple crime novels and some women's novel he found in his wife's bedside table.

Dima felt, truthfully, that he had put on a little weight during this time, but not a huge amount. Hardly any.

And suddenly August was coming to a close, and soon his wife and children would be returning. The weather was fine, just like before, only you really didn't want to count on it. At any moment, summer could tumble over into fall. You had to seize every little bit of good weather in the receding summer. But Dima wasn't seizing anything. He'd fallen into serenity. He didn't get a haircut all summer.

Gosha called exactly one day before Dima's wife and daughter were to return from the South.

"Hey, what's up?" Gosha said, a bit surprised when Dima picked up the phone. "You already back? I, uh, just called you for the heck of it, and you're here already. Have a good rest?"

"What rest?" Dima replied with a sigh. "I sat out the whole summer in the city. So I'll just have to rest next time. And how are you?"

"So what, you were *here*?!" Gosha was clearly and truly astonished. "But we were certain you'd left. There wasn't hide nor hair of you. Me, I got back a while ago."

"Where were you?"

"Where was I? I was off cursing you all summer long. Weren't your ears burning? We listened to you and went off to the Baltics. We were up to our ears in rain. There wasn't a single decent day. So we fled. And you praised that place so loudly last year..."

"Gosha, Gosha! Why is it my fault I told you that? You just weren't lucky..."

"Yeah, well you're always lucky," Gosha interrupted. "They say the weather was excellent here all summer. What'd you do then?"

"Yeaaaah... Lots to do, the usual nonsense. And I sent the family off to the sea. Had to get the kids out of the city. So, you been back long?"

"Ten days. So bored I almost went insane. No one was around. Everyone left. Too bad I didn't know you were here. A few days ago everyone returned all at once, so we all played soccer yesterday. And I noticed you weren't there. So I thought you still weren't back."

"You played yesterday? Without me? Why didn't anyone call?"

"Well, no one knew you were here..."

"Know, didn't know, would it have been so hard to call? Played without me and no one even called? Is that how it's done?!"

"We thought..." Gosha said, taken aback.

"Actually, you didn't think," Dima broke in. "You just forgot, just say it. Would it have been so difficult to dial my number?"

Dima was angry and offended. These soccer matches at the school stadium were an important ritual. And the point wasn't that it was Dima who'd originally set up the teams, and spent so much time instilling everyone with the habit of the weekly matches, followed by trips to the *banya* and lively conversations. That wasn't the most important thing. It was just that they played without him and no one called. No one! Not a single person. That is, they were able to play without him and nothing happened. And Gosha only called—by chance—the day after the game.

A few hours after Gosha's call, an old friend called. She wanted to know if Dima could talk, meaning was Dima's wife there or not.

"Sure, talk, talk, everything's fine," Dima said.

She explained how she'd had a great trip to some island, had totally rested up, and had brought back a present for Dima.

"And by the way, Dimochka, you have to see my tan," she said, and Dima gathered that his friend was gloriously and happily drunk.

"Who went with you?" Dima asked.

"We-e-ell, *clearly* I was not alone," was her answer.

The friend was truly ancient, but not in the sense of her age. He hadn't seen her for a long time and was seriously surprised by her call. But her "*clearly* I was not alone" grated on Dima. The words didn't offend him out of jealousy, or annoyance that he, Dima, had never been to that island. No! The words grated on his serenity.

Then during the evening there were a couple of business calls. Not bad calls, not even serious ones, but Dima had nothing to say. All that day, Dima didn't turn on the television, only getting around to it rather late, when he turned on the evening news. The news was unpleasant, and not the foreign news, but ours. In that fifteen-minute news broadcast he saw enough in the tense faces of the bureaucrats and deputies to know that they were all clearly lying and that nothing good was happening. There wasn't much about sports, and Dima missed the weather

　　　　　　　　　　　　　　YEVGENY GRISHKOVETS

when his wife called to remind him of her flight number and arrival time.

Dima slept poorly the night before his wife's return. It took him the longest time to fall asleep. In the morning, he brought a semblance of order to the apartment. He ran the vacuum cleaner through the center of the rooms and the kitchen. He picked up the clothes lying in the corners and so on, and then he went out to the store and bought some food and drink, so he would have something to feed them at the end of their travels. All these activities were excruciatingly difficult. Then he had to make dozens of phone calls. Everyone was returning from somewhere or other and wanted to get together and share stories.

When Dima drove to the airport, the car wasn't running well. Dima hadn't been behind the wheel for a long time, and the car was thick with dust and just didn't drive right.

But the weather continued to be nice. The blue sky and small, distinct clouds were simply sublime.... The city still seemed completely carefree and summery. The women, just as in July, wore very little clothing. Dima's eyes were caught by one feminine figure, then another. At the entrance to the airport there was some roadwork going on. There was the sound of steamrollers and other road machinery. The guys with shovels wore their orange jackets next to their bare skin. The workers' bodies glistened with sweat, and through the open window Dima was smacked by the odors of heat and burning asphalt. For a moment it seemed as if summer was just beginning.

There were an awful lot of people at the airport. Many were homeward bound, and others were seeing them off. Still more were arriving, back from somewhere and in a hurry to get their children home before the start of the school year. People were there to meet them. At the back of the hall, glass doors released flight after flight of passengers. The returnees were tanned, smiling and happy. Those waiting hugged them and picked up the children...

Dima saw a friend who was meeting someone. He was someone

Dima had known long ago, in the distant past, and he couldn't remember his name.

"Who you here to meet?" the fellow asked.

"My family. Back from the sea."

"And where were you?"

"Ahhh," Dima gave a dismissive wave, "I sat out the whole summer in the city! Where'd you get the tan?"

"Me?" the acquaintance chuckled. "I was on the roof. I spent the whole summer finishing off the *dacha* with my son, and sent the wife away. Now I'm meeting her. So how's things?"

"What things? Summer's ending and I hung about in the city. Didn't get any chance to relax at all. Well, see you!"

"Yup, take care!"

They shook hands. Five minutes later Dima saw his friend carrying two huge suitcases, and trailing behind him was a formidable woman in a light dress. The friend was smiling to himself as he walked.

Dima was suddenly uncomfortable with having lied to his forgotten friend. Why had he said he'd had a bad summer? He hadn't had a bad summer. And why had he slandered his summer serenity? He might never have such a wonderful summer again.

Several flights were delayed for various reasons. The flight Dima was waiting for was two hours late. There was no sense driving to the city, then coming back out here. So Dima loitered, wandered around, and napped in the car.... Then they announced that the flight was delayed another hour. That turned Dima sour. He thought, "Here it is the last day of summer, and what am I doing?" He bought a paper, but couldn't read. Nothing fluttered inside him. Serenity had not yet forsaken him.

He truly missed his wife and daughter. He missed his son, who would be coming home in two days. He missed them, but as he thought about them, his face was relaxed, and his head tilted a bit to the left. Even the sounds of the airport receded.

He met his family. He hugged his daughter and raised her high in his outstretched arms, then he kissed his wife. They waited for their bags, and his daughter talked non-stop, showing him this and that and even dancing. His wife said they'd suffered horribly because of the horrible delay. Dima tried to listen attentively... but in reality he was listening to the serenity within himself. How was it doing? Was it still there?

Night was falling as they drove back into town. His daughter fell asleep in the back seat—in a position unthinkable for an adult. Zhenya began listing all the things that had to be done the next day. It was made clear that in the morning they were to go and buy his daughter some shoes and plenty of other things for school. Dima nodded, smiled, and thought... No, he didn't even think, he just looked into the eyes of his serenity, so that he wouldn't forget what they looked like. For a while he'd looked at the world through those eyes—and he'd felt good. He wanted to remember those eyes after he said goodbye.

It was almost dark when they drove up to their building.

"Oh, what amusing benches they put in. Just what we need, how sweet," his wife said.

Dima looked and, sure enough, he saw that they'd installed some new benches near the entrance. When did they put them in, he wondered? Dima hadn't noticed.

"Yeah, we didn't waste our time here," Dima answered right off.

He kissed his wife, then slowly and carefully drew his daughter from the car, while his wife got the suitcases and bag from the trunk. They walked to the entrance. His daughter was sweating in her sleep. Dima held her closer; she was drooping and felt heavy and large. Her hair smelled of sun, wind and sea.

"You're warm..." Dima said to himself. "My beauty," he said almost silently.

As his wife opened the door to the building, Dima quickly looked back at the courtyard. He looked up at the top of the huge maple tree that towered above the birches and the ash. The maple was tall, very tall. Against the almost completely darkened sky he could see that the maple was stock-still, not quivering in the least. Dima winked at it, turned away, and, as he entered the building, smiled... saying a reluctant goodbye...

September 15, 2004

TRANSLATION BY PAUL E. RICHARDSON

YEVGENY GRISHKOVETS

Shelter

Alexander Kabakov

The street flew into the sky. It was as if the clouds were swimming slowly through the sky, yet, at the same time they rushed along, constantly changing their color and form. It was true theater: turn away for a moment, and you might miss the most important thing.

In the early '70s, people of his generation moved en masse from the ranks of researchers and engineers into those of elevator attendants, boiler room technicians, parking lot security guards, or mere jobless loiterers with fake employment papers obtained from a low-level boss of one's acquaintance in exchange for a dog-eared foreign edition of *Lolita* or a scratched *Sergeant Pepper* LP. As soon as they left their posts, they would sit down to write the unprintable great novel or to cover canvases with abstract yet brilliant swirls, or else with concretely merciless visions of their contemporaries' abominable mugs and grim landscapes of the Motherland... They all drank port—"Kavkaz" or "Agdam"—and strummed on guitars, singing their harmless dissident songs late into the night in basements and unkempt apartments.

But he was cautious. Well, it was not because he was afraid—although he was—but mainly because he rejected on principle this self-satisfied idleness and unfounded faith in one's own exceptionality. All the same, he went to the same parties, drank the same port—preferring vodka, but one should blend in—and conversed about art and cursed the state that held them all by their throats. With respect to the state, he was in complete accord with the others, though his reasons for disliking it were somewhat different from his friends'. As for art, he questioned its value most when he surveyed the heaps of unframed paintings that leaned against the walls or listened to a chapter of the latest immortal manuscript.

Once, his doubts got him into a fight.

It happened at a farewell party organized for some hapless graduate of the Surikov Art Institute. With his Israeli visa, he was about to depart first for Vienna and ultimately, of course, for New York City, that acme of contemporary culture. The artist had quietly worked as a trolley-bus driver and never made a fuss in the reception room of the Supreme Soviet until the time allotted for tormenting the would-be immigrant came to an end and he was finally free to leave. Now he was taking with him some surrealist canvases, re-primed and painted over with kitschy and twisted likenesses of his relatives. Everyone present had helped with the priming; the emigrant himself painted the portraits inspired by pre-war photographs of girls in berets and men in military-style overcoats. They were all to pass for family relics, but once transported to freedom, the silly portraits would be removed, revealing the true stuff, fit for an immediate exhibit somewhere in SoHo—oh, SoHo! But at the Tretyakov Gallery, a dour dame with the unmistakable stamp of KGB service upon her face, glancing maliciously at the con artist, stamped the back of each painting with the following formula: "Artistic value negligible. Not to be transported." So the painter could neither move his masterpieces from his socialist Motherland—the Motherland that gave him "a happy childhood and free education"—nor sell them, even to the lowliest of galleries, since their artistic value was officially negligible. And so the guests helped themselves to the spooky portraits, for safekeeping till better days: who knows, perhaps they could be carried across by some Western diplomats. The paintings without takers were hauled outside by the drunken, furious artist and thrown into the perpetually burning dumpster. He then doused them with turpentine for dramatic effect.

No one came to extinguish the fire. Those were quiet times, no one expected trouble, and besides, it was only a dumpster—let it burn.

Together with everyone else, our hero, who came to say goodbye to the artist—let us call him, as usual in literature, "N"—wrapped the painting he was given in some newspapers, while cursing the laws. More precisely, he was bewildered: what kind of idiots were these communist bosses? They created their own enemies. What harm could have come of letting the painter show his canvases in the foyer of some "palace of culture"? Who would have been hurt if the main gallery in Saratov—the town he had left to compete for entrance into the Surikov Institute—had bought a couple of his clever imitations of de Chirico and hung them in the room with "The Works of Our Compatriots"? Nothing, absolutely nothing would have happened to their omnivorous power, no one would have died, and these old fools would carry on kissing foreign leaders, embracing other cannibalistic regimes around the globe, and building their stinking rockets. The painter would not have left the country, filled with hatred. He would have intrigued quietly at the Artists' Union, hatching plans to get himself a new studio, and, given the opportunity, would have preached to foreign guests about freedom of creative thought in the Soviet Union. What idiots.

By midnight all the guests got sow-drunk and no one talked of going home anymore; instead, they all decided to go straight to the airport at dawn, to wave at their friend through the steel bars as he walked across to the plane that was to take him to paradise. To hell with the secret police—

let them snap their photos and file them in their shitty dossiers—enough fear and trembling! N too was going to go, although it would be more dangerous for him than for all these street sweepers and plumbers: the cadres department of his thrice-damned institute might easily receive a very unpleasant communiqué compelling it to postpone his defense or simply kick him out, under the excuse of cutting lab costs.

However, it was just then that the conflict erupted. As always when far from sober, he became unpleasantly sincere. Cornering the fresh "traitor to the Motherland" and making as if to proffer a pearl of wisdom, he plunged ahead:

"Look, old man—" N said, swaying and bumping the artist lightly against the wall, which was a bit much. "You're right—life is passing by and you should live it *there*, so as not to feel the sting of impotent regret..."

Here they both smirked at the popular adage of recent years, when so many were leaving, having suddenly "discovered" a Jewish branch in the family tree. For N, it would not have been difficult to obtain through friends an invitation from some "aunt" in Haifa—for who is to say that a Russian could not have such an aunt. In fact, only half of these exiles were destined for Israel; the rest were trying to get through Austria and Italy to the United States.

"You see," N continued, not letting go of his captive, pinned up against the wall, "You understand, old man—you'll never have an exhibit here, I agree."

They were all quite certain that there would *never* be anything here for them.

"But listen, old man—" Here, N, luckily, lowered his voice, as otherwise everyone in the room would have heard him, and he was right to do so. "What if there you don't have—you know... Eh? Not because of ideology, but due to artistic merits. You know they're honest there, don't you? What if they say no—for artistic... you understand? Just imagine—what then? Tie a noose? Look at me—I'm not going anywhere—"

He was not given the opportunity to explain why he wasn't going. He wanted to say that it was not because of the ban on exit within five years

                              ALEXANDER KABAKOV

of leaving a job—which sometimes became an indefinite ban—although, of course, that was the first and main reason; but N also wanted to explain that he was scared of freedom, which is ultimately certain to reveal everyone's true worth; for it would be frightening to find, once freed, that one was worth nothing at all, whereas here there was a perennial consolation in blaming the communists. Therefore, one ought to think a hundred times before asking for freedom and N, for example, was not ready for such an exam. At his institute, it was plainly understood that he could have defended not only his candidacy, but his doctorate too—had he only joined the party. Here, he was an unrecognized genius, whereas *there* he might end up a recognized nothing.

These thoughts were fairly insightful, and it is strange that N, a man of no particularly keen intellect, arrived at those conclusions as far back as 1972, rather than '92 or '96, when everyone realized these truths—when the other participants of that evening get-together (those that stayed behind or were still living) began to join the old women in red neckerchiefs and old men in felt fedoras in organized protests *against* freedom. That N's intellect was not so great was confirmed by the fact that he decided to share these insights with a man whose pocket contained a "certificate of divestment of Soviet citizenship on the grounds of his pending immigration to the state of Israel."

And so, before N had his say, he received a weak, intellectual punch from half-clenched fist. He was lucky not to get a real punch: the artist actually could fight. All the same, blood rushed from his nose; there was an uproar; N stood with his head tilted backward; everyone urged the two men to reconcile. No one understood what had happened, and neither N nor the artist would explain. When it was time to go to the airport and those who snoozed had to be shaken awake—when everyone began to finish the unfinished drinks, either to muster courage or to soothe the pain of the impending eternal parting, and luggage had to be pushed out into the street, and the rare morning cabs had to be seized—N suddenly decided that, although they had been reconciled, it would be strange of him to wave through the bars at his now former friend. After all, his departure was the end, so former friends it was. So, instead, N shook the hand that had punched him in the face—picked up the rolled-up canvas and calmly walked to the metro to take the first morning train home and straighten himself out after a hard night before going to work. The artist, already emotional, understood the handshake to be an additional gesture of reconciliation and took no notice of N's absence from the farewell, with its crowds, tears and inanely cheerful jokes. As for the remaining company, N distanced himself from them little by little, over a year-and-a-half or so.

Sadly, N had been right about the artist, although he did not hang himself, but set himself up well in Brighton Beach, remodeling apartments for his prosperous compatriots. There, on the wooden promenade, they met again, when N happened to be in New York on important, boring business and decided to spend the evening among near Russian speakers. The two embraced and went to celebrate at the famous "Odessa" restaurant, reminiscing about their past, except for the foolish farewells, and the painter kept trying to pick up the cheque, flashing his gold American Express.

The painting N had got at the party moved with him from apartment to apartment for many years, rolled up all the while in a scroll. When finally he returned from America, he unrolled it at last, and, as he did, the paint flaked and crumbled from the canvas—not just the top layer and the primer, but with them the hidden, subversive painting too. Artists' materials were dreadful in the Soviet era.

The clouds began to swell somewhat, to turn into thick, blue thunderclouds; filaments separated from their outer edges and disappeared into the emptiness. In the distance, the thunderclouds fell upon the street where, like a thin blade, it sliced into the horizon; from that same spot spewed white fragments of lightning.

                                          ALEXANDER KABAKOV

Thirty years went by. Everything changed. The old life vanished somewhere down those decades, and N had almost no complaints about the new life that took its place. At least not the same complaints that he had before. One could live any way one pleased, including the way N had always longed for: making lots of money in a variety of ways—and he had a knack for inventing new ways. Back when he had spent his evenings drinking with artistically inclined friends, all his schemes were good for nothing but a stint in jail, so he had settled for cursing the government along with the rest of the crowd. Now, however, all the reasons for complaining had evaporated. His friends, according to rumors that reached him, went on cursing the lack of freedom, the injustice, the pig-headedness, and the insolence of office. In essence he agreed with all of this, but now felt that these characteristics were probably—in larger or smaller degree, that was the key—innate to any state, which was shown not only domestically, but abroad as well, something he was now well familiar with. And if there was no other sort of government, he thought carelessly and typically, as he sat in an endless traffic jam that had nothing to do with stoplights or powers that be, why waste time being angry? His friends were unlucky, sure, but no one bothers them now, they live as they want and they manage okay, he thought. I, as it turns out, can...

Much had happened in those thirty years, but N had forgotten almost all of it. And if something reminded him of something he had forgotten, he would only be perfunctorily surprised—after all, so much had happened and so much continues to happen, and then ruthlessly suppress the memory. For example, his family had disappeared, but how, he could no longer remember. He had no children: he and his wife had tormented one another for years as desire wilted, and finally they settled for the inanity of "it didn't work out." But even after N had gotten used to those words, even "it didn't work out" became a part of his forgotten past. He continued to rush from place to place, earning and spending, losing and recovering the losses, without questioning for a moment that this was the only way to live, that there could be no other life but this life, though one might be more or less lucky.

For some reason, he counted everything from that year, 1972, when he separated from his company of friends. Only this accounting could, every now and then, break through his existence and possess him... could it really be that fifteen years had passed... twenty... a quarter of a century (that's crazy).... thirty.... Only this accounting truly distressed him: truly the end is near... near... who knows when, but it is always closing in...

Once, at some forum or the devil knows what, with the usual empty speeches and the all-important small-talk during intermissions, which conversations being the reason that everyone came here, to this foolish resort he had long since tired of... in the evening hours of boredom, when most were up to their ears in champagne (which he could not stand—Sovetskoye champagne had disappeared and only this thousand-dollar stuff remained), on the second day, N sat in the hall and found himself talking to one of the tarts who had been flown in for the participants on a special airplane. The girl was excessively, disgustingly attractive, but, to N's surprise, she talked almost articulately, almost without any swearing or any provincial accent, and was not at all dull. She even spoke decently in English, having at first mistaken N for a foreigner. That she was unmistakably Russian was given away by the fact that she was overdressed in an evening gown at a cocktail party, and her meticulous grooming left no doubt that her occupation depended directly upon her body.

"I would have never guessed that you were Russian," she repeated, emphasizing her surprise with a toss of her platinum mane. "By your appearance, by the way you speak English."

"Everyone can speak English these days," he replied in the flirtatiously gruff manner of a bachelor, of a man ready for anything, then for some reason gruffly mumbled, "If only they learned to speak Russian as well."

"But you are adult," she said, unthinkingly using a ridiculous euphemism for "elderly." Then: "I mean to say, middle-aged. We studied English... we, expecting to use it, but you—"

Here, she became genuinely embarrassed, as "we" and "you" emphasized to both of them that he was at least twice her age.

"And where are you from? And what are you doing here?" N asked almost rudely, in part because it fit, in part because it flowed naturally from the fact that he was offended by this "adult," "we" and "you."

"Originally, from Volgograd," she said unexpectedly simply, and N again was again surprised by the simplicity of this clearly "Premium" class professional. "But I've been living in Moscow for the past two years. I am here as an interpreter."

He chuckled in a fairly offensive manner.

"There's not much demand for interpreters here, especially for English—"

"But I am fluent in German." Now she was insulted. "And I know a bit of Spanish. And you seem to think that if a girl is attractive, then she must be, well—"

She did not finish the sentence, and he really liked that. The girl seemed still to have one foot in Volgograd, where, as she told him over the next quarter of an hour, she had been living with her father, an engineer at a military manufacturing plant, and her mother, a teacher. She took her degree, with honors, in philology or something like that, and then went to Moscow to visit a girlfriend who had already settled there—and stayed longer than planned. She spent half of her first year there unlearning her native fricative "g"—"they pronounce it in Volgograd just as they do in Ukraine. I seem to have gotten over it, don't you think?"

They had already had plenty to drink. She was drinking champagne—just as she should be, given her profession, thought N, for no stories or polished manners could convince him that she really was just an interpreter. He kept ordering cognac, shot after shot. Meanwhile, the party had quieted down, and only a few delegates were still at the bar. Laughter and shrieks of girls less cultivated than his companion could be heard from the ballroom. But, for the first time in many years, N was conversing freely and un-self-consciously, without looking for any advantage from his conversation, as if with someone he had long known and liked.

They decided to go back to their rooms and change into winter clothing, and then to meet on the central square, to see the mountains and snow in the moonlight. She, naturally, showed up in a senselessly luxurious ski outfit. He had merely changed from his dinner jacket into a sweater and mundane black overcoat. His feet were cold in his dress shoes.

"If you don't mind my asking—" she suddenly asked, after they had enjoyed the view and she had sipped a fair amount from his flask to warm herself, and they were about to start back to the hotel, though they had not yet negotiated whose room to go to. "How old are you really?"

He shivered, not just because he didn't feel like admitting to fifty-four, but also because he realized that the girl was estimating the difficulty of the job.

"Fifty-four," he said too loudly. "But what's the problem? Everything's in good shape, knock on wood—"

He felt nauseated by his crudeness, but she seemed not to have heard him.

"I want to ask you as an adult," and she corrected herself again, "as an already elderly, excuse me, person..."

He stopped walking and looked directly in her face. In the nighttime luminescence of snow, storefronts and firmament, her face seemed absolutely childlike, as if she was not twenty-five as she must have been, but only ten or twelve. How she'd found time to take off all her makeup was a mystery.

"Go ahead, *kid*," he said all of a sudden, feeling a deep sadness as his heart stammered and then beat faster. "Go ahead, ask. What do you want to know? Whether I'm married?"

She sighed.

"No matter what I say, you still think I'm a whore—and you're wrong." He noted that she cursed appropriately, too. "That's not what I wanted to ask at all..."

⌇

A downpour was unleashed. It seemed as if you were driving at the bottom of a violent river; the road twenty meters ahead melted into the sky.

Out of the water shone the dim yellow lights of oncoming cars, into the water flowed the red flickers of those going his way. They all passed him; he drove in the right lane, afraid to miss the turn in the dark. Finally, a narrow path opened up in the dark forest wall and he drove slower still on asphalt that was flatter than that on the highway.

Three years had gone by since that February night, but N was still thinking about why he was so hurt by her question, about how the two most important conversations of his life took place when he was not sober, and about how, after all those thousands of wasted evenings, the only two that he ended up remembering were when some self-satisfied wannabe floored him for decades with an awkward punch and when some clever, impudent broad asked him a question that he still didn't know how to answer.

He never saw her again. Sometimes he thought he glimpsed her face in a crowd; he would approach, smiling, but each time had to withdraw, mumbling "Excuse me, I'd mistaken you for someone else."

"Haven't you had enough fun yet?" that is what she asked him back then. N frequently asked himself the same question.

It was not a well-formed idea; it could not be called "desire"; perhaps "sensation" was the best word to describe it. Anyhow, that was the word N finally attached to what he had experienced for several years and what surfaced more and more often in the perfunctory conversations with the few contacts he still talked to in his life, scheduled as it was down to the hour and even the minute.

"If only I could go away," he would sigh, and the conversation would die down for a moment, like the flame of a lighter in a sudden light gust of air. After a short pause, his acquaintance would try to jolly him along, smirking: "What, like Tolstoy, eh? What's the matter with you? Have you lost the meaning of life?" But N would already have regrouped and answered, also with a smirk, "Well, sure, just like Lev Nikolayevich—I too shall kick the bucket en route to Astapovo station."

"There's no such station anymore. They've renamed it Tolstoy Station," his contact would retort.

But he did want to go away.

Not like Tolstoy, not from family and people; he had long left those things behind. He had seceded, putting behind him the cordon guards of habitual actions and routine words and had created inside himself something like a ministry of foreign affairs for negotiating practical matters and a ministry of defense for the protection of his borders. Any attempt to violate those boundaries was unstintingly met by a weapon of mass destruction called "money." It used to be entirely effective—he was able to pay off any aggressor, be it a woman, a relative, a friend, or a business partner. He spared nothing for his defensive readiness, expending all of his energies on ensuring his monetary preparedness.

But this would no longer suffice. He needed to walk away from himself and he no longer had the strength to maintain border security. What is more, of late his defensive systems were failing, one after the other; something was breaking down, leading to the opposite of the intended effect: people got used to being carpet-bombed with money and started responding to his assistance with attachment, tenderness, or simply incorrigible dependence. And it was dependence that vexed him most. It wasn't, somehow, they who depended on him, but he who depended on them. He was his own fifth column. And it destroyed his psychic security, and, like a dotty capitalist who built himself a deep, fully autonomous shelter in the 1950s against Russian hydrogen bombs, N kept dreaming of self-sufficiency in some impregnable bunker.

"Go away, I have to go away," he kept thinking to himself, even saying it out loud when the irony of his friends did not force him to turn the insistent phrase into a joke. But as a measure of defense, a joke was puny; the only correct, dependable resolution would be to go away.

N had spotted the place after happening to drive past it several times.

He was on his way to his country home when a traffic jam diverted him from his usual bridge and he saw this beautiful place. On another day he drove by it again. And the third time, he pulled over and got out of the car. The church stood without crosses on its cupolas. Inside, its freshly whitewashed walls shone in the daylight, and a stack of wooden beams stood in the middle. The priest puttered about awkwardly in the empty space, at times throwing back his gray head and pointing his beard toward the object of his reflections, which clearly had something to do with construction.

"You surely must know this," N said. He did not know how to to talk to a priest, so he talked as he would have done to anyone else burdened by the unexpected crises of building... "I just recently finished some renovations, so I am up on these things... You really need to buy all the materials well ahead of time... Because they go up in price quicker than labor... Over there, in the yard—"

"In the garden," the priest corrected him.

"In the garden," he repeated quickly, "there is room for an awning, to store all the materials. If you buy in bulk, ahead of time, you'll save a packet, and then, when everything's ready, you can start building. But first, you should get a specialist's estimate. And don't hire Moldavian workers."

"We have our own workers," the priest said. "Forgive me, but we have special rules about such matters."

Something made N feel that he had no need to defend himself from this man, whose eyes were calmly penetrating, though his billowing robes sprinkled with sawdust made his silhouette waver against the sunlight. This man was not about to encroach on him, tear through his defenses, entrench himself on the territory gained. He was indifferent to whether N's borders were open or closed, for he didn't appear even to notice them.

He would visit at first once a week, then twice, and gradually he assumed full responsibility for managing the renovation. Then he came up with a way to notify not only the old women in the neighborhood but also some conscientious Moscow collectors that the church was open once more and needed icons. Then he paid the full cost of gilding the cupolas.

Yet he refused to be baptized, telling the priest in an embarrassed tone that he had been secretly baptized as a child and it would be wrong to do it twice. Entering the church, he would not cross himself but would only bare his head or bow slightly, as he would when meeting an acquaintance in the street.

With difficulty, over half-a-year or so, he struggled through the Bible, skipping a lot and finding it hard to see what could possibly be holy about the repetitive passages and genealogies of the long-dead. But he read the Gospels over and over again, examining especially the divergences between the four evangelists' accounts. One day, he saw for the first time the import of a verse of Mark: "And they gave him to drink wine mingled with myrrh: but he received it not." He began to weep, seeing the Crucified reject the anesthetic in the smoldering sunset hour. Immediately, he felt embarrassed, even though he was completely alone, and wiped away the tears.

After that happened, he bought in a church for a kopek a tiny silver cross on a cord, and began to wear it.

That's how it went on, until he made his final decision, which, like all final decisions, crystallized as if by itself, so that he could not say exactly when it happened. Just a while ago, it all had been uncertain, but now nothing could be clearer or simpler. It was strange that it had not occurred to him sooner. It was so simple, exhaustive and final, that it could not be any other way.

But something troubled him still.

—◦—

In this condition, he now drove through a positively relentless rain.

—◦—

The gate was open.

The priest met him inside the gate, leaning to protect himself from the sideways streams of wind-blown rain with an old, black umbrella, its spines broken and protruding like knitting needles. In the manner of an experienced driver, he guided N with hand signals, helping him park in the garden.

"Father!" N shouted through the rain, still feeling embarrassed by this form of address. "I've signed a power of attorney for the car. Getting it all formalized is a pain in the ass, but the power of attorney was no problem, for a fee."

He was completely flustered by the vulgarity of his own words, but he had somehow forgotten any others.

"One more thing," he said, hurriedly, "the funds—I've made three deposits, to the accounts you'd specified."

They stood on the porch beneath the awning.

"Also—" He finally dared to speak of the main thing on his mind. "About my decision. You see, Father, I made it—well—just for my own benefit. There's no sacrifice in it, you understand? It's just that I want to hide, and to get saved. I'm sick of everything."

"Do not give it another thought," the priest replied with a smile. "Do not think about anything. You want to be saved? Rightly so. People have always come to the church to be saved from the world, and if you don't get away from the world, it's hard to save your soul. I could only save myself here. Do you know what I was before? I was in the navy. I served on a missile boat. No use talking about that now. Let's be saved together, eh? Live a minute without sin, and that shall be your salvation. Your room over there—we put some furniture in there yesterday— would you like to see it?"

The priest opened a small door on the right of the double doors of the church, and N peered inside. He saw a bed with a chipped wooden headboard, a plywood dresser, a chair with a torn seat, and a half-opened armoire. A cast ewer was attached to the wall; underneath it stood an enameled green washbasin on a stool. Only a dark icon distinguished the place from a typical room in a municipal motel.

"And the toilet is not far off, near the market," said the voice of the father from behind him. "And we have a fine *banya* in the village. It's open every other day… That's it. Before matins, clean up a bit in the garden. And at night, keep your ears open. Although we have a security system, it is safe here. Make yourself at home."

He turned around. After a momentary confusion, the priest backed out through the door to let N out of his room. Again they found themselves on the porch recently covered with slippery faux marble tiles bought with N's money. He made a step toward the half-opened double doors and raised his hand to make the sign of a cross.

Early the following morning, it was damp as he was sweeping in the garden, and he thought how the rain always washed the builders' rubbish across the path, and that this broom and dustpan was stupidly ineffective. I'll have to come up with a more rational way to do this, he thought.

And he thought of nothing else.

TRANSLATION BY ANNA SELUYANOVA

     ALEXANDER KABAKOV

Earplugs

Alexander Khurgin

Nelya Yavskaya[1] lived by the beauty of the world and of her environmental habitat. By nothing else. And if beauty hadn't existed and been present in the world, she would probably have died. Because she wouldn't have had anything to live by. If she'd had a pure, grand love, she could've still lived like a woman, in terms of sexual relations, that's just inherent to women; but somehow love, in the exhaustive sense of the word, hadn't come her way for a long time. Love gave her a wide berth, both the grand love and the pure one. So, after a certain point, Nelya had stopped waiting for love to happen to her, because, in the first place, she lived by beauty, and, in the second place, she understood through her own common sense that there was no use waiting for love to come into her life, since there was nowhere for it to come from. She worked in a purely female collective, where all her co-workers and all the patients were women of varying ages

---

[1] The last name "Yavskaya" is based on the word "yav," reality.

and diagnoses. With the exception of the department head and a few idiot orderlies, of course. But the department head was a jack-assed jerk, both on first impression and in his deepest essence, while the orderlies, well, they were even worse. As if you'd even want to fall in love with people like them. Nothing will come of it, no matter how hard you try, because, of course, love is cruel, you could even fall in love with a jerk, nobody's going to argue with this piece of wisdom. But there's still a limit to what love'll do to you.

Earlier, however, in her early childhood and when she was young, there had been a few specific men and Nelya Yavskaya had experienced certain elevated feelings. So, thank God, she was no old maid. That is to say, she was neither old, nor a virgin. But lately she couldn't honestly brag about the feeling of love, either; she couldn't show it in its finest form to what they call 'interested parties.' She didn't have the least bit of that feeling, in zero of its permutations; or, to put it plainer, she wasn't loved by any of the men, and she, reciprocating the men's feelings, didn't love any of them herself. So Nelya lived, taking pleasure in unadorned beauty itself, since beauty—you can make beauty independently, and with your own two hands. In contradistinction to love.

Nelya, she used to talk about it like this: "Every person," she'd say, "is the blacksmith of his own individual beauty." And, "I don't know, each to his own," she'd say, "but, for me, beauty is more than sufficient for the fullness of life and the satisfaction of my spiritual needs."

Apart from that, she was unshakably convinced, and loved to repeat, that someday, all over the world, beauty, and beauty alone, would save the world. In this, she was entirely on the side of the classic writer Fyodor Mikhailovich Dostoevsky.

Lots of people objected, saying, "What does it save the world from?"

And Nelya answered them: "From everything."

But they kept objecting, asserting, over and over, not without justification, that by now nothing can save the world, and where is it, this beauty of yours, they'd say, who's seen it around here? So Nelya would say, "Come on, what do you mean, beauty is present everywhere and all over. Wherever you look."

 ALEXANDER KHURGIN

"There's the human being, for example," she'd say, "you could even take me. My face and hair, my body—all that is the highest symbol of beauty, its incarnation in earthly life. Everyone else is, too."

"Our department head?" said those who entirely disagreed with her. "Or the orderlies?"

"The department head," said Nelya, "I agree, is a jack-assed jerk, and the orderlies are even worse. But the rest aren't like that, are they?"

"What are they like?" they asked her, and she answered, "Beautiful. How else could they be?"

Of course, people who knew her laughed at her for such talk, and for her entire womanish worldview, hinting that working in that particular department was influencing her, and not in the positive sense. And Nelya even noticed something like this about herself sometimes. Something superfluous and extraneous. For example, she loved examining the bruises left on patients' bodies after they were given shots. She would go and get lost in contemplation of them, especially when a lot of patients accumulated them during their courses of treatment, and the bruises ran together into patterns, with fantastical shapes and various colors of the rainbow, from red to violet. And sometimes there'd be bruises the shade of the sea at morning or of the sky just after sunset. It wasn't unheard of for Nelya to give a shot of the same old droperidol and then to just stand there, enchanted, enjoying the sight of the pattern. Then she'd come to, look around and say, "Oh my goodness, now what was I doing?" and tell the orderlies, "Take the patient to the ward, let her rest."

And they'd lift the patient up from the examination table and lead her away, while Nelya was thinking, "I've got to get hold of myself," she'd think, "because after all, work is work, and my personal aesthetic passions and notions might be out of place here, regardless of the fact that beauty has a place everywhere and in everything."

And Nelya would finish out her tense workday impatiently, passing the shift over to the night nurse and going off home to relax and de-stress there among the pictures. Her whole apartment was covered in them, in works of the painter's art. In pictures, that is. Nelya had cut them out of magazines over the years: from *Ogonyok* and *Yunost*. At one time, those and other magazines on society, politics and art printed inserts with master-pieces by the best artists of all times and countries. Then other publications started putting out ones that were more contemporary and better in terms of print quality. She cut these world masterpieces out, framed them, and hung them all on the walls. As a result of all this, her living room assumed the appearance of a museum of fine arts, reduced in scale. Nelya made the frames herself, with her own delicate hands. It was a sort of life-long hobby she had, making frames for pictures. In the Young Technicians store she bought cheap remnants from lumber-finishing and furniture manufacturers, small boards of all different shapes and sizes, little planks, thin strips of wood. Or she lifted whatever was lying around un-monitored or unused on construction sites. So she made frames for her pictures from all this stuff. She had a full set of woodworking tools at home, too. The last man in her life had given it to her on her birthday, presented it to her like a big joke. He'd found out from her that she made the frames herself, personally, and so he brought her a full set of tools in a special case, with little divided sections. There was nothing that wonder-suitcase didn't have in it. It really had everything. A regular plane and a smoothing plane, chisels and hacksaws, and burins, and all kinds of files, and drills and drill bits, and not one, but *two* hammers, and a little axe, and a bit brace. It had a folding rule, of course, a bright yellow one, and a marking gauge, and a spirit level, and other priceless equipment. This was the tool set that her dear Vasya Bratus took from work and brought to her. He brought it over and gave it to her. For fun and games. It didn't give him a bit of trouble to take a tool set from the factory where he worked as a senior foreman, and giving a woman this kind of gift, instead of the generally accepted perfume or pantyhose or something, was interesting for him, understandably so. To make a little joke, to be original. But Nelya, when she saw the present, she couldn't stop thanking him and couldn't stop kissing him.

She said, "Nobody's ever given me anything better in my whole life." And she said that only a truly loving person could guess so exactly and hit the nail not close, but on the head, in the bullseye.

As for Vasya Bratus, as soon as he realized that his idea wouldn't result in any happy laughter or jokes, he became annoyed, and said, "You're either sick and not feeling yourself, or you're just playing around and acting stupid. But you don't have any sense of humor in you at all," he said, "and I cannot remain for long in a close relationship with a woman who is deprived of this important human feeling," he said, "nor do I even want to." So he walked out on her on her birthday, and never came back. He didn't sit down to eat with her, didn't drink a single drop of wine or vodka to Nelya's health. Actually, he didn't even walk out, he rode off on his Kharkov Bicycle Factory bike, and the set was left with Nelya for good, as a symbol of his memory, the memory of that joking man by the name of Vasya Bratus, whom she had been hoping and counting on marrying, so as to create a family. After all, she did love him with all her heart, and always watched from the window how he'd come wheeling up to her building on his fine, light bicycle, and how rays of sunlight pierced through the wheels' spinning spokes, and how the spokes flashed silver, reflecting fans of shadow and light. The beloved man himself, though, Vasya, he sat straight and rigid in the bicycle seat, gravely turning the pedals clockwise. The bicycle transformed his legs' circular motion into forward motion and started off. And Nelya always waited for Vasya, looking at the road and thinking with satisfaction, "He really is beautiful, my Vasily, he is genuinely beautiful, especially when he's riding a bike." She also dreamed and thought secretly about how once she and Vasya were joined in marriage, she would be able to become Nelya Sergeyevna Bratus, and that that would also be beautiful. And if you made a double last name, say, Bratus-Yavskaya, or the other way around, Yavskaya-Bratus, then that would be even more beautiful and sound even better.

But her intimate dreams fell apart overnight and did not come true, because the desired Vasily, having given her the set of woodworking tools, left for the rest of his days, as they say, and didn't come back, and got married, probably, to somebody else—it's not as if there aren't a lot of willing women in the world. In any case, ever since that distant day, Nelya hadn't seen his Kharkov Bicycle Factory bicycle with the shining spokes in its wheels even once, and she also hadn't seen or run into Vasily.

On the plus side, of course, making frames for her pictures became much easier, and in every way more convenient, and they turned out much more evenly and beautifully than before. Because, in a matter like this, one that requires precision, a set of good tools is the most important condition for success and for the quality of one's craftsmanship.

So, in her leisure hours Nelya made frames, a lot of frames, since, over the years, she had accumulated an enormous quantity of pictures. The main thing was that these frames weren't just four narrow boards hammered together at right angles with nails; for each picture Nelya made a different frame, taking into consideration what the artist had depicted in the picture and what its color scheme was. If he'd depicted, let's say, a bright female figure, or some kind of Sistine Madonna, or something, Nelya would plane a capacious, carved frame, with ornamentation all around the edges. But if the picture was a man in severe shades, or a knight at a crossroads, then a correspondingly severe and simple frame was prepared, without decoration. And Nelya picked out the color of the frames, their tone that is, especially for each individual case, with a sense of responsibility, so that it—that is, the color—would underline the meaning and quintessence of the artworks and set them off, not clash with them.

So Nelya's pictures hung not only in the room, like they did back when she had just begun to put together her beauty collection, but three rows high in the hall, and in the kitchen, and everywhere that space allowed and where there was lighting so you could look at them and see what was portrayed in them. Nelya kept the pictures that didn't fit on the walls in a storage closet—a repository was what it was, thanks to which she had many opportunities for changing her exhibit whenever she wanted, according to her taste and whims. When the unavoidable moment arrived and the storage closet was so full she couldn't fit one more thing in it, Nelya started taking her pictures to work and hanging them there, all over the corridor and the wards. The first time the department head saw her autonomous acts, he said, "And what are those, if I may ask?"

                                ALEXANDER KHURGIN

But Nelya answered him, saying, "Paintings, works of fine art."

"What're they for?" the department head asked.

And she answered him, saying, "They're beautiful."

So the department head left Nelya alone and waved her off, thinking, let her do it, a little extra psychotherapy won't hurt, and everything would've been totally fine if the idiot orderlies hadn't spoiled the pictures, drawing mustaches on the women's faces and horns on the men's. They even made a hole in the mouth of the portrait of Mademoiselle Charlotte du Val d'Ognes[2] and stuck in a burned-out cigarette butt.

But Nelya had countless pictures at home, and she replaced the disfigured portraits with new ones without saying a word. Just once she couldn't help herself, however; that was when the orderlies drew something filthy onto the three ancient heroes' horses.[3] So Nelya called them idiots, and bastards, too. Called them that right to their faces, shouting, "Sick people understand the beauty of the world, and the department head isn't against it, but you heartless bastards trample all over it."

Nelya Yavskaya would come home from work physically and mentally exhausted. She'd sit down in an armchair somewhere, let's say, in the middle of the room, and look at her pictures—not all of them one by one, but the ones she felt most like looking at at that particular time. *Alyonushka* by Viktor Mikhailovich Vasnetsov,[4] or maybe Rembrandt van Rijn's *Saskia van Uylenburg*.[5] She also loved examining Alexander Shilov's

---

[2] An 1801 portrait of a young woman drawing; long attributed to the French master Jacques-Louis David (1748-1825), it was correctly identified in the 20th century as the work of an accomplished but less recognized female painter who studied under him, Constance Marie Charpentier (1767-1849).

[3] The reference is to Viktor Vasnetsov's (1848-1926) famous 1898 painting "Bogatyry" (Medieval knights), portraying the three warrior heroes of Russian folklore, Alyosha Popovich, Dobrynya Nikitich and Ilya Muromets.

[4] Viktor Vasnetsov (1848-1926) was well known for his works on Russian mythological and historical subjects; "Alyonushka" shows the folktale heroine Alyonushka alone in the forest, pining for her bewitched brother.

[5] The Dutch artist Rembrandt (1606-1669) painted several portraits of his wife Saskia van Uylenburg (1612-1642) after their marriage in 1634.

picture *Morning*[6] for an entire evening. But the best picture, the one she loved the most, was a canvas by Peter Paul Rubens, *Portrait of the Lady-In-Waiting to Infanta Isabella*.[7] On the whole, it made a greater impression on her, and she liked it better, when artists painted portraits of women on their canvases. All the artists' women came out more beautifully than their men. This was probably because the actual women they chose to draw portraits of were beautiful, not scary-looking. Well, maybe they also loved these women and painted them with love in their hearts and souls. Although Nelya couldn't say anything about that for sure, since she didn't have any reliable information about it. But it was an indisputable fact of her life that she could sit for hours examining those beloved pictures down to their tiniest features and details. Especially when it was silent all around and no external sounds came in from the street or from the neighboring apartments. Which happened rarely, obviously. Maybe late at night, but even then, not every night. Because at night, too, something was constantly happening in the area: either some neighbors would be celebrating something at home with such fanfare that even a corpse would wake up and start to dance, or some other neighbors would start settling some personal issue at the top of their lungs, or an ambulance or police siren would go off, or something else loud would happen. And in the evening, it was really bad. All different kinds of noises came raining down on Nelya from all possible directions, which, of course, did not allow her to concentrate on experiencing art and receiving true pleasure from beauty. To make matters worse, she was on one of the building's lower floors, and mothers and children usually went for walks in the courtyard, under her windows, and the mothers yelled at the children while they were taking care of them, and

---

[6] Aleksandr Shilov (1943-) is a much-decorated contemporary Russian artist (made a People's Artist of the USSR in 1985, and has been a member of the President of the Russian Federation's Committee on Culture and the Arts since 1999); "Morning" depicts a young mother breast-feeding her baby.

[7] This portrait of a young girl by Rubens (1577–1640) is widely interpreted as a tribute to his daughter, who died in 1623 at twelve years of age.

                    ALEXANDER KHURGIN

cursed at them, for their own good, using various very bad words. The guys playing dominoes, it goes without saying, also yelled at each other and argued about whether they really were stuck in a stalemate, merging together into a general chorus, and cursed each other out with choice, flowery curse words. For no reason, since it didn't make any difference.

At one point, Nelya used to go out into the courtyard and say to the mothers, "Do you really want to talk to your own children that way? Such bad words. Now is that really beautiful?"

She tried to reason with the guys playing dominoes, too, tried to appeal to their conscience and their dignity as men. "Aren't you ashamed to express yourselves with curse words? After all, there are women and children all around you."

But the mothers, walking away, didn't answer her, and roared at the children anyway, children they had given birth to, and beat them in various soft places, and the guys playing dominoes said, in their particular style, "Get out of here," they said, "Get lost."

And then, after that, they added that she was a few cards short of a deck, they said, and that she must be part of some totalitarian sect, no doubt about it. And so the end result was that Nelya stopped going out and talking to the neighboring tenants, having become convinced that the conversations were useless, and she started to stop up her ears with earplugs.

Earplugs are these special plugs for workers in factories with a heightened noise level. This strange name is easily decoded: "Plug up your ears." A maternity ward nurse she knew had advised Nelya to arm herself with them. The nurse put earplugs in at night so she wouldn't hear her husband and children snoring. So Nelya, using the nurse's experience in her own particular way, started looking at her pictures with stopped-up ears. At first, when she wasn't used to it, it wasn't very pleasant, because her head filled with a heaviness and sort of swelled up from the earplugs, but then she got to where she could stand them, the earplugs, and sometimes she even forgot to take them out, and would go to bed with them in, and then go to work like that. She'd only remember them as she was getting to work, because she'd hear what people said to her vaguely and unclearly. In short, those earplugs turned out to be a real find for Nelya, all the more so since they manifested and revealed another unexpected attribute.

After Nelya got used to using them, they became a vital, inseparable accessory to her. Without them, she felt that she was missing something, and the empty holes in her ears bothered her, and it felt to her like these holes went all the way through, that gusts of wind were blowing through them. But when the earplugs were resting in her ears, everything went back to the allowable norm, and the wind died down, leaving behind a light heaviness in the area of her neck and the back of her head, a cottony kind of heaviness, a sweet heaviness. Then a low, prolonged sound would arise in her head, generating itself spontaneously, and that calm sound would hum for a little while; it would hum until Nelya tuned herself entirely to its wavelength, and as soon as she tuned herself to it, the sound would carefully begin to separate into parts and vibrate, and change its constant tone. The fact is that music would come from that soft, lonely sound and, as it was happening, it rang out inside of Nelya, not extending beyond her person. In any case, no one else who happened to be next to her could hear any music. Nelya somehow got the idea that, if she took the earplugs out while the music was sounding inside her, it would pour out for everyone to hear, and everyone around her would get the opportunity to hear her music and enjoy its broadcast, outside, in public. But, as soon as she did that, the music inside her ceased, emitting the sort of glissando that a trombone makes when the trombone player falls asleep while playing. So, not a drop of the music seeped out or penetrated to the external world, while Nelya heard the howling, whistling wind in her ears. So she quickly returned the earplugs to their places, and the melody that had almost died out inside Nelya gradually restored itself, filling her up completely and making her happy. First it filled up her head, then her lungs, and then the remaining space in her body.

Now Nelya did everything to music. She built her frames, and looked at her pictures, and worked at work. And while she was doing this, a multitude of melodies, as it turned out, lived inside her, and they all took turns

                    ALEXANDER KHURGIN

playing, depending on what picture Nelya was admiring, and depending on her mood, and on her general condition, and basically just on everything in the world. Even on what color dress Nelya was wearing and what the department head had said to her that day and on whether the orderlies had made fun of her handmade deafness and aloofness. Because Nelya eventually quit taking her musical earplugs out of her ears both at home, and in the ward, and everywhere. She learned how to understand what people said to her by the motion of their lips, like mute and deaf people understand it, although it wasn't as easy as all that. But she learned how. Having learned that, she acquired the ability to listen to the music inside her practically without ceasing, and the more she listened to it, the more she wanted to. That is, Nelya conceived a passion for her own internal music that was almost stronger than for preparing frames and for viewing the grand masters' pictures. Of course, she felt the best, the most superb, when her eyes were contemplating the eternally new paintings while the music rang out inside her. The most elevated and harmonious effect was achieved in this confluence, and Nelya very quickly realized and became convinced that this confluence was true beauty, Beauty with a capital letter, as they say. Without her music, she would simply no longer have been able to live among people and be a member of their society. Because, if she ever had to take her earplugs out, the music inside her went silent, and Nelya's fingers almost immediately started trembling, and her mood got worse, and, under the influence of external noises and the whistling of the wind, her body was stricken with one big aching pain that was unbearable even for a woman's patient constitution. So that now, even if Nelya had suddenly started wanting to live like she used to, in the general human clamor, she wouldn't have been able to, because of the condition of her soul. What a terrible thing almost happened to her, then, because she bought those earplugs in the drugstore without any extras, just one single box. She bought so few of them because she was being stupid and not thinking about the future. And then they went and disappeared from the shelves, for no reason—just disappeared into thin air. There were probably just a lot of people who wanted to defend themselves and save themselves from all kinds of noise.

So, although Nelya used her box sparingly, replacing her earplugs only when it was absolutely necessary, let's say, when she washed her hair and couldn't avoid getting water on them, still, nothing in this life lasts forever, no matter how long you try to drag things out. What could she do? Just wash her hair less often; people say that it's not good for your hair to wash it frequently, anyway. So the issue of hygiene, at least, didn't worry Nelya very much. Instead, it was the mysterious disappearance of earplugs from the local and regional drugstores that exceptionally and severely worried her. She turned to the International Red Cross and various philanthropic foundations, and personally approached the representative of the director of the regional governmental administration. Naturally, without any results: the much-vaunted representative didn't even see her, while the Red Cross and the foundations didn't give her any real answers. So Nelya, despairing of and disappointed in the official avenues for getting what she wanted, lowered herself to the point of asking the department head for help. After all, he had connections and personal relationships in the world of medicine and pharmacology. But the department head told her, "Just stop up your ears with cotton wool, and you'll be fine. What do you need earplugs for?"

Nelya explained over and over to him that she couldn't use cotton wool to do it because cotton wool only protected her from the whistling of the wind, and didn't give her any music. But, like a talking parrot, the department head asserted that it was good that it didn't, that's the way it should be, he said, since music was just one step away from trouble, one short step. And about the earplugs he said that each and every person could exist just fine without them, that there was no special trick to earplugs. So he suggested to Nelya that she start living again like everyone else does, like how she herself used to live, that is, without plugging up her ears with some damn stuff, but just the opposite, listening hungrily to her habitat, which was full of sounds and music for all tastes, full of everything your heart could desire.

Nelya told him that her personal habitat was located inside herself, not outside, but he didn't care to get into details and wasn't willing to meet her halfway. Proving, by that very act, that Nelya was right a thousand times over to think of him as a callous person who was not beautiful in any sense of the word.

But Nelya hadn't the slightest suspicion that she would get nothing from their maternity ward nurse, Miss Polya, the one who had advised her to use earplugs in the struggle against noise. She told her, Miss Polya, everything about her hopeless situation, and didn't hide a thing—she told her both about the music, and about the way she was walking her feet off, looking for earplugs everywhere she could, and said, "Lend me just a dozen of them, of those earplugs, Miss Polya, just to get by for a little while, and I'll pay you back. With interest."

But Miss Polya answered her like lightning out of the clear blue sky: "I can't," she said. "I myself have an insufficient quantity," she said.

Nelya tried to explain convincingly that she couldn't exist, wasn't capable of it, without earplugs and said, "They create the music of the spheres inside me."

Miss Polya said, "What about me? What do they create for me, chopped liver?"

So, after that conversation had taken place, Nelya's spirits fell and she lost heart. After all, her final set would become unfit for use if not today, then tomorrow, and she'd have to take them out. And there was nowhere to get more new ones. And that meant that the end of her music, and of beauty as a whole, was coming implacably closer, and so, her own final and irrevocable end was coming. She did live by beauty alone, nothing else, and taking it away would be just the same as killing her.

And she couldn't forgive herself for not thinking to buy ten or fifteen cases of earplugs and not spending all her strength and using all her means to create an inexhaustible supply of them, so that she'd have more than enough, have them up to her eyebrows, enough to last her whole life, with some left over for the people who'd come after her and take her place. "But who knew," Nelya thought, justifying herself, "who knew that they had that kind of side effect? Nobody knew. And it was impossible to guess or foresee that there wouldn't be a single one left in the drugstores." Because, in life, there is a lot of stuff that it's simply impossible to foresee. Well, you can't foresee practically anything, if you think about it. Who could've foreseen that, let's say, an ordinary ring of the doorbell would turn out to be what these days they call a fateful event and a turning point, and also a new stage of life? Nelya, hearing the doorbell ring, not only didn't foresee anything, she didn't guess anything, either. She turned the key indifferently in the lock and opened the door to her apartment. On the threshold stood the unforgettable Vasya Bratus, the man himself...

He stepped over the threshold and said, a little hoarsely, "Well," he said, "I've come back home to you after many days and nights. And in those years I was married seven times, in addition I had a wide variety of unofficial female friends and companions, some with a sense of humor, some with other strong sensibilities, but I've never met or known anyone better than you."

So Nelya said, "I'm boundlessly happy to hear that, Vasya, but you're too late, since I don't have any earplugs. And without them life isn't life for me, and you, Vasya, aren't Vasya."

Vasya, of course, didn't understand what she was talking about, and said, "What earplugs are you talking about?"

"The ones that protect people's ears from various noises and troubles, the ones that have disappeared from all the local and even the regional drugstores like the earth swallowed them up," Nelya explained to him.

"Oh, those," said Vasya. "But what do you need a drugstore for?" he said. "Out there at the mill we're up to our asses in earplugs, if you'll pardon my French."

Nelya heard Vasya's words and didn't believe them, saying, "Is that true?"

"It's not just true," said Vasya Bratus. "It's *absolutely* true."

And then Nelya took him in her arms and hugged him and said, "Bring some. Bring some right now, without delay."

                                        ALEXANDER KHURGIN

"You want it now, you got it now," said Vasya, "all the more so since my faithful bicycle is down below, chained to the gas pipe."

"Just bring a lot of them, a whole lot of them, so that there'll be enough for me, and for our kids, and for our grandkids—enough for everybody."

So Vasya, who still hadn't understood a thing, sprang onto the bicycle seat, and the pedals and spokes started flashing under him, and his bicycle carried him off in the direction of the mill with the maximum possible speed.

And Nelya, for the moment still Yavskaya, on the threshold of the triumphant return of both Vasya and love into her life, walked up to the window and looked down through it at the road, and she also started to wait, and hope, and, of course, believe. Although she didn't quite know what in, yet.

TRANSLATION BY ANNE O. FISHER*

*I thank the following for their help with translations: Alice Ritscherle, Lars Fogelin, Christa Craven, B., volume editor Paul Richardson, and the volume's collective of translators.

All Alone
(An Excerpt)
Eduard Limonov

The old woman lay on the couch. She looked like an oversized crust of black bread that had been left in the sun for too long. She was black and, in some places, yellow. Her mouth was half-open, with broken pieces of metal teeth sticking out. Her jaw was held in place by a head scarf, but it didn't keep her mouth shut. The problem was that the old woman had died alone. There was no one with her. She died with her mouth open. The nurse who found her in the morning tried to close her mouth, but by then it had been too late. The old woman looked like the corpse of another old woman which he had seen a long time ago at a body identification center outside Vukovar, Serbia. That old woman, though, had been tortured before she died.

This old woman was his mother. It was his fault that the corpse lay there with its mouth open. If he were a good son, he would have been there with her when she died. He would have held her hand. He would have closed her mouth. But he was a bad son and that was why he only got there in the morning.

He was lucky to be able to come at all. Both Russia and Ukraine were kind enough to let him through the border. They could have easily not let him through, Russia because a court had ruled that he owed Mayor Luzhkov 500,000 rubles and the police could now stop deadbeats from leaving the country, and Ukraine hadn't let him on its soil for the past decade. His name had been on some blacklist or other, along with the names of other enemies of Ukraine, but about six months previously the list had been abolished.

The last time he spoke to his mother was six days ago, on International Women's Day. She managed only three short sentences that made any sense. The rest was the babble of her subconscious. Her last words were "Where's Bogdan?" His mother had lost her mind a couple of months before, but she had not lost her metaphysical connection with her grandson. She asked the right question: "Where is my grandson?" He, her son, had lied to her that his wife and child were staying with the other grandmother in Togliatti, yet the truth was that her only, late-born grandson was who the hell knows where, at the other end of the globe, in Goa, the capital of hippies and druggies. He had been taken there by the wife of the man who now stood over the corpse of his mother. That wife of his had suddenly turned into a werewolf. The old woman's grandson had been there for two months, staying with who knows what kind of people. Besides, his wife was once again pregnant, in her fifth month. His wife's behavior was irrational and therefore a danger to all. The old woman sensed a metaphysical tremor in the part of her no longer functioning brain that was responsible for Bogdan. "Where is Bodgan?" she asked. Not "How is he?", but "Where is he?" It was the right question.

He who stood over the corpse was not only the son of the dead old woman, the father of the kidnapped child, and the husband of the beauty who had turned into a werewolf, but also the head of a banned party, its founder and, for the past 15 years, its irreplaceable leader. He belonged to the party more than to his mother, his wife and his child. True, he had left his mother and father a very long time ago, in 1964, but what about his child? Or his wife? His wife had gradually grown estranged from him. In the end, she literally renounced him, the way wives used to renounce husbands who had been declared enemies of the people. She hardened against him to the point of inexplicable hatred and, finally, took her son and fled to a land without meaning, a place where there were more trivial Russians than gray-skinned Indians. What was she doing over there all that time? He hoped that she would be sensible enough to stay away from drugs—she was pregnant, after all. Yes, he hoped this, while recognizing that it was not in her nature to be sensible.

Yes, the party. Party members died and went to jail for a cause which he had started in prison. They were closer to him than was his beautiful wife, who had turned into a werewolf.

Women—neighbors and nurses—pulled the pillows out from under the corpse. His bodyguards, who had come with him from Moscow, lifted the light corpse of the old woman together with the blanket and carried it downstairs. There, by the front door, a light, flimsy casket rested on two stools. They placed the corpse and the blanket into the casket. They tucked pieces of the blanket under the old woman. The old woman's head rolled to one side and a pillow was called for. They ran upstairs to fetch a pillow. The funeral bus waited patiently. Several old women and men came over and leaned over the casket. As was customary, they received sweets from a bowl.

While they were fetching a pillow, he looked around and smelled the air. Spring had already arrived and the smell was damp, like between a woman's legs after she had been impregnated. The building was the residence of poor people, common people—the entire suburb of New Houses was the same. His parents had lived there for forty years. What did they do all those years? They ate, they bought clothes, they planted potatoes and they continually fixed the roof, since their apartment was on the top floor. Yuck. What a repulsive life they led, a life without events. What a smart kid he had been to run away from his hometown without so much as a backward glance, not knowing why, but following his instinct. What a clairvoyant he was, what a genius, to have run away. How well he had arranged everything. It started to rain. It wasn't raining hard, and they didn't cover the old woman's face.

They brought down a pillow and placed it under the old woman's head. It took a long time to arrange her head, which refused to lay straight. When she was alive, his mother hadn't worn headscarves, but now she had on two: one on her head and the other supporting her jaw. She would have objected to scarves, had she been arranging her own funeral. She wore hats, but a hat would look odd on a corpse. His mother wore lipstick and nail polish until her last months. In the clinic where he had spent the night, there was a bottle of nail polish next to the night table. Had she been arranging her own funeral, his mother would have certainly put on lipstick and painted her nails.

"Are you finished?" asked the bus driver. He was also the only undertaker and gravedigger. Some 13-15 people, including him—the old woman's son—his three bodyguards, a colonel friend of his and another friend, a connected local businessman who had spent an impressive number of years behind bars, the nurse and the neighbors, conceded that they indeed were finished. The driver took out the casket top from the back of the bus and covered the old lady. There were two nails prepped on both sides of the casket top. Very skillfully, at an appropriately tragic, measured pace, the undertaker drove the nails into the casket. He drove them in with style, not with small neurotic taps but confidently and sternly, several precise strikes for each. The knocking of Fate. The sound of Destiny. His bodyguards lifted the casket and slid it into the bus. He tried to offer a hand to 76-year-old Aunt Valya, to help her into the bus, but the driver halted him sternly:

"Not from here. A bad omen. Enter through the side door."

They entered the bus. His bodyguards, the nurses, Aunt Valya, two neighbors, one of whom had swollen feet. The rest piled into the connected man's Chevrolet. The driver started softly and drove competently, brushing aside space.

                                        EDUARD LIMONOV

He stared at the casket, in which the physical body of a woman who gave birth to him 65 years ago flowed away. She had called on his 64th birthday, but by the time he turned 65 she had forgotten who he was. When he called her to congratulate her on Soviet Army Day, she mumbled something unintelligible into the receiver and then suddenly said:

"Tell him his father is dead."

"Mom, it's me, your son," he said. "Father died four years ago."

"Yes, yes, make sure you tell him," she replied, and he hastened to put an end to the conversation. It was disconcerting to be staring into the depth of her abyss.

And now her final journey. Apparently, he felt the same way common people feel on such occasions, but because he wasn't quite a common person, he didn't feel it deeply. Not to tears. Not to goose bumps. Had he been drunk the night before, the odd tear might have flowed over his eyeball, causing him to blink it away, but he hadn't had an occasion to drink much. Even more than sadness (and he was indeed sad) he felt a sense of accomplishment, because the corpse had been successfully removed from the apartment and he was now going directly to where corpses were meant to be, to the crematorium-columbarium. He had almost completed what he came there to do.

He briefly reviewed the years they spent together. There was no sadness there. There was his young father and he, a remote and probably unpleasant child, even though he was undeniably smooth and, as they liked to say now, charismatic. It was the same way Bogdan, his late-born son, was likely to turn out—a stranger to all, yet seductive at the same time... He noted that a piece of carnation stuck out from under the cover of the casket. And a piece of blanket, a camel-hair blanket of the kind they no longer made. The blanket would be burned along with her and would mix with her ashes. There would be very little ash. His mother had shrunk to just thirty-odd kilos by the end. All of a sudden he felt relieved. A strange biological freedom intoxicated his lungs. It's all over, I'm all alone. All alone. All alone. Like a deep sea diver whose cables have been cut, I can swim wherever I want.

"Where are you going to swim?" he parried in an inner debate. "Why now? You have been free from them for a long time. You cut all the cables a long time ago. The old woman who died in a Ukrainian town was but an episode in your kinetic life. You have buried kids, what does the death of an old woman mean to you? Only last December you stood in a snow-covered cemetery in Serpukhov, outside Moscow. The coffin of a party comrade was lowered into the frozen earth. He was not even 23 years old. He had been killed by the police because he was a member of your party. They had cracked his skull open with a baseball bat. At the cemetery, you sobbed silently, you sniffed softly to make sure no one noticed. There were reporters there, after all. You couldn't really cry, could you, the iron leader of a banned organization? You sobbed. Yes, you did sob. No one heard you. But now, you're bringing nothing but old memories to the crematorium."

His bodyguards were silent. The women yakked nonstop about the price of cremation, which had risen, and then shifted to price increases in general. Russian women—and Ukrainian women, too—are highly effective when they come into contact with death. They know all the customs and they aren't squeamish about washing the body of a dead person and dressing it. When he and his bodyguards arrived from the train station, an entire female platoon had been busy in the tiny kitchen, tapping a tattoo with their knives, preparing salads. The corpse lay already all dressed and packaged.

They required neither asking nor hurrying. Without a thought of payment, only because they enjoy life of which death is an integral part, they gladly wash, dress, slice, cut, boil potatoes and prepare herring. By the time he got to the apartment, they had already bought ten bottles of vodka and some wine. He stared at them in amazement, as though they were some unknown tribe. Can it be that Russian women disdain everyday life and only like parties? Death is a party of sorts, too. Would they have liked to have a funeral every day?

"Damn," he stopped himself. "You talk nonsense, as usual. You have always been a crazy kid. Remember how the girls at school thought you were nuts. But things turned out just as Erasmus of Rotterdam once said:

                                          EDUARD LIMONOV

'He who is not taken seriously almost always wins.' In the end, it was you, crazy eyes, who triumphed over those girls, the young philistines. But even back then, while they appeared to disdain you, some of them were secretly in love with you."

Meanwhile, the bus arrived at the crematorium. The women were showering compliments on Valentina, whom he had called Aunt Valya since he had been a child. She was around 80 years old, but was full of life and vigor—her hair dyed blonde. A year ago, she had still been working at the same plant where she had started as a young girl after getting out of college.

The crematorium-columbarium was quiet. The crematorium looked like a somewhat awkward hangar built of concrete and glass. It could have been used to fix or park airplanes. But the columbarium had been planted with lines of short arborvitae, juniper bushes and blue firs, which would eventually grow tall and create an even more pleasant environment for the dead, emit even tarter smells, and cast even deeper, bluer shadows. As he stared out the window of the bus, he knew that it had its boulevards and avenues, and that on one of them an urn with the remains of his father, a man with an angry face, had been installed into a stone slab. When the old woman was cremated, an urn with her remains, mixed with the ashes of her blanket and clothes, would be placed next to the remains of the man she loved.

"What the hell did she love him for?" he thought bitterly. They were bad for each other precisely because he had even less vitality than she. He had his talents, he had an ear for music and could play the guitar and the piano like a virtuoso—not just a few chords, but seriously. Yet, neither of them spurred the other to conquer the world. They gave birth to him, but they never thought he would turn out to be a conqueror. Basically, they couldn't understand him, didn't believe in him and were deeply offended and dumfounded when, in 1989, his books began to be published in Russia for the first time and he was welcomed back like a big man. Journalists took an interest in him and, in the apartment his mother had just been carried from, the telephone never stopped ringing. Back then, his mother remarked to him darkly: "Your father is such a good man. Why is it that no one takes an interest in us?" A tear rolled down her cheek. He was no longer as principled as he had been when he was an unknown—he had already been spoiled by fame, so he hastened to reassure his mother with a meaningless phrase: "This is the kind of work that I do." But he thought in amazement: "They treat me like a stranger. They envy me. Yet, I'm their son. How come they don't feel that my victory is their victory, too?" It was then that he understood for the first time that everyone competes with one another, fathers compete with their children and women compete with men. Even his beautiful wife, the most beautiful wife on earth, began to compete with him like a guy. That's how things always were. He thought of her interview published in a mass-circulation paper more than a month ago, in which she got all puffed up and declared: "I'm the main breadwinner in the family." To say nothing of the grotesque exaggeration of her achievements (he had supported the family while she was pregnant and then breast-fed the baby, and after that he gave her money every day, whenever she asked, because that year she barely worked a few weeks, even though her work as actress-performer did pay better than his, a creator's), he was shocked by this division of the family into two, with her being the breadwinner and him supposedly contributing very little. And she would drag all this out into a yellow newspaper? Had she changed as a result of some crisis of consciousness? She was about to turn 34. But she had begun to turn strange a year earlier, at 33. It was then that she went to Goa for the first time, in order to "restore herself," as she had put it.

The bus stopped and they exited. It was raining. The bus with the old woman's casket drove off to unload the casket at the back entrance, at the door reserved for the dead and the staff. Before leaving, the driver had said that they would soon see the old woman and would be able to pay their respects.

"Go over there," the driver pointed to the main entrance and the rather ugly industrial doors. The passengers of the bus of the dead, they headed for the doors. Along the way, in an open space in front of the crematorium paved with slabs, they were joined by the passengers of the Chevrolet. One

of the women, the one with swollen feet, was leaning on a stick. His bodyguards helped her to the industrial doors of the crematorium, just as they
had helped her down the steps of the bus.

Once they entered, they found themselves in a kind of vestibule or
foyer, bare and unadorned except for signs such as, "Wait Here to Be Invited
to the Hall of Last Respects," "You Will Be Called" and several others written in the same stern spirit of discipline and order.

They stood there like parentheses around a subordinate clause, on one
side the colonel, the connected man and the old woman's son and on the
other his bodyguards and the women. The woman with swollen feet said
that she liked cremation and wished to be cremated herself. She even had
money set aside for it. Her relatives would be close by and would come to
visit her and it would not cost much. Aunt Valya was also leaning toward
cremation. They spoke in an everyday tone of voice and even smiled when
they felt it was appropriate. The youngest woman, the nurse who had
found his mother dead, had left them for a while and had driven away with
the driver. She had the death certificate. Now she returned, saying that, in
the old lady's apartment, somewhere in a drawer, they would need to find
documents confirming that the niche at the columbarium had been pur-
chased for two. Otherwise the old woman's remains would not be placed
together with the remains of her husband, and her photograph would not
appear next to the photograph of the angry old man.

"We'll have to find it," she said to the old woman's son.

A short compact man with closely cropped hair wearing a black suit
now came out and invited them to the Hall of Last Respects. The old
woman's son found the Hall impressive. It was a semi-dark, slightly damp
room with a tall ceiling and proportions large enough to ensure that a
handful of mourners felt orphaned and insignificant. The casket stood on
a platform by the far wall. The old woman lay in it. She once had been his
mother. The funeral director ushered them to the side of the casket. He
went to the other side and climbed the dais, which was draped with pine
branches, wreaths and ribbons. The funeral director made a speech, which
was as competent and appropriate as it was standard.

The speech explained that such and such person (he used the old woman's name and patronymic) was being taken from us, or rather was leaving us and going to the next world, and that we mourned her departure. Still, the semidarkness, the skillfully cast light and the impressive size of the room imbued his speech and the simple ritual with a larger meaning.

When he finished, the funeral director asked whether anyone wanted to say anything. Nobody expressed such a wish and so the funeral director said:

"Then, let us go up and say goodbye. Please pay your last respects to the deceased."

The old woman's son was the first to approach the body, which he did as though it was a routine task for him to pay his last respects to the dead. He was light on his feet, dressed in a black coat and a black sweater, gray-haired, looking like the devil only knows what kind of polar explorer or Captain Nemo. He came up to the casket, leaned over and kissed the scarf on the old woman's forehead.

He whispered: "So you have died, Mom. Rest in peace. Forgive me for being a bad son." The old woman lay with an otherworldly, inhuman face, like a chunk of mined ore or a broken mammoth bone in the snow. He walked away and was followed by Aunt Valya wearing a scarf on her dyed head, who said goodbye to her girlfriend. The old woman's son didn't hear what she had said to her.

"The farewells are over," said the funeral director. He picked up the casket top and covered the old woman, his mother. Funeral music sounded. Just as skillfully as the driver an hour ago, the funeral director drove confident nails into the casket. Boom. Boom. Now he drove them in all the way to their heads.

The casket suddenly began to ride upward from the platform, heading toward an opening in the wall curtained off by red velour drapes. The casket stumbled momentarily at line of the drapes, and then crushed them, disappearing with a second or third nudge into a space where it could no longer be seen by the mourners. Behind it, the drapes returned to their original position. The music stopped.

"The ceremony is over," said the funeral director.

They headed for the exit, the limping old lady with her bad feet, Aunt Valya, the other women, his bodyguards and the passengers from the Chevrolet. Once outside, in the rain, he thought that at least this problem, the one that had oppressed him for several years, turning into a nagging pain every New Year's, had now been resolved by Nature. "No person, no problem,"[1] he thought bitterly. "My mother, who oppressed me by her very being, is gone. But another mother, my son's, lingers on," he admitted to himself.

They piled into the same bus and the same driver drove them, now recklessly, back to New Houses. The old woman's son thought that at least he had accomplished his task. He could now go back to Moscow, but the moral duty to the women—the nurses and the neighbors who took such an important part in the funeral (in fact, who had arranged everything)—had to be fulfilled. A banquet awaited them, the most pleasant part of the ceremony of death, the pagan rite of sating the mourners and filling them with alcohol.

Actually, his mother was the oldest and the most enduring character in his life, a life rich in people and adventures. And the fact that she had finally physically departed this life changed nothing in an already established order. In reality, he had long since erased both his father and his mother from among the living. Even though he wrote to them from prison, replying to their letters, it was only a formality. It was in prison that he summed up his attitude to family when he wrote his treatise, Monster with Tearful Eyes. In the years that passed since then, he had no reason to alter his views. When he came out of the labor camp, responding to pressure from a lawyer friend—who had traditional values—and taking along a couple of bodyguards, he drove in the man's car to see his parents. At the border, at the Goptivka checkpoint, Ukrainian border guards scurried

---

[1] An infamous quote attributed to Stalin.

nervously to and fro when they recognized the famous goatee and eyeglasses. In the end, he discovered that he had been banned from entering Ukraine long ago, that there had been two decrees by the Security Council of Ukraine on this subject, one dated November 1999 and the other March 2003. By March 2003, he was already in jail—awaiting sentencing—so that the rationale for the Security Council of Ukraine's decree, whatever it was, was either false or absurd. But whom could he complain to? No one. His passport was stamped with a statement that he was banned from entering Ukraine until July 25, 2008, and there was nothing to be done except turn around. "You should thank us that we didn't arrest you for 72 hours. After all, you were trying to cross the border," a Ukrainian officer told him by way of a farewell. "Thanks," he replied.

By then, his father had already taken to his bed. He simply got bored with life. He was not ill, he just chose to stay in bed and let his wife take care of him. Life became difficult for her. When they neared Belgorod, riding in the lawyer's Lexus, the lawyer—a traditionalist—said that he would leave the old woman's son at a hotel and drive and bring the old woman to Belgorod. Meanwhile, his father would spend half a day in the care of the bodyguards. He was so kind, that lawyer. Had it not been for his idea, the old woman's son would have driven back to Moscow with a clean conscience. A cruel man, he could never understand this kind of sentimentality. No one had ever taken pity on him, neither the women he loved, nor the authorities, nor his enemies and rivals, of course. Hadn't they made an honest attempt to cross the border? What else could he have done?

The lawyer brought his mother over. She turned out to be a crooked, stooped old woman with a walking stick. She was very happy to see him, cried a little at various moments and described to him the physiological details of his father's condition—how she had hurt her back lifting him and how he would wet his bed if she didn't get there in time. He listened to all these horrors and considered going back to Moscow as soon as possible, where a friend had lent him a huge, bourgeois apartment, where he stayed with a 21-year-old girl who had welcomed him back from prison. The lawyer took his mother back and in the evening he and the lawyer sat at an outdoor restaurant, since it was July, and about them walked young girls smelling of young flesh. Less than a month had passed since he had emerged from the camp. Life was a holiday for him. He ate a kebab, chased shots of vodka with beer the way he liked it, used foul language and felt happy. For no reason at all, just because he had spent two and a half years behind bars.

They went up to the apartment on the top floor. Tables had been set up in the large room and food was ready to be served. Two women and two bodyguards had stayed behind. "Back so soon?" those who had stayed behind asked. "We didn't expect you back so soon. Some things aren't ready yet."

There was the usual fuss that precedes a banquet. Where is the bread? Where are the soup plates? What shall we dump the potatoes into? Common womenfolk hold men in far greater respect than educated women. He reached this uncomplicated conclusion when they placed him, the colonel and the gray-haired, connected man at the head of the table and served them vodka and food while scurrying about arranging the table and, whenever they needed it, exploiting younger men—his bodyguards. He had not been in the company of common people for so long that he kept making new discoveries, one after the other. It turned out that they had a well-defined sense of hierarchy. They had promptly arranged themselves into a small tribe, recognizing the authority of those who had more experience, knowledge and skill. In his own small family there was no such natural hierarchy, he thought bitterly. Nor was it now possible to re-establish such a hierarchy. Since last fall, the monster-werewolf who had taken residence in a beautiful actress would reach for her cell phone whenever tempers flared even slightly and would emit an ugly cry: "I'm calling the cops." She had just acted the role of a businesswoman who put her husband behind bars because he allegedly raped her, which was why she sounded so convincing. Unwilling to tempt fate, he would call his bodyguards and leave.

How had it started? ("Pass the pickles, please." "Excellent pickles!") How had she managed to turn into a werewolf? "I should spend some time thinking it over," he promised himself and stood up. They wanted him to say something about the deceased and were clinking their forks against the shot glasses.

He began by admitting that he had been a bad son, that he had left his parents early in life and lived abroad for a long time and that, after 15 years of separation, he came back to find his parents aged. He said that his parents didn't believe in his abilities, but nonetheless they helped him in those distant years when, as an adolescent, he set off to conquer Moscow. They used to send him 25 rubles every month, addressed to "General Delivery" at the Central Post Office on Kirova—now Myasnitskaya—Street. He added something else and then said again that he was a bad son to the deceased. They drank. He sat down again.

Aunt Valya, whose turn it was to speak after him, because she had known his mother for fifty years if not longer, began by defending him. It wasn't good for the son of the deceased to speak like that about himself. His mother understood that he had a different destiny, and others around her understood it, too. Nobody expected him to spend his entire life by his mother's side. Even when he was a child, they saw that he was a different kind of man, a man unlike them.

The different kind of man, in the mean time, attempted to figure out what there was in him that he got from his parents. Nothing, it turned out. Even when he lived with them, he hadn't been raised by them, but by books about travels and adventure, then by special books about history and by books of poetry. Now his character consisted of several distinct strains. One was the working habits and opinions of a hard-working writer. Up early, work at the writing desk, physical exercise, walks, one meal per day. Ascetic habits, of course. Then, when he became a Soldier, those ascetic habits stood him in good stead. His soldiering years and the time he spent at war honed his character. Decisiveness, courage, ability to make do and enjoyment of life were traits they built or uncovered in him. When he became the head of a radical party, a revolutionary and a leader, he had to get used to surveillance and eavesdropping, to prosecutors and judges. When he did time, prison became part of him forever. If you do time, you can never again be completely free of prison. It follows you for the rest of your life. In short, it was a very complicated character that sat at the head of the table next to the colonel. An insatiable sex fiend, too, but that was something few people knew, he thought, sneering, even though many suspected it.

He brilliantly if obscenely proved it before the evening was over. He declared to his mother's nurse his desire to sleep with her, grabbed her breasts and asked if he could pull out her tit. His bodyguards looked the other way in embarrassment. Old Nadya, a former neighbor, stared at the scene without blinking an eye.

He had taken a notice of that nurse the last time he came. He saw her briefly in the corridor (they were about to leave by then), and he got the sense of her feminine tidiness, and goodwill toward him, and a certain nervous excitement when he was near her.

Yet, he didn't carry his shameful conduct to the end. His infallible iron health kept him from getting completely drunk. He controlled himself and made sure that the nurse and her girlfriend got home, ordering his bodyguards to walk out with them and put them in a taxi. He gave the key to his bodyguards and lay down in the small room on a broken down old bed. His father had died there four years ago. His mother had died yesterday, in the large room. This room smelled of dust, old things and, faintly, of mothballs, the usual smell of the old. His father's guitar hung on the side of the armoire that bulged with old things. The bottom peg that held the strings in place had long since come unglued because of the heat, and the strings reared up like the depiction of a wave in a Japanese print. He thought that now he was indeed all alone in the world. There had been a time when that was what he dreamed of. But now he didn't like it much.

TRANSLATION BY ALEXEI BAYER

Oedipus Complex
(A short story)
D MITRY L IPSKEROV

To My Sweet V.G.

A guppy is swimming. Her tail is like an oil slick on the water. Her tiny body surrenders itself to the current, weaving now right, now left. The fish likes weak currents. She is trusting, light and graceful. Far too beautiful and too small for the big river full of warm water. She is probably stupid, and her life is practically worthless.

She will soon spawn. Her viviparous belly is swollen and it weighs her down and pulls her toward the bottom. Her tiny mouth moves incessantly, as though she is chewing a tiny piece of gum. She trails a black string. The string is thin but it thickens here and there. She tries to jerk herself free, but the string becomes longer and longer and coils like a snake, making it more and more difficult for her to swim, and she eventually starts to get mad. She must choose whether to try to get free or spawn. Tiny eyes and tails show through the translucent film of her belly. The mother must make this effort to provide more food for larger fish. Of course, the entire brood won't become food, but a large number will be damaged in the spawning and will be eaten and transformed into other strings.

Looking at the river from above, it turns out that there are a great number of similar little fish swimming together and getting ready to spawn. At first glance, it might seem that a quantity of oil has been dumped into the water. Thousands, even tens of thousands of guppies, those exotic fish, are about to spawn in a single coordinated effort. Still more hundreds of thousands of identical fish are ready, in their utter stupidity, to fill round fishbowls and square aquariums, to die by the thousands, thanks to inept amateur fish keepers, and to spawn in tight spaces as well as in an unlimited expanse. They all expel tiny strings, which drop to the bottom of glass bowls like black spider webs, muddying the water.

When I was two and a half years old my mother experienced a hideous shock.

One day, lying in bed and craftily pretending to sleep, I was taking great pleasure in watching my parent mete out punishment to my older sister who, being almost four years old, could not restrain herself, and, thanks to some fantastic dream in the early hours of the morning, had sent forth a brief jet, spraying not only her half of the sofa bed, but infringing upon Mother's sacrosanct half, as well. Now, Mother was heartily spanking her wet behind.

I have no idea what my dear sister's dream was about, perhaps a giant piece of hard candy in the shape of a rooster, or naked Fyodor Mikhalych straggling back to his room from the bathroom. It should be mentioned that his cyanotic belly used to scare the little girl badly when she stared avidly at our neighbor. Be that as it may, I don't want to hazard a guess whether the child's bladder had failed her from happiness or horror, but she got her punishment on the spot. When my sister's sobs had nearly stopped and I, having greatly enjoyed the spectacle, was yawning sweetly, our door flew open and two men came in. Both were young and apparently cultured. One even had a thin moustache that twisted upward. An edge of a handkerchief protruded from his breast pocket. The other was more common-looking. He now began to speak, seemingly a little embarrassed in front of my dumfounded mother. She had a dirty nightgown on, with those silly frills on the shoulders, and her right underarm was quite sweaty.

"We must apologize," said the common one. "We have burst into your room. We even have the key to your door." He took out a key from his pocket that was, in fact, an identical copy of ours.

Our building was built before the 1917 Revolution and our lock had endured from those prehistoric days, so it was strange to see a copy of our key. Mother had tried many locksmiths and they had all told her that supplies of such blanks had run out by the time our country marked Stalin's sixtieth birthday.

The one with an upturned moustache got a gun out of his pocket. Nothing like this had ever happened to us before.

"You've got a choice," continued the common one, holding the key as though it were a gun. "Either we kill your daughter or your son. You have a few minutes to think it over."

"There is no alternative," added the one with a moustache and wiped his gun with the handkerchief from his jacket. "Do not offer to sacrifice yourself, it will not work. We don't want money, either. And we are not interested in your body," he added quickly, looking at Mother as she pushed aside the blanket.

Mother was sweating so much her breasts showed clearly through her nightgown, as though a bucket of water had been dumped over her. Her right underarm was tinged with black. My sister let out another installment of urine, now surely out of fear, and began to kick her legs in discomfort. Where had it come from? She didn't seem to drink much before bed.

"Please, don't waste our time," said the one holding the key. He twisted it around a finger and assured Mother that once she made her choice, he would give her the duplicate and they would never return to our apartment.

"Otherwise we'd have to kill all of you," added the other one and pointed the hole in the barrel at my uncomprehending face. Suddenly I also had to go to the bathroom. I did not fear punishment because I was too small, and therefore I promptly emptied my bowels—to the great displeasure of our guests. They immediately began to fuss and grew jittery.

The one with a moustache kept shifting his aim from me to my sister, muttering through his clenched teeth: "Come on, come on. Make your choice." The common one squeezed the key so hard that his fingers turned white. It was getting light outside; the first ray was just about to slip from the tallest roof into our window and work was about to start at the distillery in the basement of our building. In the light of day the one with a moustache turned out to have a hairy birthmark on his hand, just like the one Fyodor Mikhalych had on his belly.

"I give you one more minute."

The hole of the gun aligned with my sister's belly button.

"The son or the daughter?" they asked the question one more time.

Everything intermingled in Mother's bed: sweat, a child's fear, horror, despair, the inevitability of making a choice and the suffering that would follow it.

"The son or the daughter?"

Mother replied:

"The son."

She shut her eyes and passed out.

I don't know why she made this choice. Maybe because a daughter is closer, she could grow up to help my mother and share her common distrust of men. Or maybe because I was still too young and it would be easier for me to die, not understanding what was happening. I don't know. Oh, how my sister's eyes lit up with genuine joy. She opened her eyes wide and raised herself on her elbows in order not to miss the moment when I was punished. She was still very silly. She couldn't be expected to understand that this punishment would be very cruel and final. That she would no longer have a younger brother to play house with. It was then, at two and a half years of age, that I knew I must never wish ill to another being, because otherwise I would be paid back with the same coin. Never rejoice when your sister gets punished, because you too foul up your sheets every night and even now you lie there sticking to the mattress.

The one with a moustache put the gun to my forehead and squeezed the trigger. A shot rang out and everything was immersed in sadness.

Ever since then I have had on my forehead a square indentation with uneven edges. I survived thanks to Providence, but after that morning my mother stopped loving me. Perhaps it was because she chose me, and not my sister.

It isn't true, of course. My mother loves me like any other mother loves her child. No one ever burst into our room and offered her such a preposterous choice. I don't even have a sister, and never had one, which always made me feel sorry and sad. Why do I have such fantasies? Maybe because I'm bored?

As to the square indentation on my forehead, I do actually have one. It measures the length of the phalanx of an index finger. When women kiss me, they always ask me why I have such an indentation. When they hear my next fantasy, they stick their wet little tongues into the hole. I'm the only person in the world who gets his brains licked.

When I was two and a half years old, I had no tin soldiers. I had ordinary nails instead. I stood them on their heads, lined them up in the corridor and played with them lackadaisically. Fyodor Mikhalych used to say that I was a bad boy, and that was why they had never bought me real tin soldiers. Once he stepped on a nail, but he didn't dare to whip me then. Father had just come home for two months and he kept his gun in the armoire. That was why our neighbor temporarily covered his shame with a waffle towel as he walked to the bathroom and why he didn't dare to whip me.

"You enjoy other people's misfortunes," I told Fyodor Mikhalych. "Don't." I added, killing one nail after another. "My sister enjoyed it so much when I was being killed, she never even got born."

Once I fell over the threshold and with all my might drove a nail into my forehead. The nail entered my brain all the way to its head. But instead of feeling pain, I felt great pleasure such as couldn't be compared to anything I had ever felt before or since. It was as though thousands of erotic climaxes were joined together. Everything felt by men and women, and by flowers as they are pollinated by a bumblebee, and by stars as they are born was granted to me alone. I rolled up my eyes, stuck out my tongue and began to wheeze. That was how my parents found me when they came back from the kitchen. Besides, my pale little face was covered with a trickle of blood. Apparently, the nail, before reaching the spot in the brain that was responsible for pleasure, hit a blood vessel along the way. In short, my parents thought my innocent soul was headed straight to Heaven. Mother collapsed, hitting a wall with her head, and Father got his gun out of the armoire. But my soul was actually nailed down pretty well and I groaned with pleasure, reviving hope for my precious life. Father stuck his gun into his pants. Mother quickly exhaled, grabbed me in her arms and hopped down the stairs to the exit like a kangaroo. Father followed her, his face contorting. Fyodor Mikhalych would have run out with them, too, but at that fateful moment he happened to be wearing nothing but his underwear. But he promised himself that when I came of age he would buy me real tin soldiers. In the event, the industry stopped making them long before I came of age, and therefore our neighbor could absolve himself of this promise.

Mother stood in the middle of an empty highway, holding me in her outstretched arms like a Madonna with the dead Child. Blood dripped from a lock of my light hair and fell onto the concrete. Disconsolate, Father sat on the curb but the horizon remained empty. The tires of a late bicyclist swished on the road and the silent horizon froze once more. Surrendering myself to Mother's arms, I breathed very softly, overwhelmed by a wave of pleasure. I withdrew from the outside world and even my mother's wolf-like howls and my father's dog-like whining could not bring me back to this base world of ours.

Several minutes later a covered military truck at last appeared on the road. Father took out his gun and threw himself under its wheels as though it were an enemy tank. The vehicle managed to brake at the last moment, a sergeant fell out of the cab in a paroxysm of swearing and a moment later we were on our way to the Filatov Hospital.

"What a blue-eyed angel," said the elderly nurse. "Such a good-looking boy. A pity he isn't breathing."

Coming through a thin partition separating the operating room from the corridor, the nurse's words served as a catalyst for action.

Mother opened the window and deliberately stepped onto the precipice.

The nail was successfully removed from my head, but my heart registered its protest by stopping for a few minutes. What is the value of life if it is emptied of pleasure? The doctors were competent enough and after receiving an electric shock my heart began to pump with redoubled force. I broke into genuine tears, unhappy to be coming back to reality, while they put Mother's leg in a cast. Her fall from the first floor window was an unlucky one and she broke her ankle.

They discharged us simultaneously, having reassured us that I would be all right. Overjoyed, my parents attempted to make love on and off until sunrise but, full of vengeful resentment, I kept piping up at critical moments. Fyodor Mikhalych's anxious voice kept coming through the door:

"Shouldn't we call an ambulance?"

This is a fairly truthful account of how I got the indentation on my head.

"Come over," my friend's voice came over the receiver. "I've got something interesting for you. Don't delay. I have another surgery."

"I'll come over right away."

I put on my pants, ran outside and hurried to the Sklifosovsky Hospital. It was early, public transportation functioned irregularly, and it took me a full hour to get to the hospital. My friend was no longer in the staff lunch room, because he was in surgery. His "something interesting" excited me so much that I got sterilized scrubs from the closet, put on plastic shoe covers, and went to the operating room wearing a surgical mask. All the operating tables were empty except for the last one, at which sat my friend. His eyes were enlarged by horn-rimmed glasses. His yellow hands, covered with rubber gloves, were rubbing iodine onto the shaved head of the patient on the operating table.

"Sorry. There was no bus."

"I see."

There was a pause during which Kazbek—that's my friend's name—made a scalpel incision on the shaved head.

"Will he live?" I asked, sympathizing with the patient. Perhaps he felt as good as I had felt when I was little, but they, acting against his wishes—

"Who the hell can tell," replied Kazbek, taking a drill from the instrument table and aiming it at the head. "Thank God it's the last one for today. In an hour, I'm going home to sleep and there is no force on earth that could keep me awake."

"So what is it?" I asked impatiently.

"Wait."

The drill successfully penetrated the skull and Kazbek gathered fragments of bone onto a special rag. Then he placed a finger into the hole he had just made and was silent for several minutes, as though he was sucking in the brain. Then, coming to, he withdrew his finger and examined it. It was red and had brain matter all over it. He said:

"He won't live."

"Why not?"

"See the fluid?" he passed his finger in front of my nose. "In our department almost everybody dies. It's the Severe Trauma department, you see. Mine is the night shift. This one got hit by a fender."

"Maybe you could try to do something for him?"

"There is no brain left in there, only mush. We'll keep him on life support, but he'll die in another half an hour."

Kazbek began to put the head back together. He covered the fragments of the skull with special glue, placed them over the hole like a mosaic, sewed the skin and, having rung the bell, walked out of the operating room. A surgery nurse hurried toward us. She smiled at the Kazakh face of the surgeon and placed a drainage tube into the dying man's mouth.

Kazbek swallowed the dregs of some tea from a dirty glass and closed his slanted eyes.

"A friend called from Cholpon Ata yesterday. They have built a gas pipeline over there. Three hours before they were due to start it, one of the welders cut the pipe open and took a mini scooter in there. He welded up the pipe and rode the scooter up and down. He kept riding in there for two hours, until they sent the gas down the pipe. Naturally, there was an explosion and so on. That was all I had to tell you."

The surgeon opened his eyes.

"What number is this one?"

"Forty nine," I replied quickly. "It's one of the most impressive ones. It's extraordinary. Thank you very much. I'll add it to my records right away. Nowadays, suicides with any kind of imagination are becoming increasingly rare. This one is a real gift to me."

"I'm going to leave this place," Kazbek stated firmly and yawned. "What have I got going here for me? I'm transferring to neurosurgery. I've been invited to Alma Ata. What do I care about this Moscow of yours? At least, there will be fewer people dying on the operating table over there. Besides, everybody over there has slanted eyes, just like me."

I wasn't listening to Kazbek. Instead, I thought how I would add his charming story to my files, which would greatly enhance my collection. I had not added such a valuable gem to it for a long time, and because of that I felt joy and elation in my soul.

After packing her things in a small knapsack and placing her breasts in a travel bra to keep them from swaying, she departed for Moscow. An eight thousand kilometer journey lay ahead of her, and she would have to travel by train and by boat. Six hours on a train and two more on a boat.

A hugely tall girl with thighs as though cast in concrete, a bright-red braid as thick as the trunk of a birch tree, and enormous breasts as large as fishbowls, she climbed on board the train and headed toward the center of Russia. She had just turned eighteen and her body demanded action.

Eventually she will become my mother, but she is, as yet, virginal and pure, and train wheels rattle, bringing her closer and closer to the present.

Hard-boiled eggs, a dismal landscape out the window, snoring neighbors in the third class car and she, unable to wash for four days. Fat lice crawling on her head, and the braid which she let grow unimpeded since she was a baby has to come off. Nothing to cover the cast-iron behind with, and tears roll down her face, washing off the freckles. Plus, her money gets stolen. It is a story that is familiar to all mothers who come to Moscow from the provinces as young women. Then there is a boat and everybody is sitting together on the deck. Because she is so nervous, it starts early, ahead of schedule. There is no water, even though the sea is right there. She must wash, or else she would die of shame. She goes below deck, where the mechanics are playing cards, and, suddenly tongue-tied from misery, she tells those obscene mugs about her misfortune. They guffaw, touch her hands, deal the cards, put the girl in play and begin to gamble for her in earnest, suddenly becoming sweaty and angry. She stands there, half-dead with fear, frozen like an elephant in hot weather, and it just ends there as suddenly as it began. The lucky runt who wins the hand slinks toward her with a bucket of water in his hand and pushes her behind the engine with his thin hands. He offers to pour water for her in a sweet voice, and lust drips from his eyes like overripe honey from a honeycomb. As if in a dream, she slowly strips her large body, uncovering her red nudity, a body that bears a natural wound. She strains her strong legs that are made for stomping in the fields and through her numbness she feels his animal gaze on her stomach. At this moment, the kind old Lord, saving her for a bright future, runs the boat onto a sandy shallow. Everything breaks up around them and falls down. The mechanics' dried-up arms break off, red-hot coals pour down on them from the furnace and their lust-filled eyes go dark. She stands alone amidst the chaos on her cast-iron feet, her head shaved, and washes her saved body. As though made with condensed milk, wholesome, not diluted by civilization, like a chunk of ice that is golden from the sun, she is saved, preserved, and she sails toward the promised shore, a future woman.

She got acclimated in Moscow by unloading freight cars for a year. She searched for love, not chaotically, like thousands of other girls her age, but by relying on her powerful instincts. She believed that her one and only love would not pass her by unnoticed but would declare loud and clear: "Here I am. It's me." Indeed, once she started library school and wrote home to her mother that she was becoming cultured, she met Yasha, a Young Communist League activist at the school. A romance began with a swarthy boy who barely came up to her breasts. There was no sin in that relationship, no touching of sensitive parts, only stories about the Far North where she had spent her childhood, Yasha's tales about community organizing and other trifles, which they followed up with ice cream and inhaled along with the spring wind of their young years. Then, when the first school break came, Yasha secretly expelled himself from the Young Communist League—an action which he recorded in the official minutes and authenticated with a stamp—sent an article about a man without a motherland to a newspaper and, having submitted these documents to the Emigration Office, soon got an exit visa which allowed him to leave for Israel for good. She was unhappy for a long time and, getting invitations from Yasha, cried entire nights on end and pined away for him, but she was not strong enough to join him over there. She had to live in the North. That was her destiny.

It didn't happen often, but people did fall in love with her occasionally. There was an excitable figure skater with a passion for everything out of the ordinary. But she waited, turning down everyone, and waiting bore fruit once more. He was common, not especially good-looking, but she gave herself to him on their first night together. Calmly like all large women, like a large boat, she plied the waves of pleasure of which I became an end and a reward. She carried her large belly the way other women carry their pocketbooks, and she gave birth to me calmly and easily. I came out like a bullet from a well-oiled gun.

"What a good boy," smiled the old obstetrician, but seeing how Mother crossed her legs he became angry. "You can't do that! What are you doing, for God's sake?"

She was embarrassed to be lying all uncovered in front of a strange man. What's the big deal, anyway?

Father spent six months at a stretch on Sakhalin Island, where he headed a geological expedition. Mother worked late at the library. After I got the indentation on my forehead, I was sent to five-day care, where I was successfully assimilated into society. Five-day care eventually gave way to a six-day boarding school, albeit with a specialization in German. At the time, Father was on the Kola Peninsula. Mother was mad at him for that and, as a result, she was too strict with me when she took me home on weekends. I was not a good student by any measure, and certainly not an angel. Picking me up on a Saturday, she checked my report card on the bus home and for the remainder of the trip I steeled myself mentally for a whipping. We came into our room and Mother got an officer's belt from behind the armoire, pulled me out of the corner by my hair, in a single powerful motion jerked my pants off along with my underwear and laid the first lash on my boyish buttocks. Opening my eyes wide, I began to cry silently. The next lash elicited an incredible scream, while the third sent my tiny fist hitting fiercely at Mother's leg. There followed the fourth and then the fifth, and so on. While I writhed in pain, Mother sat on the floor leaning her head against the radiator and stared at the ceiling. Perhaps she thought of Father, then me, who at that time felt the sweet sensation of receding pain, and then she leapt upon me like a wild beast. She kissed my skinny ass and shed hot tears, and I told her how I would be embarrassed again to show up at gym and that I didn't love her. At that moment of over-the-top caresses I adored her, but since I did feel insulted and humiliated I was childishly cruel and called her a fascist Hitlerite and she cried bitterly at night into her blanket and I stared at her spread-out breasts and they seemed to me transparent, as though made of glass and filled to the brim with water. Tiny exotic guppies swam in water, bumping against the freckled skin and dreaming of a big river. Then I went to the kitchen, got a piece of bread, came back and fed the fish. Mother groaned heavily, the fish went away, and my attention shifted to the place from which I had emerged into the world. I touched it, and it felt warm and strange, and I was taken aback

　　　　　DMITRY LIPSKEROV

because she was built so differently, as though we were strangers. She woke up and, half asleep, passed me the bedpan. My bladder deflated pleasurably and I fell asleep tucking my face under her arm, which smelled of noodle soup.

When Father came to visit, I would be moved from the sofa to the folding armchair, which was inhabited by bedbugs. They'd bite me, and the next morning I would be covered with red spots and stay home from school for a week because of a sudden allergy attack. Mother thought it was caused by nerves. That it was my reaction to Father's visits, that I was so overjoyed to see him. In fact, I couldn't have cared less for good old Dad, since I saw him very rarely and didn't remember him from one time to the next. Besides, he took my place on the sofa and pawed Mother for nights on end, while I was being eaten alive by the blood-sucking bedbugs.

On one of his visits, Father used his bonus to buy Mother a tiny Zaporozhets, a ladybug of a motorcar. At first she took it as an insult. How would she fit into that matchbox with her magnificent bodily proportions? But then, once she had squeezed into it and circled the courtyard, she was overcome by limitless joy. I was happy, too, of course, even though I was one hundred percent sure that I would not be allowed to drive it. At least I would go to the boarding school in a car, while stinky public transportation carried the rest of the world. After that, Father came to visit less and less frequently, explaining that he was too busy. Whenever he did come, he got drunk every day. When he was drunk, he would drag me to the bathroom to wash. Drunk, he would fill the bathtub with boiling hot water, put me in and start a theological discussion with himself.

"I'm not doing at all well," he would say.

"Nothing to be done," he would answer himself. "Bear your cross and have faith."

"I do bear my cross," he would add, sighing heavily. "But I don't have faith."

I would stare at him glassy-eyed and beg him to get on with the bathing. He would catch himself, fish me out with unsteady hands and, smiling like a dog that had been kicked, carry me naked back to our room.

Fyodor Mikhalych would bump into us in the corridor and, striking a deliberate pose, declare:

"You walk around naked yourselves. How come I am not allowed? Where is the equality? Where is it, I ask you?"

Father would apologize, saying that I was still small and that he was taking me straight to bed.

"You probably got a woman ready for him," the neighbor would say, growing bolder. "He is not so small. Just look at his thing."

Father would carry me to my bed and lay me down. He would then return to the corridor and, pushing Fyodor Mikhalych into a corner, pummel his stomach with his fists. After that, the old exhibitionist would weep for a long time. I would hear his bitter sniveling through the wall and pity the poor bastard, getting angry at old Daddy and the damn cross that he had to bear. Father had stopped pawing Mother, and I would soon fall asleep and dream of being behind the wheel of the Zaporozhets, running over boarding school teachers one after another.

Then, Father stopped coming completely. The last time he telephoned and said that he would be exploring without a break until he found what he was looking for. A friend whispered to Mother that he had already found a mother lode, one with two tits and a respectable-size posterior. It was on a Sunday. Next morning Mother took me to the boarding school and asked them to keep me over next Sunday. She took unpaid leave at work and filled up the Zaporozhets. She placed her breasts on the steering wheel, set her enormous feet on the pedals, started the motor and headed for Sakhalin.

By then she already had an enlarged thyroid, and her eyes, which were once normal size, protruded from their orbits. She pushed the pedals to the floor and, like a hippopotamus astride a bug, pressed forward. The middle stretch of Russia, with its churches, bad weather and scrap metal littering the fields, spooled unto her wheels one faceless kilometer after the other. She stopped only to eat, drink and answer the call of nature under the odd fir tree. The wolves stumbling upon those spots recoiled in fear from the smell of a mighty female, and ran back to their lairs without a backward glance. Only when the night sky became lit with the trinket of a moon, did she slow down, looking inside herself as though she were on the moon. Then, the road again, the crossing of rivers large and small, the jazz on the radio and the memories of Yasha. When the car broke down, she pushed it for miles to get it to the nearest service station. She lost weight, shedding her northern flesh. Sometimes she regretted setting out on such a long trip. Yet, with every passing day she got nearer and nearer to Sakhalin. Somehow she managed to find somebody high up who informed her that Father's expedition was camping very near some elevation or other, on the very spot where, some years ago, during the darkness of wartime, one man ate another. At long last, she can make out the tents, and next to one of them she sees Father, resting his foot on the carcass of a bear he has just killed. Father then watches as his gift, the Zaporozhets, stops, a woman-soldier gets out, approaches him quickly and, after a short wind-up, slaps his face. The blow echoes around the elevations. Then, just as quickly, the woman gets back in the car and, pressing the gas pedal, drives away from the monument to cannibalism. She no longer can see Father, who only a moment ago stood upright like a hero, but who now bends down and, pressing his face into the stinky pelt of the dead bear, begins to cry bitterly, like no man ever should. Next to the tent stands a woman in a wolf hat. She has a flat chest and an ass as big as a baby's fist. She stares at Father and cries, too, and nature all around them sheds tears of Sakhalin rain.

Exhausted, the Zaporozhets can bear it no longer and, at the start of the trip back, breaks apart. Mother has no regrets. She dumps Father's gift at the side of the road and, as in her youth, there is once again the train and the boat. But this time there are no lice, no unusual incidents and no hope. This time it is a tired, suddenly aged and bug-eyed woman, coming home.

That Saturday, Mother took me home from boarding school and for the first time didn't give me a whipping. I couldn't forgive her the dead Zaporozhets, as a result of which no teacher would ever be run over. But by way of compensation, she promised to take me out of the boarding school and to send me to Grandma. Fine, let it be Grandma then, whatever. I'd smoke right under her long nose. Grandma—she was Father's mother—would feel guilty toward me.

Then Mother met Zhorik the Dwarf. Well, perhaps he wasn't a real dwarf, but he was extremely short. He was also divinely handsome. He batted his doll-like eyelids at Mother. He worked as an actor in the theater. It is a known fact that, in the old days, it was a sign of great sophistication to make love to various abnormal people. Even queens amused themselves with dwarves. To say nothing of Mother. Besides, they said that Zhorik was a talented actor but had an excessive weakness for the female sex. He had mounted every actress at his theater and he was very proud of himself, the little devil. He lived with Mother for six months. Then, he got the title role in a play about the French Revolution. The rehearsals were brilliant. At the end of the play, a guillotine was set up on the stage and a crowd of frantic women was supposed to chop Zhorik's character's head off. At the last moment, a doll would be substituted for Zhorik so that the scene looked extremely realistic, complete with blood and fainting fits in the audience. But on the opening night all those previously mounted actresses stuck the real Zhorik's head under the sharp blade instead of a doll. His head was severed from his body, rolled down the stage and fell into Mother's lap, since Mother sat in the front row. The audience screamed and employees at the mortuary worked hard to sew the head back on. After that, Mother was overcome by sadness and joined a team of skydivers. She spent almost a full year boning up on theory and, when given an opportunity to jump, did so without a parachute. She turned spectacular pirouettes in the air, spun around and fluttered like a bird. Witnesses claimed that had it been an official competition, the previous world record would have surely been shattered.

Mother's first parachute jump became the first case of an imaginative suicide in my collection.

"So that's the story, Galya."
"Did they ever find those two?"
"Are you kidding?"

                                                   DMITRY LIPSKEROV

"And what about your sister?"

"My sister? Oh, my sister. Well, she grew up, got married and went to live abroad."

"This is so amazing. How could your mother do that to you?"

"What would you have done in her place?"

Galya is a short woman with a bird-like chest. She listens to me holding her earlobe between her little fingers and sighs sadly, showing uneven teeth. She is older than me, but her neck is like a girl's, with soft, smooth skin. But when she gets excited, two veins appear on both sides of her neck. Seeing them, I realize that she is older than me and that she has already had a life and that now it is nothing but an echo. She sighs sadly and I can't tell by looking into her eyes whether she believes my stories or not. The important thing is that she doesn't accuse me of lying or being childish. Well, experience is important. She lies in a fetal position. She is wearing an undershirt and panties. She takes them off only when she is in the shower or when there is absolutely no way to keep them on. It's a whim or a habit with her. Her body has no flaws, or at least none that I could find as yet. A man needs a woman to have a flaw that makes her different from all the other women. When he finds such a flaw, he tries to conceal it. The very thought that somebody else knows about this flaw plunges him into a murderous jealous rage. Imagine a woman with a perfect body and you'll see that there is nothing to conceal in her. A perfect woman is a mannequin.

"Is there anything about me you don't like?" Galya asks.

"There is something I don't like about all women," I reply.

"What?"

"Myself."

"What do you mean?"

"What they think of me is always worse than I am in reality. I like myself to be good, because in reality I'm worse."

"I don't get it."

"I don't either."

She changes position, turning to the wall. Her shoulders bend backwards and become sharp. I'm sorry to be looking at her with an artist's eye. Not the slightest desire stirs in me. My dear little nail did its job and discovered a source of pleasure compared to which a woman is only a charming diversion. She is a mannequin when she is perfect and a mannequin when she is not. This is why they love me, because of what I think of them. It's a shame that the nail discovered it but the surgeon covered it up.

Galya's husband is a cosmonaut. He has been on a mission for an entire year, spinning around the Earth. He is a future hero, maybe even a hero twice over. I have never asked her about him. Let him go up there to spin even thrice, it's an important task. Galya sniffs loudly. She has a stuffed nose. In outer space, a stuffed nose would be a disaster. Imagine if you blow your nose and fail to catch the stuff, you might be hit by it a week later. Taking a shower is also a problem.

"What do you do for a living?" asks Galya

"Nothing."

"What do you live on?"

"I got an inheritance from my grandmother."

"Why are you her heir and not your father?"

"Father found gold. He doesn't need money."

"Aren't you bored?"

"I have a collection."

"What do you collect?"

"Postage stamps. Nothing is fun in life. Life is boring. No matter how you look at it, no matter how you spin it, it's still boring."

"I used to keep fish when I was a child."

"Guppies?"

"Yes. Guppies, too."

When you have nothing to talk about it's better to say nothing. Why did Freud think a man seeks a woman who resembles his mother?

Draping my dressing gown over her shoulders, Galya heads for the shower. She doesn't need to cover herself, only to protect herself from the cold. Dear Fyodor Mikhalych. Where are you now? Can you see anything

　　　　　　　　　　　　　　　　　　　　　　　　　　DMITRY LIPSKEROV

from up there in heaven? Do you care about us and our little vanities? Do you still show your belly, or maybe everybody up there is an exhibitionist, too? Your dream has come true. Naked, you stand upright in formaldehyde at the Institute of Physical Culture, and visitors admire you. The five hundred rubles they paid you for your cadaver were sent to your daughter. How come you never spoke of her? She lives in your old room with her husband the cosmonaut, and now she went to take a shower. Should I tell her that you were an exhibitionist who earned the right to show his magnificent body forever? I doubt she'll understand. In some ways, women are hopelessly stupid. Your neck bears a telltale mark of a rope. You are number forty one in my collection, even though your departure from life was ordinary. But the end result in this case is more important: a giant vial with a unique object.

I like your daughter. She is quiet and tender and can be taught all kinds of things easily enough. Her husband, who went on an extended spin around the Earth for the sake of science, never even had time enough to get her pregnant. All in all, he never liked to waste sexual energy, sublimating it into the Universe. Well, someone has to correct another man's mistakes or finish the job that another man left unfinished. Why shouldn't it be me, if only to honor your memory? Besides, I've turned out to be a good teacher. I'm as cold as frozen steel. My feelings never get ahead of my sober mind and no passionate moan ever elicits an echo in me. It is the greatest achievement in sex. Remember the old metronome in your room? I use it to set the optimal tempo. Of course it is only good at the initial stage, but you've got to get through it first, right? Naturally, as an old sensualist, you would have understood my experiments with fruit juices. I buy them in vast quantities and pour them into the bathtub, first the heavy ones that settle at the bottom, then the light transparent ones that form the top layer. Into that colorful cocktail, the largest I've ever seen, I immerse the subject of my lessons. Even then, your daughter does not part with her panties and her undershirt. Well, it does add a certain charm to our studies. Unfortunately, we had to abandon the juices. They gave Galya a skin rash. But in other ways she undoubtedly has made strides. I have taught her to copulate in public, at the beach, for example, or more precisely in the river, while you're surrounded by dozens of swimming citizens. You stand in the water up to your waist and the girl presses herself against you, as though she is cold. This is when everything happens. The trick is to keep up a bored face. Well, old goat? Are you spinning in your vial yet?

"Who are you talking to?" asks Galya. She is toweling her wet hair.

"I'm thinking of your father. He was a great man."

"I'm sorry not to have known him well," complains Galya, gathering her hair into a pony tail. "Mother used to say that he was a bad man."

"All mothers are selfish," I say with great conviction. "Whenever something goes wrong, they turn the kids against their fathers. He was a great scientist. He discovered free matter in himself. When he died, all his papers were removed by his colleagues. Fyodor Mikhalych had clearance at a very high level. Like Lenin, he has been embalmed and is being kept at a secret lab, to make sure his fellow-scientists don't forget him. I only found out that he had clearance after he died."

We sit for a while with mournful faces, paying homage to the memory of the great scientist.

"What should I do when my husband comes back?" asks his daughter when she's done mourning.

"What do you mean?"

"I won't be able to be with him as before. You've taught me so much."

"You shouldn't worry. Weightlessness makes men impotent. You can divorce him," I suggest.

"But I love him," she sighs, putting mascara on her eyelashes.

I need to go out on business. I get dressed, pat Galya on the cheek and walk down the stairs into the fall day. I walk to the notary public, thinking of my business. Then I wait in line for an hour and, finally, when I'm invited to see the notary, I explain to him what I need him to do. He stares at me in surprise, unable for a long time to understand what I want. Then, when he does at last grasp it, he firmly refuses. I try to explain to him that there is no risk, that the paper will have my signature and that he will only have to notarize it. As to the standard fee, we could always find a way around it.

At last the document is drafted, the notary puts away a portion of my grandmother's legacy and I depart completely satisfied.

"Your health, Kazbek," I raise a glass of champagne. "I hope your slant-eyed mug soon finds its way to Alma Ata."

We drink to celebrate my birthday, and he tells me that he has already submitted his resignation and has only a few more days left to pick half-dead brains. He invites me to visit his native land one day in summer, to swim in cold natural pools and to taste a kebab roasted over saxaul firewood. It certainly sounds enticing and I accept. We raise our glasses to Kazbek's relatives, a huge number of whom inhabit the steppes of Mangghyshlaq. I listen to his nonsense a little longer, and then take out the notarized paper.

"You see, I have this problem–" I start from far away, so as not to scare him off. "I have a professional question to you as a neurosurgeon."

"What kind of question?" sings Kazbek, accompanying himself by plucking the strings on a saaz.

"How should I put it– Well... Is it possible to find in the brain the mark of an injury inflicted twenty five years ago? For instance, the mark of a shell fragment?"

"Of course it is," the singer replies easily, suspecting no trap.

"Can you do it?"

"What do you need it for?" asks Kazbek more cautiously, tossing the instrument on the bed.

"You see, I want to find that spot in my brain... I'm a little bored."

I eye my friend steadily. He understands that I am not joking and turns serious.

"You're crazy," says Kazbek after a pause.

"You must help me. I could come at the end of your shift, you'll open up my brain and implant a small tube, so that a nail, when it is inserted into it, could hit the same spot."

"No."

"Think of it as though I have been run over by a car."

"No."

I hand him the document, which is damp with sweat.

"This will protect you. It has a stamp and a signature of a notary. You'll need it if I die. You're a great surgeon."

Kazbek is adamant in his refusal and I'm forced to keep describing to him the senselessness of my existence until morning. Finally, when the night comes to an end, he agrees, saying that he will do it for me but, turning pale and looking not at all like a Kazakh, warns me that he will never shake my hand again and that he no longer wants me to come and eat kebab in sunny Alma Ata.

"When?" I ask.

"The day after tomorrow," he replies.

He stops shaking my hand that same morning.

All women can sense trouble. Galya lies next to me but she is awake. At night she took off her undershirt and panties, but I found no flaws in her body.

"Think of it as though your husband were back from outer space," I say to her angrily.

"Why?"

"And make sure you visit the Institute of Physical Culture. They have a very interesting exhibit over there."

Galya goes to her father's room, where he used to sob after getting a beating from my progenitor. I lie staring at the ceiling. The minutes just before sunrise are very sad and dark. Couldn't someone call me and tell me about a wonderfully imaginative suicide?

Next evening, after purchasing a red wig at a consignment shop, I go to the barber shop and get my head shaved. That makes the indentation on my forehead seem even bigger, and passers-by stare at me. I put on the wig and, having covered the distance to the hospital on foot, appear before Kazbek as a buffoon. Unlike me, he is gloomy, but, having given me his word, he decides to keep it without fresh objections. I wash myself thoroughly in the hospital tub, rub myself down with a stinky liquid and put on a sterile white floor-length hospital gown. Kazbek rolls me to the operating room on a gurney and transfers me to the operating table. I try to make jokes, but the Kazakh doesn't respond and speaks only when it is absolutely necessary. To prevent my head from jerking around, he ties it to the handles and inserts a wooden plank into my mouth, to keep me from biting my tongue. He thoroughly covers my skull with iodine and asks:

"Should we begin?"

I blink and start to inhale the anesthesia.

Twenty-eight, twenty-nine, thirty... They swim out one after the other. Their little bellies are no longer burdened, and the school, enlarged by the newly born, lazily swims down the wide river. The water in the river is very blue, its current is almost imperceptible, and the fog envelops it like gray hair.

In the middle of the river, barely touching its surface, lies a beautiful woman. Her pale body blends with the fog and almost floats on it. Her large eyes are shut and a small vein throbs near her nose. Her chest rises noticeably with each breath. A bird has landed on her right breast. Apparently it mistook the tiny brown nipple for an apple pip and is now at a loss what to do. The woman draws her right knee slightly to the side and at the bottom of her belly a little red sun lights up.

The school of guppies swims through the little sun and the woman parts her lips with pleasure. Startled, the bird takes wing and disappears in the fog. The woman smiles and touches the throbbing vein with a finger. She is being pulled by the current, and the fish, the bravest of them, hop onto her belly in order not to fall behind. The woman's skin seems touched by a rainbow and she laughs gently from a pleasant tickling sensation. The small caravan swims into the night and the fog thins out and settles like down.

The woman turns over on her stomach and slowly swims to the shore. Her back is wrapped in red hair down to her buttocks. She comes out of the water and gently shakes the stragglers back into the water. She walks away, a large woman on the soft grass. Then she pushes off and slowly floats in the air and turns pirouettes under the black heaven like a skydiver in the sky.

Coming out of anesthesia is hard. My head is like a cocoon, wrapped in yards of bandages. I touch it and feel a small metal tube in my forehead. Good boy, Kazbek. He found the tiny spot and opened up a path to it for me. Now I need to get out of the hospital as fast as I can, lock myself in my den and—I hope nothing interferes. God forbid some cosmonaut's wife should wish to spin around you like an abandoned satellite.

The door opens and Kazbek's slanted eyes stare at me. I smile at him in gratitude. He makes his way to my bed moving slightly sideways and, taking his hand out of his pocket, hands me a small package tied with a blue ribbon.

"What is it?" I ask, barely able to move my tongue.

"A gift."

He tosses the package onto my bed and leaves, closing the door tightly behind him. I unwrap the bright paper and find myself with a nail in the palm of my hand. It is brand-new, and it has a dull shine and a checkered head. A perfidious Kazakh. He thinks I won't be able to fight temptation and will make use of his gift right away. Meanwhile, he will spy on me through some hidden hole and conduct an experiment. No way. I'm tricky, too, I can hold out, I can wait and resist the temptation until the right time, and then—

I get out of bed, find my clothes in the bedside furniture, change and, after mouthing an excuse to a flustered nurse, go down to the exit. At the taxi stand, people let me to the head of the line. I get into the seat and close my eyes. At my house, the driver wakes me up, announces that we've arrived and kindly wishes me to get well. He doesn't know that I'm the healthiest person on earth. He doesn't realize that in a few minutes I'll be fortunate enough to feel the kind of pleasure no man has ever felt on this unhappy planet of ours. Squeezing the nail tightly in my hand, I climb the steps to my apartment. The most important thing is for the exhibitionist's daughter to be out. Like a mouse, I sneak into my room and shut the door tightly. I lie down on the sofa and, staring at the walls, try to steady my breath. Here it is, my nail. I squeeze it in a suddenly sweaty hand. As if alive, it strains to get into my brain. I close my eyes, raise my hand and place it into the little tube. One moment longer. One more. I should press a bit harder on its head. What the hell is happening? Is it too short? Of course it is! Back then I was a child, and since then my brain must have increased in size three times over, so that the nail is too short to reach the spot. I slide down from the sofa and crawl on all fours to the armoire. Mother's knitting needles are still in there; she used to knit sweaters for me. This one will certainly do the job, the one with a sharp end. It's long enough for an elephant's brain. I lean against the armoire and with an unsteady hand struggle to insert the needle into the tube. My hand shakes and the needle tears through the bandages on my head. I need to calm down, count to thirty and steady my breath. Carefully now. Here we go. It's in. It's about to start.

I sit there with a knitting needle in my head and nothing happens. I crawl to the phone and dial the number of the Sklifosovsky Hospital.

"You're a bastard," I say to Kazbek in a whisper.

"Why?" he asks.

"You tricked me. You're a loser. Nothing happens."

"I did what you asked me to. It's the right spot."

"You made a mistake. You're incompetent. All you're good for is to cut carcasses. Not human ones, either."

"Wait a minute," Kazbek interrupts me. "It's the right spot. I didn't make a mistake. I did everything correctly."

"Why don't I feel anything, then? Why?"

Kazbek breathes into the receiver as he ponders the answer.

"You were a kid back then," he says. "Your brain was clear, like an unexposed film. Everything you learned was new and unexpected. What your child's brain subjectively perceived as pleasure became transformed into commonplace once you have grown up. Only your memory preserves the sensation. In reality, it is a very ordinary spot. It is not responsible for the pleasure function. You had to understand this in order to come back to earth..."

He keeps telling me other things, too, but I start crying like a hurt child.

Except now the hurt is no child's hurt, it is far more cruel than a mother's whipping.

Galya comes in. She sees my bandaged head and my bandages that are wet with tears. She stands there staring and me, and suddenly she also begins to cry. Either she feels sorry for me, or else she thinks of her cosmonaut husband.

"Get out of here," I say to her.

"What?" She doesn't get it.

"Get lost, and quickly. Scram. Don't stare at me. Your Daddy was no hero of national security. All his life he was an exhibitionist and a dirty old man. Now he is at the Physical Culture Institute, in a vial of formaldehyde. Go cry for him if you want."

Galya leaves. I take a carton of matchboxes from the closet and until evening scrape sulfur off their heads. I fill an entire glass with sulfur. It is brown and has traces of wood in it. Then I take out a fresh sheet of paper and write the number 50 on it. It will be a nice round number for an imaginative suicide in my collection. I fill out the sheet and file it. Then I put the glass with sulfur in it into my pocket, grab an oil can and a length of dry string and go out. My gait is straight and my step is steady. I reach the river, stick the nozzle of the oil can into the tube that leads to the spot in my brain and empty the sulfur into the oil can. I stick in the string, climb onto the parapet, stare at the water for a moment and, striking a match, light the string.

I'm swimming down a blue river, lazily moving my fins. My little tail is like an oil slick on the water. Hundreds and hundreds like me swim behind me and we are a rainbow on the water.

In the middle of the river floats a beautiful woman with a large white chest. She is all white, all of her. Only at the bottom of her belly glows a tiny red sun. I lead the school toward it and, slipping through its rays, become born anew.

TRANSLATION BY ALEXEI BAYER

      DMITRY LIPSKEROV

The Heart of a Snark

SERGEI LUKYANENKO

The dark wood of the deck was damp, rough to the touch where the salt had eaten into it, and very, very warm.

Robert perched on a coil of harpoon line. He took out his cigarette case and lit up. These were real cigarettes, Earth cigarettes. They'd been properly frozen, so they hadn't lost their shape or taste.

The clients were late. They were always late, even if they needed to scramble, even if it was down to a matter of days and hours. Everything was new to them: the sky densely shrouded by violet clouds, the mountain peaks to the west, the boundless ocean to the east, the narrow strip of city between the foothills and the shore...

They called the city a settlement, and Robert couldn't fault them for that. He had seen Earth cities, on video. To earthlings, Lazarus City was no such thing.

Miguel hailed him from the next boat over, wanting a cigarette. Robert nodded. Miguel called to one of his boys, but the youngster was picking over the standing rigging as only a child in love with the sea can, checking the shrouds and stays centimeter by centimeter. Miguel gave up, walked down his gangplank to the dock, and came aboard the *Bad Rap*. Robert held out his cigarette case. Miguel lit up and hunkered down on the deck, at Robert's feet. For awhile, no one said anything. They were looking northward, to where birds were flitting uneasily over the landing pad.

"I'm hearing there's only four," Miguel said.

Robert shrugged. A ship came from Earth every three months. Sometimes it brought upward of a dozen clients. Sometimes, very rarely, just one or two. But Robert couldn't remember a time when no one came.

"Dennis told me," Miguel explained. "His sister works in the scheduling office. You know her?"

"Yep."

Robert spat over the side, and Miguel winced in disapproval. If a boat was near to shore, spitting or dropping a load into the sea was a sure way of riling fate. But Robert did spit into the sea. And at fate too. Robert was younger than Miguel. But things always went his way. And they were friends.

"Somebody's going to lose out," Robert said.

"Jose," Miguel said with certainty. "There's no client for him."

They glanced to the right, looking at the *Lucky Break* as if they had never seen it before. Jose's boat really wasn't a confidence-booster. Once upon a time, it had been a robust, reliable felucca, but a couple of years ago it had lost a mast. Jose had never bothered to replace it, so now his boat had the look of an inordinately large single-masted balancelle. Compared with a shipshape sloop or cutter, it was clumsy, but in comparison with Miguel's little ketch, it was a lumbering mess.

"There's no client for Jose," Robert agreed.

They had finished another cigarette apiece before the earthlings showed up on Port Street.

Miguel hopped to.

"May you spend this night with the neighbor's daughter," he wished Robert as he went.

"She's hideous," Robert replied.

There were four clients. The few crew members who came with them were in uniform and easy to spot. Robert liked the look of one of the clients: a sturdy kid, dressed right and carrying nothing but a small traveling bag, and he wasn't eyeballing everywhere. That one wouldn't be a lick of trouble on board. The second one was in a wheelchair, laboriously propelling the nickel-plated push rims round and round. A ship's steward was right there with him, helping him along. Robert just shook his head.

And then there was a lad and a girl. Or a man and a woman. It didn't matter. There was no way to figure out the age of earthlings. They were walking together and it was immediately obvious that they would be staying together.

"Three clients," Robert said to himself.

The earthlings came up to the dock. Miguel and his boys stood on their boat's stern, and the other crews fell into line too, best face forward.

Robert didn't get up.

The one in the wheelchair chose first. He rolled up to the ketch and gave an imperious wave. Miguel and his older son went down to help. They left the chair on shore and carried the invalid aboard.

The kid who was doing it right picked Daniel's sloop. In his mind, Robert gave him the okay on that: best boat, best crew. He also saw how rapidly the guy's eyelids were twitching. And he wished him luck.

Then the lad and the girl boarded his sloop.

"Your name's Robert," the girl said. "You were recommended to us."

Robert nodded. On rare—very rare—occasions in the past, he'd refused a client. He couldn't always explain to himself why. But if he didn't like a client, he'd refuse.

"We want to hire your boat and you," the girl went on.

"You know the rules?" Robert asked.

"Yes."

"A thousand credits. No more than three days. No guarantees. If we don't find a snark or if we find one but can't kill it, I still get the full fee. On board, my word is law. If there's work to be done, you'll work."

The girl nodded. She seemed to be in charge here, but Robert looked at the young man, meeting his firm, steady gaze. He nodded too.

"You'll bring no more than a hundred grams of metal with you," Robert went on. "Best to bring nothing at all. No technology. Absolutely none. No electrical devices or energy sources. If you have anything implanted, the hunt'll be a washout."

"We know," the girl said. "The snarks sense metal and electromagnetic fields. Right? I had an implant, but I got it removed before lift-off."

"Those are all the rules?" the young man asked. There was an assurance in his voice that inspired trust. People with that kind of voice are used to getting things done by persuasion; they don't even have to tell anyone what to do.

"Yes."

"We agree."

Robert took another second. Once a captain had chosen, he couldn't just call off the hunt.

He liked them. So what was bothering him?

"How old are you?" Robert asked.

"I'm twenty-six. Alina's twenty-seven." He paused, then added, "We're husband and wife. By the laws of Earth, we're a hundred percent legally competent."

To Robert, that was important. He had nothing against rejuvenates, who could look like teenagers when they were a hundred years old. If a person had the means to prolong his youth and was enjoying life, why not? But rejuvenates seemed unpredictable to him. A mature mind in a youthful body is sketchier than old wine in a new bottle.

"Then we can shake on it," Robert said, standing up.

The lad had a strong, reliable, masculine grip.

"Thank you for your confidence, captain," he said earnestly. "We're all yours. My name's Alexander the Younger. But you can call me Alexander."

"I'll call you Alex. Alexander if you earn it."

"Deal."

By evening they were five miles off shore, on a northward tack. Snarks love the cold. After twenty-four hours in that direction, given a good following wind, the odds for success would go up.

Miguel's ketch was also heading north. He was almost twice as far from shore and had overtaken the *Bad Rap* by seven or eight miles.

Robert didn't care. A snark hunt was always the luck of the draw, and it didn't matter who was first to the hunting grounds. And the fact was, you didn't always have to go that far out, because snarks could be caught right by the dock. Or you could roam the northern waters for months but never once see, rising above the water, a head atop a thin, white neck with big eyes and wreathed in stiff, trembling quills.

Still, the odds were better in the North.

The cabin door banged. Robert had encouraged his two hunters to get some sleep, and they'd had a good six hours. Now Alina was coming up on deck. Her face was fresh, squeaky-clean. Probably she'd brought some moist towelettes with her, because the only sink was in the galley.

"Good evening, captain," the woman said.

She went aft without waiting for an answer. Not arrogantly, as if she owned the place and was just giving a servant a casual "hi," but like a level-headed woman who didn't need to distract a man just to make small talk.

Robert smiled. He took out a precious cigarette and lit up. Then he looked back.

Half-hidden by the mast and the rigging, Alina had dropped her pants and was hanging over the stern. Sheepishly, Robert turned around.

Women had to be told how to take care of business at sea. They were usually incredulous, and often they'd hold it in for half a day. And, whatever else happened, they'd make a big thing about everyone not looking.

This woman was acting like a seasoned sailor.

Good clients.

Which of them was sick? And with what?

Cancers could be cured on Earth. Almost every kind. And nobody with a horrific late-stage cancer would act so calm or look so healthy.

The old man in the wheelchair probably had a rotting spine. It was a painful, difficult thing, but might not be terminal for decades.

The kid who'd gone with Daniel had cysts from the twisting sickness. When there was that much blinking, that often, the bugs were within three or four days of hatching. Either Daniel would find a snark by then, or those bugs would eat the guy's brain.

But these two?

Robert thought a little, while his hands kept doing what they did. Tighten the halyard. Look at the sky. Glance at the compass card. Turn the wheel two points to the west...

They were both sick, he decided. Which meant it was Michelaux syndrome, a sexually transmitted disease. Unbearable pain, paralysis, and a death that could come at any moment.

No worries. The odds were still good. He thought about the men, women and children who had sailed on his sloop. The sick, the crippled, the paralyzed, the mad. They had all needed one thing—a snark. The heart of a snark. And they had almost all got one.

Robert figured he would make it in time. Usually the ones he liked made it in time.

Alina came up, stood near him, and took a pair of binoculars out of her pocket. Robert eyed them suspiciously, but they were the right kind: ceramic and glass, not a single metal part, no chips, no batteries. Alina raised them to her eyes, followed Miguel's little boat for awhile, then took to scanning the desolate shore. Usually Robert hustled women off the bridge. But for this one, he was making an exception.

"On the shore," Alina said, "there are animals like seals but with long necks. Are they snarks?"

"Snark pups," Robert replied.

"Oh!" Alina stared at the shore for a time. "I didn't think they'd be so ... graceful," she confessed. "Or that there'd be so many... Why can't we catch a pup?"

"They're easy to catch, very friendly. The youngsters love playing with them."

"Did you?"

"Sure. You can swim with them. Way out to sea. They understand when you want them to go back. You can play ball with them too."

"They're not ... rational, are they?" Alina asked.

"Like dogs. Or dolphins. A commission looked into it and concluded they aren't rational."

Robert didn't give her the details. That the commission had been made up of a couple of dozen old, sick scientists. Or that they had returned to Earth hale and hearty, their minds clear, and with not a thing ailing them. Earth medicine could make a man young again. But not even it could cure everything. Only snarks could cure everything.

"So why don't we hunt the pups?" Alina asked.

"You do know that the snark doesn't really have a heart?"

"Of course." She glared at Robert. "They have a vascular circulatory system. What we call a heart is an integral hormonal gland through which... Yes, I get it!"

"The pups don't have the same hormones as the adults. They go to sea when they're five years old. At seven or eight, the thing we call their heart is fully functional. You can tell, because they grow their quills then."

"I get it." She lowered the binoculars. "Shall I spell you, captain?"

Robert hesitated. He was not used to trusting so quickly. And on top of that, she was a woman.

"Are you up for it?"

"I'm well trained. Crewed yachts for a year."

"Which ones?"

"A sloop like yours. I selected the *Bad Rap* before we left Earth."

Robert looked her in the eye and stepped away from the wheel. She took his place.

"Hold this course. The shoreline runs almost due north. Stay five miles from shore. Keep an eye on the sky. It's often squally here."

"Don't worry, captain."

Robert went below, to the wardroom. He was sure that Alexander would still be sleeping, but found him standing at the stove in the tiny galley. The partition was drawn back, so Robert could see every move he made.

On the even flame given off by a coal briquette in the small range, a heatproof glass saucepan was simmering. Wielding two long knives, Alexander was at the little table, cutting up a fish. Up went the matte gray blades, hung in the air for a fraction of a second, and came down to slice gently into the hepu's oily flesh. Blood and slimy chunks of guts, along with bone fragments, should have been splattering out from under the knives. But instead, something amazing was happening. The knives were taking thin cuts of fish and flipping them into the air; one blade briskly removed skin and scales, while the other split each cut into two slim slices and tossed them aside, to join the rest of the fish slices lying on a plate.

Robert knew how sharp a knife would have to be to carve up the compact, clingy hepu flesh like that.

"Are they metal?" he asked.

"Ceramic," Alexander said, not turning around. "They're good knives."

Robert loved good knives. He had a Solingen from Earth at home—a good knife that had cost him fifty credits. But he couldn't even guess how much these knives went for.

"Hepu isn't the best fish there is," he said apologetically. "I brought it because it keeps well... But I've got sea-glog too. It tastes better."

"No problems," Alex mumbled. "No problems. We'll make something of this."

Robert thought for a moment, then sat down. Sleep could wait.

Those astonishing knives had turned the hepu into one small heap of meat and another of scraps. Alex swept the scraps into the garbage pail. He carefully wiped the knives off on a cloth and slid them into a belt sheath. Robert frowned. When they had boarded, Alex had not been wearing that belt.

"Hepu's best fried," Robert said. "Boiled hepu isn't good at all."

"No problems," Alex said again.

   SERGEI LUKYANENKO

A little canvas bag came out of nowhere and from the bag came some mauve pongo leaves. Alex dropped five of them into a saucepan. Sniffed the steam. Added another leaf. And a small pinch of salt.

Robert shook his head. No one ever boiled fish with pongo leaves. That was guaranteed to make it inedible.

And what came next made no sense at all. With two little sticks like the chopsticks that the colony Orientals ate with, Alex picked up a sliver of filleted fish and plunged it into the boiling water for three seconds, took it out, and slung it onto a clean plate. So sushi was on the menu?

When all the fish had been in and out of the boiling water, Alex poured some of the liquid from the pan, squeezed a lemon into what was left and sprinkled it with half a cup of powder—like flour but mauvish-gray—and a few pinches of dried herbs. Some of the herbs had a familiar aroma. Some were in small glass jars, and probably from Earth.

"Any minute now," said Alex, although Robert hadn't said a word. "I know you're hungry."

There was a frying pan set to one side. Alex removed the inverted plate that served as a lid, revealing a stack of thin flatbreads. He must have cooked up those tortillas earlier... He put a couple of fillet pieces onto a flatbread, topped them with two spoonfuls of sauce, and rolled it all up. The sauce had thickened and gone blue. Nothing fit to eat could be a color like that.

But it did smell good.

"This one's for you, captain." Alex handed him the wrap and started rolling another for himself.

Robert took a careful bite. The flatbread was still warm; the fish and sauce in it were hot.

Good. Very good! He would never have believed that hepu could taste so good. The sauce might have looked horrendous, but it went down smooth, with a light, tartish note that brightened the oily fish. Before Robert knew what he was doing, he had finished the wrap and had even licked off his sauce-smeared fingers.

"Here you go, captain."

A plate with two more wraps was set in front of him, and Alexander took another plate (how did he put them together so quickly?) topside.

Robert ate, cleaning the drops of sauce off his fingers with his tongue. Superb! A man doesn't have to be a good cook. But if a man does cook, he should cook superbly. A man should do only what he can carry off superbly. Women are good at everything else.

He peered into the galley. There was a little fish left, two flatbreads, and some sauce in the pan. He realized that it was there for him. He poured a glass of cold tea from a porcelain teapot. Drank it thirstily. Then he made himself one more wrap and went up on deck.

And stopped short.

A mile dead ahead, a snark neck swayed above the water. The open mouth was turned to the sky. A thin, barely audible sound carried over the waves. The snark was singing. Alex and Alina, their arms around each other, stood at the wheel. The sloop was heading straight for the snark.

But Robert knew why snarks serenaded the sky.

"Alex!" he barked. "Reef the sail! Squall's coming!"

The snark's song was bewitching, especially when heard for the first time. Robert had to shake Alex to bring him out of it. He grabbed them both by the shoulders and turned them around. A churning bank of violet clouds was rapidly bearing down on them from the ocean side. Off and on, the clouds were stitched through with a white flash of forked lightning that made no sound. The song grew louder.

"It's close!" Alina yelled. "A snark! Do you see it? A snark!"

The woman's eyes were merrily mad.

"Go to your cabin!" Robert pushed her away from the wheel. "Get a move on! Dog the hatches and secure your things!"

The violet clouds had fast covered up the sun, which was setting into the sea. It was suddenly dark and cold. Another bolt of lightning sparkled in Alina's eyes. Thunder rolled. The snark was singing, rejoicing, triumphing. The pale flame of a corona discharge danced on its quills.

Alina took one last look at the snark and dashed below. The wooden hatch banged shut. Alexander was already out on the weather side, leaning against the boom while he reefed the sails. He was almost done, so Robert didn't go to help. He fastened a lifeline to his belt, glancing dubiously at the buckle. He should have replaced it but there was no time now...

"Lifeline!" he yelled. "Alex! Tether up!"

Alexander heard him. Under the captain's exasperated eye, he lunged for a belt and, with the moments ticking away, buckled it and secured the line to the mast.

And it was on them.

The *Bad Rap* slid along a wave crest, hovered motionless over an abyss of black glass. And slammed down, in a cloud of salt spray. Then shot upward, its bow caught on another wave. The sloop was playing on a giant's swing set.

Robert laughed, holding onto the wheel for dear life. There was no sun. The sky was foam. The song had died away. The frigid water...

"Captain!"

Alexander had struggled to him along the galloping, bucking deck. He grabbed him by the shoulder. Robert read his lips, not hearing the words: "How much longer?"

"Five ... ten ..." To get his point across, he took his hands from the wheel for an instant. And the ocean got in with a sneaky punch against the bottom of the sloop's hull. The next wave that had come to lift the *Bad Rap* up suddenly fell apart. The boat that had been loping up now wallowed downward. Robert was pitched up by the impact and realized that he was suspended in the air, like a cartoon character with the floor pulled out from under him. The deck, covered with seething, streaming water, was falling away from him. Black walls of waves capered all around, gloating. Alexander had grabbed the masterless wheel, gripping it hard with both hands.

But the brief instant of surreal weightlessness passed. Robert flopped down, his feet hitting the deck at an angle; he had his hands on the wheel for an instant before he was jerked away, dragged across the deck, smashed into the port rail ... and heard the lifeline give way, with a moist popping sound. The unbuckled belt flew past, as if the lifeline were a rubber band wanting nothing more than to snap back.

Robert felt his feet slipping between the deck and the rail. He clutched hopelessly at the damp deck, but his fingers just slid. He knew that he would be able to catch hold of the rail on his way overboard. Where he would hang for the ten or twenty seconds it would take for the next wave to come and sweep him away...

Something stabbed through the air and drove softly into the deck. Robert hadn't seen a thing but his hands instinctively clenched around the handle of a ceramic knife. Alexander put back the second blade he had unsheathed and took the wheel again. For a few seconds, Robert dangled there, clinging to that knife. Then the deck tilted forward, and he sprang to his feet, dashed over, made a grab for another belt that was tethered to the mast. And buckled it.

Alexander was steering the sloop straight into the waves. His stance was tense, he had no real feel for the boat, and he was doing everything the way the books said. But for now, nothing more was needed.

Robert stayed by the mast, letting Alexander spend the remaining minutes piloting the sloop through the storm. The squall was ending as quickly as it had begun. The clouds had moved shoreward, dropping a brief downpour as they went, the lightning died away, and the waves subsided. Somewhere far to sea, the snow-white spot that was the snark glittered, then disappeared into the waves. After a storm, snarks dove deep, for an hour, for five, for ten hours.

"The lightning's power they drown in ocean depths." That was from a poem that Robert had studied in school. Actually, it was far more straightforward than that. The snarks used the electricity they had stored up to stun fat deepwater crabs that were completely invulnerable in their armor but helpless against a high voltage discharge.

Poets always lie.

Robert went over to Alexander and clapped him on the shoulder. The lad dragged his eyes away from the calm ocean, as if still waiting for another wave.

"You did well," the captain said simply.

Alexander nodded. He looked to shore.

"The squall's gone," Robert said.

Alexander nodded again. "And so has the snark," he said. He unbuckled his lifeline and went to the knife embedded in the deck, rocking it back and forth to get it out.

"There'll be another."

Robert and Alexander split the night watch, and Alina didn't argue. When morning broke, Alexander was at the wheel. He was on a northerly heading, navigating by the sun. Call it happenstance or an irony of fate, but Earth's sun was to this planet what Polaris was to Earth. A yellow glimmer over the horizon. The world from which he had come and to which he would return. Or would he? Alexander felt the doubt growing, overwhelming him. The noisy cities, the trackless forests, all the good things civilization had to offer... where were they? Had they even really existed? There was a sloop sailing through the night, a wind filling the sails, a black sky spattered with stars, cold water lapping against the sides, there were snowcapped mountains to the west.

But the ocean grew lighter, the clouds to the east flared pink, the sun— almost the same as Earth's sun—broke from the water. The wind freshened, the sea glittered, the waves strengthened just a little. The pink balls of floater-urchins that had bobbed all night on the surface grew dark, took on water, and began to sink. Alexander watched them thoughtfully. He had heard that floater roe was tasty. It would be very difficult to harvest them from the sea floor, but then at night, when they were drifting from one feeding ground to another, all you would have to do is throw a net overboard and by morning it would be full of urchins and random tatters of fish.

Alexander decided they would drop a net that evening.

Robert came up on deck, bringing a cup of hot, fragrant coffee and some croissants warmed in a frying pan, cut open and filled with jam. Alexander sipped the coffee skeptically, but liked it. The locals had managed to get coffee to grow in the foothills, almost at the snowline. Alexander had smiled when he saw tourists buying up their sacks of beans, but now he decided to take a kilo or two of his own back to Earth. The croissants were a let-down, though; he didn't care for the local grain at all. But the jam was good.

Every planet had something interesting to offer.

"How do you feel?" Robert asked

The squall and the broken belt had brought them closer. It wasn't quite a friendship yet, but it wasn't the relationship of master and man either.

"I'm frozen," Alexander said after a moment's thought.

Robert gave an understanding nod. Michelaux syndrome. Capillary spasms. Icy hands and feet...

"We'll get a snark for sure," Robert said.

"Is it true that a snark can only cure one person?" Alexander asked out of the blue.

"Bull," Robert replied. "The only thing is, the hormones lose their potency in a hurry. And they're unstable. A snark heart can't be frozen or preserved. It has to be eaten within thirty minutes of the kill."

"Of the harvesting," Alexander corrected him

Robert shrugged. He didn't do word games. Words couldn't change reality.

"One, two, maybe five," Robert said. "Probably no more. But every patient doesn't have to get his own snark. That rumor was started by greedy captains. It's dishonorable."

"So we could all have gone out on one boat?" Alexander wondered.

"The bigger the boat and the more people on board, the more leery the snark will be," Robert replied diplomatically.

Alexander nodded, satisfied with that answer.

They caught sight of the snark at noon. Perhaps it was the one that had sung before the storm. Perhaps it was another.

The snark was swimming to shore, with Miguel's ketch in pursuit. It wasn't exactly a hot pursuit, though. Snarks could swim deep underwater for several hours at a time, too fast for the swiftest schooner to overtake. But this snark was playing tag with Miguel's ketch. Perhaps it had played that way as a youngling in the surf, with noisy, naked children. Parents love to see their children playing with snark pups. First, the children are in no danger. Second, even small snarks leak some sort of fluid that keeps the children healthier.

And third ... well, snarks that have played with children are easier to kill.

"We can beat him to it," a wound-up Alina said. "Captain?"

Robert silently shook his head. That was too stupid to merit a reply. Captains didn't horn in on each other's prey. Not even if clients were waving wads of cash.

The client would eat his snark's bleeding heart and lift off, to Earth, Eden, or Olympus. The captains had to live side by side until the next ship docked. Had to walk the same streets that led to the same taverns. Their wives and daughters would meet in the stores and at market. On Sundays they would all sit together under the pastor's reproachful eye.

Some things are too costly to sell.

The snark was having fun. It was a young one, no more than twelve years old. It would jump half out of the water and race ahead, then arch about, round the ketch, and settle into the stern wave. Miguel wasn't even trying to keep up with it. He was simply waiting until it felt like swimming closer.

Robert stood on his bow and waved to attract Miguel's attention. He placed his arms crosswise, then dropped the left while extending the right horizontally.

Alexander and Alina watched him silently.

The gesture-language was no substitute for radio but about as good ... about as good as signal flags. Miguel went to his client, who was seated in a roomy wooden lounge chair fastened to the deck. Asked him something. Asked again. Shrugged. Came to the side, flailing his arms in the signal for "no."

Robert had thought as much. The old man with the rotting spine didn't want to share his snark heart. He apparently believed that one snark could cure only one person.

"They don't want to hunt together," Robert let his clients know.

Alexander and Alina weren't put out. They just stood there, watching the movements of the graceful white beast. Now the snark was circling the ketch, now it was lazily backing water as if bored with its game, now it dove and stayed down for several minutes, now a limber white torpedo flew out of the water alongside the ketch.

Miguel flung a harpoon, while his sons hurled javelins, to bleed the beast and tire it.

The harpoon slid along the smooth hide and fell into the water. The javelins seemed to have missed their mark too.

The snark let out a thin, indignant cry and dove, swimming a good half-mile underwater before surfacing—right by the *Bad Rap*. Fear must have thrown it off. The flippers slapped the water, the long neck stretched out, the snark's head drooped by the gunwale, and it looked at Robert with frightened eyes.

Robert spread his hands helplessly. It wasn't his snark.

The beast ducked gently into the water and disappeared. Robert sighed and steered his sloop away from the shore. The *Lucky Break* stayed put, spiraling out in the vain hope that the snark had been at least lightly wounded. Robert could hear Miguel swearing and the old man's shrill voice. He winced.

"Beautiful," Alina said unexpectedly. "Good heavens, how beautiful it is."

Robert winced again. That was no way to think, or talk. You mustn't admire a creature that you're about to kill and eat. One time, a woman client of his had called off the snark kill after seeing one for real. She called it off, and flew back to Earth to die.

"It's a strong beast," Alexander said. Now, that was more like it. "Robert, make for the shore."

"Why?"

"Because I'm asking you to."

Robert turned the wheel, steering the sloop toward the craggy shore and leaving the ketch to continue the search for its wounded quarry.

   SERGEI LUKYANENKO

"If we come across that snark again, can we take it?"

"Once we're two miles distant from the ketch. And if they call off the pursuit."

"Uh-huh," Alexander said. "Robert, head for those cliffs. I'll handle the sails."

Robert stood at the wheel, not asking any questions.

"I've been sailing for thirty years, ten of them solo," he announced after a while. "I know snark habits. They don't take cover close to shore."

"The snark isn't close to shore," Alexander replied. He was standing by the side, looking into the foaming water.

Robert brought Alina over with a glance, left the wheel, and leaned over the side.

The snark was swimming under the boat, hiding in the shadow that the *Bad Rap* cast on the sea floor. Pressed down by the side wake, the quills fluttered around its head like hair.

"Clever brute," Alexander said. "Since we didn't attack it, we must be safe haven. Can you hit it?"

Robert laughed. "Down there? I don't have a harpoon cannon. Mine's manual. If it surfaces..."

"Ready the harpoon," Alexander pushed.

Far astern, the ketch stopped sailing in circles. It came about and continued northward, to the land of ice-floes and snarks. Robert took the harpoon from its case. Secured its cable. And hefted it in his hand, remembering the feel of a weapon ready to kill. A ceramic blade on a solid wooden shaft; a sturdy nylon line. Snarks were agile and quick, but not outstandingly strong or hardy. The whalers of Earth's olden days had had a far harder time of it.

"Take up the sails," he told Alexander. "If we stop, the snark'll surface."

Alexander worked with the rigging, while Robert stood at the side and watched the snark.

It was steadily slowing, to stay in the boat's shadow. But the sloop hove to, rocking on the waves. The snark began turning in place. But the sloop's bow slowly pivoted toward the sun, and the shadow shrank...

With a strong stroke of its flippers, the snark surfaced. From the water rose a head wreathed in quills, a long neck, and fore-flippers that beat the water hard and fast. The dark eyes gazed at the captain. The snark made a quiet mewing sound.

Robert raised the harpoon.

The snark's eyes narrowed. Blue sparks blazed on its quills. Clients often thought that it was about to attack the harpooner then. Dimwits. The electrical discharge was only dangerous in the water. It was like a cry, a soundless cry above the threshold of hearing.

Robert flung the harpoon. Twenty centimeters of razor-sharp blade pierced the snark's neck, the serrated tip emerging on the other side.

The snark began to flounder. Robert had started out by making the line fast, leaving only a short length free to run. The snark couldn't even fully submerge, so it arched and floundered alongside.

"But it's suffering!" Alexander shouted.

Robert tried to tell him that this was actually a good thing. The shock would activate the hormones, increasing the heart's healing power. But Alexander wasn't listening. Taking out his astonishing knives, he bounded over the side. He jumped right onto the snark and slid down into the sea, carving two deep furrows into its body. There was a gush of dark crimson blood. The snark was immediately, strangely calmed. It gave a few more flipper strokes and went limp in the water.

"Done and done," Alina said. She was eyeing the bloody stain and the motionless body with complete calm. "It's bad to torture an animal for no good reason. Wait, though—are there any sharks here?"

"God forbid." Robert had seen movies about Earth's swift predators.

"Ropes down here!" Alexander called. He was swimming around the dead snark, in the spurting blood. "Stop wasting time!"

They threw ropes, strong nylon ropes, over the side, running them through the blocks. Down below, Alexander smartly trussed the snark's body, impressing Robert all over again. This man was so good at everything he did.

Then Alexander clambered back on deck, giving off the sharp, disquieting smell of blood. All three hauled on the ropes, lifting the body aboard. This was a strong, healthy snark that weighed at least a ton. Still, all snarks were strong and healthy. Nobody had ever seen a sick one.

They sluiced the deck with three buckets of water, to wash away the blood. Robert stretched out his hand and Alexander obediently handed him a knife, which Robert ran along a flipper several times, to get a feel for the blade. It split the flesh like a sack of grain.

"Go ahead." Alexander was eager now. "Go ahead, captain!"

Robert ripped the snark's belly open, drawing another spate of blood. The insides were still pulsating, the shrunken veins contracting. The lung sacs quivered.

Moving the guts aside, Robert took the snark heart in his hand. It was lurking behind the lungs and really did look like a huge heart, bigger than a bull's, with a whole cluster of vessels running to it.

Robert first cut the fibrous bands and membranes that held the heart in place in the chest cavity. Then he separated the vascular branch.

Once removed from the snark's body, the gland didn't resemble a heart so much. It was a flabby, spongy mass honeycombed by thousands of capillaries. That organism's only gland. The elixir of life. The cure-all incarnate.

"Done." Robert plunged the gland into a bucket to wash off the blood. Very quickly, just to make it look a little better. The hormone-rich blood inside the gland was best left alone. "Eat it raw. Don't be scared. To top it all off, it tastes good."

"We know," Alexander said. "Will you have some?"

Robert shook his head. He wasn't sick, and a snark heart isn't eaten just in case.

"Eat."

He went up on the forecastle. Stood a while at the wheel, then went to the bow. He watched the receding ketch through his binoculars—an ordinary pair, nowhere near as good as Alina's. Miguel was probably still wondering where his snark had gotten to. After a moment's thought,

Robert decided that he would have to tell him, regardless. No one had known until then that the snarks even knew how to hide out.

"Captain…"

Alexander had come up to him, holding a plate in his bloody hands. On the plate were thin slices of snark heart. Clients didn't usually have that kind of self-control. They ate the heart just as it was, snatching at it, sinking their teeth into the pulp, choking and gagging on the salty concentrate of life.

Robert thought how well they must be now, that brave, competent man and that brave, competent woman. The sickness had left their bodies. The snark's death had been their gift of life.

"You have to try this! I was sure it would need lemon."

The snark heart was indeed dotted and sprinkled with something. Robert took a small slice and tasted it.

Delicious. Robert had eaten snark heart three times. Once out of curiosity. Once when he had broken both legs; the fractures had knit together in two hours. And another time, when his own heart had started to go bad and the doctor had presented him with the choice of taking pills for the rest of his life or eating snark heart.

Of course he had opted for the snark heart.

Robert took a second slice. What was that seasoning? Herbs of some kind… And the lemon…

"When we were told that snark heart was really good to eat, the first thing I thought of was lemon juice," Alexander said. "Lemon juice, mint, and just a touch of sugar. Hardly enough to taste. Interesting, yes? It's a pity it can't be grilled…"

"How sick are you?"

"What?" Alexander popped another bloody lump into his mouth.

"How sick are you? What did you want the snark heart to cure?"

"We're not sick!" Alexander shook his head in vigorous protest. "Captain, don't worry! We're completely fit. We're foodies. We like to eat well. We heard that snark heart isn't only a medicine, it's a delicacy. Except a thousand times more expensive than black caviar or foie gras. We're rich.

　　　　　　　　　　　　　　　　　　　SERGEI LUKYANENKO

We can afford it. So we flew here, and the flight was well worthwhile, I can see that now. It's phenomenal, captain!"

He turned and went to join his wife. Rigid, Robert looked at them, those two figures standing over the bloody, gutted carcass. Like two scavenging birds over a beached snark.

Then he came to the dismal realization that if he tried to give Alexander a sock on the jaw, he'd get socked right back. And if he jumped overboard and swam to shore, they would serenely sail his yacht to port.

"Come and join us, captain!" Alina called to him.

He sat on the deck and lit up. The tobacco was strong—strong enough to make his head spin and calm him down.

The thought came that he would have to go through more of his cigarettes on the way back.

There were no winters here. After a long, warm, dry summer, just a short season of cold rain.

It had been raining going on three days. They were sitting in a tavern, gazing at the mournful boats in their berths.

"Relax, pal," Miguel said. "Fate was born blind. They could just as well have come to me. Then I'd've been the dimwit."

"A snark's life taken for a human life," Robert replied, "that's honorable. I just have my sail and my harpoon. The snark can get away. But to take a snark's life just for the taste?"

Miguel hoisted a heavy mug and gazed into the thick, dark beer.

"I'm drinking this beer just for the taste," he said tactfully.

"But you didn't cut out a snark's heart to fill your glass!"

Miguel nodded. He took a pull of the beer. Got out his cigarette case and offered one to Robert. He had had a good season and could buy all the smokes he wanted, big family or no big family.

"The old man who had me looking for a snark will live a hundred years now," he said. "I asked him what he was going to do when he was home and well. He said he'd get the rejuvenation. And collect a bunch of lady friends. Innocent lasses. That's what he likes best. He has plenty of money and doesn't have to work for it. Robert, does it really make a whole lot of difference who we killed the snark for? A guy and his gal who like to eat offbeat things? Or an old man who wants to hump young girls twenty-four seven?"

"You're trying to make me feel better," Robert said quietly. He was slightly plastered. It had been a week since he had come back from his last trip out, slightly plastered.

"Sure I am," Miguel agreed. He finished his beer. "Sure I am. And you've had enough to drink. We're people, not angels. We're always chowing down on someone."

He stood up, threw three heavy silver coins onto the table. And made for the door, but on the way there, he turned around.

"Robert!"

The captain of the *Bad Rap* lifted his head.

"It's not just the snark that doesn't have a heart, you know," Miguel smiled. "Neither do people."

TRANSLATION BY LIV BLISS

                                                 SERGEI LUKYANENKO

The One-Day War

Vladimir Makanin

When a young woman doesn't show up until the very end, somehow, there's no room for her, no need—and so, all the more naturally she appears at the beginning, immediately, here and now. She was a St. Petersburg taxi driver, definitely young, friendly, energetic, but fated to work on that very night. (In general, female taxi drivers are spared from nights. Shifts are rotated.) And her very first passenger sent her straying down unlit and half-lit streets. He was alone, somber, and without a suitcase or any other kind of bag. But it went alright. She let the sulker out and drifted down the deserted streets on the outskirts of St. Petersburg.

Noticing a streetlamp and some well-placed fir trees bravely standing over the road, she slowed down. It was right by the sidewalk, and there was no one in sight. Turning the car off and not forgetting to take the keys (watch out!) the young woman hopped out of her car towards the trees.

The street slept. Just one window was lit in the building across the street. An old man was glued to the glass, intently staring off at nothing.

He hadn't been fully asleep when he was woken up. He'd been jerked from that sweet, elderly dream state, when you're half-asleep and you start to believe that, at any moment, your strength will return to you. How he waited for it! These last rays of will are nocturnal, inarticulate, and they slip away; they're yours and not yours. You can't tell whether you're dreaming them. Whether they're a momentary illusion, teasing you.

It was a late night telephone call that woke him up. Of course, he shouldn't have answered the phone so late at night, but he jerked out of bed, hurried his hand towards the receiver, and listened (for the hundred and first time) to a rude voice calmly say, "Oh...It's you...your time is SOON," laugh and hang up.

The old man lingered for some time, holding the phone, listening to the insolent dial tone that spilled from it before putting it back in its charger base. That's what they called it now: "putting it in its base." In his day, they'd used the unpleasant verb "to hang up."

He could go back to bed and perhaps fall into a vivid dream state. Laying down on his right side, he could perhaps find something funny about his soft bed and himself: an old man, putting his phone in its base after a conversation.

But before he did this, taking advantage of his brief nighttime clarity, he went up to the window. The time of the moon! He turned his gaze to the darkened, empty street. He saw a taxi. Suddenly, the car stopped and a female driver stepped out and hid in the trio of firs. She took care of her needs there. The old man didn't see her and didn't guess at what she was doing. He only saw her happy face as she reappeared alongside her car and, raising her eyes, assessed her surroundings. She looked at the building across the street and, naturally, at the window—and at him.

Her gaze lasted a second or two, but the old man was already cheered. She waved at him as if to say, "So there are two of us wide awake, you and I, in this slumbering St. Petersburg night." Perhaps, her wave was also to apologize for the trees and her need—it happens, what can you do? The palm of her hand lit up in the light of the moon, or the street lamp. Petersburg had already started freezing over, though it was autumn. Light

                                          VLADIMIR MAKANIN

was strictly conserved, as was heat, but that single streetlamp was always on near the building where the old man lived.

The taxi drove off, but the old man stayed by his window, heartened by the least bit of human contact. He spent day and night locked in his room. He was under house arrest. The old man, you see, was a former President.

He was not alarmed when something warm pressed at the back of his leg a minute later. He knew that it was the eager face of his companion looking for affection—the sturdy head of his dog. His dog and no one else. Remaining by the window, the old man tousled his dog's ears, to which the dog tersely and joyously replied, "Ouuu-ouuu."

The room's echo returned the dog's "ouuu." As though some other dog was answering from afar, thought the old man, an echo from across the sea. From very far away.

Downstairs, at the lobby entrance to this building, there was a table, chair, a telephone, and the strong male musk of security guards. The night guard was on watch—if anything happened, he'd whistle. Next to him was the door (wide open, naturally) to the lounge where three or four strong and, naturally, armed, young men snored. The ex-President was in no way dangerous from a security standpoint. Even if he were at liberty, there was nowhere for him to go. He was no longer mobile enough to flee.

Essentially, the only person guarding him was that night guard. He was also a geezer, and lonely. He suffered from insomnia, and had asked for the night post in order to give the young men a chance to sleep.

There was a song from his faraway youth, a song of his grandfather's generation, where voices cried out to the heavens: "Leeeet the soldiers sleep..."

And they slept. The security guard's mind wandered, considering this and that, not at all concerned with the ex-President—why should he be watching an old man? At the same time, his nightly show of empathy couldn't be generalized. It was like this in every country! The global pursuit of influential old men (the basis and engine for modern public life) made sense to the guard. That's what the powerful deserved. Everyone gets theirs! Another's misfortune isn't always a source of pleasure, but with these powerful men, it isn't for nothing that their downfall warms our humble hearts. It's entirely because of who they are. We're no ex-Presidents, we're just old men. They don't write about us in the papers. And we're delighted in our insignificance. (The only thing pursuing us is our old people smells. And the smirks, perhaps, of our smart-aleck grandchildren, who think that we already reek of death...) The old man he was keeping guard over got what he deserved. After all, wasn't he human just like everybody else? Didn't he commit his share of little sins on his way to the top?

With this last thought, full of severe justice though not self-reflective (yet), the guard fell into a weak and steady state of nocturnal nirvana. Not sleep, but peace.

The peace of mind of the guard, like the peace of mind of many security guards, rested on two facts: first of all, when he worked he got bread and heat—heat at home. Another was the sedative he took every day. Every evening he'd drink (slowly) from the television... This had to do with the world. Even after the One-Day mass hysteria, we Russians had something left. There were a few SS-series missiles left behind, just, just in case.

The modernized ballistic SS-21, commonly referred to as the SS-series, had a calming effect on just about everyone. It was well-known. As soon as it was launched at some hypothetical aggressor, the missile, playfully even, divided into ten parts. And it packed a ballistic surprise: along with the "hot ten," it also shot out exactly forty light-weight dummy missiles. They called them dummies. But it was because of these dummies, indistinguishable from self-guided missiles when in flight, that the number of missiles released grew to 50: 40 + 10.

We've always feared death from above: first it was thunder and lighting, then the wrath of God, and now, on top of that, missiles! Since the time when we were cavemen, everywhere we went, we've planted our little lightning rods. Prayer is a charming shield, one of the strongest we've got, but it's not by prayer alone that we live these days. This is why (not only because of the SS-series, though it seems to have started with it) there is a universal and universally acknowledged project: to suspend a thousand satellites over the Earth that will track and monitor any missiles splitting through the air. It is an international project, for the peace of mind of many nations. Isn't that the most important thing? Isn't it the perfect lightning rod for our overgrown cave? Isn't it the

fulfillment of all of our dreams?...

to quote a famous poet from the newspapers back then. And the cave passage ended with the feeling of being a part of the world, or rather, a participant in world events—this captured the hearts of all of the war-wearied public, without exception.

Only the first hundred satellites took any time to launch. The second and third hundred followed soon after... then the dynamic fifth, the seventh—it all made quite an impression! (A spectacle even. All of us have good imaginations). It looked like some grand New Year's display when, branch by branch, they weigh the tree with golden orbs of light. They scattered them around the corners of the room—and onto the very ceiling!—even (the mischief!) strewing them on the houseplants. The last little lights are hung up here and there, anywhere they fit, then with one fell swoop all of them are illuminated at the same time—what a show! The laser light display of the satellites, hundreds upon hundreds, lit up (what a show!) in order to monitor the launching of our or somebody else's—anybody's—self-guided missiles. The elderly security guards of the world can sleep on the job in peace. As they should. And let them!... What else do old men have (when they've worked their whole lives) other than night shifts, illnesses, and nagging thoughts about national security?

The final, tenth hundred satellites were being sent into space, Russia seemed stable and comfortably Europeanized, when suddenly the conflict erupted. Religious conflicts, said the papers, never end, because their sparks are fanned by the little winds of history. There's always a small heap of embers, smoldering.

In Russia's patchwork tapestry, it could be Tatars, Bashkirs, Chechens... It was merely by chance that it was the Tatars... that government clerks, tending to minor but necessary affairs, happened to hit a nerve, spot-on (the newspapers were straightforward with "insulted"), offending Tatars' religious beliefs—theirs and not anyone else's. But that's what happened. The wheels of history, in such cases, slightly adjust themselves. The first robins were the youth in Tatarstan. Kazan students donned green, Islamic armbands and started organizing meetings here and there, sitting on streetcar and trolley tracks, and then, without any warning, one day—in the middle of the day, no less—they blocked the Kazan-Moscow train line. They called the students the "Green Robins."

University administrators did not deal with the situation in the best way they could, summoning and giving free reign to the police. *When the infidels get aggressive, the true believers, praise Allah, get militant.* This was confirmed the next day by the thousands in the streets and by the fury of the fire that night, raging in the oldest, most holy mosque in the city. Most likely, the fire was started unintentionally, but History likes chance best of all. Unfortunately and irrevocably, it happened that the Russian President was right then at an international summit. His council of deputies, directing operations from Moscow and clearly at a loss, deployed armed forces to Kazan. In crawled the tanks, and things began to look very familiar. Then the familiar became the course of things: shots fired at rooftops, into open windows. Shooting in the streets... The students set tanks on fire and immolated themselves. Photographs and footage of the violence appeared in newspapers and on TV around the world. The world wobbled... and started shaking...

It was the 21st century, but like the previous century, people seemed to lack the necessary experience to know better. We knew how it *shouldn't be...* The West, by decree of the UN, demanded that Russia withdraw its tanks from Kazan. They would be replaced by international peacekeeping forces, guaranteed to maintain neutrality in the long-term national and religious conflict. The Hague got involved in a familiar way. Even more familiar was Russia's response, advising the world to keep out of its internal affairs. The wheels were in motion (they only needed the slightest push!). Good will and the constancy (or inconstancy) of good will are, unfortunately, independent faculties.

                                                VLADIMIR MAKANIN

The West vacillated—should they or should they not penalize Russia for its actions, forcing them to comply with the UN's resolution—a decision made by the world community, after all! The West could, say, launch just one missile attack—strategically and only destroying the economy, sparing civilians. As it was written afterwards in *The Guardian*, the experience of Russia and the West collided. Russia had Chechnya (which was analogous to Tatarstan) while the West had the wonderful (and similarly victorious) experience in the Balkans. The West knew what was what. It was time to strike at the economy of the offending country and bleed it dry. They would shut off the gas and oil pipelines, shutting down factories, bridges, power stations, mines, and so on. It was time for punishment without declaration of war. The country would survive—opposition forces would come into power.

This was an especially potent plan of attack, since Russia's energy resources were extended over great areas and too closely resembled airy summer spider webs. In the folk tradition, spider webs in summer portend fair weather. After the first, precise blows to gas and oil supply lines, Russia (plunged into primeval winter) will be destroyed in terms of energy and forced onto its knees. No man or nation can say "no" for long once it is on its knees.

The "thousand satellites" system was by this time fully functional.

Certainly, the possibility of a counterattack by the diabolical SS-21s was analyzed and planned for. The anti-ballistic missiles lay in wait. Statistically, in the best case scenario, Russia would only launch ONE AND A HALF indestructible missiles. However, missiles tend not to fly in halves (so ONE).

One missile will be launched—the rest would be intercepted and countered. The concussion of the explosion at the moment of interception would be powerful enough to knock that one main missile off its course. Dummy missile! It'd wobble helplessly in the air. A joke! It is unlikely that its free-flight trajectory would land it in Europe or Asia; most likely it would end up safely in the boundless waters of the Pacific Ocean. And incidentally, it could even drop smack down on its own territory, in the dark taiga of Siberia. What could be better? What more could you want?

The most grievous errors are always the simplest and the most human.

Who would have thought that Russian colonels (in their national laziness) could not be bothered to gather up "used" missiles from the fields and forests after each SS-21 trial? It boggles the mind! These large metal missile shells, crumpled and contorted, could not be reused. (These monsters were now only good for the scrap heap). At some point, army officials (without the knowledge of the Ministry) cut the number of dummies launched by a factor of three. Naturally, after conducting trials, they would correct their laziness (their "human error") arithmetically—all the totals were simply multiplied by three.

Intelligence regularly reported that the Russians were multiplying their number by a fixed factor of three, but in the West, this was interpreted as the Russians exaggerating their success. It was thought that they just wanted to appear stronger and more threatening than they really were. Which can be expected from any individual or nation preparing to receive the first blow.

As it turned out, NATO and Russia struck at the same time, the launches separated by mere seconds. The war came and went. *Le Monde* reported that the interval between the missile launches was so small that, had the course of events been any different, it would have been impossible to determine who had struck first.

The journalist allowed himself a popular comparison: the missile face-off (before the attack) reminded him of two aggressive cats on a rooftop striking the "devil's pose"—arching their backs. A cat sets its fur bristling in order to look bigger, and more muscular. So, you know, that when you looked at him, you got scared.

The missiles, prepared for launch, continued the journalist, collided in the atmosphere like frightening bristled fur. However, for the people (whose roof is the sky), the factor of three that seemed mythical proved to be all too real.

It wasn't one and half missiles that were launched (which would have meant ONE missile, since missiles don't fly in halves) but *four and a half* (which meant THREE).

And with that, the missile attack reached its conclusion. The day of war ended, by evening the war was considered one day long. What enormous, "expanded" Russia, with its long, long winter looked like without power is hard to imagine. What happened, perhaps, was not catastrophic, but it wasn't life, either. Russia was cut off "from oil, gas, and coal—back to logs"; from the third millennium back to the first.

And, amazingly, there were still missiles left over.

The West did not want to keep fighting, either. The French left NATO, kicking and screaming. They couldn't forgive their leader. Europe could not stop blaming the Americans, even though America was hit the hardest.

One of the Russian missiles that was not countered, as it had been supposed, ended up sinking in the Pacific Ocean. It splashed somewhere into the calmness of the waves.

The second one's crooked trajectory landed it in Europe, in neutral Switzerland, though luckily it only destroyed a small patch of happy trees somewhere in the Alps. Superpowerful, it killed only a bit less than one thousand locals and, on top of that, about a thousand pretty skiers on vacation.

Only the third missile (the last of the "lucky" ones) reached America, destroying almost half the city of Chicago in one fell swoop. Chicago. A population of two million. The missile, as though in a daze, reached the very coast of America before splitting off into its component parts and shed them, blasting, where it could—mostly into the sea. But one of these self-guided little pieces made a sudden detour towards Chicago.

This third missile, unlike the others, was called "crazy," even though, by missile logic, the crazy one was the one that merely caused a slight disturbance in the Pacific.

That was the damage. *(According to France-Presse.)* Plus, of course, gas- and oil-deprived, freezing Russia.

Horrified by the Chicago disaster, Americans blamed their President. They impeached him—honest taxpayers of all ages repeated the same thing to every newspaper and camera: "How could he? How could he?"

Very quickly, he was run out of government. Now he was an ex-President.

On top of that, they rushed him to court. Across the country, petition after petition gathered signatures: to court with him! To court! A war that lasted one day couldn't change people in their essence. Rather, as those mean-spirited philosophers maintain, the most important crowbar in the democratic process has always been the citizens' proclivity towards indicting eloquent old men at the end of their careers.

Say what you will, this is the only manifestation of *Judicium Dei* on Earth—and its only equal.

They prosecuted Pinochet, they prosecuted Honecker, they got Kim Yes Yes and Kim No No, little old man after little old man—sent to the corner, one and all! Without an ounce of sentimentality (instead, the cold of self-righteous discipline), the TV screen broadcast their sad, pathetic faces to the whole world. All of it was done for our sake. Publicizing the defeat (Look at him! Just look!) of yet another little old man—is this not our humble civil triumph? And isn't this, seriously, our daily (or nightly) spiritual food? And why not the answer to our prayers? Our brief, frightened prayers about the future (our own future)—our prayers in front of the blue candles of our televisions. We're only human, and our TVs are our humble churches. We stand on our knees in front of the television and we pray.

They even took former chancellor Kohl to court! The number one German, the fatty, the one with the great big jowls! They didn't end up convicting him, but they beat him up rather good, anyway. Perhaps, they were in a bit of a hurry. They rushed it with him just a little bit—then they let him off. The most important part of an indictment (this must be kept in mind) is to wait for the helplessness of old age. Why tear at the healthy? Who needs their big fat rosy cheeks? Instead, we must await feebleness, flabbiness—show us the impotence—and (the minute a man is pitiful) off to court with him! The moment of truth is the moment of impotence. Otherwise, the truth of truths isn't just. (And, we must admit, it isn't very fun.)

It's important to get to the bottom of things. After all, it's specifically *this man's* sickly gaze that we need to see. We need his spittle out of the corner of his mouth... his lawyers... his relatives. Hobos with placards—all of this is part of the process, it hypnotizes us, already gaping in front of the screen—it's a ritual. They're carting *him,* who was once so powerful (in front of screaming crowds), around in a wheelchair! At least once, on a weekend (towards the evening) we need this—to sigh and turn our spirits to this, to have a look...

In Warsaw, a local crazy ran around town with a new monologue. (He found out that they were taking Jaruzelski to court.) "Panie! It's a trick! We keep on prosecuting the false ones! Take a close look at them, panie— you'll see right away! Mock-up men—imaginary dictators! Neither one way or another—*we'd loved the real ones...*"

Of course, certain wiseacres believe that prosecuting old men at the end of their careers is only the petty revenge of a crowd that, unfortunately, has few joys in life. These very wiseacres (unwittingly, or even wittingly) defend the despicable little old men. They would never acknowledge the grandiosity, the sheer beauty of the process. They're only good for wanting Kantian ethics, duty and the stars. And where can you find Kantian ethics? Up your ass, is where. There's no such thing.

We've learned to approach justice from another angle—the earthly one. We know everything we need to know. It (the truth) is very simple. No matter who our leader is, he's a bastard. *And he'll finally get what he deserves.*

People freezing here and there (in Russia) also separated their leader from his presidency. It was time to call him to account. Yet Russia, in the One-Day War, by a mere second, ended up on the defending side. So the simplest thing to do was to continue pursuing the actions against former President R (Russia's "R" was the easiest thing to call him), in order to make him answer for the tanks and blood spilled in Kazan. There was nowhere to hide.

Former President A (the American), aging, was left completely alone, expect for his dog.

His wife died, his children had long since moved to opposite ends of the country. It couldn't be helped that the children became estranged: who'd like it if, day after day, their father was savaged in the papers. Not to mention the damned TV, where, in anticipation of the trial, everyday there were new lies—and malicious ones at that!

President A's dog, on the other hand, did not read the papers nor sniff at the blue essence of the television. The dog was named Ivan. This was this custom—to name large and powerful dogs popular foreign names, preferably from enemy states. It was believed that Ivan was the most popular Russian name.

Former President A (the American) would hardly touch his breakfast. The same went for the papers: glancing over the fresh headlines, it wouldn't have even occurred to him to read further. However, he would gladly get down on the floor and wrestle his formidable dog and scratch it behind its ears. Rolling around on the thick carpet, the aging ex-President would speak with easy bitterness to his dog, "Just the two of us, Ivan. You and I, and nobody else."

But a little happiness crept into his voice. The dog had become a dear, familiar creature. It understood everything.

Other than the long (and probably happy) games with the dog, former President A spent his days occupied with unpleasant affairs: he had to concern himself with his future. How little he wanted to do this! (He didn't even want a future—the hell with it!)

His people would come, leftovers from his former team, the whole old royal guard. Over coffee, ice cream, and a little whiskey, they had a long and downright difficult talk about how to stall the court proceedings. They couldn't get around them, of course, just like they couldn't get around democracy itself. But maybe they could stall things... Make the process drag on interminably (maybe even torturously so, but nevertheless). This was the order of the day—it seemed to all of them that this was the most important thing they could do, their only chance.

Even a small, professional team is a busy organ—it requires regular financial upkeep. The money that former President A had saved over the course of his life was going into these trusted hands, into their pockets, and being dispersed into the "pits" these hands were digging in the path of the Court.

The last of his savings were something like ice cream, melting in his mouth. The money was like coffee at the bottom of the cup. Finishing up their discussion (and the coffee, the ice cream, the whiskey) the trusted people would leave him by noon.

There was a computer screen at the ex-President's headboard with a graph of his life and a graph of his money. Both graphs reflected prognoses. Both lines were falling downwards with each passing second, as though racing against one another. The same kind of calculating device (so that it wouldn't get lost) could also be found on his desk. And another one was lying around on the carpet by his dog.

"What do you expect? Once the money's gone, the trial will start. But will it happen in my seventieth—or my seventy-fifth—year?" the former President asked his dog, lying back down on the carpet and picking gray strands of fur off his great body as though it were a giant daisy.

Ivan only turned his nose towards the window (in the direction of the unconquerable calculating machine).

By this time, on the other side of the world, former President R (the Russian) was also elderly and completely alone. For health reasons, his wife lived in Crimea, where the air itself was full of iodine vapors, and (more importantly), it wasn't as freezing. His two adult sons had moved away, picking a small town somewhere in the Urals to raise their families and live the kinds of lives that least reminded them of who their father was. Sometimes the sons would meet on a Saturday or Sunday, get drunk and loudly (but not too loudly) complain of the ingratitude of their fellow countrymen:

"They (the people) have forgotten everything good our father did for them."

Or:

"They (the people) remember every bouquet that they themselves ever brought him."

But what is the point of breaking sons' hearts and lamenting the whims of the people when, century after century, they (the people) do not think on their situation without taking causality into account. They (the people), in their simplicity, lay the blame for all of Russia's present troubles on the shoulders of the ex-President—namely the destroyed electric lines and the oil and gas pipelines.

The Hague—they couldn't give a damn about it! They (the people, the countrymen) were soothed and comforted, even a bit diverted, by the fact that the Hague tribunal was looming over their ex-President, as though it were a phantom, albeit an increasingly real one. More and more insistently, it was putting him at fault for sending tanks into Kazan ages ago. The grandeur of the self-propagating procedure! A decade and a half had passed, two Russian Presidents had come and gone, but still, The Hague, year after year, continued to accumulate more and more evidence supporting that old crime. The proceedings turned abruptly serious. Finally (by regular mail) a subpoena came summoning President R for questioning.

Russia had been vaguely waiting for something and hadn't yet given up its ex-President into the hands of The Hague, though he had long been under house arrest and could not leave the St. Petersburg city limits. They were waiting for the diligent Hague to gather all of the facts. But even more so (and everyone knew this) they were waiting for the ex-President to become senile.

Ex-President R was not a man of great means—his savings were melting away like ice cream, inching down like whiskey in a glass. However, he too had a team of sorts. A few devotees considered him a Great Man who had tried to restore Greatness to Russia. These passionate supporters were few in number and, of course, poor. But friends are friends, and these could spend hours on the phone with the ex-President, say, after breakfast, boosting his spirits.

And the ex-President had breakfast completely alone, not counting his dog Jack. By Russian custom, dogs have popular American or German names. Whether the name is American or German depends on the winds of history.

Breakfast was brought directly to the ex-President's table, since he was not allowed to leave the house to go to the grocery store or the deli. He drank tea with milk, ate two light rolls, cheese, and salami. As a former athlete, the ex-President limited the amount of meat he ate in the morning. He would eat the roll and the cheese while feeding the salami to Jack.

Like many aging men, he did not stand on ceremony when talking to his dog:

"Is it fun, Jack, to win the battle against cholesterol?"

Jack didn't answer, but leapt to catch a slice of meat in his mouth.

"Even idleness doesn't depress me anymore, Jack!"

There was no treat for him and so the dog, with his mouth free, could hold up his part of the conversation. He joyously replied, "Ouu-ouu!"

The ex-President reached out and scratched Jack behind the ear.

While ex-President R was awaiting the Hague tribunal, ex-President A (the American) was waiting for the verdict of the American Supreme Court. Both Presidents fiercely resisted. Neither considered themselves guilty. And both, from newspapers and television, learned various details about each other's lives.

Their being old men inspired a special kind of curiosity in them: which one of them would get trapped first? There was no getting around the fact that their names were inextricably linked in History, with its One-Day War—the blame was theirs to share—but each one of them had their own dues to pay: so which one of them was more guilty? Of course, this was an empty question, and put rather sportingly—neither one really had any hope of absolving themselves of any responsibility. On both sides of the Atlantic, a grand process had set slow-moving and angry packs after them—but who would be caught in the chase tomorrow? Who, with fur flying, would be caught by his weak aging calf?

If the Russian ex-President were to fall first, would the American be able to feel somewhat justified? (Of course not, unfortunately. A brief illusion). It'd be the same thing vice versa... However, no one wanted to be put on trial first. Thus, the ex-Presidents were again competing, albeit indirectly. Both considered this fact with a smile. Both understood very well what nonsense these thoughts were—how little it all meant! But human lives (especially the lives of elderly humans) consist of insignificant things.

Both waited... Each one of them suddenly remembered their health. It was essential to stay in good shape for as long as possible.

The Hague tribunal finally got the evidence it had long sought—that during the unrest in Kazan, the President had called Moscow three times from the summit he had been attending. Some special services operations were found (paid for) that could accurately confirm (though not in writing) the contents of those phone conversations—the date, the time, even the very minute they happened! The Russian President spoke—but what could he have spoken of in those days if not Kazan? What else could he offer his powerful support staff but the advice to send tanks in reaction to the unsatisfactory outcome of the talks?

Like clockwork, the leading newspapers of the world again lit up (in red) with images of Kazan— with the orange sunflowers of tanks burning in the streets, and with the red buds of self-immolating students...

Blow for blow, ex-President R (or rather his team photographer) answered the challenge with haste. The photographs they had to offer perhaps were not as flashy, but they too meant war.

The ex-President's devotees, the same three or four of them, saw to it that the ex-President got a second, simple, one-bedroom apartment in the same Petersburg building. (They weren't able to get one at the same entrance as the guards, but they got one nearby.) Not of significant means, they'd all pitched in the money to rent the apartment for the ex-President so that he could practice his former favorite sport—martial arts. In that small apartment, they set up a very small gym with tatami mats. Once a week, on Tuesdays, he would train. His faithful followers were trying to raise his spirits, reminding him of his former days. One of the devoted agreed to be the "dummy," a weak sparring partner, whom the ex-President would throw over his hip onto the mat. The ex-President had once been capable of executing this move with some skill (everyone knew this), but now, his loyal friend had to more or less throw himself onto the mat headfirst of his own volition. The faithful man risked his neck every Tuesday.

After the training session, the ex-President would be so weak that he had to be taken back to his room in a wheelchair. The exit with the wheelchair was executed with the utmost precaution, lest it be observed by the greedy eyes of the press. The ex-President was wheeled out in the thick of dusk. Rolling him from building to building, his helpers would dress, or rather bundle, the ex-President in a gray, nondescript cloak with a large hood that hung over his face.

The newspapers were chomping at the bit to get a picture of him looking weak, but still alive—millions of people had to see for themselves how much better were their lives (their millions of lives) than the life of one who had been above them.

He's being rolled to court in a wheelchair! This has and always will inspire great satisfaction in TV viewers. It's best if he also has a tick of some sort—all the better if his glass eye is shaking from terror. Not bad at all! And there's the strand of saliva dripping right on the blanket the security guards have swaddled him in (out of pity)... and from the blanket, the silvery thread reaches right to the floor.

However, the faithfully devoted, the three or four of them, disseminated photos in which the aging ex-President, in a fighting pose, threw a well-built opponent down onto a mat. It was impressive. The man, with a glassy look in his eyes, was flying somewhere far into the corner. The newspapers printed the pictures, but not eagerly. The readers were only irritated by such photos—life is short, how long can a person read the newspaper and watch justice be postponed again and again!

The Hague, after a few of these pictures were published, slowed down their procedural rush. The judges shrugged. Of course, the Russian Ex wouldn't be going anywhere. Time and Democracy stop for no one.

However, one still had to wait until the President stopped throwing his sparring partners into corners. What a sight it was! The caption under one of the winning pictures of the Russian ex-President, slamming his dummy onto the mat with the greatest of ease, read simply: "Who's next?"

In the prolonged biological one-on-one with Time (and the implicit one-on-one with the Russian ex-President), the American Ex was also strategically placing photographs in newspapers, and, more effectively, on TV. His Texan friends (also only a handful, the last ones left) made it seem that the ex-President, donning a cowboy hat, was barreling down the dustiest local road on horseback. This happened a half-mile from any curious onlookers. He himself couldn't sit in the saddle anymore. A dependable corset-harness was constructed for him out of parachute wire—it went from the saddle right up to the armpit of the rider on his left side—the rider, presumably, was filmed and photographed from the right.

The ex-President galloped for nearly ten minutes, during two of which he looked passable. After his ride, however, he shut down. The only reason he didn't actually collapse was that he was strapped in so tightly. He was carefully removed from the horse and carried to the car. All day at home, they carefully blew dust off of him. He was completely out of it for a day and a half, not recognizing his friends, sitting in his chair with his mouth agape.

However, the two minutes of his brave ride lit up television screens worldwide.

It was enough to stall the court proceedings—it even put a halt to tallying the votes from Chicago, Illinois. The ex-President's lawyer, in a public statement (immediately following the release of the footage of the ex-President on the horse), was able to use the fact that the votes "for" and "against" were not tallied by hand. The lawyer insisted on a recount. It would be more fair, more humane. After all, we were talking about *one of ours,* a man who gallantly sat astride a horse, nonchalantly holding the reigns with one hand...

But in some states they were fairly burning with a desire to put him behind bars.

    VLADIMIR MAKANIN

The lawyer was planning to contest the hand recount as well, declaring the challenge to one staffer after another. He would (in a retreat this time!) invoke the propensity for human error. He would emphasize the biases held by various re-counters. Untrustworthy government employees—they're a dime a dozen! Their mother or father (or fiancée) had been killed by the "crazy" missile. How could this person be expected to correctly place the tallies "for" and "against"?

By this time, the war was being called the "one-day misunderstanding," "an unfortunate accident," "a historical comma," and so on. The moral of the story being that it needed to be forgotten as quickly as possible. People from Chicago and the surrounding states were still escaping to the East and West—as far as possible from the strontium and enriched uranium fallout.

The world expressed its sympathy. Unscathed Europeans, Swedes, Germans, Spaniards all called Americans to their safe shores. Even the freezing Russians invited them with open arms. The utter cold (even the Siberian cold) was preferable to acute leukemia. Those who, for one reason or another, could not house Americans, expressed their sympathy in kind words. Letters upon letters were sent so that the victims wouldn't lose their fighting spirit. The largest number of letters came from Hiroshima.

The ex-President was the recipient of a very different variety of letters, ranging from condolences to insults, from every corner of the States. All Americans were familiar with this address, "To the Texan who couldn't multiply by three." Even schoolchildren knew of his ridiculous error.

He had no place contending with Russians if he couldn't even do basic arithmetic.

In Europe and in the far reaches of Africa, when children learned how to multiply by two, they would already start giggling in anticipation of the threes, knowing their teachers would soon take the opportunity to back up their lessons with an example from recent history.

He, the man who hung the sky with strategic missiles, was being called an opportunist! He, who had laid awake night after night in those terrifying times, was being accused of being carefree—and guilty of the death of hundreds of thousands... Or, they were incapable of seeing that his decision and his will was indeed their own decision and their (and no one else's) will. They (the people, his countrymen) did not want to think for a minute that turning their thoughts in this direction would be seeing the truth. All they wanted to do was see him in court. Without hesitation, posthaste, they wanted to see him as a salivating old man. They were already intoxicated by the pursuit—out of the gates, no holds barred. Life in prison would not be enough. Some thought he would get 21 years, one source calculated a total of 322... The people relished these figures, but they were too small... Far too small.

Sometimes, he would get phone calls (in the middle of the night), and people would outright scream at him about his approaching trial, "It's coming soon!"

Sometimes, it would be as though they were asking for information, "Hey, buddy. I was wondering, where's half of Chicago?"

Obviously, they were referring to the half of the population of the city that had died in the One-Day War. The victims had died instantaneously, within two or three seconds of impact.

The question "Where are they?" was purely rhetorical. Some religious members of the population persisted in posing the question in the sense that the massive destruction of Chicago had given the Lord a job that was both unfathomable (to us) and urgent. He was responsible for each individual soul! Some were intended for heaven, others for hell... We would be perfectly capable of taking apart the concrete ruins, clearing the brick and the rubble, but could He, sorting through such a great mass of the fallen, separate the millions of sinners from the righteous?

Since the time (recently) when philosophers, and with them other wise men, realized that Time was a man-made construct, created for its convenience (so that comparisons could be drawn), since that time, Time had become simply time. Tick-tock, tick-tock. For this reason, any troubling idea could now be replaced by a set of rules and regulations—fine-tuned and infallible Procedure. Why should humanity wait for the hand of Time

　　　　　　　　　　　　　　　　　　　　　　　VLADIMIR MAKANIN

to judge? It wasn't enough—let time do its job—just time, just a day, a month or so, even a year or five. Tick-tock. We'll get what's coming to us.

So, in sadness, thought the old security guard—the same one sitting in the entrance of the St. Petersburg building where the ex-President was under house arrest. The former Petersburg engineer (though that was so very long ago) and current security guard yawned at his nighttime post; he was bored, but at least he was warm! Exhausting his own insomnia, out of sheer idleness, the old man contemplated Time... and the fate of the former President... and how sorely old men were defeated (finally, his thought turned on something important!)

Why, he wondered in the still of the night, does this chase reek of spiritual carrion?... Indeed, indeed, a good and naïve question (while in Russia whole blocks are freezing to death!). Right now is the perfect time for this question... at this very moment. That untalented, self-aggrandizing, jeering, heartless horde—what are they so happy about? And why do I, an old man, who has no love for them, take them seriously? Why do I, so full of trust, run ahead with them into our common future?...

He spit off into the corner of the room. Old men are grumpy and rarely happy with the present.

"Who's next?" The question underneath the picture in the newspapers appeared forebodingly poisonous.

Newspapers flocked out from St. Petersburg, again full of pictures of the Russian ex-President. This time, he was not in karate uniform towering over tatami mats. His torso was no longer belted by that familiar black belt. And he wasn't throwing anybody over his hip. This time, the Russian former President was in a wheelchair, out of it, with his characteristically glazed-over eyes and a half-open mouth. One of his devotees was pushing his wheelchair forward with difficulty, hurrying to disappear into the courtyard of the building complex.

One of the faithful had not been careful enough. It was a Tuesday, and they were taking the ex-President (and ex-fighter) home from his practice room. One of them let the hood fall, revealing the old man as he really was. It's possible that the hood was simply pulled off by the wind. But it is also possible that somebody who was aware of what was going on had been bribed and "accidentally" pulled the hood off the ex-President's face. Someone had been bought off. A photographer couldn't have landed in the bushes outside of the building of his own accord. And two more near the building gates, with flashes. Somebody's extra cash had done its job. (As they had also done in the American case. As soon as an old man is betrayed, someone nearby is in the money. As reliable as snow in winter).

The photograph of the weak old Russian man was greeted with sighs of relief and even cheers of long-awaited victory. People in cafes jumped out of their seats and waved bundles of newspapers over their heads: finally! He didn't get away! See what he really is! His time has come!... The Hague immediately set a court date. The Russian government, as is their wont, was still dissatisfied. They remained reluctant to give up their wilted ex-President just like that. But there was already talk of Russian officials making some secret deal with one of the Baltic states. They (*NATO members* despite it all) were prepared to kidnap the ex-President and put his extradition on their own cool consciences. From Petersburg to Tallinn? It was just a stone's throw away. And from Tallinn to The Hague, on a good private jet—he wouldn't even have time to finish his coffee!

All of the calculators—on the desk, the rug, and the one by his bed— were telling the American ex-President that his hard-earned money, set aside for his battle against Time (with the approaching Court), had been spent. It would no longer be difficult for someone to pay one of his entourage more than he could pay them. Someone's loyalty was bought. At first, all bribery suspicions fell on Gary, an old boozer (one of his oldest friends). Gary, embarrassed, shot himself. The man who had really betrayed the ex-President to the photojournalists ran off to another state without looking back (and from there, he wrote his memoirs justifying his actions).

But there was no fixing things. That black Tuesday (the very same day that the Russian ex-President was hit), the American ex-President fell off a horse. The feeble cowboy couldn't even stay in the saddle for a minute. And right then and there, hiding in the bushes, some rake of a photographer snapped the picture.

The pitiful, lost face of the fallen American greatly resembled that of his Russian colleague. This coincidental day (a Black Tuesday for both), the journalists also began to call The One-Day War—one which both old men had suddenly lost.

American newspapers, more than others, disseminated images of the lifeless expression on his face. The old man, with a confused look and an open mouth. Steps away from the grazing little horse, he was slobbering like an infant and being lifted up, carried, pushed away in a wheelchair (resembling the Russian one), so he could get home and to bed.

Now even the formerly neutral states were voting to take him to court as soon as possible. The Head of the Supreme Court set the long-awaited date.

The night passed like any other, the night when the American ex-President put the phone *back in its base* and decided not to be upset by the rude voice—he even tried to smile. And why not? The moon was high! He went up to his window (just like his transatlantic counterpart) and looked out at the still nocturnal landscape. This was not one of the worst minutes in his life. It was a good minute! It's not very often that the heavens allow old men moments of such clarity, and a modicum of strength. When it does happen, it is at night.

On the street—on the opposite side of the road—he saw a cheap car stop and a girl hop out of it. This was maybe fifty feet away from him, maybe more, but his sharp though elderly eyes saw it all very clearly. Looking around and deciding that the coast was clear, the girl ran behind some bushes on the side of the road and disappeared from view. She was probably relieving herself. It happens!

Happy, she returns to the car and (raising her eyes) notices the yellow glow coming from a window in the building across the street, framing a man's silhouette. It's night. The street is asleep. Just in case, the girl gives him a friendly wave. The palm of her hand lights up with her motion—hurray! Hurray!

The ex-President sees (in the silvery moonlight) that she is young. He sees that she is well-built, with a good figure. Through the veils of old age, he remembers something, and whispers to himself, "If only I could screw her right now."

He feels no desire to get closer to her. His psychoanalyst once taught him to do this—as soon as he sees a young woman, he has to say how he wants her—as though he was letting himself lick the very desire! That's how a man can stay young. This gives him the strength to fight for his life. Though it didn't end up helping the psychoanalyst. He was dead. But maybe that was because he was unlucky, thought the ex-President. Or maybe he didn't see pretty young women often enough.

The old man returned the young woman's friendly gesture. Her car set off into the night, and a moment later it disappeared. She was gone. There was nobody else left. She was gone... but at least the dog was still there. The ex-President felt how behind him, pressing to his shaking leg, the dog was begging for attention.

Without turning away from the window, the old man reached behind with his left hand and pet the dog's head.

"Ouuuu—ouuuu," the dog answered, swooning from affection.

The room's echo quivered. And, as though from the other side of the world, the other end of night, the cheerful whine of another dog replied, "Ouuuuu—ouuuu!"

TRANSLATION BY BELA SHAYEVICH

VLADIMIR MAKANIN

Trash Can for the Diamond Sutra
(fragment)

Marina Moskvina

And here's another interesting novella about an unexpected enlightenment, whose events began unfolding right before the Great Fatherland War. Back then, the same kind of "black Marias" would drive up of a black night, not only to the doors of such unfettered personages as my grandpa Stepan Gudkov, and others who were teaching their fellow citizens Pure Land Buddhism, but also to the doors of the most absolutely normal residents of the towns around Moscow, people who didn't stand out in any way.

Now several esteemed and respected figures will pass before your eyes, figures not related to me by blood. However, they were Stepan and Matilda Ivanovna's close neighbors at the *dacha* in Kratovo, therefore the threads of these people's fates are weaving into the pattern of my narrative all by themselves.

And so, to begin: a mother and child, Matilda and Stepan's neighbors, lived in Old Bolsheviks village. Their last name was Bronstein.

One fine day they come along and arrest that mother, Sara Naumovna Bronstein, and send her off to a camp for political offenders. What's going on, you might ask? Well, it appears that they had started suspecting poor Sara Naumovna of being in a very bad situation; to be exact, they suspected her of being a close relative of Lev Borisovich Trotsky, the oppositional Party member and main Trotskyite, whose real last name, it turns out, was Bronstein.

But Trotsky didn't have anything to do with this Sara Naumovna! All the more so since by this time poor Lev Davidovich, hiding from Yosif Vissarionovich somewhere, either in Mexico or in Brazil, had been killed, on the order of our Soviet government, it seems, by a man who had been worming his way into his trust for a long time. He came over, drank tea with jam, and acted as though he wanted learn the way of the world from Lev Davidovich, dip into his encyclopedic knowledge. He was so polite, so charming, and had such a totally open heart, that the awfully suspicious Trotsky, who by the way already suspected they'd try to assassinate him, relaxed his watchfulness completely, and became warmly attached to the nice young man and always gave him the very best seat and the very choicest food.

And that one chatted with him, chatted away on different philosophical topics, until one fine day the right moment came along and he whacked his respected friend and teacher in the head with a hatchet.

The arrest of our Sara Naumovna Bronstein, the innocent bearer of that low-prestige last name, was an echo of that distant Mexican event. They slapped a good solid sentence on her, too, for such a little thing!

Anyway, I won't be talking about poor Sara, or about Mr. Lev Trotsky, but about Aunt Sveta, Sara Naumovna's daughter, who back then wasn't an Aunt at all, but a young girl, who at one fell stroke had been divested of both her mother and her bright future, seeing as how she'd acquired the status of the daughter of an enemy of the people.

But I should tell you that, regardless of her unhappy fate, Aunt Sveta was a great lover of good jokes and witty anecdotes when she was young, and, due to her jolly disposition, she even attracted the attention of a very thoughtful student from the Institute of International Relations who was studying to be a diplomat.

Of course, Aunt Sveta fell desperately in love with that future representative of our country abroad, and so, every time they met, she'd go and shower him with jokes and stories about all kinds of things, so that their love would grow ever stronger and more enduring with each passing day.

They were even going to get married, but suddenly she was arrested. There was this article in the Criminal Code, "for the slander of Soviet power."

They asked Aunt Sveta, "Have you been telling this joke?"

Having learned from bitter experience, she answered firmly. "God, no! I'm hearing it for the first time. And I'm actually amazed that you can bend your tongue to pronounce such words about the wise leaders of our Soviet government."

At this, the door opens and her beloved comes in and says, so gently, even a little reproachfully: "Sveta, what are you saying? Don't you remember how we were standing on Mayakovsky Square, and how the trolley was so late, and you told it to me?"

They led the student away, and he kept on studying to be a diplomat, an envoy of the Soviet land; but they locked up our Aunt Sveta.

So there they were, doing a whole lot of time, Sveta and Sara Naumovna, and neither of them knew anything about the other. Then they were both rehabilitated. Sara Naumovna died soon after that and was buried in the Novodevichy cemetery in the wall of faithful Leninists.

But by now, Aunt Sveta wasn't the same person she was before. She was often sick, didn't talk to hardly anyone, and lived alone for many, many years in that same building in the town near Moscow, the one they'd both been taken from, and whose door had been closed and sealed.

Once, all of a sudden, she put an ad in a newspaper for lonely people and singles. She said, blah blah blah, I'm looking for a life companion, I'm not young, but I'm pleasant-looking, I love good jokes and witty anecdotes. And she got an answer: "intellectual and cultured, blue eyes, former Navy officer, Captain First Rank, now retired, by the name of Nikolai Mikhailovich Oreshkin."

They met. Oreshkin showed her photographs of himself as a young man, where he was standing with other officers on deck; they all had such serious faces, with the thin coating of the eternal on them that you get in black-and-white group photographs, and there was the ocean out past the ship, and seagulls in the clouds.

The cries of the seagulls, frozen in the sky, stirred the hope for simple human happiness once more in Aunt Sveta's soul. She liked the magnificent valor of this Oreshkin, maybe not a young man anymore, but not feeble yet—the valor manifested doing battle on the Black Sea with the Fascist German invaders. And she liked his warm, from-the-heart generosity: when they first met he brought her cake, champagne and flowers.

In short, they got married.

She treated him with kid gloves; he was the apple of Aunt Sveta's eye.

But suddenly he manifested a strange quirk of character.

To Aunt Sveta's enormous anguish, he was constantly collecting grains, pasta and matches to tide him over in the dark days of old age, although they were both getting respectable individual retirement benefits, those of an innocent victim of Stalin's repressions and a veteran of the Fatherland War. Alas, this psychologically unbalanced captain would run with feverish eyes to the grocery store and use both her pension and his to buy up tons of grain and pasta.

They didn't go to the theater, or the museum, or ride the little tourist tram along the river, just the two of them, like she'd always dreamed of doing; and they didn't go to the forest in autumn to rustle the fallen leaves, and they didn't go skiing in winter, not even once a season! God, no.

Nikolai Mikhailovich Oreshkin turned out to be totally insane, and now there was absolutely nothing she could do about it.

He crammed the kitchen cupboard full of grains and matches, then he stuffed the clothes closet and the linen cupboard full, and he even took to hiding bagfuls of boxes behind the stove and in the ceiling storage space, and by now grains were packed into every corner of the room: rice, buckwheat, millet and special Artek-brand millet porridge for children. The long and the short of it is that he filled up the entire apartment with his strategic reserves.

Poor Aunt Sveta Bronstein, horrified, watched her living space shrink and observed what kind of person her chosen one was.

Everyone told her to throw the scumbag the hell out, that executioner of innocent babes, that wolf in sheep's clothing. But no, she didn't throw him out, she didn't even confront him with accusations; clearly she was hoping, up to the very end, that she could get her extremely sad life in order.

So when only one little patch of space was left free of pasta, grains and matches in all her familial home, she sat down on the floor, crossed her legs, and placed her hands in prayer position on her breast; having sat that way for about three and a half weeks, she entered peacefully, soundlessly, and with Christian humility into Nirvana.

At this, all of Old Bolsheviks village was filled with the unusual perfume of flowering orchids. You could smell the aroma for several days, in the course of which her body, sitting up with a very straight back, looked alive.

But Captain Oreshkin, the unobservant naval officer, didn't notice his wife's absence right away. Only after a month had gone by, when the mailman brought them their government pension checks, did he start to call her name and look for her, finally stumbling over her body, sitting in deep peace and calm submissiveness in the labyrinth of bags and boxes.

Then this quasi-respectable Nikolai Mikhailovich turned to the mailman and said, "Svetlana Ilyinichna isn't feeling well, see, she's sitting right over there? Something's not right with her head. I'll sign for her and give her the money when she comes to!"

That happened once, twice, even three times. But the fourth time the mailman got to suspecting that something bad was going on. Horrible rumors started going around the village, and a doctor came in and certified the cessation of breathing and heartbeat. So Aunt Bronstein was sitting for, let's call it half a year, just like she was alive, with a beatific smile on her lips, and no smell of decay.

A bunch of TV crews showed up, and then newspaper and magazine journalists rushed over, they blew it up into a big sensation, and it leaked through to the foreign press, and what an unwelcome brouhaha it started for Nikolai Mikhailovich!

Just then, Oreshkin discovered a court summons right there in his mailbox for unlawfully pocketing Aunt Sveta's pension for four months, when she no longer had any need of financial assistance.

So this was all to say that when somebody rang the doorbell, he knew they'd come for him, and he would never see the dark days of his old age, which he'd tried to provide for—maniacally, day in and day out—in pasta.

Oreshkin trailed dejectedly over to open the door and froze: an unfamiliar Indian in a turban was standing at the threshold. "Greetings, Nikolai Mikhailovich," he pronounced, pronouncing his *r*'s with a little bit of a French accent. "My name is Swami Bodhidharma. Please accept my apologies, but answer me in the name of all that's holy: is it here where, for several months, the incorruptible body of your wife Svetlana Ilyinichna Bronstein has been located?"

"What's my wife's body got to do with you?" asked the captain, surprised.

"I have arrived from India with a secret mission," said Bodhidharma, "all the details of which I will relate to you as soon as we go inside and there's nobody else around."

Nikolai Mikhailovich looked his Indian guest up and down, from his turban to his toes, with enormous suspicion. But he didn't find anything that would've given him a reason to slam the door shut in his face. On the contrary, this Hindu was remarkable for his unheard-of politeness and courtesy, the kind you seldom come across in our central Russian region, especially when they start dragging you to court and a district policeman is coming by every day.

"Why not? Come in," said Oreshkin. The agile Hindu slipped swiftly inside and, nimbly maneuvering through the bags and boxes, made his way to the body of Svetlana Ilyinichna.

"So it is true!" he said. "It is SHE!" Then, performing a countless number of prostrations, he began lighting incense sticks.

"You'll set the place on fire!" said captain Oreshkin anxiously. "I've got boxes of matches in here."

"My dear friend!" Bodhidharma pronounced triumphantly and ceremoniously. "I will explain everything to you now. The point of the matter is that your wife, Svetlana Ilyinichna Bronstein—she is the earthly incarnation of the goddess Devi."

"Of what goddess? What are you talking about!?" said Oreshkin, amazed.

"Of Devi, the goddess of love!" said Bodhidharma. "The symbol of womanhood, the life-giving womb! She is the mate of Shiva, the Lord of Worlds and the God of Gods..."

"So that means that I'm... the incarnation of Shiva?" Nikolai Mikhailovich asked, dumbfounded.

"Oh my, no," Bodhidharma burst out laughing. "You are Captain Oreshkin, which, taken for what it is, is quite nice. However, once she turned up in your world, she waited her whole life for her beloved, the radiant Shiva, lost among the worlds."

He continued, "She might not have remembered that, but in every man she loved (there were two of you), she was looking subconsciously for the true essence of Shiva, that is, for the miracle-filled Universe. But, as if just to spite her, instead of her divine mate, she came across two very nervous and fussy earthly beings; one was an informer, while the other... ," he paused and threw a penetrating glance at the mountains of grains and pasta, "... was a hoarder!"

"If you came here from distant India to shower me with insults," captain Oreshkin flared up, "then I'll throw you out the door double-quick. But tomorrow your goddess Devi is scheduled to be cremated, which will be followed by burial in the Wall of Old Bolsheviks in the Novodevichy cemetery in the same niche as her repressed mother, Sara Naumovna Bronstein, who they still suspect deep down of being Trotsky's relative. I can just imagine what would happen if they found out in Lubyanka about this love affair with Shiva!"

"Don't put her in any Communards' Wall!" begged Bodhidharma. "Give her body to me! I will pay you well for it."

"That's another question entirely," said Nikolai Mikhailovich, softening. "I just don't see what you want her body for?"

"Look, this is a picture of Shiva," the Hindu held a portrait with some kind of strange figure drawn on it out to Oreshkin, "half a man, and half a woman."

"One of those, eh?" the former Captain First Rank, now retired, noted disapprovingly.

"Don't take this the wrong way," said the Hindu to the offended Nikolai Mikhailovich. "It's Shiva and Devi. The goddess Devi isn't just his wife. She is Shiva's other half. If a couple loves each other, then the deeper they enter into it, the less and less they remain two people, and the more and more they become a complete whole. And there comes a moment," Bodhidharma continued to Oreshkin, "when the summit is reached, and it only *seems* that there are two of them. The boundaries of duality are overcome—listen carefully to this thought, Nikolai Mikhailovich: their bodies are different, but something that is beyond the boundaries of their bodies unites. And that is the single reality of our life experience that brings us closer to God... For many centuries we made no sculptural representations of Shiva. We made only phallic symbols, *shiva lingam*. But a Dark Age has come upon us, Nikolai Mikhailovich, and people don't understand the language of formless things. Now we need a clear and simple representation, one that opens the Path toward consciousness of the treasured wisdom. So if people see the body of Shiva and the body of Devi, then the meeting of these great lovers in the Dark Age of names and forms will unite yin and yang, the female and male essences, in the minds of all living things; it will return the lost Universal Harmony to the human consciousness; it will serve to awaken the Truth in the soul of every living being."

"I'm going to go nuts!" said captain Oreshkin. "Let's get back to the point here."

"We have come right up to the point," said Bodhidharma. "Shiva, the God of Gods and Lord of Worlds, is sitting in a serene pose in the cave of Agna Parameshwara, on Mount Kailash, in India, and his presence has been there throughout the ages until this very day. A temple has been built right over this cave. Shiva's body will soon be placed there. But we've been missing the earthly incarnation of Devi. What good is Shiva without his Devi? Nobody would even bother to bow to him. Without her, nobody will even admit that it is he, people will say he's an impostor. So we've been waiting, just in case she turns up. And so she did. We've been reading in the *Daily Telegraph* about this case of yours. We've been asking the astrologers and fortune-tellers, and they all answer as one, 'Yes! It is SHE!' Even the photograph—well, to tell the truth, it's hard to see, it's a copy of one from the Russian press. But there can be no doubt that Svetlana Ilyinichna Bronstein is the earthly incarnation of the goddess Devi."

Swami Bodhidharma took his canvas sack and started untying it. "Look," he said, "these are rubies, emeralds, diamonds: Hindus took up a collection for this enterprise and sent me to you in Soviet Russia. I hope we can come to some kind of agreement."

"Well, now," answered Nikolai Mikhailovich, with that same well-known awareness of his own dignity that a citizen of the Land of the Soviets famously exhibited whenever he entered into conversations of this kind with rich foreign tourists. "Of course, I wouldn't give my dear Svetlana Ilyinichna away for all the money in the world. But considering that you have this entire philosophical foundation worked out for it," he added quickly, "okay then, you can take her, and you hand over your rubies, diamonds and emeralds on the double."

At this, a Gazel van drove up to captain Oreshkin's window and let out two stocky Hindus carrying a stretcher. They carefully carried Sveta Bronstein out of her father's house and loaded her into the van.

As they were taking her away, the entire village of Old Bolsheviks came pouring out of their buildings. Everyone was amazed at how well our Aunt

Sveta had kept! She was a young girl once again. A golden light was surrounding her, and calendula and peony petals were falling from the sky.

The only one to pay no attention to her, just as before, was Captain Oreshkin. He took the money and precious stones and ran off to buy grains, matches, and pasta.

The local old-timers say that when his place was full to bursting of all that stuff, and he sat down in the middle of it, satisfied, because now the black old age wouldn't take him so easily, suddenly hundreds of kilograms of rice, buckwheat groats, millet and special Artek-brand millet porridge for children came crashing down onto his head.

Nobody ever heard anything else about the retired captain Oreshkin, while meanwhile Aunt Sveta is sitting with the God Shiva in profound Nirvana on the holy mountain of Kailash, promoting the awakening of Truth and Universal Harmony in our callous hearts.

TRANSLATION BY ANNE O. FISHER

MARINA MOSKVINA

Ontology of Childhood

Viktor Pelevin

Usually, you're too caught up in everything going on with you in the here and now to suddenly start remembering childhood. In general, the lives of adults are self-contained and—how can I put it?—don't have any free space to put feelings about things not happening right around them. But sometimes, very early in the morning, when you wake up and see something really familiar—even a brick wall—you recall that it used to be different, not the same as it is today, even though it hasn't changed at all since then.

Over there is a crack between two bricks—in it you can see a hardened ribbon of mortar curling like a wave. Not counting those years when, for variety's sake, you lay down to sleep with your legs the other way around, or that really far-off time when your head was still gradually receding from your feet and the morning view of the wall was undergoing small daily shifts—if you don't count all that, then this vertical whitecap in the crack between two bricks was always the first morning greeting from the huge world we live in—both in the winter, when the wall was permeated with cold and sometimes was even covered with an amazingly beautiful silver patina, and in the summer when, two bricks up, a triangular, ragged-edged sun spot appeared (but just for a few days in June, when the sun goes far enough to the west). But in the time it takes for them to make the long trip from the past into the present, the objects that surround you lose the most important thing—some completely indefinable quality. I can't even explain it. Take, for example, how days used to start out: the adults left for work, the door slammed behind them, and the entire huge space all around, the infinite multitude of objects and arrangements, became yours. The do's and don'ts no longer applied, and it was as if things relaxed and stopped concealing something. Take anything at all, the most ordinary thing—even a plank bunk—upper, lower, it makes no difference: three parallel boards, a metal crossbar underneath, and three rivets sticking out of every bar. Anyway, if there were even a single adult nearby, I swear, the plank bed would somehow shrink, become narrow and uncomfortable. But when they went to work, it was as if it got wider, or maybe it was just that you could finally get comfortable on it. And each board—back then they didn't paint them—would take on a pattern, and you could see the tree rings that once upon a time were intersected with a saw at the most unimaginable angles. Either they disappeared when grownups were around or it just didn't occur to you to pay attention to such things when you had weighty talks about work shifts, production norms and imminent death playing in the background.

The most amazing thing, of course, is the sun. Not the blinding spot in the sky, but the stripe of air coming from the window in which fuzzy dust specks and the tiniest coiled fibers are suspended. Their movement is so circuitous and graceful (actually, in childhood you see them swarm with amazing clarity from a distance) that it starts to seem that there's a special little world that lives by its own laws, and maybe you yourself used to live in that world, or maybe you might still be able to enter it and become one of those glistening, weightless specks. But again: in fact, that's probably not it at all, but there's no other way to say it, you can only get so close. It's just that you see camouflaged realms of total freedom and happiness. The sun has an astounding ability to pick out all the very best from among the little that it is able to touch as it moves from the upper corner of the first window to the lower corner of the second. Even the iron-clad door says something about itself that lets you know that you don't have anything to fear from what might come out from behind it. And the stripes of light on the floor and the walls are saying that there's nothing to fear. There is nothing frightening in the world. At least that's how it is so long as this world is speaking with you; later, at some incomprehensible moment, it begins to speak at you.

When you're a child, you usually wake up to the morning swearing of adults. They always start the day off swearing, and through your continuing dreams their speech seems strangely drawn out and glutinous, and from their intonation you can clearly sense that both the ones doing the yelling and the ones standing up for themselves aren't actually experiencing the feelings that they are trying to express through their voices. It's simply that they themselves have only just woken up and they haven't yet come out of their dreams—even though by now they don't remember anything— and they're trying to convince themselves and others as quickly as possible that it's morning, life, there are just a few minutes to get ready, that this is all real. And when they succeed at this, they link up with one another. The last of their morning doubts vanish, and they're trying to find a more comfortable place for themselves in this hell that they have only just entered so precipitously. And from swearing they move on to jokes. And so long as there are some minimal differences, which they have learned to see, the fact that they all share a common fate becomes irrelevant, and it's no longer important that they will all croak here, it's just important that someone sleeps on the top bunk and far from the window. The main thing is that you understand all this when you're still quite small, when you'd never be able to express it out loud—you understand it from the voices of adults that reach you through your morning half-sleep. And this seems amazing and strange, but then all the world is still amazing, and everything in it is strange. And later you have to start getting up along with everyone else.

At first, grownups bend down from somewhere up above and present their face to you, stretched out into a smile. Evidently there's a law in effect in the world that compels them to smile when they talk to you—it's understood that the smile is forced, but you realize that they aren't going to harm you. Their faces are frightful: pockmarked, with spots and stubble. In some ways they resemble the moon in the window—the same degree of detail. Grownups are easy to understand, but there's almost nothing to say about them. Their relentless attention to your life can become loathsome. They don't seem to be asking for anything: for a moment they drop the invisible log that they've been carrying all their lives in order to bend down over you with a smile and then, once they're done, pick it up again and carry it on—but that's just how it seems at first. In fact, they want you to become what they are, they need to hand over the log to someone before they die. They weren't carrying it for nothing. In the evenings, they get together in groups of several people and beat someone—the one being beaten up usually plays along with the ones doing the beating, very subtly, and for that they go a bit easier on him. As a rule, they don't let you watch this, but you can always hide among the plank beds and see everything through the standard centimeter crack between the boards. But later—and although there is still a long time between the moment when you're watching the entire procedure from your hiding place to the one when it will happen— later, for the first time, the day will come when you yourself will be writhing on the floor amidst flying feet shod in boots of felt or *kirza*[1] trying to play along with the ones who are beating you.

When you first start to read, it's not the text that steers your thoughts, but your thoughts that steer the text. The tear always runs through the most interesting part, and if you find out from a piece of newspaper how the audience greeted comrade this and comrade that with applause, you start thinking what real big shots these two must be if even their comrades give them a special greeting with some kind of applause. And you close

---

[1] A multilayer, cotton-based fabric treated to resemble pigskin that is used to make military boots.

your eyes and start to imagine these comrades and the applause, and you manage to live a whole little life that is completely hidden from those sitting on the neighboring cans. And all this thanks to a piece of newspaper the size of one side of a tea box and imprinted with the sole of a boot. And if an actual book falls into your hands, that's an experience unlike any other. And it doesn't matter what kind it is—there aren't many of them here, five or six, and you read each one several times—and the reason it doesn't matter is that each time you read the book differently. At first it's the words themselves that are important, and they're all immediately followed by a flash of the thing they denote ("boot," "can," "quilted jacket") or a meaningless, gaping blackness ("ontology," "intellectual"), and you have to go to one of the grownups, which is something you'd always rather avoid, so as a result ontology turns into a flashlight and intellectual turns into a long monkey wrench with a changeable head. The next time you start to wonder about entire situations: how a certain person tramps heavily into the stinking closeness of a kitchen and with strong worker's fists clobbers the simpering, odious face of the waiter Proskha. There isn't an adult who, after reading this, wouldn't for an instant turn into that righteous guy, the worker Artyom, every time the usual foul-breathed circle gathered around the latest victim, one after another taking a little step forward and putting all their hatred toward the simpering, waiterly thing flailing about in the center into their blows. Probably there has never been a single beating where righteousness did not triumph. And later—the third time—you find a description of how on the top plank bed some girl is breathing hot and heavy, and now that's the only thing you notice. You have to grow up quite a bit before you understand just how dull and squalid all that you managed to read so many times really is.

You're happy in childhood because that's what you think when you remember it. In general, happiness is recollection. When you were little, you were let out for the entire day and you could go down all the corridors, looking wherever you wanted and wandering into the sorts of places where you might be the first person since the construction workers. Now this is a closely guarded memory, but back then—it was just: you walk along the corridor and feel sad because winter is starting again and it would almost always be dark outside the window, you turn a corner, and just in case you wait while two foul-mouthed sheepskins lumber along an adjacent corridor, and again you turn into the door that is always closed, but today is suddenly wide open. There's some sort of light at the end of the corridor. It turns out that along the wall here there are two stout pipes covered in plaster and even painted. And at the end, there, you can see light and a metal trapdoor is open, below something is humming, and when you carefully bend over the trapdoor you see some huge blue machinery that is shaking and droning ever so slightly, and beyond it there are two more of the same, and nobody in sight: you could even climb down the ladder right now and find yourself in that magical space that's quaking from all the power concentrated here. The only reason you don't do this is that when you have your back turned they could close the door at any moment, so you head back, dreaming of one day making your way here again. Later, when you start to come here every day, when taking care of these unsleeping metal turtles becomes the nominal purpose of your life, you often have the urge to remember how you saw them for the first time. But memories wear off if you use them too often, so you keep this thing—about happiness—in reserve.

Another memory that you hardly use at all is also associated with the conquest of space. This is probably something that happened earlier: one of the side corridors, a winter day (the window is already bluish: it's starting to get dark), silence throughout the entire, huge building—everyone is at work. It seems that truly nobody is there. This is obvious from the way everything looks. Grownups change whatever is around them, but now the dusky corridor is uncommonly mysterious, nothing but shadows—it's even a little scary. They haven't turned on the lights yet, but it's almost time, and you are able to indulge in a rare pleasure—running. You start running from where the fire emergency instructions are posted in the corridor's dark dead end (the instructions are very strange—a picture of an axe, a fire hook, and a bucket, done in oil paints), and for a while you zigzag along the corridor, savoring the freedom and ease with which you can force the wall to incline, advance, or retreat—and all because of the tiny little commands you're giving your body. But the most astounding thing, of course, is the turn to the right into the short branch of the corridor that ends in a window covered with wire mesh. A whole twenty meters before you get to the corner, you heave to the left wall, and when you catch a glimpse of the laminated door marked Valve 15-S across the hall, you peel away from the wall and, tracing an elongated arc, lean sharply to the right—and these few seconds when your right side is almost suspended over the floor tiles give you freedom unlike anything else. Then you easily fly through the remainder of the corridor and, sticking your fingers into the wire squares, you look out the window: it's already dark, and over the fence, whose posts are topped by tall hats of snow, a few cold blue street lights are glowing.

Noises coming from outside the window are of a completely different nature than those that are generated somewhere inside the corridor or on the other side of a partition. The difference is not so much in the properties of the sound itself—loud or quiet, sharp or muffled—but in what brings it to life. Almost all noises are produced by people, but noises that originate inside a huge building are perceived as if they were the intestinal rumblings or the cracking joints of a huge body—in other words, since they are so familiar and explainable, they're of no interest. But what comes from beyond the window is almost the only evidence that a whole other world exists, and every sound from there is extraordinarily important. The auditory picture of the world has also managed to change a great deal since childhood, even though its main components remain the same. Take an ordinary sound from outside the window: the distant, resonant pounding of metal on metal, about two or three times slower than a pulse. It has a very interesting echo: it seems as if the sound is coming not from any single point, but from the entire arc of the horizon all at once. The very first thing this pounding was—back when you could still sleep past the general wakeup—was the time scale or even the external point of reference that gave the grownups' evening tussle and the morning face-smashings their necessary duration and sequence. Later, that measured clang turned into the beating of the world's heart and remained so until such time as someone said that it was the sound of piles being driven into the ground at construction sites. Also among the sounds you can make out the drone of far off machinery, the wail of the switch engine in the sorting yard, voices and laughter (very often of children), the hum of airplanes in the sky (there is something prehistoric in that hum), a sound generated by the wind, and, finally, the barking of dogs. They say that there used to be a way to communicate with the person in the next cell (there was just one person per cell—it's hard to believe such a thing is possible): the person in the first cell began to tap on the wall in a particular way, encoding his message in the sequence of taps, and he got a response from the person in the next cell using the same code. This must be a legend—why would you make up a special language when you can talk things over just fine at the work sites? What's important is th idea—conveying what you want to say by tapping some combinations that seem utterly meaningless through the wall. Sometimes you think—if our Creator wanted to tap back and forth with us, what would we hear? Probably something like the distant sound of the pilings being beaten into the frozen soil—definitely at regular intervals, because using the Morse code or something like that just wouldn't seem right.

The more grownup you are, the less intricate the world becomes, but there is still a lot that's incomprehensible. Even the two squares of sky in the wall (sky if you sit on the lower planks, but from the upper ones you can see the tops of distant smokestacks). At night you can see stars through them, and during the day you see clouds, which raise quite a few questions. The clouds have been with you since childhood, and so many of them have been born in the windows that you're always surprised when you encounter something new. Now, for instance, in the right-hand window an expanded pink fan is hanging (it's almost sunset), consisting of a multitude of feathery stripes—as if made by all the world's aviation (incidentally, I wonder what the earth looks like to those who do their time in the heavens), and in the left-hand one the sky is outlined as if with a crooked ruler. It turns out that today the infinitely distant point from which the wind blows is straight opposite the right-hand window. That probably means something and you just don't know the code—there you have it, tapping back and forth with God. There's no mistaking it. You also can't mistake the meaning of what's going on when a fuzzy spot appears on an opaque November cloud, a pale irregular triangle (you've seen it before, one summer morning on the bricks near your face), and from its center the sun is shining through fast-moving bands of fog. Or in the summer—a red hill that takes up half the sky over the horizon (only from the upper planks). There used to exist many things and occurrences that were ready to reveal their true nature at your first glance—actually, almost all of them. When a photograph of the prison taken from outside (presumably from the watchtower over the candy factory zone) was passed around, it was hard to understand what the older cons were so stunned about—was this really the most amazing thing they'd seen in their lives? The eternal piece of bad cake, the familiar stench from the cans, and naïve pride in the abilities of human reason. But you can tap back and forth with God. After all, answering him just means feeling and understanding all this. That's what you think in childhood when the world is still being constructed out of simple analogies. Only later do you understand that you can't talk with God, because you yourself are his voice, gradually becoming more muted and quieter. The same thing is happening to you, if you think about it, as happens with someone's shout that reaches you from the courtyard where they're playing soccer.

Something was happening with the world where you grew up, every day it was changing a little bit, every day everything around was taking on a new shade of meaning. It all started with the sunniest and happiest place on earth, home to people slightly ridiculous in their attachment to *kirza* boots and black quilted jackets—ridiculous, and all the nearer and dearer for being so, it started with the joyous green corridors, with the cheerful play of the sun on the peeling wire mesh screen, with the desperate twittering of the swallows building their nest under the eaves of the tin workshop, with the festive roar of the tanks crawling on parade (even though you can't see them through the fence, you can tell by the sound when it's a tank going by and when it's a self-propelled gun), with grownups' chorus of laughter in response to some of your questions, with the smile of a guard who runs into you in the corridor, with the wagging tail of a huge German shepherd running up to you. Then the very best things begin to gradually fade: you begin to notice cracks in the walls, the awful stench from the food unit, particularly disgusting because it's there every day; you begin to guess that beyond the fence you've known since childhood with its freshly puttied pockmarks there exists some sort of life—in other words, with each new day there are fewer and fewer questions about your true fate that remain unanswered. And the less that remains hidden from you, the less grownups are inclined to forgive you your purity and naivete, and it turns out that even seeing this world is enough to sully you and implicate you in all its abominations—and in the evenings frightening things turn up in the blind alleys of corridors and the dark corners of cells. And out of the rippling fog of the childhood that is receding from memory, an understanding emerges—as if the focus had been adjusted—of the fact that you were born and grew up in prison, in the filthiest and most putrid corner of the world. And once you have thoroughly understood this, you come under the full force of your prison's laws. But so what? The point is that it is not people who thought up the world—however they might try, it is not within their power to make life for the lowliest prisoner any different from that of the superintendent. And what difference does it make what occasions it if the happiness manufactured by souls is all the same? There is a happiness quota allotted to a person in life, and whatever might happen, you can't take that happiness away. You can talk about what's good and what's bad only if you at least know by whom and for what a person has been engineered.

Objects don't change, but something disappears while you're growing up. Actually, it's you who loses "something," every day you irreversibly pass by the most important thing, plunging downward—and you can't stop, you can't halt your slow freefall to nowhere—all you can do is pick out the words that describe what is happening with you. The opportunity to look out the window is not the most important thing in life, but you still get upset when they no longer let you into the corridor—you're almost an adult, and by the holiday you'll get *kirza* boots and a quilted jacket. Of the multitude of panoramas once available, you now only have constant use of one (you can see the same thing out of both windows at slightly different angles), and you can only admire it if you tilt a short bench against the wall and stand on the edge of it: the courtyard enclosed by a short cinder-block fence, two rusted busses—probably just the remains, resembling dead wasps—yellow membranes empty on the inside, the long building of the neighboring prison with its semi-circular brown roof, and beyond that, the really far-off prisons and the sky, which occupies the entire remaining portion of the quadrangular opening. The things you have seen every day for many years are gradually transformed into monuments to yourself—to what you were once upon a time—because they bear the stamp of feelings that belonged to a person who has almost entirely vanished, a person who appears inside you for a few moments when you see the same thing that he once saw. To see—what this really means is superimposing your soul on a standard imprint on the retina of a standard human eye. They used to play soccer in this yard, they fell, they got up, they kicked the ball, and now all that's left are rusted busses. In truth, since you started to go out to work with the others you've been too tired for anything inside you to come alive that's even capable of playing soccer on your retina. But whatever universal change of underwear might lie ahead, nobody can deprive anyone of the past they saw (the former you, if that means anything at all), standing on the teetering bench and looking through the window: a few people are passing a ball around, they're laughing— their voices and the sound of feet hitting leather reach you with a short delay, one unexpectedly breaks out ahead of the others—he's wearing a green t-shirt—and moves the ball toward a goal made out of two old tires, shoots, falls, and disappears from view, and the cries of the players reach you. Amazing. In this very same cell a little prisoner once lived who saw all this, and now he is no more. Apparently escapes are sometimes successful, but they are always shrouded in complete secrecy, and where the escapee is hiding, nobody knows, not even the escapee.

TRANSLATION BY NORA SELIGMAN FAVOROV

VIKTOR PELEVIN

Joe Juan

Ludmila Petrushevskaya

The things Joe told about himself got no reaction from his listeners—none whatsoever. Everyone sat there dumbly, eating and drinking, unable to take in his information.

He's an old friend. What's more, the host of the gathering, the head of a family, is his employee. And what does Joe do? He comes in and laughingly relates that the twelve-year-old daughter of his other friends (name not divulged) is sleeping with him. How do you react to that? You can't just say, "You're a child molester," or "Joe, you're a criminal!"

It's awkward. What should you do? Run to the police? Inform the girl's parents? That would be even more horrible. On the one hand, this is a terrible tragedy for the family. But on the other, if you put Joe in jail, you bring all the shame of a trial on that little girl.

Plenty of girls sleep around at a young age. The same things go on everywhere—in town and country, at children's camps.... As long as the parents don't know, everything's fine. Much knowledge is indeed much grief.

The girl will grow up and get married or get by somehow, and even then she'll need to avoid her parents' scrutiny, their insane shadowing of her, their accusations and tears.

And after all, Joe is a friend, and a proven one. You can ask him to fix your washer or sewing machine. He won't refuse. He'll take a friend's ailing wife in for X-rays. Joe hired the very host at whose home this information was made public, lifted him out of night duty at the regional hospital to the position of research fellow in his laboratory.

So it's impossible to object or to condemn. Therefore, we choose to see our friend's sex life as his own private business.

Or his fantasies. After all, nobody has stood over his bed with a flashlight.

But alas. His chatter is absolutely true.

By his own account, Joe is a comforter of women. He bangs them all; no one is turned away. (The friends' daughter called him herself. She said she would come to his car, told him to drive to the doorway of her building at 1:00 AM and wait until her parents fell asleep. Then, in the car, she climbed right onto him. "What are you doing, child?" was all he said. And everything went smooth as butter. Either the girl was already experienced, or she had been watching porn and had decided to try everything herself. That's why she didn't squeal. We have to believe this. That's how it happened. Joe doesn't lie, he's too lazy.)

He's screwed everybody. Unhappy women passed his phone number from hand to hand. Often it was pregnant women with their caprices, or the mentally ill. He would go to the addresses they gave. Once, he returned to work and cheerfully told everyone that he had just fucked a pregnant woman while a cat wailed in the bathroom giving birth.

On the other hand, these were all new liaisons. Used channels could not be reopened. To put it simply, there was never a second time. He said himself that he "worked more with extremeties," and pointed to his tongue with a snigger.

The people he said this to laughed more or less naturally, but their hearts constricted.

　　　　　　　　　　　　　　　LUDMILA PETRUSHEVSKAYA

How do you receive such information as, "Andryukha climbed on top of her and I worked from behind." How?

But he lays it all out like he's under oath, no matter where he is or who is there. He also shared the very private information that he takes naked Polaroids of all of his women, the kind that develop instantly. And almost none of them refuse, he says. Each takes the photo as a gift, and he carefully keeps the second copy in the camera and later puts it into an album. Does each one actually think that hers is the only copy, that it goes no further? Because that album is his main bait. A big reason women flock to him is to feast their eyes on those indecent pictures of their acquaintances; and they look through it with delight after their own fuck and photo shoot.

Maybe it was all because his father held a high position in this small college town. People might have expected that the son would provide protection, help for the future, etc., since the father held the strings to the distribution of apartments, defense of dissertations, personnel rolls and job assignments, trips abroad, funding... everything.

But this son—who gave himself the name of Joe—without, it may be assumed, ever considering why he got away with everything, nonetheless made use of his position and did as he wished in a virtually vanquished city.

The friends who heard his startling confessions in their own kitchen—they too in some way depended on the storyteller. That is the only possible conclusion. Indeed, they were an impoverished, intellectual family, whom he had helped. Perhaps he had also done some good turn for the ill-informed parents of that lively young girl.

And this family also had a young daughter, and might have feared the writing on the wall... but no.

They chuckled at his tales out of habit.

And yet it is absolutely certain that no idea of his father's omnipotence entered Joe's reckless head.

He lived completely on his own and didn't see his father for months at a time. The father went to Moscow on the weekends, and the son would settle for those same days in his bachelor apartment, a small dark lair with an enormous six-legged bed. There, in that apartment they, father and son, sultan and scion, had a so-called color organ, which Joe mastered and gave demonstrations on for everybody, roaring with laughter. Various colors lit up according to the major or minor key, or even the melody played. Joe invented a great deal himself, which came in useful later, after his arrest and deportation to the "zone." In the prison camp, he quickly fixed up a color organ for the convicts' disco.

To say that he was a modern Don Juan would be a stretch. In the first place, this all took place during Soviet times, and everything surrounding Joe's sexual acts was a rare novelty. All the equipment, a separate apartment, his own car, his father's indulgence.

It was a novelty also that Joe feared nothing, that he related his exploits himself, not even concealing his modest sexual abilities.

In other words, it was neither his personality nor his special qualities that drew women to his den. And certainly not love.

But the facts remain: Joe faced no obstacles, either from the powers that be, or from the female population.

They did not merely not refuse him, they called him themselves. They flocked to him. The whole town laughed.

Joe had all this success. Joe, carelessly dressed, always unwashed, with dirty shoes on crooked, worn-down heels, with machine oil always on his hands. Joe, smelling of sweat. Joe, who was always naked at home. (He wore swim trunks when he had guests he didn't know.) Joe, brilliant inventor for the everyday world, who had only to approach a broken machine for it to begin to work. (It would often continue to work only in his presence).

By the way, is it possible that Joe, in telling all to everyone so candidly—insistently even—is it possible that he was trying to atone for his sins immediately afterward by means of these public confessions?

This idea occurred to people only after his tragic death.

In any event, he only became a religious thinker when he was in prison, mathematically proving several unprovable things—more on that later.

Joe's male friends loved him because he could fix anything that didn't work, and also for his generosity in buying liquor for all, and for his constant readiness to receive guests who came with girls (excepting only those times when he would answer the phone with "I'm here with a buddy"). He was a party guy in those days. The only emancipated man in the system.

All around him, people lived their tense intellectual lives: the town was a research center after all. They read forbidden literature like heroes of the underground, organized philosophical debates in kitchens, made forbidden copies, like spies, of the works of forbidden philosophers: Berdyayev, Frank, Ilyin, and Fr. Sergius Bulgakov.

Eventually, literature published abroad made its way to these readers, hitting every circle: everything from the most inoffensive (Becket, Joyce, and Kafka, for example, which were banned in the Soviet Union for no particular reason), to the most virulently anti-Soviet.

The town authorities knew absolutely everything about the escapades of the professor's son. However, infractions of a moral nature were overlooked in artistic, literary and (especially) scientific circles.

This was the party line, expressed once by Joseph Pock Mark[1] in the words, "I have no other writers for you," when he was informed by his retainers that debauchery reigned among the workers of the pen. There really were no others; these ones had to be kept, and the words of the Kremlin leader laid for all time the foundation for the Soviet system of indulgence for sinners in the creative unions and scientific associations. One had only to adhere to the party line, and that was all. Everything else was quietly permitted.

For example, these engineers of human souls—as they were named by that same Joseph with the pitted face and withered arm—might be called (as witnesses) into the matter of the underground writers' bordello on Preobrazhensky Street, where young girls were lured; moreover, the way that affair came to light was outrageous: one of the treasurers of this children's brothel lodged a complaint that a certain union secretary hadn't paid his dues for half a year! Girls of twelve and fifteen were sent to penal colonies,

---

[1] Stalin

the madame was given a six-month suspended sentence. Nothing happened to the writers.

Two young investigators from Rostov-on-Don who exposed the pedophilia affair (what's more, it involved the participation of an honored writer and took place in a vault at the edge of an old graveyard, no less) were forced to leave. They were transferred to Krasnodar.

A young prose writer who molested thirty-six boys (he led a literary circle for the Pioneers) did get eight years. But he wasn't an important writer, he was small fry; also the parents raised a storm and filed complaints.

You can imagine what was said about academic society when the names of such geniuses as Dau were mentioned, whose wife, under the threat of the so-called 'fine' being withheld, was forced to make the beds for the stray women her husband brought home. (In revenge she used dirty linens.) Much was also known about artists. For instance, one lefty sculptor lived with a pair of little twins. Well, what of it? We have no others. Everything ran according to the rules established by Joe Pock Mark.

However, as the actors expressed it in the old days, with the passage of time, "the weight hit the floor." Joe slept with both the adult daughter and the young wife of a very influential official—that is, he behaved no worse than Khlestyakov,[2] whom Gogol, however, did not give the opportunity to join with both the wife and daughter of the governor, although it's entirely inevitable in the final act.

Joe meticulously inserted the photograph of the wanton wife in his album and showed her just as she had flaunted herself for him to all who wished to see. The city was in ecstasy.

Just then, after giving herself to Joe and viewing the album in reward, the daughter of the official recognized her stepmother and triumphantly informed her mother. The wise divorcée, however, forbore to spreading rumors out of concern for her daughter's reputation and her own future.

(A few words here about the town itself: almost all of the streets bore the name of Lenin. They had been connected on the map in an outpouring

---

[2] Main character in Nikolai Gogol's *The Inspector General.*

                                    LUDMILA PETRUSHEVSKAYA

of service to the ideal, and Lenin Street went wandering, flipping, diving, and winding sideways through every neighborhood. This was a gift from the authorities for the commemoration of our leader. Later, in some country settlements such as Peredelkino, near Moscow, they handled the name nicely. It's always a complicated business to change addresses and rename streets. Maps have to be corrected, new signs made, confusion managed in the post office.... There, instead of "Lenin Street," they modestly hung signs that read "Lena Street," as if in honor of some woman by that name.)

And so, Joe Juan, gallantly emerging every Friday evening from his Moscow-plated car on Lenin Street, walked the brink, defying circumstances with his very way of life.

He informed everyone of each latest conquest immediately and loudly, like a cock on a fence. It was one of his duties to serve society by means of the utmost openness before it.

And we must give our hero his due: the community raised no objections. Everyone accepted the goings-on as normal; nobody said a word to him about the poor child whom he picked up nightly at an address known to all, though she was the daughter of mutual friends.

What was going on? What was done, as they say, was done. The act of pedophilia had been completed and repeated. What's to do now—report it? Let the girl be sent to a penal colony? No and no again—it is for none to judge. Evil will come in this world, I will not be the means. I will not be an informant. Not I.

Thus, the city laughed (not the sea, as in Gorky).

However, the impatient official's daughter could not restrain herself. She carried the news of his new wife's unfaithfulness to her cuckolded father.

There instantly arose an urgent need for a search. That is, for a warrant. That is, for an arrest.

Up until now, the petty authorities had been meekly tolerant. They were all so-called 'milk brothers,'[3] made kindred by Joe the Joker. They were forbidden to meddle with science; they were to ignore infractions. Don't hang out dirty linen, don't bring shame on all of us.

Joe was arrested a week after the investigation was launched. Grounds were produced in Moscow, in the laboratory he headed. Nothing was taken into account—neither the good work of the collective, nor the inventions which Joe had been trying to register, expending great and mostly useless efforts in the sluggish patent office.

What did they arrest him for? On a ludicrous charge. All in all, that technical bungler had signed documents for the disposal of old equipment but hadn't destroyed anything. In the first place, Joe was too lazy for such dull business as sledge-hammering last year's data monitors, burned out radio tubes, and unused measuring devices. In the second place, he saved almost everything, like a slovenly housekeeper. It might come in useful in the future—and at that time, there wasn't a spare nail to be bought for love or money. This was a period of massive shortages. Joe even acquired, at his own expense, transistors from people selling them outside the Pioneer store. (This was later declared to be purchasing stolen goods, and he got two additional years for it.)

The city underwent a wave of searches. They claimed to be after forbidden literature, but they were actually looking for those Polaroids. They wanted to remove and destroy the town's disgrace.

Joe was sentenced to seven years' hard labor in the camps with permission to write two letters a month. In one year of prison he suffered beatings, rapes and interrogations that lasted from sunset to dawn. Apparently, he was forced to name everyone who read 'forbidden' literature—and who wouldn't speak, if the consequence of refusing was to be thrown to the homosexuals? Strangely enough, however, mass arrests did not follow. None of the locals were touched; they let the whole thing blow over. The town authorities didn't want a loud political scandal that would attract a pack of low-ranking KGB officials, eager to earn their stars.

Joe was given one indulgence: he spent some time in the hospital with a suspected heart attack and two broken ribs.

---

[3] Suckled at the same breast.

    LUDMILA PETRUSHEVSKAYA

The doctors did not confirm the diagnosis, and he was returned to his cell.

There, he proved the existence of God logically and mathematically. That was his scientific work. Hoping for nothing, he sent it out in one of his letters.

His short new life began there, in prison: the life of a rigorous religious ascetic and martyr.

And for all of the time allotted him, he loved only one woman, his little Juliet.

After seven years, when his term was about to end, she joined a convent.

TRANSLATION BY LISE BRODY

Grandmother, Wasps, Watermelon

ZAHAR PRILEPIN

Grandmother was eating a watermelon.

It was a marvelous August treat.

Our large, loving family was digging potatoes. I remember to this day the cheerful sound the potatoes made as they struck the bottom of the pail. The pails had holes in them and couldn't be used to fetch water. Their only remaining use was the most important one: carrying potatoes over to the potbellied sacks that stood at the very edge of the garden.

The potatoes made a dry gurgling sound as they poured quietly into the sacks. A dusty, damp smell came from the sacks. They'd been crumpled up in the shed for a whole year.

The bags were also torn, but not a lot; sometimes a small, light-hearted potato would poke itself out of the thin tear on the side. When the bag was picked up, it would jump out onto the ground and burrow into the soft black earth, and nobody would ever give it another thought.

It was a sunny day, but the sunlight was already full of August and its slow, honeyed leave-taking.

I kept catching myself thinking I wanted to stand and look at the round sun for a long time, as if we were parting before a long, happy voyage. I probably just didn't feel like working.

I thought a bit, then said that digging potatoes wasn't really man's work, but nobody agreed with me. My mother, my aunt, my sisters, and even the neighbor woman who'd stopped by to help opposed me.

Only my grandmother took my side.

"Of course not!" she said. "When did men ever poke around in the ground? This is woman's work. Go and lie on the grass while we dig. You're carrying those sacks over there, you'll strain yourself."

My grandmother said all this with her unvarying sweet irony, but all the women began yelling anyway, waving their hands in the air and vying with each other to say it was precisely the men who should be digging in the ground, since there was nowhere else they could be put to use.

The others, the grown men, meanwhile, weren't working. Grandpa was tinkering with some scythes in the courtyard, peening and honing them. My father had gone to the market and was apparently in no hurry to get back. My godfather—my father's brother—was lounging near the tractor.

He'd tried to start the tractor in the morning but had done something that made it stall out for good.

Our neighbor, Orkhan, a refugee from the South who drove a tractor for a living, happened to come by an hour later.

He was a good man and never understood when someone was joking with him.

My godfather viewed him very kindly and helped him out of a spot when he could. Except, whenever he had the chance, he tried to have a little fun with Orkhan.

"Hello, Orkhan," Godfather hailed as Orkhan passed by.

"Hello," said Orkhan drily, anticipating as always some kind of shenanigans from my godfather.

Godfather was the picture of unusual busyness, and donned a serious, anxious face.

"Listen," he said hurriedly. "The women are in a rush, and I still have to feed the pigs. Can you get the tractor started, Orkhan? Just get it going, and I'll be right back."

Orkhan didn't have time to answer before Godfather scampered away in his reckless slippers to the courtyard. Everyone except Orkhan noticed that, after circling around the yard, Godfather crept over to the window in the shed where the manure was tossed out.

After some hesitation, and despite the ridiculous request—why couldn't his cheerful neighbor get his own tractor started?—Orkhan slid into the tractor. A minute later, the tractor roared, coughed, and then fell silent again.

Godfather had already had time to run back to the garden, his eyes bulging.

"What the hell did you do, Orkhan? Huh? Do you work with tractors or not?"

Orkhan gave it another try, but this time the tractor was completely silent.

Orkhan crawled out of the tractor and circled around it several times, frightened. Godfather wouldn't back off, embarrassing Orkhan every which way and demanding he fix the damage right away.

"I worked on it yesterday, Orkhan!" yelled Godfather. "You saw me doing it! What did you do that it crapped out? Fix it!"

"I have lunch, and then again I work!" said Orkhan, choosing the Russian words with difficulty and trying to sidle away, but Godfather could not be deterred.

"What work? What am I supposed to do? You broke it, you fix it. That's not a neighborly thing to do, Orkhan. Is this how your people back in the Caucasus treat their neighbors?"

Ten minutes later, Orkhan lay under the tractor, his hairy legs twitching the flies away. Godfather had taken up a post nearby, smoking a cigarette, one arm thrown behind his head.

"Some tractor driver you are, Orkhan," he said softly. "No kind. You can't do anything. Started up a tractor, right away it broke down."

"Huh?" said Orkhan from beneath the tractor.

The women laughed. Only my grandmother pretended she didn't understand what was happening.

My father came back from the market, bringing three healthy watermelons with him; after scooping the flesh out, you could have crossed a small stream in each of them.

Oh, the crunch of watermelon, the blazing, icy inside, the black seeds... Nobody could hold back when my father hacked open the luxurious, weeping fruit.

Hastily finishing their patches, the women collected around the watermelon and fell still, transfixed.

Only my grandmother kept on nimbly digging potatoes, raking the earth with her strong hands.

My mother went to get some white bread; the soft inside is good with watermelon.

"Gran!" my sisters called to my grandmother. "Come on already!"

"I'm coming, I'm coming," she responded, but finished her patch, took the pail to the still unfilled sack, skillfully grasped its edges, and poured the potatoes in. Everyone else would have needed help with this simple task, one person maybe holding the sack while another poured the potatoes, and even then they sometimes fell on the outside. But not my grandmother, she'd gotten used to getting by alone.

Orkhan was also called to have some watermelon, but he'd finally got the tractor going and immediately set off for work without even glancing in at home. My mother barely caught up with him. She'd put a parcel together with eggs, a generous slice of sausage and bread, and a bottle of milk, and gave it to him. I hadn't even noticed when she brought it all to the garden and placed it in the shade under a bush.

We ate the watermelon, gazing at each other with happy eyes. How else can you eat watermelon?

My mother spread out a pretty red and black oilcloth, my grandmother sat nearby on a stool, and my father stood.

Drawn by the icy smell of watermelon, wasps began descending one after the other and circling over us, intruding and dangerous.

My father was the first to give in. Wasps were really the only thing in life he was afraid of. Once, when he was drunk, he'd been stung, and he, a healthy man well over six feet, passed out. By nightfall, his head had become huge and pink and his eyes had disappeared between enormous, puffy eyebrows. He almost died.

"I'd better go have a smoke," he said, and disappeared behind the tractor. The wasps flew after him, but then returned, displeased with the iron and the smoke.

"Always smoking, always smoking," my mother said after him.

Cheerfully waving the wasps away, my godfather followed my father. By his face I guessed the men were about to take a nip from the stash that was probably hidden somewhere in the tractor's iron crannies.

My godfather's wife watched his back attentively, suspecting something. But just then a wasp lighted on her face and she got distracted, and started bustling about and waving a handkerchief.

Annoyed by the wasps, my sisters yelled and ran from place to place, and my mother tried to frighten the pushy insects off.

I tried to keep my composure, but I didn't do well either. I blew on some wasps that had settled on a watermelon. They didn't detach themselves for long, but made an annoyed circle and almost landed on my head.

Only my grandmother sat motionless, slowly raising the red sickle of watermelon she'd been served and smiling as she nibbled the luscious fragility. The wasps crawled over her hands and over onto her face, but she didn't notice. The wasps settled on the watermelon, but when my grandmother bit into the flesh they crawled further away, avoiding her teeth and lips at the last minute.

"Grandma, you have wasps!" I looked at her admiringly.

"What?"

"There's wasps on you!"

"Well yes, it's sweet for them." She laughed, really only just noticing the wasps.

"Why aren't you afraid, they could bite you!"

"Why would they bite me?"

Grandmother raised her beautiful hand with its slice of watermelon; two or three wasps crawled along her arm and two more sat on the rind, feeding on the trickling sweetness.

She bit off the watermelon and yet another wasp, who had lighted on her cheek, simply flying away with no hard feelings, made a circle, and landed somewhere in the grass by the watermelon rinds.

Everyone became nervous and quickly dispersed. Grandmother sat quietly alone.

In the morning, discarded watermelon rinds have a slovenly look, their white insides turned to gray and the flies crawling along them in place of wasps.

That's how the village of my memories looks now. As if someone had scooped the honeyed flesh of August out of her, leaving the gray behind along with the last of the flies.

Everyone died. The ones that didn't die were murdered. The ones who weren't murdered, finished the job themselves.

My sisters were flung several times against a corner and were scattered someplace far away.

The only ones left were my grandmother and Orkhan and his Russian wife, whom he beats every day for drinking.

The gardens where the sap of life seemed to have just been churning beneath the earth had fallen silent, overgrown by unfamiliar grass. No vigorous potatoes rumbled onto the bottom of the pail.

We entered the village in my white Volga, moving through the dust we raised, a strange and unusual thing here, as if we were on the moon.

Grandmother's tired arms trembled rather than flying up in delight. She got up to greet us, blinked away a tear, and smiled.

She saw my wife for the first time. They immediately started speaking like two women do, while I was quiet and stroked the walls.

"Women's work is invisible," my grandmother said to my wife.

"Women's work is invisible," I repeated to myself, and went outside with a cigarette.

This is what my grandfather built: a fence, a shed, a porch, a house.

My father painted the pictures in the house. They show: my grandfather, the house, the meadow, the orchard.

My grandmother's heart, broken into several pieces but still alive—there you have the persistent work of men.

By not moving or bustling about in the rare moments when it was possible to enjoy a small sweetness without moving or bustling about, she'd lived through an enormous life. Glancing back, a mortal gaze couldn't distinguish even the first bend in the road, after which had come thousands of others.

We weren't able to live like that.

"A woman serves, but a man lives in fear, except he hides his fear," I heard my grandmother's quiet voice say from beyond the opened door. "A man can't understand a woman's life; nobody has any pity on us. And we can't spot a man's struggle."

"His struggle?" asked my wife.

"His struggle, his turmoil, his pain," grandmother explained.

"A woman lives in service, but a man lives in pain... Or maybe only mine were like that, I don't know." She sighed and fell silent.

My wife and I left the house and went down to the river. We crossed over a bridge that was barely alive and climbed up a hill. An enormous wasteland was visible from the hill.

"Even the sun is aching and sagging, like a dislocated shoulder." I said this out loud.

"What did you say?" asked my wife.

I didn't say anything. And she asked me again. And again I didn't say anything. No reason to repeat every stupid thing.

My wife sat motionless, enchanting and mortally beloved by me.

Just wait, I'll break your heart too.

Night was already falling when we returned. I walked ahead and she hurried behind me. I knew it was hard for her to walk fast, but I didn't stop.

I sat down on the grass by the river. Nearby there was a rowboat, old, dried out, dead. It was beating against the jetty, bobbing slightly, moored with a rotted rope.

I dipped my hand in the water, and the water flowed between my fingers.

With my other hand I grasped the grass and the earth that held my loved ones, who so recently had been so cheerful, so loving, and so sweet; and suddenly I felt an angry sting and a burning in my palm. Cursing foully, I brought my frightened hand to my face, not understanding a thing. I turned around and glanced at the place where I'd been grasping the earth, and in the grass lay a wasp. I had crushed it.

My hand began to swell up and sting. A dull pain began growing in my palm, just as if the wasp had settled under the skin and was thirsting to break free, swelling everywhere and releasing its hot, burning, wasp blood beneath my skin.

After getting back to my father's house, I was in a hurry, didn't finish my tea, and practically ran outside and started the car, even though my grandmother was still chatting with my wife.

I drove, holding the wheel spitefully with my injured hand and pressed mercilessly on the gas, winding down the black road.

We got back at night and I fell right into bed. Clutching my head with my hands and dropping off, I suddenly heard the beat of my heart. It was hurried and stubborn. I dreamed of a moored rowboat beating against a jetty. Tuk-tuk. Tok-tok.

Just wait, we'll cast off soon. Soon we'll sail away.

TRANSLATION BY DEBORAH HOFFMAN

  ZAHAR PRILEPIN

Fog

Dina Rubina

1

The alarm clock chirped gently; its first attempt to raise Lazarus was doomed to failure.

Then the chirp became a tapping out of three little bells—a kind of do-mi-so into his temple closest to the nightstand... But even this wasn't yet the real torture. After the inquisitional arpeggio, a vulgar cancan would burst forth, and he couldn't allow that...

"Arka!... I have to take off in three minutes!"

Arkady worked his hand out from under the blanket and, without looking, found the hateful button and gave it a push.

"What time did you get in last night?" Nadezhda asked, standing in front of the mirror, arranging several strands of Bedouin beads on her sweater. She loved large, garish Eastern jewelry that Arkady couldn't stomach. Sometimes he would ask her, "Why are you always jingling with necklaces, like the fifth wife of some lame Bedouin?"

Odd that he hadn't become a misanthrope, given this damned life of his...

"Around 4 AM...."

"Something *amusing* once again?" She stopped in the doorway with only one boot on. She held the other in her hand. Still lying in bed, Arkady regarded his wife through the bedroom door. At last he pushed the blanket away abruptly and lowered his legs. Greetings, new day: how on earth shall I ever get through you?

"Yes, suicide. A young woman did away with herself and in a very unusual way... But don't you go blabbing about it at your drug store. Nothing's known for sure."

"Who did? Where?"

Nadezhda, it seems, had forgotten that she was planning to "take off" three minutes ago.

Arkady was silent. He grinned bitterly, brushing his teeth in the bathroom; she waited for him to spit.

"Maybe you remember that old policeman Walid... we met him in Acre, at the harbor, after the picnic for Yulka's last birthday."

"I don't remember," she said. "And?"

"It was his daughter. The older one, unmarried... She was getting on in years, about thirty-five... There's a younger daughter, and now she can get married. It's their custom that the younger one can never marry before the older..."

"Well, so what?" asked Nadezhda, already feeling irritated. "Why are you so upset? Did they do her in, or what?"

He gazed through the window and sighed: a wall of fog—literally, as if someone had planted a thick gray shield a foot away from the house. The round light near the balcony seemed shrouded in cotton and looked like an opaque white apple.

"How shall I go today?" Arkady asked himself. "What? What did you say? Did her in? It looks like it..."

"Lordy!" cried Nadezhda, standing in the open doorway. "'Why do you stand there swaying, mountain ash so slender?' You said yourself this kind of thing happens all the time—*they* choke, stab, and burn their women just like flies! So, what now?"

"Enough, get going, you'll be late," he muttered.

Nadezhda loved to delve into his "tender psyche," more suited for teaching music to wunderkinds than dealing with charred bodies.

"Wait..." she even took a step back into the apartment. "You can't interrogate him, can you? Didn't you tell me that cases concerning policemen are handed over to the Ministry of Justice?"

"Nadya!" he cried cheerfully, pulling on his sweater. "Give up selling enemas. Come join my investigative team! You know the law so well that even I envy you."

She left, slamming the door.

That's it; he should be leaving for the weekly section meeting, especially since he'd have to feel his way through the winter fog. But he kept lingering... five more blissful minutes... A cup of coffee in his own kitchen...

Well done, Nadka, the star pupil with a fantastic memory. Yes, most likely the case would be handled by the Ministry of Justice. But, at this stage of a preliminary investigation, he'd be the one to sweat over it, that is, his group, by no means very large. Safed was a small town; only him and two sergeant investigators—that was the total brainpower on hand.

The book that his daughter had been glued to for the last five days was lying on the table—*Witches and Wizards*. Charming title.

While finishing his coffee, he reached squeamishly for this masterpiece with a bearded old man resembling a shaman on its glossy cover. He opened it to the table of contents. Yes, of course... "Black Mass"... "The Fire of Satanism"... "Witch-hunts"... very, very nice! A merciless beating, that's what his own fourteen-year old witch deserves, especially given the work she still owed in mathematics, if memory served correctly.

He thumbed through a couple of pages at random. It was all crystal clear, the usual collection of trash, casually combining a bunch of items from some provincial Russian newspaper together with some articles

from scientific journals. Yes, indeed... "Witch-hunts in Western Europe."
Good Lord, why does the child need this stuff? What does she see in it?
"In the town of Braunschweig so many bonfires were built on the square
for public executions that contemporaries compared the place to a pine
forest. During the decade of the 1590s, there were times when 10–12
witches were burnt in one day. The town council of Neisse built a special
oven in which, over the course of nine years, more than a thousand
witches were burnt to death, including children aged 2 to 4 years old... In
the free imperial city of Lindheim, the period from 1631–1661 was noted
for unusually cruel persecution. Women suspected of being witches were
thrown into pits, 'witch towers,' and tortured until they..."

He slammed the book shut, stood up, put on his shoes, and began to
tie his laces...

And while he was putting on his uniform jacket, walking out the
doorway into the damp cotton of the winter morning, turning on his
windshield wipers and warming up the engine... scenes of last night's
events floated before his eyes as if surfacing in the pea-soup fog.

Walid's spacious, slightly empty, and quite spotless home, with photographs of old men in gilded baguette frames on the walls... In the middle of the large living room on the first floor stood a small stove with a
whole set of copper pots; the smallest had traces of coffee that had boiled
over, still warm.

Walid and his son were sitting on opposite ends of the sofa, uncon-
cerned with the appearance in their house of all these new people; they
were totally withdrawn as they were supposed to be: *men in mourning*.

The deceased was in a room on the second floor, lying in her bed,
covered up to her chin with a blanket. The high collar of her green
sweater made her lifeless face appear sallow.

The younger sister, who had been weeping, was wearing a long
djellaba and a white headscarf covering the lower part of her face; she
was sitting hunched in an armchair, following the investigator's strange
shuttling around the room out of the corner of her eye.

"So, yesterday she was still alive and well?" Arkady clarified for the third time.

As if on duty, the girl began howling again. He waited, looking at her with patience and compassion. Because of the headscarf that concealed her lips and chin, her lovely large eyes somehow reminded him of the grandfather clock in his grandmother Katya's house not far from Moscow, under which he took naps during his childhood summers.

"Alive and well, yes, indeed," she confirmed earnestly. "Only she was sad... She kept saying that she was fed up with life, and asked that I look after her, because she felt that she might do something to herself."

Arkady, who had completed God knows how many circles around the room, stopped opposite the girl.

"And why didn't you look after her?" he asked sympathetically.

"I did, I did, but then I dozed off..." she replied. "And when I woke up in the morning she was dead."

Aha, that's why those eyes reminded him of the grandfather-clock: all the while, the girl kept his partner Varda in sight; Varda had just spread her large frame in the armchair next to hers and, it seemed, wouldn't have minded having a snooze. Oh, Lord, could he last until she left on her pension next year, so he could request a bright lad as a new partner, whom he could send on endless errands and not have to rush around everywhere himself! During the last few years he'd come to feel sorry for Varda and didn't bother her unless he had a good reason. What could you say? The old girl had accumulated a respectable résumé: thirty years in the same job. By the way, she had very good intuition and a woman's amazing memory for apparel; she could tell you without hesitation who was wearing what when she happened to bump into someone accidentally in the supermarket last year. Once this ability did play an important role in the investigation of a hopeless matter, and Varda made sure that no one ever forgot about it. Thus, the fat woman had become a living legend even before her retirement. However, the one thing she was lacking was a brain. But right now she was needed, even though she was dozing off: Walid and his son, even though distraught, immobilized by the unexpected commotion in their house, would never let any man be alone with the young girl.

He was still wandering around the room, waiting for the mobile crime lab he had summoned. He paused several times and stared at the sallow face of the deceased, emaciated by prolonged suffering... It seemed to him that some inhuman torment had taken up permanent residence in this body, already abandoned by its soul, and continued to lacerate its victim.

He turned and went into the gallery that surrounded the entire second floor.

The countryside was sinking into sleep...

The edge of the new moon on the surface of the deep sky and a tiny star not far from it seemed like features on someone's partially-covered face, perhaps a brow and a mole on her cheek. The smell of manure and smoke wafted in, a dog was barking rudely in the courtyard, and somewhere on the hillside people were firing guns from the rooftop. Apparently someone was celebrating something—*they* never miss a chance to show they keep guns in their houses.

Arkady took out a cigarette and lit up.

In the room behind him Ron Degen was already at work with people from his lab; in the gallery his serene voice could be heard indistinctly—he was chatting with Varda. These pathologists, Arkady thought, always have such an even temper and such soft voices, as if they were cultivating orchids rather than disemboweling stiffs. Especially Ron, who never raised his voice. It'll be interesting, however, to see what he says about this case.

An experienced specialist, Ron could usually determine on the spot whether it was necessary to perform an autopsy. If so, it would always mean a scandal.

Not one of the nationalities living here, not one of numerous ethnic groups, liked the idea of handing over one of their dead for an autopsy. There had to be special circumstances. Take the ultra-Orthodox Jews—

they'd do the devil knows what to avoid autopsy. They'd steal the bodies of their relatives from the morgue or the hospital. That fact in itself didn't mean anything suspicious.

Besides, this family wasn't strangers. Both Walid and his son Salakh were policemen...

The son had strange, transparent eyes—the color of green grass, beautiful, but ever so slightly crossed; the impression was that he was looking right through you. And his left eye had developed a twitch, as if he were winking at someone behind your back.

They say that the dead sister had raised him from infancy—his mother had passed away very early. So that *she* was like a mother to him. No wonder the regular patrol police, summoned by the ambulance crew, decided not to drag out the case, but to shut their eyes to it; after all, it was a family drama. Why should they barge into someone else's private affair? It was only sarcastic David, always and everywhere suspecting unnatural death, who insisted on calling in an investigator.

Well, we'll get him to work with us instead of Varda. Why not? We'll send him to take requalifying courses... He's a lad with brains and principles... True, he's an incorrigible character. Never mind, never mind... we'll come to terms.

Now they were faced with the most unpleasant task, that of forcing the relatives to sign a form granting permission for an autopsy.

But maybe they should have it their own way with this family matter, he thought... A clan comes and a clan goes, and nothing ever changes in these villages with their age-old way of life, whether it's a governor-general of the Ottoman Empire sitting here, a British commissar, or the supervisor of an investigative unit of the Israeli police. A young woman did herself in, or else her relatives helped her... it's even possible that the victim and the executioners collaborated in this noble action... One may, of course, get lost in this dangerous maze that goes by the name of "the restoration of family honor," and, smashing everything in sight, consider oneself an arbiter of justice. But not one of the 1500 or so men and women living in the village will sympathize with the victim and say thank you to the police. On the contrary!

Still, it's interesting, what this unfortunate girl did…

Ron came out onto the gallery, leaned up against the railing, and said in a low voice:

"But there are still marks on her neck indicating strangulation."

Arkady took a last drag on his cigarette, crushed the stub against the baluster of the stone railing, and tossed it away.

"We'll take the body," he said.

He turned to look at the door into the room lit by the bright light of a five-pronged chandelier; from here, because of the dark night, it resembled a stage. There, as before, Walid's younger daughter was sitting in her armchair, her eyebrows raised in suffering above her impish little eyes.

"Wait here," said Arkady, walking past Varda. "I'll try to do this myself, in a nice way… They're both packing."

⟊

All week the damp murk hovered above the hills of Galilee, with ragged clouds clinging to the stubble of evergreens. Then it was clear for three days in a row, and the earth started to steam and breathe… From the heights of Safed, the Sea of Galilee seemed like an oblong, convex lens. From such a viewpoint it became entirely evident that the earth was round.

Here and there light pink smoke crept along the folds of deep hollows, as if someone were baking potatoes; it was simply the blossoming of almond trees.

But towards the beginning of the next week the rains poured down and once again forgot to clean up after themselves; wisps of steam were left hanging in the air… They wouldn't disperse.

On Monday, the results of the autopsy arrived from the Institute of Forensic Expertise, known simply as "Abu-Kabir," in as much as it was located next to the well-known holding cell of the same name.

Arkady was looking at the bare, thorny bush of bougainvillaea outside the window. In the summer it was lush and glowing—you glanced out the window and it was a sight for sore eyes! Now it shivered all alone in the wind, its long thorns piercing the clouds of cotton wool.

The tedious pauses, timid sobs, and lonely, lost harmonies: Debussy, the études—that's what this long-lasting fog was like. Debussy's études, which my music teacher, the late Stanislav Borisych, had been so fond of...

He dropped his eyes to the autopsy report and reread it. He ran his fingers quickly along the edge of the table.

He missed the musical instrument that his accursed life did not allow him to touch even for a minute; he often would tap out some passage onto any surface where his hands found themselves. He had played Debussy's étude at his beloved professor's funeral, in the great hall of the conservatory, where coffins were usually placed for farewells...

Why was it, why precisely during these periods of winter fog did the memory of Stanislav Borisych come back to him so often?

He scratched behind his ear with a pen.

According to the experts' conclusions, my dear ladies and gentlemen, the unmarried girl (in his mind he thought of her as an "old unmarried girl") had in no way been "alive and well, alive and well" the night before... She'd been dying for four days before that, in a terrible, agonizing manner. It was a real pleasure to read what our friends from "Abu-Kabir" had scribbled: both paralysis of the respiratory system and a scorched esophagus—an absorbing story, may the devil take you all. The main thing was, her death was caused by heart failure; apparently, she couldn't endure the suffering.

He recalled the convulsive twitch under Salakh's eye, the father's in-flexible cheekbones, and the tear-stained face of the pretty younger sister, awash in expectations.

The older one was unattractive, with angular features and a nose that was too long. During her life, however, all this was probably softened by her feminine charm.

Hmm... yes... expert opinion on poisons was in general the main issue in this case. There are no more than a couple of specialists... and in fact, there are two of them: one was Russian, the other, Argentinian—two cheery guys. The work is hellish; every investigator begs for quick results. And the results themselves, to put it mildly, are ambiguous.

In our case: during the last four days, the poison in the body had managed to recede... Now go figure out what she was poisoned with... So, clearly we have to be more ingenious, take evasive action given a tight budget, find the means for sending a tissue sample to London, to FFS—not an inexpensive luxury; after all, it was a commercial firm, that superb lab...

By noon the gray mist had not exactly dispersed, but had somehow moved, begun to stir... and flowed like blancmange.

From the window of the little wood-panel house where the police headquarters was located, the slope of the nearest hill became visible, with its rust-red rows of low grapevines, bare in winter.

The air became brighter and more cheerful, too; outlines of houses, a minaret, and a hotel tower arose in the silvery ripples. Pale blue Atlantic fir-trees stood along the edges of the roadway, taking in air like powerful grenadiers; during his childhood he had known them as "Kremlin trees"; finding them here in the hills of Galilee, he let out a deep sigh and settled down to live. Even though it had been proposed to him more than once that he transfer to the Central District.

But he loved old Safed, its steep hill where stone steps lead up to the sky or give out suddenly in the middle of nowhere; where structures of five, seven, or even nine stories seem nailed to the cliff like starling houses by someone's powerful hands and—when you glance down from the road—seem to be hanging in the air. Where at twilight enormous lamps like cockades flood the air with light like yellow honey, and townspeople decorate balcony railings, shutters, lintels, and even stone fences in light- and dark-blues, which, as is well known, ward off demons, dybbuks and ghosts from one's house.

Here at every step you see bumpy, colored glass. People place it in windows, doors, and lattice fences; you look here and there and you're touched by all the shades of dark-blue, red, violet, green and yellow. When you wake up in the morning in just that kind of old house, when the resonance of red and sun-yellow burst through your high, vaulted window, uncontrollable joy rushes into you with all its wind and brass instruments: you've awakened in paradise—transparent, multi-colored, celestial paradise!

But it's still a long time until summer.

Along the road home he made a detour to go past his favorite light-blue alley of Atlantic firs. That always improved his mood...

Winter in the hills—there was a book with that title he'd read in his youth. The author was named Wain, it seems. The hero in it was also always searching for someone, wandering around, wandering in the fog...

His daughter Yulka was home already. She was stretched out on the sofa reading a book. But eighth grade, by the way, had a rather difficult program of studies.

"Oh, Papa!" she said cheerfully. Her father didn't often stop by at home in the middle of the day.

"I've got only a half-hour," he said. "Daughter, fix me a little something to gulp down quickly!"

"I can heat the *borshch*," she said pensively, turning the book over and laying it aside on the sofa.

"Don't treat books like that! How many times have I told you?"

"Pa... you turn the gas up under the saucepan yourself, okay? I want to finish reading this one page..."

Without taking off his shoes, Arkady went into the kitchen and swearing, took the cold saucepan out of the refrigerator, wedged into his arm some jars that had started to tip over on the shelf as he grabbed the soup... He put the saucepan on the burner and thought, is it worth taking off my shoes for only half an hour? He didn't take them off.

They ate in silence; the father thought about his business, the girl continued to read to the end of her chapter.

When she jumped up to answer the telephone, Arkady turned the book so he could read the cover: bah! It was the same *Witches and Wizards*.

This would be a good time to hold an edifying conversation with her, but Yulka was gabbing with her girlfriend, and it was already time for him to go. He left to the sound of his daughter's peals of laughter. It was interesting how the soft uvular "r" in her Hebrew instantly yielded to the hard trilled "r" in her Russian. He wondered if any changes in the structure of the larynx occurred in bilingual children... That would be something to study, instead of searching for traces of poison in the internal organs of the murdered—yes, murdered, he would prove it!—woman.

He walked out of the entryway, sat in his car and drove to work. Today he still had a lot of things to do. Stop by the courthouse, review budgetary issues with the men, conduct an investigative experiment with this young jazz musician who'd "accidentally" killed his neighbor. Write a request to the criminal lab in London... And not to forget: one of his two investigators, Yoni, wanted Arkady himself to interrogate a psycho, or a guy pretending to be a psycho, the owner of a falafel shop who lured schoolgirls into his back room and showed them various pictures, for which they ought to cut off precisely that body part which he had shown to the girls... The main thing was that, at his interrogation, this psycho stared wildly, with eyes the size of plums, and, leaning his torso over the table, *shouted* in a mysterious whisper, that he'd received these pictures *on command, by fax—from a matchbox!*

                                             DINA RUBINA

All of a sudden he decided to drive through the village. Simply to have a look, to see what was up, he said to himself.

It often happened that he couldn't explain to himself why he took one or another unnecessary action, which, in addition, used up time in what was already a day boring enough for him to smoke five cigarettes. He took these steps... not "intuitively"—he couldn't stand that feminine word—but rather as a result of his musical education. There suddenly arose before his eyes an image of the "Bechstein" piano keyboard in his very own classroom number 24, where, before his lesson in composition, he used to seek out the harmonies almost blindly: he would touch the keys, and a triplet would quiver in the upper register... the left hand would support it with a chord... and all of a sudden something resembling a melody would emerge, or—as the late Stanislav Borisych used to say—a fresh musical idea...

So here it was, a fresh musical idea: to drive through the village and drop into the snack bar not far from Walid's house, the one with the large picture window... To have a look around... And, at the same time, to grab a little something to eat! Nadezhda's vegetable borshch never filled him up completely.

"More pita and *labane*," he said to the lad behind the counter. "And don't stint on the *zahtar*! More, more, pour it on!"

The lad smiled and showed his white teeth, scooped up a spoon of *labane*—something like sour cream, but with a sharper taste—and spread it generously on the surface of a large *lafa*—Druze-style pita, not hollow, but more like lavash baked on an iron stove and shaped like a tent. Like a sower of seeds, he sprinkled the white edges with dark green *zahtar* powder and sesame seeds, fragrant with flavor. The circular movement of his wrist produced a thick stream of green gold from the rubber tip of the bottle—local olive oil. Then he rolled up the *lafa* bread.

Arkady sank his teeth into the springy softness... Scrumptious!

During the last few years, he'd grown accustomed to the local food, and lately, when he happened to travel abroad, he would miss it a great deal; in restaurants, he would grumble and criticize refined French and Italian cuisine. In general, these fifteen years spent "among the lands," in the Hills of Galilee, in endless rounds from one Arab village to another, Druse or Cherkessian, hadn't exactly altered, but had somehow deepened, fermented his whole being, just as the local air is fermented by the curdled fog during the winter.

Sitting next to the glass window, its outside surface splattered with dried mud, he observed the typical village street—as much as the patchy murk would allow him—leading up the hill, winding and narrow, where it was hard for two cars to pass. Just then two cars almost sideswiped each other. The drivers honked their horns, gesticulating furiously and cursing...

"Is that Walid over there, in the car?" Arkady asked lazily, indicating the road.

Of course, Walid couldn't be in that car. For the last five days, he and his son had been held in an investigative confinement cell. Arkady himself had interrogated both of them. Without much success. They both kept firmly to their story; alas, Jamilya had done away with herself. In general she was inclined to be unhappy, poor girl, ever since birth. Not unlike her late mother... In a word—a family matter...

Today was the last day when the suspects could be legally detained in custody. Tomorrow he would be forced to release them for lack of evidence, that is, to admit defeat. "Evidence of what?" he asked himself, chuckling. That they forced the girl to hang herself first, and then they made her drink some agricultural poison? (That's what the boys at the lab believe.) And what if she had made the decision to wipe herself off the face of the earth in such an awkward manner?

"No," said the lad, glancing at the whitish haze behind the glass, as if it were possible to make anything out. "In the first place, Walid has a gray Subaru..."

He didn't say what was in the second place; he held his tongue. Especially since an old man came in from the cooking area; he was wearing a *galabiya* and a white headscarf wrapped around his head as women do. On the right side the fabric encircled one protruding hairy ear. The old man held a red nectarine in his hand and with a small knife was removing its reddish ribbon of skin.

"Walid," he sighed... "Walid..."

He was so attractive in his dark-blue *galabiya* with a snow-white scarf on his head and shoulders, with his full salt-and-pepper mustache, and the shiny red fruit in his hand.

Arkady was lost in admiration.

"Walid is very sick," the old man said at last. The young man glanced up at him fleetingly, without turning his head, merely squinting.

"Sick?" Arkady nodded his head sympathetically and respectfully. "I thought I saw him not that long ago."

"Sick, very sick." The old man cut a neat red section of the nectarine and using the sharp tip of the knife, conveyed it to his mouth. He chewed it slowly and set about cutting another piece. "His heart's sick. Last Wednesday he had an attack. My nephew—he's a doctor—saw Walid and said: 'Let's go to the hospital!'... But he didn't want to!"

Arkady looked at the old man... It seemed as if this was true. *They could all cover up, but to make up details, to invent a nephew-doctor! Not likely... Then what do we have, my friends? If last Wednesday the doctor visited the patient at home... and the poor maiden was already dead... then... four days earlier... it turns out the doctor examined Walid at the very same time the daughter was upstairs dying in agony!*

Well then, that's a quite fresh musical idea, Stanislav Borysych, my dear...

He remembered how Walid, opening his bovine eyes wide and grabbing his chest, had tossed the autopsy form on the floor and cried, "Don't do this to me, Arkad!!! Don't you do this to me!!!" Yes, what was most painful was that this family wasn't strangers... And it appears that the father really did have a weak heart.

Now to have Varda confirm the existence of the nephew-doctor, and the main thing—the time frame!

He stood up, put some coins down on the counter, and asked for a can of orange soda. It wasn't worth it, of course, buying this carbonated junk; he'd have heartburn again that evening.

Then he left...

The fog was growing thicker in the sky. In clear weather, Safed resembled a white nest on its hill. But now only gray mist hovered over the peaks of dark hills. That meant that up there, on top, it was pitch dark.

He dialed Varda's number on his cell phone and said:

"I'll be there in about twenty minutes. Have them bring in the younger son... Salakh."

2

After opening the door quietly, he entered the apartment and, in the darkness, without removing his jacket, tiptoed into the kitchen. It was a little brighter in there: the light from a streetlamp outside the window stretched lazily to find at least a few meters of the front garden. At the same time a slice of damp light shone on the medicine chest by the wall.

It was amusing to grope around in cabinets in one's own kitchen, like a thief at night...

He reached his hand deep onto the upper shelf where there was supposed to be a jar of baking soda, but the sleeve of his puffy jacket brushed against some bottles: he began to pull his hand out and... damn!!! The sound of broken glass crashed in the silence of the sleeping house like the explosion of a shell on an artillery range.

There you have it... All because he didn't turn on the light, not wanting to wake anyone... so ve-ry thought-ful! Now go ahead, you asshole, turn on the light, take off your jacket, and clean up the mess of glass and the soda. And suffer with that damned heartburn until morning! Meanwhile, there were only two hours left until morning...

He started sweeping, while behind his back could feel Nadezhda standing in the doorway. But he didn't turn around, allowing her a minute to *normalize* her mood.

   DINA RUBINA

"Go-oo-od Lord," he heard the usual, sleepy voice. "What time is it, huh? Am I ever going to have even one peaceful night's sleep? What mischief are you up to—heartburn again?"

He suddenly choked up in gratitude: what a sweetie, she remembered about his heartburn!

"Nadya," he said and sat down on a chair with his back to her, broom in hand.

She approached, embraced his head, and pressed it against her soft bosom, quickly stroking his forehead, cheeks and throat with both hands... muttering something, in an almost sing-song voice...

She had nice hands, Nadezhda did; they radiated something or other. Even a visiting psychic from Nizhny Novgorod who performed here last year in the Palace of Culture, the one who conducted mass hypnosis séances for women who wanted to lose weight, even he had said that she possessed some special gift.

And in a few minutes Arkady really did feel a bit better; the poisonous spasm in his chest that had made it hard for him to breathe was relieved. He bent his head to one side and gratefully squeezed his wife's hand between his shoulder and his burning ear.

"I spilled the soda," he said guiltily. "Such terrible heartburn, Nadya, it reduces me to tears!'

"What's soda have to do with it?" she cried. "What utter nonsense! Here, take some Alka-Seltzer," and she filled a glass with water, began to stir a tablet into the glass, repeating something he'd heard from her a hundred times—that it was all nerves, it had nothing to do with his esophagus, that sooner or later all normal people become accustomed to such work, that it's absolutely normal for normal people, understand? That, after eight years, he shouldn't give a damn when a run of the mill *wog bumps off one of his own...* But he can't get used to it in any way, and no tablets can ever help him—you remember what happened last year, when there were shoot-outs in the village near Akko, and the bastards from one band murdered a three-year-old infant from another band, and your section was the one to conduct the investigation, do you remember? You stopped sleeping and went reeling from wall to wall... You just have to quit this damned police work once and for all. How many times do I have to tell you?

Then she couldn't help remembering his late mother, who insisted that after his third year he leave the conservatory and enter the law faculty. She was concerned about his earning a crust of bread, of course. A crust of bread is a good thing, lodged in the throat of the whole family! And now, if you please, you can see the result—soon he'll wind up in the madhouse! If only he could have a job in a normal office, make out wills, try insurance claims—no, he's managed to get into the thick of it, in the middle of this criminal brutality!

In half an hour they were back in bed, although the alarm clock would soon send out its loathsome sound...

Arkady didn't feel in the least like sleeping, and, skipping the hours of exhausting interrogation that would be impossible to convey in words—Nadya, it was like explaining a Mahler symphony note by note—he started telling her about things from the moment when Salakh, the younger son, the deceased sister's favorite, whom she'd taken care of—telling her how he behaved during all those hours, what self-possession, what will-power—how he blanched at the photograph of the dead Jamilya suddenly tossed onto the table, then his face grew pinched, and he fell silent. Only the spot under his eye twitched and pulsed.

And in the ensuing silence Arkady said to him:

"So... Be a man!"

He lowered his fist to the table heavily, like the lid of a coffin in which they bury the deceased, and he said in a muffled voice:

"I've had enough... Start writing!"

"That's how it went down, Nadya, this business. His sister had fallen in love with a poor soldier and had begun meeting with him... The soldier was about fifteen years younger than she was, and the father would never give permission for her to marry someone like that. It was impossible for her to go on meeting him, extremely dangerous; the relatives would quickly snitch on her... She used to leave the house at night in men's clothing, a black cloth wrapped around her face."

"Insane... Medieval! A masquerade," Nadezhda said.

So rumors began to circulate in the village, someone had seen a stranger in a black mask. At last, her own uncle bumped into her one night. He grabbed her, tore the cloth off her face, recognized his niece, and was stupefied... He spat right into her face and immediately went to see Walid. He told him everything. That very day Jamilya was sentenced to death. She lived only another three weeks after that.

"How medieval!" Nadezhda repeated in a fit of temper.

Propping herself up on her elbows, she peered into her husband's face. She suffered for him... He lay there on his back, and using his elbow to shield his eyes from the light of the bed lamp—very cozy, but still too bright at this moment—he spoke in a monotone that became hoarse at night, barely moving his lips. At times he seemed to be dozing, his voice would drop to a mutter, but Nadya didn't want to stop him, understanding that he was in the process of *healing*...

"Apparently the uncle couldn't restrain himself and told his wife everything, even though Walid had begged him to *hush it up*... And she spread it around to her sisters, and then it made the rounds... The rumors proliferated, and one fine day..."

... The most interesting thing was that he could imagine with absolute clarity and accuracy that fine day, one of those when nature in the Galilee delicately reacts to the early, fragile warmth, still only February, and almost overnight miraculous grass of a piercing green color, almost hysterical in intensity, penetrates the red softness of the earth—as a result of a thick covering of pale-yellow mustard plants.

That morning Salakh went to see his older sister and said:

"I can no longer face the shame. One of us has to die."

Jamilya leaned back against the wall, as if he'd pushed her. She closed her eyes.

They stood facing each other in that room where both sisters lived, where their mother had previously fallen ill and died. And where after their mother's death Jamilya used to bathe the young Salakh, because the room was sunny and warm.

"I will," she said. Her thick, masculine eyebrows instantly appeared black on her chalk-white face. "I'll be the one."

"How?"

He stood before her, a tall, strong man, a twitch quivering under his eye, more likely, a small scar; when he was three, standing on the staircase, Salakh turned when his sister had called him and he fell; it was a miracle that the eye itself wasn't injured. She carried him on her back until he was five or so and she remembered those warm hollow places under his sharp knees, when, pausing in the middle of a game, she would hoist him up into a more comfortable position.

"How will you do it?" he repeated insistently.

"I'll swallow pills," she whispered.

"I'll give you two hours," he tossed back. "In two hours I want to find you dead!"

He left, got into his police SUV, and for the entire duration of her death sentence, drove around the village, furiously turning the steering wheel, terrifying hens and dogs.

Two hours later, he turned into the courtyard of their house. Getting out of his car, he glanced around and saw a wide open hand, then another, emerge convulsively from the well in the middle of the courtyard... and grab onto the stone edge; then the drenched head of his sister appeared, her eyes protruding, lips trembling...

For a few moments they looked at each other—he and that horrible, pale-yellow face with a burning red stripe on her neck.

He rushed forward, ran to his sister, caught hold of her under her arms and helped her climb out.

"What can I do, what?" she muttered, hanging onto him, weeping and spluttering, just like a child. "I took twenty Vaben tablets—and vomited... I went to hang myself in the cellar—but the rope broke... I jumped

　　　　　　　　　　　　　　　　　　　DINA RUBINA

into the well—but it was too shallow and I merely got hurt. What can I do? Tell me, what? So, you kill me, kill me!"

"Let's go," he said and dragged her into the cellar where sacks of fertilizer stood in a row along the wall; a skull and crossbones were depicted on each with the words: "Danger, poison!"

She collapsed onto one of the sacks, with her wet dress clinging to her; she sat there, staring ahead senselessly. Water was dripping from her hair, her face was blue from the cold, and her nose stuck out as if from someone else's face. Two murky streams were flowing slowly from her nostrils.

Salakh took a large measuring cup from the shelf, scooped up crystalline powder from an open sack, poured in some water, stirred it, and handed the cup to her.

"Drink!" he ordered. He stood over his sister and watched as, choking, she swallowed the fatal swill.

She vomited at once.

Then he mixed more chemicals with the water and once more ordered her:

"Drink!"

She drank and straightened up... She staggered... Slowly she began to climb the cellar stairs... But on the threshold she fell flat on her face.

Salakh called his other sister. She came rushing down—in a moment she understood everything and shrieked! But when he slapped her across the face with the back of his hand she quieted down and began to help him willingly, her red cheek burning.

Together they lugged the body upstairs, undressed her, dried her with a towel, dressed her in a green sweater with a high collar to hide the marks left by the rope, and lay her in bed...

"Four days and four nights she suffered agonizing torments in silence," muttered Arkady. "Agonizing torments... Finally her heart failed."

The day, as always, began with a conference call. Arkady listened to the voices, recognizing each one even before they identified themselves.

"Greetings, Akko."

"Hey, Karmiel, what's up?"

"Last night we had... (two spoons of sugar, please)... Last night someone broke a store window on Herzl Street and carried off only a few small items—most likely it was some kids making mischief... And one young lad was wounded in a skirmish at a discotheque... Other than that, nothing much..."

"Good morning, Rosh-Pina, Rosh-Pina... we have something to report. You remember, in December a vagrant froze to death in a grove by the gas station..."

He listened to the voices... noted on his pad what had happened last night in the Galilee, at the same time trying to accept and come to terms with his own morning news, not that it was resounding, but an hour before the beginning of the investigative experiment, Salakh retracted his confession of his sister's murder, declaring that he had given evidence under the duress of the investigators and that in fact he was completely innocent of any crime—Jamilya had committed suicide of her own free will, for the sake of his family's honor, since she was unable to bear the disgrace.

So what? He, this gallant policeman, could sincerely consider that the truth. After all, he had only *helped her to die*, just as she'd asked. Had it not been for his pallor at the sight of his dead sister's face, so tormented by suffering...

"Safed! What's up with you? Why are you so quiet? Hey, you turkeys! Have you fallen fast asleep there in your fog?"

He coughed. He began speaking quickly and calmly...

Then Arkady conducted the routine meeting. He wrote down recommendations on various cases, distributed them among those very same *turkeys*—Varda (who was soon to retire) and Jonah, who, even without Arkady's errands, was kept awake every night by his five-month-old twins... After lunch, which he didn't eat, he left for the prosecutor's office, to refresh his memory on an unsolved case he'd worked on a year ago. Then, already almost evening, he went to see what had been recorded on the surveillance cameras...

From time to time the image of a scar pulsating on Salakh's face arose before his eyes, and the heavy hammer of his fist dropped from his side onto the table: "Write!"

That's it. I no longer have the right to keep him behind bars. No one would extend the arrest order, no one... You lost, old man, it happens, in the sense that West is West, but interrogation is merely interrogation, as much as you feel like ripping his guts out, so he could understand how his sister died. Very well, resign yourself to it... All the same, the case will be handed over to the Ministry of Justice; people there are serious... who knows, perhaps...

At home, very late that evening, refusing supper, Arkady remembered that he hadn't eaten all day. And, what was more interesting, he still didn't feel at all like eating.

His heartburn was right there; a soldering iron was leaving its black burn mark somewhere down his throat...

But you can only remotely imagine what that poor maiden suffered before her death...

He looked in the medicine cabinet and hurriedly mixed a tablet of Alka Seltzer in water so that Nadezhda wouldn't see, or else she'd latch onto him with all sorts of questions. He went to lie down for a minute in the bedroom, just as he was, still fully dressed.

There, he could hear the amusing and poignant music of the French composer Kosma; his wife and daughter were watching an old film with Pierre Richard. In the darkness, Arkady's limp hand came across the cover of a book lying upside-down on the bedspread. He stretched out his arm, turned on the bed lamp and discovered the same glossy rubbish that

Yulka had yet to finish. That miserable wretch is abusing a book again! Squinting in the half-dark room, he ran the angry glance of his eyes scanned down the page: "In France, the persecution of witches began very early. One of the Jesuits at the time wrote, in 1594: 'Our prisons are filled to the brim with witches and wizards. A day doesn't go by when our judges don't sully their hands with their blood...'"

Desperate rage suddenly seized Arkady by the throat. He swung his arm and, in a frenzy, hurled the stupid book on the floor.

Have you gone crazy, or what? Why on earth are you obsessed by the medieval execution of this unfortunate maiden? You have a whole truck-load of similar affairs. Why, just last Friday in a small grove near Akko, once again they found the charred corpse of a woman in a car... Another "restoration of family honor." They've lived that way for centuries and will live like that for another hundred centuries. Do you intend to reed-ucate them? How the hell do you know, you unfortunate West-is-West, that in their place and in their skin, you wouldn't kill your own Nadezhda, or even Yulka here, because she doesn't take good care of her books?

But he couldn't come to any agreement with himself. He kept imag-ining the younger, pretty scoundrel walking to and fro past her sister's bed for four days and four nights... Those shifty little eyes... She served coffee to the doctor who was treating her father. And all that time she was waiting for her liberation—observant, rapacious, lively, steeped in anti-cipation of her new life. The scoundrel! Most likely her hand had already been asked for in marriage.

When Nadya, after guffawing to her heart's content with Yulka over Pierre Richard's naked rear end, came into the bedroom to take off her housecoat and put on her pajamas to go to sleep, she found her husband lying dressed on the bed, crimson from the heat, with cruel, half-closed eyes. He was muttering something, either in a dream or a delirium...

"Arka, are you sick or what?" she asked anxiously, leaning over him.

He ground his teeth and said distinctly:

"The scoundrel!"

　　　　　　　　　　　　　　　　　　　　　　DINA RUBINA

After languishing for five days or so with a ferocious flu, such as he hadn't suffered since third grade, when the Hong Kong virus had begun to ravage the world, he received notice that he'd been called up for training in the reserves; and, as always, he didn't exactly rejoice, but he did experience some mild excitement, as he did before a vacation. Though being with the armored troops, where he'd served until becoming platoon commander, was by no means a restful stay in a sanatorium.

Last year the training took place in Elyakim—right here, not far from home. They lived in tents, slept in their tanks for three or four hours, were dog-tired, but—strange to say—he always returned home as if he'd had a vacation—sun-tanned, feeling tranquil, and madly in love with Nadezhda.

In the morning, Arkady went to the office, received his form and "Galil" assault rifle, and an hour and a half later he was having dinner in Elyakim...

Just before dawn, he finally fell asleep for about fifteen minutes—more likely, it only seemed that he slept... on a bend in a dusky village street, a soldier could be glimpsed, and then he disappeared behind the café window in clouds of fog... Oh, yes, a soldier... What does a soldier have to do with it? Nobody has any need for him...

When the alarm clock started chirping, he was still lying on his back, covering his eyes with his elbow.

Trees were already racing each other to bloom; here and there the white breath of almonds was floating through the air. On the steep slope where a flock of spotted chocolate-brown and white goats was grazing, the purple lining of the damp earth peeking out from under the grass. After the series of rains, the grassy hills, with their outcroppings of black basalt, seemed to have been coated with egg-yolk, forming little islands of yellow gorse and small lakes of yellow clover... In these large platters of fried eggs, the poppies looked like sprinkles of red pepper.

A moist wind brought the sharp fragrances of newborn herbs from everywhere—thyme, mint and basil; all of this uneasy abundance was joined with the odor of food from the large tent where the dining area was located.

In the transparent air, distant mountain ridges were arranged in layers, one after another, with such graphic precision of line, it was as if the fog of the previous days was merely cleansing powder that some meticulous housewife had used to scour the sky, mountains, roads and houses; yesterday, all muddy traces had been washed away by the plentiful rain; and today, wherever you looked, everything was spick-and-span, sparkling all around.

Arkady tossed his head back and gazed up at the sky where, for some five minutes, he followed a loose ribbon stretched across the fresh thick layer of blue enamel behind the barely visible dragonfly of an airplane.

When he lowered his head, temporarily blinded by the bright sun and the blue sky, the first thing his cleared eyes beheld was his Salakh, the one who was under investigation. Standing not far off, in front of the next tent, in uniform, with the same "Galil" in his hands, he was staring at the investigator with a sullen, sarcastic glance.

Well, yes, Arkady suddenly remembered, during the interrogation he mentioned that, a year ago, he'd been released from the army, where he'd served in an armored unit.

For several moments Arkady looked into the slits of Salakh's squinting green eyes, turned away, and went into his own tent.

About ten minutes later he was summoned to the commander at headquarters, a little house standing on pylons. The commander was sitting at the table and dejectedly crunching a biscuit from his rations.

"Arkad... sit down." He was silent for a minute, carefully examining under the light a plastic container with *tehina*. "Listen," he said at last. "So, this Salakh... is it true he's someone you're investigating?"

Arkady turned away from the commander, toward the window—there on the shining smooth surface of ultramarine, the remaining feathery vapor trail from the fighter plane was still fading away. Or maybe it was new clouds already gathering again?

"Yes," he replied. "So?"

"He just came to see me and said that he couldn't vouch for himself, that's what... He said, you understand, I've got a weapon in hand... Moreover, he looks like the type who... What do you think?"

"What am I supposed to think?" Arkady burst out.

The commander opened the container, took a little *tehina* on his knife, placed it on his tongue, and concentrated on tasting it.

"Why does their *tehina* always taste so sour to me?" he said pensively. "I understand they don't serve my mother's *tehina* out here, but at least it could be fresh!"

He sighed, put aside the knife and container, got up from the table, and began to dig in the cardboard carton in the corner, bending over it and breathing heavily...

Over the last few years Gaby had sprouted a sizable belly. A long time ago, he and Arkady, standing side-by-side, had successfully completed two difficult operations in Lebanon, but, after the army, Gaby re-enlisted for additional service, completed officer's training, and now he was a major.

"You know," he muttered, without turning and continuing to rustle the wrapping paper, "perhaps I'll send both of you home, out of my fucking sight, just to be safe... It'll be more peaceful that way."

"How?" Arkady was dumbstruck. "When?"

Gaby straightened up; the large, protruding whites of his gray eyes shone brightly on his reddened face, just as they did in his youth, some fifteen years ago.

"Right now," he said. "Shlomy over there is leaving for the base in half an hour. He'll drop you off. Hand in your weapon and uniform... I've released that maniac already..."

The bus to Safed didn't leave for another forty minutes or so. So they waited, both of them: the investigator and the man under investigation. They sat on wooden benches opposite each other, holding identical cans of Goldstar beer, tucking their legs under the benches identically. They even seemed to be wearing identical jeans.

The central bus station was spinning, its bustling merry-go-round pouring forth streams of eastern songs from every hawker's stand: trading, wailing, bargaining, deceiving, offering weed in a whisper; copper coins were ringing in beggars' cups, threatening God's vengeance on the stingy.

The scum of the town, our contingent...

As in many countries, it wasn't the well-to-do classes of the population who used public transportation.

In those few hours, when they were handing in their uniforms and weapons, and as they were making their way, each on his own, to the bus station in Haifa, the weather had once again started to turn sour. Apparently, this endless February fog hadn't run its course. The sky soon clouded over with grey, and the dark mass kept growing thicker and heavier, as if some sort of excavation work was going on above...

They were sitting and glancing at each other. Salakh, outwardly serene, relaxed, was clearly satisfied with how things had turned out. Taking a sip of beer from his can and tossing his head back to swallow, he stared intently from under his half-closed eyelids at the investigator, even smiling. Even so, it was impossible for Arkady to get up and walk away, to wait somewhere else until the bus arrived.

But the main thing, it was impossible to explain to anyone who's not from around here why that was so impossible! Why his own humiliating significance held a can of beer in his hand and how Salakh tossed back his head to swallow, and how he was staring... It's simply that here, my dear West-is-West, one has only to live as little as half one's life in order to make sense of even the first thing about this unspoken language of glances, gestures and signs.

After the beer, Arkady wanted to pee before setting out, but here, too, he waited until Salakh couldn't hold it in, and then followed him. So they both stood over the urinals not far from each other...

Salakh chose a seat not too far towards the back of the bus, and Arkady forced himself not to turn around even once, sensing the stern, venomous gaze behind the back of his head.

Salakh got off at his village. He walked jauntily through the bus to the front door, and, as he got out, hesitated briefly on the steps, as if unexpectedly, cast a swift, slashing glance at the investigator's face, and grinned broadly... Once more Arkady forced himself to look directly into those grass-green eyes for two or three endless seconds.

That's all... What can you do here? Nevertheless, again and again he sorted obsessively through scenarios in which he could prove Salakh's guilt. Why, as a matter of fact, only *his* guilt? What about the father, the sister-hyena, silently watching over the last sigh of that one, *the other one*, with traces of rust-red death on her neck? Well, he said to himself, in that case, one third of the local population should be serving time in jail... Leave it, leave it alone, he moaned in Nadezhda's muted voice, they've lived like that for centuries. Have mercy on your own soul, fried in a saucepan of constant heartburn!

After getting off in Safed at the last station, he exhaled a little cloud of steam and looked around.

Three young Hasidim followed him out of the bus, all tall, slim, in black coats and black hats with cylindrical crowns. Each one held a covered black umbrella with a semicircular handle. Two were leaning on them, using them as canes.

Conversing softly in English, the young men looked around and set off up the road, circling around the unprepossessing box of the bus station. The hilly road crossed through a young wooded grove. And for several moments, as they climbed in a line into the smoke-blue, opal clouds, these detached and tangential figures reminded him of a drawing by Daumier.

The last things to vanish into the little gray lake of fog were their hats.

And these people are foreign to me... Everyone's foreign to each other in this foggy world here...

He felt like a drink.

As a matter of fact, he felt like getting drunk.

It was not often that he resorted to that strong and fast-acting treatment for desperate rage. All right then. Right he was... It's a good thing, Nadezhda thinks he's now somewhere in training, supervised, and well cared for.

He took a taxi to the center of town...

The fog prevailed here, too; mountains shrouded the town in a black wave, the highest ridge, by the mountain Meron, threatening to swallow and carry off into the infinite all the pitiful rubbish of human habitation: houses under tiled and flat roofs, with remains of rusty fittings and satellite dishes; remnants of stone walls and fences; shops shuttered by corrugated metal vandal screens, cars, bikes...

On Montefiore Street, winding down the hill, streetlights shone through murky halos. In the violet mist, the minaret of the former mosque, with its tiny little balcony encircling the cone, was barely visible.

Arkady settled with the taxi driver, walked through the arc and went down the stairs into the large, tiled inner courtyard of the Permanent Art Exhibition. Doors of various galleries and all sorts of drinking nooks led from here, large and small. At the moment, only one bar was open; he went in and ordered a drink and some nuts—many drinks and lots of nuts. He settled in, steadily downing his cognac and observing through the glass wall infrequent figures fording the well of the courtyard. Wading into thick clouds, a passerby stood rooted to the spot in confusion, as if trying to locate a reliable tussock in the middle of a swamp, then set off with uncertainty, as if swimming, unintentionally sweeping the air with his arms.

In the winter all the inhabitants of this town were transformed into sleepwalkers.

Well, it's time to go home. Ask the bartender to call a cab...

Didn't you get plastered, like the last swine, you disgraced old man?

"Hey, pal," said the bartender, wiping the counter and aligning tall goblets made of dark red glass, which reminded him of the tall young Hasidim in the fog, "are you okay?"

"You bet I am!" Arkady replied distinctly, raising his right hand.

"I see," said the bartender. He was what people call a chubby fellow—so friendly, bustling, never sitting down, even for a minute, although, besides Arkady, there wasn't another soul in the bar in this filthy weather. "Have you loaded up for the night? You know, we're only open until one o'clock... So you can stay here another half hour if you like."

"Don't worry," said Arkady. "I won't cause any problems."

"God forbid!" cried the fatso. "That never occurred to me... If you like, I can show you another little place—and you'll remember me for a good long time."

Arkady smiled warmly and sarcastically:

"What sort of new place do you plan to show me in our village?"

"You'll see," he replied and spent the next twenty minutes or so puttering over the counter, rubbing it with some sort of polish, loading dishes in the lower drawers, cashing out the register, and jingling his keys.

At last, he took off his jacket emblazoned with the name of the bar, put on a long raincoat over his sweater, and turned into an elegant, middle-aged city-dweller.

"Let's go," he said and pushed open the glass door into the fog, after which, for ten minutes or so, he patiently secured the stubborn lock without hurling one word of abuse at it.

That's the sort of patient fellow he should have on his team of investigators, Arkady thought.

They climbed the stairs to the square, where buses carrying groups of tourists were usually parked during the day. The whole square seemed to be rushing about in an agitated whirl of clouds. In all this restless motion, the square first unveiled a stray tomcat wandering along the stone fence of someone's studio, then the roof of someone's Audi parked temporarily on the corner, or the pale, preoccupied face of a late pedestrian.

"Well, I turn to the right," said the bartender. "But you look here," he said and grabbed Arkady by the shoulder, turning him slightly in the direction of some small alleys sunk in fog and dimly lit by streetlamps. "You climb up as far as the Synagogue of the Sacred Ari... go a little further to the first street on the right. It's not even a street, just a little dead end... The third house from the end, it looks like it's all locked up, and the shutters are closed... It appears as if no one lives there, but next to the lemon tree there are some stairs leading down to the cellar. The door is blue, iron... Push it and go in. It's easy."

Arkady couldn't recall anything resembling a café or bar in that little dead end.

"What's there?" he asked.

"Well... it's something like a *caravansery*... Cabalists gather there, all sorts of amusing folks... Sometimes there're as many as five, and other nights, the place is empty. But you can ask for wine from the owner—he's a night owl. If you really need it. And the wine, let me tell you, is special; they make it themselves from grapes gathered at night during a full moon, while they sing their own sacred songs."

"Really? And by any chance will I turn into an angel while I'm there?" Arkady asked.

The bartender slapped him on the back and said amiably: "Not exactly... The owner's an old man. His name is Duvid Azis. He doesn't ask for recommendations. He'll see through you like an x-ray machine!" He laughed and waved him on: "You can send him regards from Avi, that'd be me."

Arkady dutifully proceeded up to the Synagogue of Rabbi Isaac Luria, a cabalist, merchant, philosopher and wizard, in popular memory—the Sacred Ari—who lived here during the sixteenth century, knew all about miracles, and was buried in the local cemetery.

Even though you'd learned the stone tangle of old Safed like the fingers of your hand, on a foggy winter night you could easily get lost in its loops and knots, its unexpected turns and dead ends, its insidious alleys. The fog fools you, mixes up and changes the location of houses and streetlamps; the customary topography of familiar streets slips away, dumbfounds you; turning at the corner of a building, instead of the usual staircase to the upper street, you come upon a stone well and a huge wooden tub that were never there before: and just you try to find it tomorrow! The fog, like a dream, opens doors slightly and allows you to glance into the endless space, but if you cross the threshold, the depth vanishes, a puddle squelches beneath your foot, and a blind wall rises up before your very eyes with traces of blue paint on stone joints. You see an arrow with a sign for "local Safed cheese" and you head off in the indicated direction to purchase some famous sheep or goat cheese with garlic, caraway or dill, and a few olives in the bargain, and three hundred grams of halvah with nuts... But after turning three times and winding up in a series of passages and courtyards four times, you find yourself back at the same sign with the arrow, now with its point pointed right at you.

After wandering in circles for about twenty minutes in search of the required dead end, and without finding anything like it, Arkady wound up in an enclosed courtyard with some sort of synagogue he couldn't identify; in his annoyance, he wanted to turn back already, but there in the corner he noticed some narrow—only half a meter wide—worn stone steps that certainly led to the lower tier of streets; he recalled that precisely here—yes, yes, of course—there was supposed to be an almost vertical passage down.

Descending the steep stairs, he stumbled into the courtyard of a small bar, long since closed, climbed over the gate, and found himself on the famous tourist street of galleries, shops and restaurants... needless to say, all locked up and ensconced in fog.

When he made his way through the murky waves of yellow street-lamps, hardly moving his feet, to the house that the bartender had described to him, it turned out that indeed the windows were shuttered tight and completely sealed; not that the house had been abandoned or boarded up; obviously it had been strongly secured against the fog, the way a submarine seals its hatches in a storm and dives to the bottom.

But a lemon tree, and such a prolific one—covered with large fruit, the color of malachite in the light of the nearest streetlamp—was indeed growing next to the wall. Arkady went down to the low blue door leading into the cellar and pushed it open; it gave way easily and after crossing the threshold, he froze in amazement, then straightened up slowly.

I certainly got plastered...

It was a rather large cellar room, with a vaulted ceiling of small stones, like those in many old houses of this town, half forgotten in the heavens. It was lit not by an electric light, but by thick candles in four large, seven-pronged candelabras, placed on two casks, and a single square table in the middle of the cellar, at which two men sat facing each other.

Arkady immediately thought of them as *black and white*. The younger one, *black*, wearing the usual attire of a Hasid—a long black coat, hat, and a black beard touched with gray—sat over an open book, its pages folded to resemble two large waves on clean wooden boards with no tablecloth. There was nothing special about him: a typical figure from the streets of Old Safed.

But the other one, *white...*

Arkady had only read that such people still exist. He was entirely white. From head to foot, from gray curls tinged with yellow under a fox fur cap, to his white socks and white shoes with buckles, looking as if they'd been rented in the costume shop of some theater. His caftan was more of a pearly or smoky color, like the underside of a large seashell or a piece of old ivory, and sewn from special Syrian silk, of the rarest kind, produced only in Aleppo, and imported as contraband.

Between these two figures, sunk in deep serenity, stood two goblets and a large bottle of wine without a label. Everything was fashioned of thick, locally made green glass, which, because of the wavering flame of the candles, gave off thick yellow patches of light.

Neither *white* nor *black* turned his head, most likely neither had noticed the door opening. They continued talking...

"Hey, young fellow," someone on the left said quietly.

Arkady turned around and saw a tall old man standing in the corner near a counter, rather, behind three wide boards resting on two casks.

The old man was probably the owner described by the bartender; Arkady was surprised how long it had been since he'd been called a *young fellow*...

"Close the door, will you," said the old man. "Or else the fog'll come crawling in and bring the damp in with it."

He was slow moving, very gaunt, with a white knitted cap on his bald head; he resembled the Tatar yardman of their Moscow home at 6 Lesnaya Street...

Arkady greeted him, wanted to state his name and convey regards from Avi, but with a nod of his chin, the old man indicated the two men sitting at the table, and pulled out an old bentwood chair from behind the counter, shooing away the sleeping cat:

"Sit here."

The cat jumped down onto the floor, stretched itself out, and arched its back. She turned out to be a calico with three vivid colors: black and white, with red patches, and a striped tail like a country floor mat. The red patches on her back appeared orange in the lively flickering of the flames. But the most astonishing thing about her was her roguish expression, exactly like a harlequin mask, divided vertically into two halves, black and red. And the black half was blind and paralyzed, while in the red half one focused eye glimmered in the candlelight.

The old man, apparently, was engrossed by the conversation between the two, *black and white*. Automatically, almost without looking, he took a goblet of blown green glass down from the shelf and an unlabeled bottle, silently poured a little wine, and placed it on the board in front of the guest. He moved over a plate with a tall pile of small pitas, soft as pancakes.

Arkady tore one in half and began chewing eagerly; he took a swallow of the wine... He'd gotten hungry while searching for this strange place.

In a few minutes, he began listening to the voices of the two men and pricked up his ears because they were talking in some language that remotely resembled Hebrew... Aramaic, perhaps? However, from time to time, their speech cleared up a bit; it felt like when the wipers cleared the watery scum from his windshield, or when someone cleaned the sweaty lenses of his glasses with the hem of his sweater. Then Arkady began to understand more or less the meaning of their words...

So, it was some ancient texts that they were commenting on.

Black's voice, muffled and curt, supplied the counterpoint, but maintained the rhythm and set the pace for the conversation; *white's* voice, on the contrary—musical and richly intoned—would ascend and then descend to a heartfelt recitative. *White* spoke in long, expressive phrases, a bit theatrically, helping himself with well-rounded movements of his hand at the end of his phrases.

"Look, it says here: 'Who is this serpent that flies through the air and goes without a guide, whereas the ant between its teeth receives pleasure from this, the beginning of which is in society, and the end of which is in solitude? Who is this eagle, having fastened a nest to a tree, that doesn't exist? Who are its fledglings, having grown, but are not among creatures created in this place, but where they were not created?"[1]

With all the exoticism of his attire, *white*, as opposed to *black*, seemed simpler and more animated. He had a broad, duck-like nose, keen, jovial little eyes, a developed thorax, and strong calves. He could easily play the role of an older musketeer in some trashy Hollywood film, but outwardly he resembled Rembrandt, from the self-portrait where he's holding his homely, tow-haired, but beloved, wife Saskia on his lap.

"'Who are they that rising, descend, and descending, rise, two comprising one, and one equal to three? Who is that splendid woman on whom nobody rests his gaze, whose body is covered and revealed, who goes out in the morning and hides during the day, who puts on adornment of which there is none?'"

What is he babbling about? Or have I drunk myself into a state of complete stupefaction?

From time to time, Arkady groped for the bottle on his left and poured himself some wine, rather weak, but tasty—it wasn't clear what was sacred about it...

It was just fine that no one here took any notice of him, and that he was in no one's way. The old man, absolutely engrossed by the conversation of the other two, only occasionally turned to the chance guest and smiled at him absent-mindedly. From time to time, after one or another point was made in the heated disputation, the old man clapped his hands, tossed his head in mute ecstasy, and winked to himself as if to say, "Hey, look how clever I am!"

Only now did Arkady realize that the table stood in the middle of the room for a purpose; it was like a stage, a podium for such theological disputes.

---

[1] From the cabalist book *ZOHAR*.

"On the first day of creation when the Most High created darkness before light, the pre-element of fire is implied by that point, that which, before its appearance in our world as real fire providing light and warmth, remained cold and dark..." *Black* uttered these words slowly, the way a stutterer talks who has overcome his defect.

"Correct!" exclaimed *white,* and once again gestured with his arm, either in sympathy with what was said, or in support of his own words. It was the same way a conductor signals the strings to begin playing.

"There's a hint of this in the Book of Deuteronomy. It is said of the Revelation at Sinai: 'and thou didst hear His words out of the midst of the fire,' and then again, 'And it came to pass, when ye heard the voice out of the midst of the darkness.' Rashi's commentary on the word 'Darkness.'"

"What are they talking about?" Arkady asked the old man. With a raised hand he signaled Arkady to keep silent, and when *black* leaned over to flip through the pages of the book, he whispered in explanation:

"The idea is that, comparing two different accounts of one and the same event, they can grasp its essence... You ought to listen, listen to them! He's an important man, a great scholar from Jerusalem. His ancestor on the female side was the Maharal of Prague. Do you know who the Maharal was, blessed be his name? He was the great Cabalist who created the Golem..." He nodded his head with enthusiasm. "An important man... But *our fellow* isn't bad either!"

Arkady wanted to clarify which one of them was *our fellow,* and which one was from Jerusalem, the descendant of the Maharal, but said nothing. What difference does it make, he thought.

Meanwhile *white* continued with genuine animation, like an actor reciting poetry:

"But here's what Ramban writes: 'The second time in the same paragraph, the word *darkness* is used in its usual dictionary meaning as the absence of light, not as the indication of the pre-element of fire. At the very moment when light was divided from darkness, darkness and light

                                                    DINA RUBINA

became new entities. In the same way, the Most High had concealed the original light, having made it inaccessible to the impious, who—He knew—would appear in the future. And He predestined it for the righteous in the future world. Where is this original light preserved?"

"But both light and darkness are necessary to manage the world," *black* said, raising his voice slightly. "Rabbi Samson Raphael Hirsch of Frankfurt wrote about this: 'Light reveals objects in their individual existence, while darkness, temporarily hiding painfully harsh influences, makes the interaction of substances possible, strengthening their effectiveness...'"

God, did I get smashed...

Resting his head on his arms, Arkady managed to mentally compliment the wonderfully comfortable boards lying across the casks. It was better than any table and they smelled like summer: wood... wine... bread... How did it happen that, having lived in this town for so many years, he knew nothing about Duvid Azis's cellar and might live even longer knowing nothing about *black and white*? He could've missed them talking in the golden mist of this foggy winter night, the night in which darkness was mixed with light.

The tri-colored cat with the harlequin face jumped up onto the boards and lay down next to his elbow, as if she'd been sent by the old man to watch over the guest.

Occasionally, the old man stroked his back with his heavy soft palm, and shook him lightly, as if checking to see whether the guest was sleeping soundly, having downed half a bottle of the full-moon-song wine of the Cabalists of Sacred Safed...

But it seemed to Arkady that it was precisely at this moment that he heard and understood everything, without missing a single beat, not one profound nuance, not one additional interpretation; every one of *white's* words was illuminated by the sunny clarity of meaning, and every one of *black's* words shrouded essences and objects in the shadow of doubt.

Arkady felt that he must, absolutely must pose the question that had tormented him for the last few years: if the Most High, who was so concerned about the *manifestation of objects in their individual existence*, nevertheless permits the murder of one object by another, then shouldn't the aforementioned Most High *be hauled into court as an accessory to the crime?*

But he didn't have time to ask.

All of a sudden they both started to sing! In an authentic duet—a bass and a baritone tenor—with splendid intonation, as if they'd spent long nights here rehearsing. The melody reminded him somewhat of Bloch's *Nigun*, that passionate, desperate monologue of a violin hovering over the background; and Arkady was not at all surprised; of course, it should be like that. Where else, if not in music, would light and darkness be irreproachably combined, not canceling, but enriching each other?

They didn't sing of Day and Night, but of Morning and Evening—that's the beginning and the end, the end and the beginning, the eternal circle of knowledge. "Erev"—evening, the time when the outlines of the world blend together. "Boker"—morning, the time when things become distinct from one another, making it possible to discern their differences, to sense their boundaries, to perceive the dimensions of things, to experience in one's soul the beauty and splendor of the world...

...When he raised his head from the leaden weight of his arms and leaned against the curved back of the chair, dawn had already lit up the colored, bubble-fused glass of the two narrow windows over the door, casting long stripes, red and blue, on the small stones of the vaulted ceiling.

Doves were outside, calling at the dawn.

The four large candelabras, encircled by congealed tears of spent candles, stood in the same place on the table; above one holder curled smoke of the last spluttering flame, just like a belated argument in a terminated disputation.

There wasn't a soul in the cellar, but the large book still lay there, its pages still resembling two large waves. The bottles of wine stood on the shelf; on the boards in front of Arkady lay one lone lemon, lit softly by the greenish gold light of dawn.

On the floor, its tail spread out like a country floor mat, the silent cat with the harlequin face was diligently licking its red paw clean.

A vigorous shuffling sound reached the half-open door of the cellar—perhaps the old man was sweeping outside the house. He should thank him for his hospitality, but the strange night he had passed for some reason yielded only silence.

Groping around in his pockets, Arkady placed all the cash he had on the smooth boards. He had the vague feeling that the old man was not expecting any money, but he had to live off something! He placed the lemon he'd been given into his jacket pocket, waited until the sweeping quieted down, and then left the cellar.

He walked through the little streets at dawn, along endless stone fences with traces of blue paint, through a new, unfinished district of Breslav Hasidim; he gratefully gnawed on the very sour, tart lemon, puckering and smiling—how appropriate!

He emerged on the ridge of the mountain, near the old cemetery perched high above the road.

During the night, the fog had cleared; down below, sparse traces of the passing night floated like foam in a washtub...

On the neighboring mountain he could see the remains of some former houses, overgrown with hasty, greedy grass. The old graves descended along the slope into the damp, shimmering shadow of the valley, as if interrupting its triumphant march in a reverie, gathering in groups of three and four. It was the way clusters of people formed in a funeral procession, little groups chatting as they marched.

Below, they grouped together in a small stone flock, a part of them adorned with blue paint, in the very oldest section of the cemetery. On the small stone square, near the grave of the Sacred Ari, stood three tall black figures rocking back and forth—they had already started in on the first prayer...

From the depths of the valley arose a fog of Syrian silk, rising to the sky, melting over the mountains.

Morning was coming, *the time when things become distinct from one another, making it possible to discern their differences, to sense their boundaries, to perceive the dimensions of things, to experience in one's soul the beauty and the splendor of God's world...*

Arkady remembered how that fellow, handsome and unrestrained, before the funeral of his sister, had demanded an expert opinion on whether she was still a virgin. And Arkady wrote that she was, thinking about the blue-eyed soldier. In such cases Arkady always wrote that the deceased was a virgin.

He imagined how men young and old were sitting in the cemetery in their blue coats, in *galabiyas*, in their high round hats... They were waiting silently for the moment when, in a loud voice, the sheik would start reading aloud the expert's opinion, utter a prayer, and everyone would raise their hands, raking the air, then splashing their faces, as if with water, stroking their beards slowly.

"*Al-lah irkham-m-ma!*" the men will chant in a constrained, stern manner, from the depths of their souls. "Have mercy on her, O Lord!"

March 2007

TRANSLATION BY MICHAEL R. KATZ AND DENIS KOMAROV

  DINA RUBINA

Anyway

Dunya Smirnova

Why oh why did I dislike him so much at first? What's not to like about him, except for the good things? Authority. I don't like authority. No, that's not exactly true. It's not that I dislike higher-ups, but I do like it when they pay attention to me. And the way he came in: a young snob with slender fingers. And those shoes. Suede, without the tiniest little spot. And his foot in an expensive sock. Two feet. Ankles like my husband Valery Ivanovich's wrists. Ooh, what a stud. The iron!—it's sticking! Didn't I ask them to clean it? Now, just one stack. Just this one stack, and then I'm done—enough! This other stack, I'll give it a shot tomorrow. In fact, how about a shot right now? How I love that little shot, when they're all asleep! *How I adore—the deep-blue of your wonderful eyes—how I desire*—What was it that I just *desired*? Ah, I desired a drink. Shh!—the goblets are all in Kuvakin's toddler's bedroom. Not a clink. Aah, here she is, sleeping, all rosy-pink. Is it possible they would really call her "Toddler Kuvakin" at the daycare? "Toddler Kuvakin, everyone has to stand in pairs—do you need a special invitation?"

I need a special invitation. I need for him to look at me in a special way. He does look, of course. But not enough, no, not nearly. Goodness, does it have to glug so loud! They call it "white," but how could it be white when it's yellow? It's the bottle that's white. The bottle is clear, the stuff is yellow, and everything together is white. Like the light in a light bulb. My husband Valery Ivanovich will never find my stash. It is amazing, the extent to which a man can be lost in his own home! You could hide a child from him and raise it somewhere in a cupboard. He wouldn't even notice! It would grow till it grew a mustache and began to steal Valery Ivanovich's ties and bring women overnight—into the cupboard, of course. And Valery Ivanovich wouldn't know a thing. He is a dear, serious, good man. How can I hurt a man like him? But I'm going to have to hurt him. Oh, I will have to. Another glass, perhaps? Let's just finish this shirt, and then, the drink. This is who I am: I am an honest, decent woman, a mistress of the house, a mother, a fantastic employee. A Wonder-Woman. A Mamin-Sibiryak. A Rostov-on-Don. Now let's have another one, let's just put this on a hanger first. Let's see. What do we have here besides the pickles? Ah, here's a little apple for a chaser. I was just thinking of something interesting—what was it? Him. What if I got to work a little early tomorrow? He enters, and there I am, all fascinating, with exquisite ears. Laughing. But, on the other hand, how could I let him, being the decent woman that I am? That is, as soon as I'd let him, I'd stop being a decent woman. That's not fair. That's not playing by the rules. But who knows, he might not even ask. He'll ask. Inevitably. And if he doesn't—it's his loss. But I would then remain a decent woman. Well, it would, of course, be a pity, a big, big pity. *And happiness had been so near.* Ooh, I can't even think about it without this tiny bubble rising up out of my belly and bursting in my throat. No, no, no—no more fantasies, no more thinking! What a darling dress she's got on. She looks so utterly touching in it, with her childish neck, with those fine hairs at her temples. Toddler Kuvakin, my precious little girl. Let's iron the sundress, and then another glass. Oh, but it's a ways to go until the sundress! And I'm going to do the towels first. I'm sneaky that way. And mind you, I'm not here to drown some sorrow. The last time that happened

     DUNYA SMIRNOVA

was ages ago. I drank with Alka. But it was no fun with her, once she got going about her cooking pots and her shoes. What she's got with shoes is nothing short of a fixation. He only has gorgeous shoes. I like it when a man has serious shoes. That's important.

It's sticking again! If you don't clean it yourself, no one will. Better to buy a new one. Tomorrow, I'll buy one. That's it. One more.

All warm and hollow inside. My joy rolls back and forth down inside of me, like a tiny glass bubble. If I lean sideways, it rolls like a marble—my joy, my youth, my strength. My love, still fresh, unsullied. Tearless. Joyful. Goodness, how quiet it is here.

It's odd, Valery Ivanovich isn't snoring tonight. Let's go take a look how he is in there. Asleep. Covered up to his head—only the forehead and the nose are peeking out, and his foot is stuck out. Let me cover him. My dear husband, thirty times dear and two hundred eighteen times familiar. What is it that I, little slut, want to do with myself? My poor little monkey, my husband. Do you remember how I tore my own hair, how I waited for you when my phone got disconnected, and you didn't know and kept calling and couldn't get through? How desperately in love I was. And now I'm plotting to betray you. And I will, my heart knows—there's no way out of it. I just can't give him up. All my thoughts are about him. Not the same thoughts I think of you, but those deeper ones, inside the glass marble. That's how it is with you and me now. The main thing is for you not to know anything, not to get hurt. Forgive me, Valery Ivanovich! I will make it up to you, every little bit. I'll be your slave. How pitiful you are.

Good Lord! I forgot the iron in there! I run, right up against that goddamn corner—there will be a bruise for sure.

Thank God it didn't fall. Alright. What next? The handkerchiefs. They're nothing, a piece of cake. Is that all? Nothing else to iron? I thought I wouldn't finish this heap for the life of me. But I've finished! I've ironed everything—just look what a good girl I am. Now let's put it all away, and then a little sip before bedtime. I will get some sleep, wake up refreshed, in a spotless, beautiful home, put on my heels, my makeup, open my brand-new perfume, and, jingling the keys in my handbag, run through the lovely

May-time city, through the familiar streets, to work, where the heavy door waits with a tight coil and a cool handle, and then—the wide staircase, the room with a bay window, and he, my beloved, in that room. My beloved and incomparable—whatever else happens, however it happens. Anyway. His favorite turn of speech: anyway.

Tomorrow it will be sunny. I know.

                                                    DUNYA SMIRNOVA

Black Horse With A White Eye

Vladimir Sorokin

They were scything and also preparing for haymaking, the four of them resting between passes in completely different ways, each in his own manner.

Grandpa Yakov finished clearing three swathes in a row and pronounced, "Rest time!" He exhaled loudly and fell on one knee, grasping a bunch of felled grass with his swarthy crabclaw hand and wiping the scythe with it. Taking a whetstone from a leather case tied to his belt, he began quickly sharpening the blade, muttering something into his straggly red beard. His oldest son, Phil, or Fee-yul as everyone called him, was always drowsy and taciturn, with the same red beard as his father and the same firm, short hands. He laid the scythe on the grass and went to the edge of the meadow where Dasha and her mother were sitting under a young oak. Taking a few swallows from a lindenwood flask, he wiped his face with his shirtsleeve, squatted down on his haunches and just sat, looking around and squinting. Grisha, the middle son, whose narrow, thin face resembled his mother's, repeated after his father, "Rest time it is!" Breathing wearily, he took his scythe and headed toward a linden tree that jutted up in the middle of the meadow and had been cleft by lightning; he sat beneath the half-withered tree and sharpened his scythe a bit. The youngest son, Vanya, a skinny, narrow-shouldered, large-eared, freckled lad of not even fifteen, was using a small scythe appropriate for his height and always lagged behind the other mowers. He leaned his scythe on his shoulder and went over to his middle brother, where he lay on his stomach beneath the linden tree, propping up his sharp chin with two rough little fists and waiting for Grisha to finish his own scythe and sharpen his small one as well.

Dasha sat under the oak, leaning her back onto it and looking at the scythers, the meadow, the beetles, the bumblebees, the butterflies, and a lonely hawk that from time to time glided through the blue expanse above the meadow and the forest. Dasha liked the way the spotted hawk would circle so smoothly and then suddenly hang in the air in one place, quickly flapping its wings and peeping a complaint like a chick, before dropping abruptly down. Her mother sat nearby, leaning against the other side of the oak and knitting a stocking out of gray goat wool. From time to time she stood up and used a rake to turn over the cut grass, which hadn't yet become hay. Then Dasha would take her nutwood stick with the forked end and help her mother do the turning.

The Panins had a good meadow. It was level, smooth, and close to the village and the main road.

They'd been assigned it back in '35, thanks to the old chairman, her mother's relative.

It was only the first day the Panins were scything. For a fortnight, the entire village had been scything, raking and mowing the collective farm fields on the right side of the Bolva. They'd been lucky with the weather; it was a hot June with a dry wind, and as Grandpa Yakov said, "Plenty of hay on such a day."

Dasha had turned ten the day before. Her grandfather had woven her a new pair of bast shoes. Her father had given her a clay whistle and

　　　　　　　　　　　VLADIMIR SOROKIN

her mother a white scarf with a red fringe. Dasha was pleased. She stowed the scarf in her grandmother's trunk and went to the scything in her room-to-grow shoes, taking her whistle with her. Each time her father came under the tree to take a drink and sit on his haunches, Dasha would get her whistle out of the front pocket of her print dress, which had been sewn in Zheltoukhi by an itinerant tailor, and whistled. Her father looked at her approvingly and scratched his beard, smiling with his eyes. He was a quiet man.

Her mother was also not very talkative. Grandpa Yakov was the only one of the Panins with a lively tongue.

"So Dasha, how are you walking there?" he asked along the way to the haymaking. "The shoes don't let you walk; do they cover your ass too?"

Everyone laughed. Dasha grasped her grandfather's crooked, work-darkened finger with its thick black nail and ran alongside him, her new shoes scraping along the dusty road.

When the mowers had finished a third of the meadow and the sun was hanging in the sky and beating down upon them, Grandpa Yakov made a dismissive wave:

"Lunchtime!"

The mowers threw down their scythes and flocked beneath the oak. While they were drinking greedily and passing a flask back and forth, Dasha and her mother spread out a torn piece of burlap and began unloading provisions from a plaited basket. Half a loaf of rye bread, a bunch of green onions, a dozen baked potatoes, a crock of baked milk, a small piece of fatback in a scrap of rag and some salt in a paper twist.

"Bless us O Lord…" exhaled Grandpa Yakov wearily, took the loaf, pressed it to his chest, and began nimbly cutting off hunks of it using a big, old knife with a darkened wooden handle that had been worn thin.

The brothers each took a piece and immediately began eating.

Grandpa Yakov crossed himself, dipped a hunk of bread into the salt, took a bite, grabbed a long onion, crumpled it, thrust it into his mouth, and began chewing very quickly, which made his straggly beard quiver comically. Dasha liked looking at her grandfather while he ate. It seemed to her he'd suddenly turned into an old, helpless hare. The brothers ate somewhat seriously, as if they were working, becoming drearier and gloomier. The youngest, Vanya, had somehow during the meal suddenly grown up into a man like his father and Grisha.

Mother cut up the fatback into eight pieces and passed them out to the men. The fatback was old and yellow; the hog had died last summer from some unknown disease and they'd only gotten a new piglet in the spring. But then there was the cow, Docha. And she gave a lot of milk.

Mother set the crock of baked milk in the middle of the cloth, passed out wooden spoons, pierced the dark brown crust that had hardened on the mouth of the crock with her spoon, and stirred it:

"Eat up y'all..."

The flesh-colored milk was mixed with the thick, white sour cream that had gathered on the top. After bolting down the fatback, the men slipped their spoons into the crock. Dasha and her mother waited for them to finish scooping, and thrust their spoons in.

The milk was cool and tasty. Dasha spooned it up, slurping loudly, and began eating her bread. She liked the yellow flecks of butter in the baked milk more than anything. At home they only churned butter for Easter, when her grandmother made buckwheat pancakes. The butter smelled very tasty and melted right there on the pancakes. There was never enough of it.

Her mother ate as she usually did, without hurrying, holding a spoonful of milk over her palm, swallowing quietly, and leaning her small head, wrapped in a faded dark-blue scarf, docilely to one side.

The men slurped down the milk, snuffling loudly.

"The dew dried up mighty fast today..." Grisha muttered, wiping milk off his chin. "Scythin' when it's dry, it's a real..."

"Heat like 'is, how else?" Fee-yul broke up a baked potato, dunked it in salt, and took a bite.

"No mind. We'll git it down in time," said Grandpa Yakov, quickly slurping his milk.

"Long as it dries all the way through." Dasha's mother scooped out a large dollop of sour cream and held it out to Dasha. "There you go, eat the top."

Dasha licked her spoon and placed it on the burlap. And took the spoon from her mother with both hands. It was filled to the rim, overflowing with sour cream. Thick and white, it just barely fit into the new wooden spoon, seeking a way to crawl over the edge. Dasha brought the spoon to her mouth carefully. The sour cream settled, quivering. Its top sagged. A ray of midday sun penetrated the oak leaves, fell on the rounded white mound of sour cream, and flared up. The yellow butter flecks in the sour cream shone brightly. Dasha opened her mouth. And suddenly a dark reflection fell across the tenderly shining whiteness. Dasha looked around.

A black horse was standing nearby.

Dasha gave a start. The sour cream tore itself away from the spoon and plopped down onto her knee. And everyone saw the horse.

"What the..!" Grandpa Yakov started in surprise and squinted.

The horse shied sideways from the sitting group, stepped away, and stood a bit off, swishing its tangled, black tail. It was a deep raven color, stocky, with a wide chest and bones like all peasant horses, a large head, small ears, and a thick, shaggy, long-untrimmed mane. The mane was thick with burrs. Horseflies buzzed over the horse's glossy back.

"Mother o' mine..." sighed Dasha's mother, crossing herself and placing a hand on her small chest. "What a fright I got, the devil..."

"Whose mare is she?" Grisha stood up.

"Not our-uns," said Grandpa Yakov, laying down his spoon. "Black' uns weren't never raised around here."

Grisha walked towards the horse, pulling a strap out of his trousers on the way. Standing sideways, the mare turned her nose toward him, bending down and extending her nostrils. And everyone noticed at once that her left eye was completely clouded.

"Look, she's blind in one eye!" Grisha smirked, approaching her. "Don't be afraid, don't be afraid."

The horse jumped to the side. And turned her left side.

"Grisha, go to the left, where her blind eye is," advised Grandpa Yakov. "She must've strayed over from Bytosh, the vagrant."

"No Dad, she came from the gypsies." Fee-yul scowled at the horse and started to get up. "They set up camp again in Zheltoukhi. That's where she ran from. Raggedy and stanky."

Grisha approached the horse carefully, making the strap into a loop and holding it behind his back. But the horse jumped away again.

"Eh, you varmint..." laughed Grisha.

"Holeup Grisha." Fee-yul broke off a piece of bread and went over to the horse. "There you go, raggedy girl, take it..."

Moving in tandem, like hunters, they began carefully closing in on the horse from both sides. The horse fell still, twitching her small ears and snuffling a little. Grisha and Fee-yul began moving very slowly, like in a dream. And Dasha became very uneasy for some reason. Her heart began to pound. She held her breath and watched how craftily they were approaching the horse, her father with a piece of bread on his palm, and Uncle Grisha with a loop behind his back.

"Don't be afraid, don't be afraid..." murmured Grisha.

The men came quite close, then stopped. Fee-yul held out the bread almost to the horse's nose. Grisha tensed and bit his lip. The still horse snorted and ran headlong between them. The men flung themselves on her, clutching her mane. Dasha closed her eyes. The horse neighed.

"If only they didn't catch her!" Dasha implored suddenly, without opening her eyes.

She heard the horse neighing and the men cursing.

Then the neighing stopped.

"Aw, your mother..." said her father spitefully.

"Wild bitch..." said Grisha.

Dasha realized they hadn't caught the horse. And opened her eyes.

In the meadow stood her father and Grisha. The horse was gone.

"And you morons!" said Grandpa Yakov angrily, waving his hand at them. "Can't even catch a horse."

"She's wild, Dad." Grisha began placing the strap back into his slipping trousers.

"Running around the forest like a tramp." His father picked up the bread that had dropped and walked over to place it on the burlap.

"If she's blind and wild, what good is she?" muttered Dasha's mother and began spooning the sour cream from Dasha's lap.

Dasha's knees were trembling.

"What's with you? Did you get scared?" Her mother smiled.

Dasha nodded her head. She was *very* glad they hadn't caught the horse. Her mother held out a spoon of sour cream to her again. Dasha took it and swallowed the thick, cool sour cream greedily. The men who had jumped up sat down again, grasped their spoons, and took to slurping up the rest of the milk. The wild mare's appearance and disappearance had stirred them up. They started talking about horses and the gypsies who stole them, about the useless new chairman, about the stable roof that had fallen in on the collective farm, about buckwheat and the clover on the other side, about the nighttime cutting in the glades near Mokry and about Mokry carpenters, and suddenly began arguing over whether it was better to split shingles from a stolen pine in your own shed or in Kostya's bathhouse.

Dasha wasn't listening to them. After the horse had run away, she felt better and lighter.

"Dasha, what're you sittin' around for?" Her mother said, adjusting her crooked scarf. "Go pick us some berries."

Dasha stood up unwillingly, took an empty basket, hung it on her shoulder, and went to the far edge of the meadow.

"Don't go far," said her father, licking his spoon.

Dasha went first through the stubble, her new shoes rustling loudly, then through the standing grass, frightening the chattering grasshoppers. The grass had warmed in the sun, and her legs were hot in it. Dasha crossed the entire meadow and looked back. The men had gotten up to scythe. Dasha pulled her whistle out of her pocket and whistled loudly. Her mother waved a hand at her. The birds in the forest surrounding the meadow answered the whistle. Dasha whistled again. She listened to the voices of the birds. She whistled. She put the whistle away and went into a sparse wood at the narrow end of the meadow. There was a young stand of birches there with clusters of strawberry plants in it. Dasha went in under the birches, took the stiff bastwood basket from her shoulder, placed it on the grass, and began picking berries and taking them to the basket. There were a lot of strawberries, but nobody had picked the entire patch yet. Dasha plucked the ripe and the not-so-ripe berries and dropped them in the basket, eating the bigger ones herself. The strawberries were sweet. Dasha picked the strawberries from one clearing, then carried the basket into another. Suddenly a bird took wing from beneath her feet, fluttered its wings, flew off, and sat on a birch tree. Dasha pulled out her whistle and whistled. The bird responded with a slender, jerky peep, just like a whistle. Dasha was surprised. And whistled again. The bird answered. Dasha went up to the bird. The bird took wing, flew off, and lighted somewhere again. Dasha had time to notice that the bird was spotted, like a hawk, but much smaller. Dasha whistled. The bird answered. Grandpa Yakov had told Dasha that birds have their own language, but only holy people and bird catchers can understand bird language.

"The whistle speaks bird!" Dasha whispered.

She wanted to ask the bird about life in the forest and about the treasures her grandmother said were guarded by the hunchbacked forest-spirits. She went through the birch stand toward the bird, blowing on her whistle. The bird answered.

But, after letting Dasha closer, it took off again and flew away, fluttering its wings.

Beyond the birch stand an old thick pine forest began. The bird flitted into it.

"Come back here, you nuisance!" shouted Dasha, like the grownups did at an unruly animal.

She thought the bird had flown to its nest, like a chicken. And nests were always set up in quiet places so there wouldn't be any hindrance. That must be where the bird's nest was, in the dark pine forest. It'll perch there, settle in, and tell her about the treasures, and show her the secret places. And she and Daddy could get a shovel and go and dig it up. And buy a horse. And ride it to Lyudinovo. And buy all kinds of good things there.

Dasha walked out of the birch stand, made her way between two enormous hazelnut bushes with their warm, soft leaves, stepped over a crumbling tree overgrown with moss and dried-up toadstools, and raised her eyes.

The fir wood stood before her in a shadowy wall. Dasha entered into it. The tall firs closed in over her head. And the sun was hidden. Her shoes were suddenly able to step softly. It was cool and very quiet inside the wood. Dasha whistled. There was a faint bird peep in the depth of the wood.

"Oh, you..." Dasha muttered, and moved toward the whistle.

She walked between the fir trunks over the soft earth strewn with fir cones and needles. All around her it became still more gloomy and quiet. Dasha stopped. Up ahead in the half-gloom the fir trunks pressed closer to each other. It seemed to her that there, up ahead, was night. And that she could enter into it. It was dreadful. Dasha glanced back to where the birch stand bathed in sunlight was still visible. There, in the meadow, her father and mother were waiting. But she had to find the bird. Dasha whistled. The forest was silent. She whistled again. The bird responded from up ahead. And Dasha moved forward, into the night, toward the bird's voice. She strode along the soft earth, rounding and touching the rough trees, skirting tree stumps, tearing spider webs, and stepping through dry branches. And suddenly she arrived at a completely straight alleyway. The stout firs stood in front of her in two rows, just as if someone had planted them long, long ago. The firs were enormous, old, and half-dead. Their trunks, eaten away by beetles, gaped with dark hollows and spreading crevices filled with petrified resin. Dasha entered the alleyway. It was completely dark up ahead. Decay wafted from there. Dasha whistled. The bird responded. Dasha went down the alleyway. The shadows thickened, and the powerful fir branches wove themselves together above, hiding both sun and sky. Up ahead something small and white appeared.

"The bird!" thought Dasha at first, but then she remembered the bird was spotted.

The small whiteness was hanging in the middle of the alleyway.

Dasha went closer to it. It hung motionless. Then disappeared. And reappeared again. Dasha went quite close. The white disappeared again. And reappeared. Dasha watched attentively. And suddenly she noticed that the small whiteness was the clouded eye of a horse. It blinked. Dasha looked at it some more. And saw the entire black horse. The same one. The horse was standing in the dark alleyway. It was barely visible in the half-gloom. Its black body seemed to merge with the shadowy air that smelled of needles and resin.

Dasha stopped still.

She wasn't frightened at all. But she didn't know what to do.

The horse didn't move at all. Her lips weren't chewing and her nostrils weren't drawing in air.

"Sleeping?" thought Dasha, and looked at the mare's healthy eye. Damp and a deep violet, like a plum, it was looking somewhere off to the side. Not at Dasha at all.

"Don't be afraid," Dasha pronounced.

The horse gave a start, as if she'd woken up. Her nostrils exhaled air.

"Don't be afraid," Dasha repeated.

The horse stood as motionless as before. Dasha carefully extended her hand and placed it on the horse's lips. They were warm and velvety.

"Don't be afraid, don't be afraid..." Dasha stroked the horse's lips with her strawberry-sticky fingers.

The horse slowly lowered her head. She sniffed the needly ground. And fell still with her head lowered. Continuing to stroke the horse's lips and nostrils, Dasha squatted down on her haunches. The clouded eye was quite close. Dasha stared at it. The eye was not entirely white. The middle was dark with a small black pupil ringed in slender darkish blue. Dasha brought her face close to the unusual eye. It blinked. The horse stood as motionless as before, her head lowered. Dasha examined the eye. It reminded her of a tube their teacher, Varvara Stepanovna, had brought from

     VLADIMIR SOROKIN

Lyudinovo and showed them in class. The tube was called by a long grown-up word that started with a "k" sound. Dasha didn't remember the word and called the tube a "carol-carol." There was a small hole in the tube. You had to look into it while turning the other end of the tube toward the light. You could see a red flower in the tube. If you turned the carol-carol, the flower turned into different flowers, and they became so many, and all of them were so beautiful and so different that it took your breath away, and you could spend your whole life turning and turning that tube.

Dasha peered into the horse's eye.

She was sure everything in the horse's eye was the whitest of white, like winter. But there turned out to be no white at all in the white eye. To the contrary. Everything in there was red. And there was so much red stuffed in the eye, and it was all so large and *deep*, like the whirlpool by the mill, and it was so very-very-very *thick* and *greedy* as it sat oozing and *threatening*, rising up and swelling like dough. Dasha remembered chickens' heads being chopped off. And the sloshing red throat.

And suddenly she clearly saw a Red Throat in the horse's eye. And there was a lot of it.

And Dasha felt such dread that she froze, like an icicle.

The white eye blinked.

The horse took a breath. Her whole body gave a start. She snorted. Lifted her head, noisily drawing the shadowy air into her nostrils. And without paying Dasha any mind, went into the deep wood.

Dasha stayed squatting on her haunches, not breathing. And suddenly she *realized* she would never in her life see that black horse again. She had walked out of Dasha's life like out of a barn. She wandered, snuffling a little. And soon disappeared from sight among the trees.

Dasha sat on the ground. Her hands sank down onto the fir needles. And her terror passed immediately. Dasha felt wistful somehow. She felt terribly tired. And very thirsty.

She stood up and went toward the light. Leaving the forest, she squinted from the bright sun. In that time it had become still hotter. She found her basket in the field amid the birch stand, hung it on her shoulder, and went to the meadow.

The men had reached the middle of the meadow with their scythes. Her mother was turning the hay. Dasha went up to her.

"Well, was there good pickins?" Adjusting the scarf that had slipped over her eyes, her mother glanced into the basket and started laughing. "That's it? A lot!"

"I looked into the horse's eye. There's a red throat in it." Dasha said, and unexpectedly broke out in tears.

"What's with you?" Her mother took her in her arms and touched her forehead. "My girl got overheated..."

Dasha's mother carried her, crying, under the tree and sprinkled some water on her. After crying herself out, Dasha drank her fill of water and fell into a deep sleep. When she woke up she was in the arms of her father, who was carrying her home to the village. The sun had set, the cows had arrived home and were lowing, and the dogs were barking.

Her grandmother and three-year-old brother Vovka were waiting at home. Night was already falling as they sat down to supper by the kerosene lamp. Grandma pulled a kettle of warm soup out of the stove. They ate it with freshly-baked bread, silently. Dasha swallowed the soup greedily and chewed the fresh tasty bread. Her mother touched her forehead.

"It's passed..."

"Grandma's girl got overheated!" Grandpa Yakov winked at Dasha.

"A touch o'sun, you know how 'tis..." nodded her solid-bodied, wide-mouthed grandmother.

After eating, everyone headed off to sleep in different places: Grandpa Yakov in the garden, Grisha and Vanya to the hay loft, mother and little Vovka in the cottage, and Grandmother on the Russian stove. Dasha's father, yawning, started putting out the copper-bellied lamp with its tasty smell of kerosene. But Dasha latched on to his pantleg.

"Daddy, what about the page?"

"The page..." her father remembered, and smiled into his beard.

Every evening Dasha tore a page off the calendar that hung on the wall near the clock and the wooden frame with photographs. In the frame were her father in a soldier's uniform, her mother and father with flowers and kissing doves drawn around them, Grandpa Yakov with a rifle during the First World War and him again with the old chairman at a fair in Bryansk, a KV tank, Stalin, Budyonny, and the actress Lyubov Orlova.

Dasha's father lifted her up and she tore a page from the calendar.

"Go ahead, read what tomorrow will be," her father said, as always.

"June twenty-second...Sun...day..." read Dasha aloud.

Her father placed her back on the ground:

"Sunday. Tomorrow we'll go scything again. Sleep!"

And he gave her a joking swat on the ass.

TRANSLATED BY DEBORAH HOFFMAN

The Novel
(A Tragedy)
VLADIMIR VOINOVICH

Not long ago I wrote a tragic novel about the life of émigrés. The novel is called… Actually, I can't remember what it's called; I'll have a look at the manuscript and write in the title later.

Although it took me about two and a half years to write the novel, I can't say I pushed myself particularly hard. The work generally flowed easily. All I had to do was write one line, and another would immediately write itself in my imagination, and after that a third one. I experienced no difficulties in describing nature or the state of the characters, while the plot unfolded as though of its own accord.

The storyline, incidentally, was extremely simple. A Russian émigré writer discovers that his wife has been cheating on him with his best friend, an artist. He kicks up a stink, and she has no other option but to leave him for the artist. As soon as she leaves, he realizes that he can't live without her for a single second. He calls her, and she immediately returns, because she cannot live without him. But once she has come back, she realizes that she can't live without the artist. The situation is made more complicated because the writer and the artist cannot live without each other. The three of them curse and swear at each other, and then declare their mutual love. They try various ways of resolving the problem. Either the writer throws the woman out of the house, or the artist does. Sometimes she leaves one for the other of her own accord. Sometimes she leaves both of them. Sometimes the writer gets sick of both of them and goes away, but cannot hold out and returns. Another time, the artist goes away. Then they decide to live together, all three—and live suffering from jealousy and hatred. Then they realize that they should all actually split up. It ends up with all three of them wearing formal evening attire in the artist's workshop. They put on a record of Schubert and drink champagne by candlelight. The champagne, of course, is poisoned.

That's the novel in a nutshell. I wrote the last full stop about a month ago, and straight away took the manuscript to my publisher.

Yesterday the publisher invited me round. We sat in soft, leather armchairs in his office, which is hung with portraits of his best writers (my portrait, of course, is among them). Between us was a coffee table, on which lay a book, title side down.

Before starting the conversation, the publisher offered me something to drink: coffee, cognac, whisky, beer... I asked for a coffee. He poked his head round the door and gave an order. His secretary brought the coffee, then left us. Stirring the coffee, the publisher looked at me carefully and said:

"Listen, Vladimir, you've written a wonderful novel!"

"Yes," I said humbly. "I think so too."

"I cried while I was reading through it."

"So did I," I admitted.

"And the last scene, when they drink poisoned champagne by candlelight while listening to Schubert, is sublime. There's nothing like it in world literature."

"Yes," I agreed. "I thought so too."

"Now, Vladimir, listen to me carefully. The thing is, we already printed this novel two and a half years ago."

I was surprised. "You printed it before I'd even written it?"

"No, no. We haven't reached quite that level of sophistication yet. Two and a half years ago you wrote this novel, and we published it. It was a huge success, it got rave reviews, you won an award for it and gave a marvelous acceptance speech at the ceremony."

"That's impossible," I exclaimed. "Do you really think I can't remember what I wrote?"

"I don't think anything," he sighed. "But here is your manuscript, and here is your novel in printed form."

He turned over the book lying on the table and held it out to me.

I felt ill. I saw that the printed novel, just like the manuscript, was called… Now I can't remember what it was called. I'll have a look later and tell you then. Confused, I put the book and the manuscript into my briefcase and went home, forgetting to say goodbye to the publisher. At home I pulled out the book and the manuscript and began comparing them. As I was reading, I wept.

Interestingly, not only had I written the same novel word for word with the same title and the same number of chapters and words, but even the punctuation marks were the same throughout. This was even more surprising, as I'm usually pretty haphazard with punctuation.

I cried all night. I cried over the awful misfortune that had befallen me. How, I wondered, could this have happened? I'm not yet old enough to be struck down by such total senility. For two and a half years, I had written this novel straight through, passionately and in a fit of inspiration. I had smoked thousands of cigarettes and drunk gallons of coffee. Everything had turned out so well that, by turns, I laughed at my creation, or showered myself in tears, or slapped myself on the back, exclaiming: "Way to go, Pushkin, you son of a bitch!" And what of it?

When it was nearly morning, I decided that I would go to see the doctor as soon as I got up. Of course, the illness was at an advanced stage, but even so, there must be some medicine for it—some kind of anti-sclerotic or whatever it's called.

It was already getting light when I finally fell asleep.

After waking up, I decided to postpone my visit to the doctor. Never mind, I thought. I've just wasted two and a half years for nothing. To hell with them. It's a shame, of course, but I'm not going to spend my time going to see doctors. I'll get started on a new novel straight away instead. Especially as I have a splendid idea that I've been nurturing for two and a half years. The plot is extremely simple. A Russian émigré writer discovers that his wife is cheating on him with his best friend, an artist. He kicks up a stink, she leaves him, various other collisions happen (I still haven't thought of everything yet), and it ends up with all three of them getting together in the artist's workshop, putting on a record of Schubert and drinking poisoned champagne by candlelight.

Actually, I've got everything all thought out already, and in about two or maybe two and half years I'll probably finish this novel.

TRANSLATION BY PETER MORLEY

VLADIMIR VOINOVICH

Rehabilitating d'Anthès

VIKTOR YEROFEYEV

I arrived in old Soultz-Haut-Rhin at about three in the afternoon, when the French finish their "second breakfast" and stroll out of restaurants with wooden toothpicks in their mouths. Unlike Obernai or Colmar, Soultz is a moribund, remote and extremely poor Alsatian town. On the central square under a hulking Catholic Church, I searched for a parking place among French compact cars. I noticed that my new silver Audi with German plates was drawing covetous stares from the locals.

I asked one, who had the red nose of a lover of dry wine, "Where is the D'Anthès Museum?"[1]

---

[1] Georges-Charles d'Anthès (1812–1895) came to Russia and entered military service after the 1830 revolution in France. In 1836 his father granted permission for him to be adopted by Baron Heeckeren, the Dutch Plenipotentiary to the Russian court, a convert to Catholicism and a bachelor, after which d'Anthès added de Heeckeren to his name. Welcomed in Russian high society, d'Anthès flirted openly with Natalya (née Goncharova, also called Natasha) Pushkin, the wife of the poet Alexander Pushkin (1799–1837) and then married Natalya's sister Yekaterina (called Katya and KoKo) in 1837. Rumors, anonymous letters and talk about the relationship between Natalya and d'Anthès eventually led to a duel

He pointed me in the right direction with an unfriendly wave of his hand. In just five minutes I was walking into the museum, under the intent gaze of two French girls, who were sitting on a bench and eating ice cream, their splayed legs in blue knee socks. I bought a rather expensive ticket from a dark-haired woman who was some kind of museum guide and quickly realized that the museum was only partially about d'Anthès. The first floor had local history. The third floor, where I didn't go, had some kind of Israeli exhibition. But the second floor was dedicated to d'Anthès and his family.

I immediately saw an outsized portrait of the Baroness de Heeckeren d'Anthès, née Yekaterina Goncharova, in a ball gown and holding a lorgnette, painted by the decidedly mediocre artist Henri Beltz in 1841. It said that she married d'Anthès on January 10, 1837, which meant that Pushkin dueled with him in the midst of his honeymoon. Judging by the portrait, Yekaterina was an unattractive, long-nosed brunette with oily hair. True, the portrait had sumptuous breasts painted rather poorly by Beltz, but all the same Yekaterina seemed lost and vague, and in her eyes was the question: "What am I doing here?" If you put Yekaterina in a bikini on the beach at the resort of Koktebel today, she would sit out her whole vacation alone, gazing romantically at the bay, unless some local hot-blooded Tatar with gold teeth first drank down a Tatar's Dream cocktail (one part vodka and one part white port wine) and went into ecstasies over her pale northern skin. Yekaterina Goncharova's deeply cracked marble gravestone was leaning heavily against the wall next to her portrait, as if there were no other place for it. This disconcerted me. It was as if the Last Judgment had already come and the dead had crawled out of their graves. I must have turned around as if looking for an answer when the dark-haired museum

---

between Pushkin and d'Anthès on January 27, 1837. D'Anthès fired first and mortally wounded Pushkin, who died two days later. D'Anthès was arrested, but was later pardoned and banished from Russia. Yekaterina joined him in Europe.

[2] *The Gabrieliad* (*Gavriiliada*) is a poem satirizing the Virgin Birth of Christ, which came to the notice of the Russian authorities in 1828. Although Pushkin denied authorship, the poem is generally thought to be have been written by him.

     VIKTOR YEROFEYEV

guide glided towards me. She had the most suspicious resemblance to Yekaterina Goncharova.

"Shall I give you a tour?"

"For free?" I blurted out.

"Are you Russian?"

"Why do you think that?"

"You look like Pushkin."

"In what way?"

"You have expressive eyes."

"I never noticed."

"All Russians look like Pushkin."

"I think I'll just walk around on my own."

There were two portraits of Georges d'Anthès. One was a flattering silhouette portrait of him as a young man, the deep black of his profile reflecting his role in Russian culture. The second image of d'Anthès was a nearly photographic likeness. Good God, in his old age d'Anthès looked exactly like Turgenev.

The dark-haired woman spoke again. "Isn't it true that he looks like Turgenev, while his name reminds one of Dante?"

"Everyone looks like someone else here," I grumbled.

She took my words as an invitation to talk.

"Here is a copy of the anonymous letter that named Pushkin as a full member and historiographer of the Order of Cuckolds."

In the same display case was, for some reason, the 1924 French edition of *The Gabrieliad*,[2] the only book by Pushkin in the entire museum. I recalled words from that poem which undermined the foundations of the church: *There is no Zeus. We have been made wiser....*

"Is that supposed to be a dig?"

"The Baron was very pious. Pushkin was the only man he killed. It's quite possible that the Baron was the Instrument of Fate. I have proof that Pushkin was grateful to him for that."

I couldn't take it anymore. "What are you talking about? I came here for a specific reason. My cultured mother asked me to spit on the grave of d'Anthès."

The guide picked up on my phrase. "I shall spit on your graves!" she said, laughing.

That was the name of a novel by Boris Vian, which didn't have anything to do with either Pushkin or d'Anthès.

"The cemetery closes soon. We should hurry."

I looked at the two well-known color lithographs of Pushkin hanging by the portrait of Yekaterina Goncharova. I surreptitiously winked at them and went towards the exit. She stopped me on the stairs.

"Write something in the guest book."

I declined, but after a moment's thought, I took my time writing "Bitch!" in big letters on an empty page.

"Bitch!" the woman read aloud with a funny accent. "Thanks to Russian tourists, we've started to learn Russian here. You ought to read what they've written."

I wasn't original. The guest album was filled with Russian indignation. Students from Arkhangel University penned, "We are disgusted to the bottom of our hearts by your criminal gunshot!" "Shame on the murderer of our 'Everything'!" was the comment of a conceptualist poet from Smolensk. "Why?" asked the Russo-French Society. In addition to multiple "bitches," there was also "whore!", "faggot!", "jerk!", and even "fascist!"

Refreshed, we left the museum and walked to my car.

"Every year there are more Russian tourists. It's like the floodgates have opened. They come by the busload. They go to restaurants and recite Pushkin by heart. This is improving the economy of Soultz, and we are considering becoming sister cities with Pskov or the Pushkin estate museum at Mikhailovskoye."

"That will never happen," I said.

"Oh, yes it will," she said, nodding optimistically.

"What's your name? Agnes? Fine, Agnes," I said. "The Russian nation, as you see, hates d'Anthès."

          VIKTOR YEROFEYEV

"Thanks to that, he is probably the most famous Frenchman in Russia, next to Alexandre Dumas. Imagine if you had killed Louis Aragon in a duel of honor. You'd have been famous in France."

"Ridiculous! Why would I have wanted his Elsa Triolet?" I said with disgust.

"Why do Russians have such good cars these days?" Agnes asked as she slipped into my Audi.

"We work a lot."

Agnes pointed to the sign on the corner. "d'Anthès Street," she announced proudly.

"Once people know the truth, they'll change it," I replied.

On the way to the cemetery, we stopped at the d'Anthès family estate. We pulled up next to a gloomy gray building that looked empty and long abandoned. Enormous trees grew in the park. The only light came from a window in one of the wings of the palace in a new restaurant called Pushkin.

"That's a kick," I said with satisfaction. "Where's the d'Anthès Restaurant?"

"It went out of business. Remember this palace well," Agnes said. "It was here that Pushkin met with d'Anthès."

I looked at her as if she was crazy, and her resemblance to Yekaterina suddenly began to gnaw at me. At one point I even wondered it was wise to go to the cemetery with her, but I didn't know the way and was afraid I'd get lost.

"You Russians," said the city museum guide, "love to hate everyone. How you hated the tsar, Jesus Christ, Trotsky, Tito, De Gaulle, millions of enemies of the people, and finally Stalin! But now? With that Slavic generosity of soul, you've rehabilitated all of them, and now you venerate them. The time has come to rehabilitate the good Baron Georges d'Anthès. He is our town benefactor. He was the best mayor—there was no one better and there never will be. He restored old buildings and put in a sewer system."

"He bore the mark of a scoundrel!" I cried. "Why did he come to Russia if a sewer system awaited him here?"

"Why? He was a young dissident who didn't accept the outcome of the 1830 revolution. With his aunt's help he came under the protection of the Russian imperial court. Pushkin wrote well of him in a letter to his father. He was handsome and intelligent, and he wielded the pen as well as he did the sword—"

"Stop it," I said.

"We're here," Agnes said.

A sign read: "NO DOGS IN THE CEMETERY ON OR OFF LEASH."

Alsace is truly lovely, and I understand why Germans still come here to weep over their lost territory: All the cities still have their German names, and the population speaks German as well as they speak French. The Rhine valley, covered with vineyards, was beautiful; the noisy creeks wending down the soft green mountains to the Rhine were beautiful; the country roads, pastures and farms were beautiful; the dusky sky over our heads was beautiful. And the cemetery where we found ourselves was also beautiful in the Alsatian way. It was modestly elegant without fuss, with stone crosses cracked by moss and covered with crawling spiders. The exception was one French artilleryman who wished to be buried under a monument depicting a large, old cannon with trunnions—a structure more appropriate to the New Maiden Monastery cemetery.[3] But everything else had succumbed to quiet, faded mourning. I began to imagine the honorable grave of Russia's enemy built on the money of a grateful town. I was getting vexed at his posthumous well-being when Agnes led me to a strange graveyard ghetto.

Yes, that's what I'd call it—a ghetto, although nothing in this corner of the cemetery looked stereotypically Jewish. But neither did it look like anything around it. All the graves in the Christian cemetery were properly aligned from West to East, toward salvation, but the dozen identical graves of the d'Anthès family, like one single grave of the *damned*, lay with their heads to the North. The new marble gravestones and small marble crosses placed over the d'Anthès family—who had obviously been moved here and

---

[3] The New Maiden (Novodevichy) Monastery cemetery is the final resting place for Russian and Soviet luminaries, many of whom are memorialized with elaborate monuments.

         VIKTOR YEROFEYEV

reburied after the descendants of the family went bankrupt in the 1960s—seemed to have been knocked askew, as if someone had been tossing and turning under them for a long time. They reminded me of children's paper boats sailing this way and that in the spring. Amidst this funereal uniformity I had no trouble finding the resting place of the murderer Georges and the nearby grave of Yekaterina, who died giving birth to her fourth child on October 15, 1843. There was also the grave of the "shameless pimp," the Dutch envoy, whom Pushkin literally skewered in his scandalous letter. On Yekaterina's grave lay a small, painted metal rose that, to be honest, did little to adorn it.

"Why aren't you spitting?" Agnes teased.

"They're already *damned*," I said.

"Can you sense that?" she asked, this time quite fearfully.

For some reason I felt ill at ease again, so I walked towards the cemetery gates without answering. The sun was setting. It was May in Alsace.

Agnes got into the car. "Now do you see why d'Anthès must be rehabilitated?"

"I'm sure he'll be awarded the gold star of a Hero of Russia soon. Do you want to have dinner at the Pushkin Restaurant?"

Agnes didn't reply. I didn't insist. It was time for me to leave this backwoods and go to Paris. It was a long ride. A Frenchman told me that d'Anthès had never once taken Yekaterina to Paris.

"There's a better restaurant about 15 kilometers up the mountain."

We drove up into the mountains. It was beautiful again. We drove in silence. We pulled into the parking lot and went into the restaurant. Everyone looked at us, as they do in a village. For dinner we ordered escargots *à la Bourguignon* and frog's legs in an herb sauce. We drank a local Riesling from a tall bottle.

"Are you offended by something?" Agnes suddenly asked.

I shrugged.

"I have the text of the conversation between Pushkin and d'Anthès."

"I'm not a Pushkin scholar. I'm not part of all that. My mother asked me to come and spit on his grave. When did they meet?"

"Just before d'Anthès died."

"But Pushkin didn't kill him—he missed! Stop it, Agnes. You have beautiful, large breasts. Why are we talking about Pushkin?"

"It's a secret story. I've never told anyone." She was trembling. Could she be a witch? I drank some Riesling and prepared to listen—probably to my regret.

"Like all distinguished men, d'Anthès had a hard time dying. All the medals, honors, titles and ranks—none of that meant anything anymore."

"Except for the sewers," I chortled.

"Pushkin said that to him, too."

I ate my frog's legs, drank some wine and didn't say anything.

"D'Anthès rang his bell. An old valet with puffy eyes walked into his bedroom. D'Anthès lay on his bed and said, 'Gustav, do me a favor. Bring me a pear liqueur and ask KoKo to come in.'

"'What did you say?'

"'I mean the Baroness,' d'Anthès said.

"Without any sign of surprise, Gustav said, 'I'll bring you the pear liqueur, but I can't summon the Baroness. She's gone into town to shop.'

"'What is she buying?'

"'A little of everything,' the servant said evasively, realizing that the Baron was delirious: the only wife in the family named KoKo had died fifty two years ago. Gustav soon reappeared with the pear liqueur, but his expression was, to say the least, extremely disturbed. 'Monsieur Baron,' he said as he handed him a tall glass, 'the mistress has indeed stepped out, but a monsieur insists on speaking with you, despite your indisposition.'

"'The mayor?' d'Anthès said, rhetorically raising his eyebrows, expecting, as any vain man would, that he'd see some sign of concern from the authorities on his death bed.

"'No,' Gustav said hesitantly and stared at him wide-eyed. 'It's Monsieur Pushkin.'

"'Well, let him in,' d'Anthès said calmly.

"Pushkin walked in. D'Anthès looked him over. They were still in different age groups, only they had traded places. D'Anthès had been thirteen years younger than Pushkin, but now he was forty seven years older. Therefore he, a senator of France, allowed himself to be somewhat familiar in addressing Pushkin.

"'Why, it's my brother-in-law. Hello there. I've been expecting you for a long time,' d'Anthès said, gesturing at the armchair by the bed. 'Too bad you've come when I'm not feeling quite well.'

"Pushkin sat down in the armchair and casually crossed his legs. 'You're dying.'

"'I know. I'm no fool,' d'Anthès said with a sad laugh.

"'That's exactly what fools say,' Pushkin said with a wave of his hand.

"'Alexandre, don't speak for posterity. I should hope that our talk won't be taken down in minutes. Everything about our relationship is examined through a distorted magnifying glass. Have you come to hear me repent?'

"'I've come—'

"D'Anthès interrupted him. 'I'm glad that you've come,' he said and sailed along the river of French eloquence, 'Because of you, all my life I shuddered whenever I heard someone speaking Russian. I truly wished Russia would go to Hades. I forbade my daughter from learning Russian. She made a scene and it was all terribly unpleasant. My misfortune was seeking the protection of my illustrious aunt in Russia instead of in Prussia. The Marquis de Custine wrote a very accurate book about you Russians. But that was after you. After you, a great many things happened. In '37 there weren't even photographs, and this year cinema was invented. Do you know what a telephone is? An automobile? You don't even know what electricity is, or the Paris Commune! And soon we'll have aviation to replace God. Nietzsche writes that He is dead. You could have lived on and on...'

"'Poetry needs neither aviation nor electricity,' Pushkin said.

"'Well, yes, that's for sure,' d'Anthès said and continued, 'Poetry needs female droppings that can be shaped into verse. You had more than enough of them, and you slipped on them. My dear man, you don't have to show off your genius, not to me. My ancestors were the best friends of the local peasants. The world needs d'Anthèses as much as it needs Pushkin. Otherwise the duel would have come out differently.'

"'I came to forgive you.'

"'Forgive me? How about I forgive myself for a start,' d'Anthès said with an officer's coarseness.

"'It was all Natasha's fault.'

"'No, my friend, you're mistaken. You didn't love her. You loved a pretty window-dressing. You thought Natasha was a little fool and told her how to live, while I accepted her as she was. We were born the same year, we had the same scent, we understood each other almost without words—we were horses from the same stable.'

"Pushkin didn't respond.

"D'Anthès continued. 'I was afraid that you'd kill her when you learned that she loved me. You did know that she loved me.'

"'Did you sleep with her?'

"D'Anthès burst out laughing. 'Pushkin! Are you a great man or not? What difference does it make? I won't say.'

"'So you did?'

"'I always knew that poets weren't men. You're slugs. My dear Alexandre, let's be honest. She didn't love you—that's a fact, and you predicted it all in *Onegin*. You had bad sex that you described with rare candor in verse. Natasha was all that I loved in Russia. Once I was with my son in a theater in Paris and saw her. I didn't go up to her, but I pointed her out to my son and said with great affection: "That's your Aunt Natasha."'

"Pushkin couldn't contain himself. 'What about Katya? Was she also a horse from the same stable? Katya, the woman Karamzin[4] railed at for her incredible stupidity on every street corner?'

"'I don't understand who is supposed to experience cosmic love—a poet or an officer? I felt cosmic love for Natasha. Katya was like expensive faux leather. When I slept with her, I imagined Natasha. They both knew it. And, besides, I saved your honor by marrying her. But you were a stupid idiot! You ran all over town screaming at the top of your lungs that a Frenchman was fucking your wife. Even Zhukovsky[5] told you to stick it up your

   VIKTOR YEROFEYEV

ass. You were disgusting: You were delirious, and you insulted everyone. You wanted to kill me. You ruined my life.'

"'You flouted it. You went all over St Petersburg with Natasha and Katya in a sleigh.'

"'I was twenty-five years old. When we were together, you didn't exist. I didn't even know your poetry. At the balls, who were you? A caricature of a man!'

"'But I'm a great Russian poet.'

"'Dostoevsky, Tolstoy, Turgenev and now that—that one who imitates Maupassant—what's his name? They are great, too. You aren't the only one. Poetry, Pushkin, is one thing, but a woman—a woman is just an ass.'

"'That's the homosexual in you talking.'

"'It doesn't matter. It's no longer the crime it was in Vigel's time.[6] Natasha came along and turned my homosexual head. That's how much I loved her.'

"Pushkin sat up in the armchair. D'Anthès took his time finishing his pear liqueur. Then he admitted brusquely, 'I didn't respect you. You weren't for the Tsar and you weren't against the Tsar. You weren't a Decembrist, but you weren't exactly *not* a Decembrist. You weren't for Russia and you weren't against Russia, like Chaadayev. You weren't for promiscuity, but neither were you for fidelity.'[7]

---

[4] A. Karamzin, son of the prominent historian Nikolai Karamzin, was a friend of Pushkin.

[5] Vasily Zhukovsky (1783-1852), poet, critic and translator, who was close to Pushkin.

[6] Filipp Vigel (1786-1856), civil servant and memoirist, friend of Pushkin since their youth. Pushkin wrote about Vigel's homosexuality in his letters.

[7] The Decembrists were a group of Russian aristocrats and officers who staged a rebellion against the assumption of Nikolai I to the throne in 1825. Pushkin did not take part in the rebellion, but was close friends with many of the participants. Pyotr Chaadayev (1794–1856) was a philosopher who asserted that Russia had no past, present or future and had made no impact on world culture.

"'But you, on the other hand, always had dirty hands—in love and in politics,' Pushkin said with revulsion. 'Perhaps you remember the elections in Colmar? You falsified the results. You were caught.'

"'I was the youngest senator in the Second Empire.'

"'Second Empire, Third—who cares? D'Anthès' finest achievement on earth—a sewer system.'

"'We are the bearers of a great civilization. Thanks to us—computers and star wars. But you Russians haven't changed—you're still wallowing in shit.'

"'Shall we duel again?'

"'I'll kill you again,' the host laughed peaceably. 'All normal people are d'Anthèses. The truth of life is on my side.'

"'You're going to hell,' Pushkin said.

"'Says the author of *The Gabrieliad*? Oh, stick it—'

"Pushkin got up and went to the door.

"'Wait.'

"Pushkin stopped.

"'You said you came to forgive me.'

"Pushkin didn't respond.

"'Why?'

"Pushkin didn't say anything. He had nothing to say. By the time Pushkin closed the door behind him, d'Anthès was dead. He died without repenting."

Agnes burst into tears. I tried to console her. She cried harder and harder. She sobbed. The entire restaurant stared at her. She was hysterical. She began to tear at her face with lilac-colored nails. Night had fallen. Who are these people? Why am I here in these primeval Alsatian mountains? She was entirely transformed. She was sitting before me in a ball gown and holding a lorgnette but without her Orthodox cross, which was in the display case of the city museum. It was Yekaterina Goncharova, the woman whom contemporaries called an ugly broomstick, urging me to rehabilitate her husband, the Baron Georges-Charles de Heeckeren d'Anthès, the woman who had left St. Petersburg after

                                        VIKTOR YEROFEYEV

Pushkin's death and the court's banishment of the Frenchman, to join her husband in Europe on April 1, 1837, and stay with him forever.

TRANSLATION BY MICHELE A. BERDY

The Storm

Leonid Yuzefovich

They never ran or shouted or fought in class. Things never reached that point, thank God. They just would chatter, squirm, drop things, throw stuff back and forth, rip up pieces of paper, and roll their pens and pencils across their desks. The noise these forty-five fifth graders produced could not be broken down into its component parts; the undifferentiated rumbling struck the ear with a combination of a savage harmony characteristic of a rain's rumbling, or a waterfall's, and its irritatingly importunate, almost mechanical timbre.

"Quiet, children!" Nadezhda Stepanovna shouted. "Today we have a visitor, Dmitry Petrovich Rodygin. He will talk to us about traffic safety rules."

She rapped her pencil on her desk—not in front of herself but in front of Rodygin, so as to draw their attention to him.

"Quiet! I'm ashamed of you!"

Rodygin thought she should be ashamed of herself. Not all that young, she ought to have mastered discipline by now.

"You go ahead. I'll do this myself," he told her as gently as possible.

Nadezhda Stepanovna moved reluctantly toward the door. The noise did not abate.

"Wouldn't you like to learn something new?" she began in the very voice she hated in herself. "I don't believe that. Vekshina here, for example, I'm sure she does."

Top student Vekshina, a little girl with a big nose and short hair sitting at the first desk, drew her head into her shoulders, frightened. Without too much of a stretch, you could interpret that as her nodding in agreement.

"Then why don't you say something? You have to have the daring to defend your convictions, even if the majority doesn't share them. Stand up and say, I'm interested! Don't keep me from listening!"

Vekshina stood up, convulsively squeezing her apartment key, which hung around her neck on a cord, like a cross, and turned silently toward the window. Rodygin couldn't help but look in the same direction. Outside it was September, damp and warm, and green leaves were brushing across the glass. For a leaf to turn yellow and fall, as it's supposed to in the Urals in late September, the weather has to be dry and clear, with morning ice on the ponds and a ringing underfoot. Lately, something in nature had been out of kilter, as it had been in manufacturing.

When Nadezhda Stepanovna finally left, he smiled another half-minute, lulling their vigilance, and then suddenly barked, "All right, stand up!"

They were surprised, but they stood up.

"You stand up badly, sloppily. Sit down."

They sat down, clattering their chairs and shoving.

"You sit down badly. Stand up!"

This time they stood up a little better, but someone in back giggled, and a wad of chewed up paper flew out blindly from the side and hit the blackboard with a characteristic, criminal sound.

Rodygin didn't look for the perpetrators.

"Mark time," he commanded. "March!"

Those in front marked time languidly between the rows. They were choking with laughter, their cheeks were puffing out, their eyes popping, but they did march. The ones in back, aware of their position's advantages, barely shifted from foot to foot. This went on for a little while, but Rodygin marked time implacably, like a metronome, tapping his index finger on the ridge in the desktop. Eventually they got in the groove.

"Well done!" he praised them. "You may sit down."

They sat down as quietly as elves so they wouldn't have to stand up again. He praised them again.

"Well done. You sit down well."

Rodygin began all his talks on a quiet, lyrical note intended to create an atmosphere of mutual trust, then he moved on to business, and in conclusion he would tell a few engaging but thematically related stories from the back pages of *Behind the Wheel* magazine. For starters he told them about how, when he was a child, he and some other boys had, for three kilometers, chased the first automobile ever to drive through their village. "At the time, automobiles were special, and you saw them as rarely then as you do horses now. Now everyone rides in cars, but have many of you ridden horses? Raise your hand if you have."

Everyone but Vekshina had. Some had ridden at the racetrack, others at their grandmother's in the country or at a Russian Winter festival, as the recently rehabilitated Shrovetide was now officially called. Vekshina said she'd ridden a pony at the zoo, but that probably didn't count.

"Yes, it does," Rodygin ruled on her case and moved on to business.

He took out a notebook, put on his glasses, and started reading the figures on childhood traffic injuries. National figures were classified, but the ones for the district, city, and even the whole province were open. Adults were impressed by the figures themselves, but the graphic thinking of fifth graders required more concrete details, so Rodygin told them about events to which he personally had supposedly been witness. "This sweet, curly-headed little boy ran across the street where he wasn't supposed to, was run over by a truck, and had to have his leg amputated."

"How far up?" came a practical question from by the window.

In reply, Rodygin flicked the pencil across his hip, showing that the leg as such simply ceased to exist.

"Don't show it on yourself," Vekshina warned him.[1]

"This has been a tremendous tragedy for the victim's parents," he summed up, "and for him personally. An eleven-year-old cripple, just your age. And why did it happen?"

"It was his own fault," the same dauntless voice answered from the same window.

"It happened," Rodygin said, frowning, "because this little boy didn't know anything about braking distance."

He explained in detail what braking distance was, what it might be at the speed limit of sixty kilometers an hour for various means of transportation and depending on the weather—on dry asphalt, wet asphalt, and black ice. Then he recommended writing down these facts, and he started slowly dictating as he paced between the rows.

Some, including Vekshina, took them down assiduously. Some moved their lips, trying to remember, but most pretended to be writing them down or remembering them. Two daredevils in the last row didn't even pretend.

Finished dictating, Rodygin talked about the ability to judge distance. If your ability to judge distance was good, you wouldn't get run over, because you could easily determine the distance to an oncoming car, correlate it to the braking distance, and then decide accurately whether to go or wait. Naturally, all this happened automatically, which meant you had to be constantly training your distance-judging ability.

"Here, for instance," Rodygin proposed, squinting. "Tell me how many meters it is from the blackboard to the opposite wall. But quickly."

---

[1] A Russian superstition. It is bad luck to demonstrate on your own body how someone else was injured.

The answers fell in a broad range. He heard them all out and then, without any particular hope, asked, "Has anyone in your class ever been run over by a car?"

It turned out someone had. That spring, Filimonov had been knocked down by a motorcycle and had missed school for a week.

"Stand up, Filimonov!" the girls started whispering. "Stand up, they're talking about you!"

Filimonov stood up. A little boy with big ears wearing a school uniform, he felt as if the usual world had been left far below, while he himself had sliced through the protective film head first, like a fish pulled out of the water, and was now gasping for air, suffocating from horror and loneliness. But he had not written down or remembered the braking distance of the IZh-Planeta motorcycle that had knocked him down near the Nature's Gifts store. Filimonov had been drinking tomato juice, a wonderful gift of nature at ten kopeks a glass, and the salt was free. When he went flying toward the grass and saw blood on his shirt, his first thought had been that the tomato juice was spilling out of him.

"Now we're going to ask Filimonov how many meters it is here."

"Where?" a cheerful boy sitting at his desk asked.

The same question could be read in the eyes of many, including those who had already answered him two minutes before. In that time the problem had been driven from their minds.

"From this wall, where the blackboard is, to that wall," Rodygin pointed patiently, and his gaze shifted back to Filimonov. "So, how many meters is that?"

Filimonov took a deep breath and whispered, "Twelve."

"Louder. So everyone can hear you."

"Twelve meters."

"Well, let's check. My pace is exactly eighty centimeters. So how many of my paces should there be?"

The silence of the grave fell. Finally one girl, after doing the calculations on paper, raised her hand, stood up, and answered in full.

"There should be fifteen of your paces."

"Smart girl," Rodygin rewarded her. "Now, count."

He took up his starting position, that is, pressed the backs of his boots right up to the baseboard, and, starting on his left foot, stamping out his pace, moved down the aisle.

"One," the off-key chorus thundered, gathering strength with each step. "Two. Three . . ."

All of a sudden, at the fourth step, Rodygin realized distinctly that it would be exactly fifteen paces, no more and no less. At that point he firmly lengthened his fifth step, and his sixth even more so, and his seventh and eighth leapt to nearly a meter and a half. His height allowed him to do this imperceptibly, moreover his distracting gesticulations played their part.

"Ten," the chorus thundered.

"And a half," Rodygin added magnanimously, and silence ensued.

Filimonov was looking at the partition with glassy eyes. He was done for. He was a bad judge of distance, and that's why he'd been run over by the motorcycle. And he would be again.

"There, you see?" Rodygin told him with kindly reproach. "Sit down."

Filimonov sat down. The girls were looking at him with compassionate curiosity, as if he were a candidate for a corpse.

Feeling light pangs of conscience, Rodygin slowed down at the wall and then started back.

"The years will pass," he said as he walked. "You will all grow up, you'll labor honestly in the economy, and you yourselves will be able to acquire an automobile for your personal use. Who wants to have his own personal automobile? Raise your hands."

Once again, all hands went up, except for the smallest boy, who was dressed worse than the others and who said he already had one, and Vekshina, who didn't say anything. Failing to pry an explanation out of her, Rodygin resumed.

"But remember one thing from your school bench. Never, under any circumstances, get behind the wheel drunk."

To help them visualize it, he sketched a picture in broad strokes where the heroes were plucked straight from life. "Here is Vekshina, a mama herself now, pushing a stroller down the sidewalk." Rodygin paused for the giggles to flutter through the class, as was to be expected. Innocent giggles, mostly, but a few girls sniffed shyly, looking down, and from off to the left there was a cautious male cackle. "They already know," Rodygin thought sadly. He himself had learned about this much earlier, but for city children, who had no contact with farm animals, the knowledge was fairly early, and not on the best authority, of course.

Vekshina didn't know yet, and Filimonov had heard a thing or two but had his doubts. Grownups certainly weren't going to go around doing the foolish things eighth graders did. You could expect anything from them.

In an intriguing tone, to distract their attention, Rodygin hastened to inform them that Vekshina had been at the infant feeding center. She was calmly pushing her baby in her stroller, while a few blocks away, still indistinguishable in the stream of cars, there was a speeding car behind whose wheel sat Filimonov. He was coming back from a birthday party where he'd had more to drink than tomato juice.

Filimonov grinned, flattered.

Now, feeling no pangs of conscience whatsoever, Rodygin reminded him that he was not a good judge of distance, and, after the birthday party, he was a terrible one. In addition, a storm had just passed, the asphalt was wet, and the braking distance had increased. Filimonov pressed on the pedal. Too late! Red, the color of blood, struck him in the eyes, and the car bore down unstoppably on the crosswalk where the happy mother was pushing her stroller.

Brakes squealed outside and Vekshina screwed her eyes up tight. Her daughter's name was Agnya, and she was a chubby, swarthy little girl in a lace-trimmed pink satin coverlet. Not blue, under any circumstance; blue was for boys.

Crash! At the last moment Rodygin had Filimonov run into a bread van. No one was injured, thank God, but the residents of an entire neighborhood had no bread. And in the morning they had to go to work. What would they have with their tea?

This problem worried everyone. Several suggestions were made as to what exactly. On the list were cottage cheese pancakes with sour cream, regular and potato pancakes, biscuits, waffles, cookies, and even breadfruit. You could easily grow breadfruit trees in apartments for just such times, a flabby boy with jug ears said with Jewish aplomb.

Vekshina took no part in the discussion; she didn't care. She was thinking about why Nadezhda Stepanovna had decided that this lecture would be more interesting for her, Vekshina, than the other kids. She had had her suspicions before, but when Rodygin started explaining the punishments applied to drunk drivers, all her doubts fell away.

Vekshina's father had worked at a motor transport company as a long-distance trucker. Three months before, while moonlighting somewhere outside of town, he was given some home brew and vodka, and on the way home he crashed his ZIL into the road crew shed and fought with a policeman. Her father went to jail for fifteen days, his license was revoked, and he was demoted from driver to mechanic. They could survive the fifty-ruble pay difference, they'd done worse, her mother said, but as a mechanic her father started drinking. Drunk, he ran to the garage and tried to get his ZIL out of its bay. The guard had already caught him twice, and the third time they threatened to take him to court. Her mother was constantly telling everyone about this because she had to share her grief with someone. Vekshina begged her not to tell Nadezhda Stepanovna, but then she got told, too. Vekshina felt like ripping the key off her neck, throwing it out the window, and never going home again.

Outside, an almost completely green leaf from an American maple was gliding down to the lawn. She couldn't figure out why such a green leaf had torn off its branch. In its place Vekshina would have hung on a little longer. She remembered the leaves would soon turn color and start falling one after the other and be springy underfoot. You could jump on them from the fourth floor and not get hurt.

"Three years . . . five years"—Rodygin's prophetic voice hovered over her—"for a serious accident . . . ten years. . . ."

Stepping silently across the fallen leaves, her father was walking toward her from the prison wall. He noticed the stroller and asked, "Boy or girl?"

"Agnya, your granddaughter," Vekshina answered, and she and her papa hugged and quietly wept for joy.

2

Tea was being made in the teacher's lounge, and Nadezhda Stepanovna was sent out to the grocery nearby for a cake. Physicist Vladimir Lvovich, with whom she had had a casual office romance, was in charge of the till. She was happy to go to him for the money.

On the desk in his lab, a battery of half-liter jars containing clusters of garish blue crystals sparkled. Ninth graders had grown them over the holidays from a copper sulfate solution. These same crystals always showed up here in September, like a final greeting from the departing summer. With a breathtaking look, he had reconciled Nadezhda Stepanovna to the idea that the ruby in her silver ring had not been hewn from mountain veins but had also been born in a glass beaker.

She had hopes that Vladimir Lvovich would want to go with her to get the cake, but he didn't. Taking the money, she went back out into the corridor. Sixth period was under way, and the free spirit of the break reigned everywhere. Children were sitting on windowsills, although that was strictly forbidden by the "Rules for Pupils" that hung on every floor, and they were in no hurry to hop down when she appeared. They knew she wasn't going to drive them away. "You want to be nice at my expense," Kotova, the head teacher, told her. When Kotova walked down the hall, the windowsills were vacated instantly, but behind her back the kids' butts plopped down on them triumphantly once again.

On the third floor, Nadezhda Stepanovna walked up to her classroom door and listened. The silence of the grave reigned on the other side of the door, like during a midterm exam. She was hurt that Rodygin had succeeded with such ease. She opened the door very slightly and peeked through the crack. Vekshina was fiddling with her key, and she looked rather dejected. Remorseful for having troubled her with her demagoguery, Nadezhda Stepanovna caught her eye, then kissed her palm, opened it flat, brought it to her lips, and blew. The fluffy little cloud of her air kiss sailed toward Vekshina but didn't reach her. A cheerful boy who had sat under his desk for the entire first half of the lesson shot it down with a wad of chewed up paper blown through a small tube.

Nadezhda Stepanovna didn't see that; she had already gone out. Rodygin heard the familiar sound and understood its origin but decided not to let himself be interrupted.

"In our country," he said, "drunk driving is punished severely by the law. Very severely, but still not the way it is in some foreign countries. Children, there are states on the planet where drunk drivers are immediately sentenced to death."

"They should be, too, those lushes," said a chubby girl who had developed early and who had dabs of brilliant green ointment on her chin.

"What's your name?" Rodygin asked her.

"Vera."

"Children, do you agree with Vera?"

Filimonov raised his hand.

"All right"—Rodygin was pleased—"express your opinion."

"May I go out?" Filimonov asked.

"I thought you wanted to answer my question."

"I'm feeling sick," Filimonov said.

Rodygin looked the class over quizzically, trying to tell whether he was lying or telling the truth, but he couldn't.

"What am I going to do with you! Go."

Filimonov went out into the corridor and headed for the bathroom, but after two steps he realized he wasn't going to make it. The tomato juice he'd drunk last spring at Nature's Gifts was welling up in his throat. He turned back, ran out on the front steps and dashed around the corner, where he threw up.

Right next to the sidewalk the earth had been dug up and workers were laying felt-wrapped pipes in a ditch. Filimonov sat down on a step and started breathing deeply through his nose, just like his mama had taught him. There was the smell of electricity.

<h2 style="text-align:center">3</h2>

Nadezhda Stepanovna smelled that ominous smell suffused through the air, too, but her memory wouldn't supply the right name for it. Hurrying to get back before the break, she jaywalked and was still running late. The grocery was already closed for lunch and the entrance was blocked by a sullen, middle-aged woman in a white coat. Nadezhda Stepanovna did not feel like groveling. In search of something that could take the place of a cake, Nadezhda Stepanovna headed for the small, improvised market near the streetcar stop. More than a dozen old ladies were sitting in two rows on overturned crates; in front of them there were colorful cans of berries and paradise apples; asters and gladioli stuck out of bottles, and limp autumn mushrooms lay in pitiful heaps on spread newspapers. One granny was selling fly agarics meant either for gourmets who had the patience to cook them in seven changes of water or for ulcer patients who had lost faith in patent medicines.

Nadezhda Stepanovna cut through the market and, in front of the last old woman, saw a chipped enamel pot filled to the brim with tiny, reddish black berries. She didn't even realize they were bird cherries right away. The woman could only have been selling them out of total despair.

The fly agarics, even those looked more appropriate here. Bird cherries hadn't been considered a berry for a long time, and Nadezhda Stepanovna hadn't eaten a pie filled with them in nearly twenty years. And what pies they had been! The light crunch of crushed stems, the marble veins on the crust, and the fragrant violet pulp inside.

"How much?" she asked.

"Fifty a glass."

Nadezhda Stepanovna took a ruble out of her purse.

"One, please."

"Take two, I don't have change," the old woman said, taking a crude and incongruously large cigarette out of her tiny sunken mouth, which looked like the mouth of an aged doll.

Lately, Nadezhda Stepanovna had given more and more frequent thought to her own old age. She wasn't going to have a family, that was obvious, and she probably wouldn't have the nerve to bear a child without a husband. After retiring, the ideal scenario for her would be to live in the city in the winter and spend the summer at a teachers' boardinghouse. They had a boardinghouse for deserving education workers in the north of the province, in the ancient district center, where she had taken the children the summer before last on a field trip. Sheltering in the shadow of St. George's Church was a formidable two-story house with a bay window and curved glass cold frames on the roof. At one time it had belonged to the owner of the local porcelain factory, a patron and eccentric. He'd had a pool put in where two Nile crocodiles swam and fed on fresh fish from the Kolva. As local residents told the story, one of them had quietly starved to death during the revolution, and the other was shot during a kulak riot, in which Old Believers who took no pity on foreign creatures actively participated. The first was buried in the garden, and the second, stuffed, was the basis of the district's ethnographic museum collection, but there was to be no rest there either, even after its death. Like any dumb creature, it lived outside history; on the other hand, by its death it inscribed itself into the context of the period and reflected the singularity of the historical moment. Therefore, for half a century it had been dragged back and forth multiple times between the regional history and natural history departments.

All those years, the pool had gone empty, and all kinds of junk had been dumped into it, and snow and flax seeds had swept through the broken bays, but not so long ago those holes had been patched, soil had been lugged in, and now there was a hothouse there. The deserving education workers raised flowers and also vegetables for their board. Nadezhda Stepanovna had become friends with two of them. She sent them Indian tea, candies and cards on International Women's Day and Teacher's Day, and once, when someone was going to town, they had sent her a bouquet of marvelous white chrysanthemums that almost didn't wilt on the way. For more than a year, this modest boardinghouse surrounded by taiga, prison camp zones,and timber lots had seemed like the dwelling place of peace, the one place in the world where she could set her heart on going.

Holding the paper cone soaked with berry juice as far away as possible from her new raincoat, and berating herself after the fact for taking a fancy to bird cherries she absolutely did not need, Nadezhda Stepanovna crossed the plank across the ditch dug next to the school. Here sat Filimonov on the step. By now, he was breathing through his mouth because he'd suddenly come down with a runny nose from sitting on the stone step.

"I felt sick," Filimonov announced from a distance, so that she wouldn't think he'd been sent from class for bad behavior.

"Lord! What did you eat?"

Filimonov listed everything. Nadezhda Stepanovna and all the children had eaten the same thing in the lunchroom, but no one had felt sick, not even Vekshina with her weak liver.

"That's odd. Why would that be?"

"I don't know," Filimonov said, although he did have a vague idea as to the reason.

"Does your stomach hurt?"

"No."

Squatting, Nadezhda Stepanovna placed the cone on the step, took a handkerchief from her purse, and started wiping the crumbs from a Kuntsevo roll off Filimonov's cheeks. She held his sweet cheek with her other hand, so his head wouldn't wobble. Then he was told to go back to class. He went, and when Nadezhda Stepanovna stuck her soiled handkerchief back in her purse she noticed that her wallet was missing from the side pocket.

4

Rodygin looked out the window, waiting for an answer to his question. Through the leaves of the American maples he could see the gray, five-story prefab buildings from the 1960s and the more recent white, nine-story ones. Smokestacks poked out between them here and there. The closest was the oldest. Laid from what was now brown brick that had never felt the hot breath of sandblasting equipment, it curved and broadened gracefully toward the foundation, like Khiva's famous minaret of Kalyan, which Rodygin had seen when he was in the army.

No one else had raised their hand, although he had given them plenty of time. He had to give the answer himself.

"Well, children," Rodygin said firmly, "I for one don't agree with Vera. The death penalty is an inadmissible measure of punishment. Punishment is supposed to reform a person—if, of course, there is any hope of reforming him. Turkey, for example, found an original solution to this situation."

He told them how in Turkey, when they caught a drunk driver, they made him walk thirty kilometers. Policemen would follow him on motorcycles so that he didn't get any ideas along the way about stopping or sitting down somewhere cool.

"I personally think that in this case we could learn from the Turks," Rodygin said, and he looked at Filimonov's empty chair.

This was said in that confidential tone that had once invariably bewitched him in these kinds of situations—the tone of someone who not only had access to privileged information but who, out of respect for this particular audience, was permitting himself to say what he would, of course, never tell another.

A terrible Turkish heat coalesced in the classroom; scorching air rose from desks to ceiling in quivering streams. Directly ahead of her, Vekshina saw the rocky road, white from the terrible heat, receding beyond the horizon. Dragging himself down it, staggering from exhaustion, was her papa. His shirt had stuck to his back and his hair was gray with dust. Sweat was running into his eyes, which he raised to the skies from time to time praying for rain, hoping to discern, far away, that tiny cloud which, as tends to happen in southern countries, was bound to turn into a storm cloud before long. Right behind him, mustached policemen in claret fezzes were riding huge motorcycles with curved horns that bellowed and glittered under the merciless Turkish sun. They were trying to nudge her papa with their front wheels. *Schnell, schnell!*

Biting her lip, Vekshina took her pencil case out of her book bag, and from the pencil case a piece of chalk, and imperceptibly whitened the ridge on the desk. From time to time, Rodygin leaned up against that ridge, and she had hopes he would get his trousers dirty.

The lesson plan had been exhausted, but Rodygin made it a point of honor to finish strictly on the bell. The noisy thanks of little listeners released to their homes ahead of time did not warm his heart. Also, since they had begun talking about drunk drivers, it would be useful to talk about how they were dealt with in Singapore.

"Now in Singapore . . ."

Rodygin stopped because Filimonov was squeezing through the door sideways.

"May I come in?" he asked.

Without answering, Rodygin turned to the class.

"Children, what did he forget to do?"

"Knock?" Vekshina's neighbor guessed.

"Did you hear?"

"Uh huh."

"Then go out and come in the right way."

Filimonov went out, carefully shut the door behind him, and knocked three times from the corridor.

"Come in," Rodygin responded hospitably.

The door opened and Filimonov crossed the threshold and froze.

"Well, go on," Rodygin encouraged him. "What should you say now?"

"May I come in?"

"You already did."

Filimonov heaved a sigh of relief and headed for his desk, but Rodygin, like a hypnotist, kept him back at a distance with a held up palm. Filimonov could feel something invisible and stiff poking into his chest, like a stream of air from a fan, only narrower and harder. He took a step back toward the door.

"Now you need to ask permission to sit down," Rodygin hinted.

Filimonov was silent. He could tell the bell was going to ring soon. The bell always started with a tickling in his stomach and then rumbled in a weak echo from floor to floor.

"Why don't we start all over from the beginning," Rodygin suggested. "Go out one more time and knock."

"I felt sick! Honest!" Filimonov said.

"Please," Vekshina pled, "let him sit down!"

She knew from personal experience the infinite loneliness that can grip you when something starts to hurt in school—your head or your liver. Recently, in history, her nose started bleeding. Nadezhda Stepanovna had her lie down on the couch in the teacher's lounge, and she lay there the whole period looking at the ceiling and thinking about death.

Now, to keep from crying, she had to think of something good immediately. Vekshina started to think about New Year's. For the school holiday party, her mama had sewn her the prince's costume from *Cinderella*, and her papa had bought her a glass ashtray in the shape of a slipper at the Gifts store. The party was held in the gymnasium, and the tree stood on an old turntable and was starting to turn at 33 rpm when Father Frost struck his staff on the floor. Nadezhda Stepanovna, dressed as the Snow Maiden, sat right down on the floor, removed one felt boot, took the crystal slipper from Vekshina, who had been carrying it idly back and forth near the wall bars, and made a hilarious attempt to put it on her foot. Everyone around was laughing, only Vekshina for some reason felt like crying and, as always, the bitterer the source, the darker the tears that rose inexplicably in her throat.

Rodygin gave Filimonov a wink.

"Vekshina is petitioning for you. Understand, you nearly ran her and her baby down in a state of drunkenness, and she's already forgiven everything. That's a woman for you! Come on now, go out, knock, and speak up like a real man."

   LEONID YUZEFOVICH

Filimonov went out again and the door shut. Rodygin got ready to give him a friendly pat on the head when he walked by. The soft burr of Filimonov's hair would tickle the skin of his palm.

A minute passed and no one knocked. Rodygin strode to the door, opened it cautiously, and then flung it wide open. Filimonov had vanished, the corridor was deserted in both directions, and it was growing dark outside, getting ready to rain. A broom was propped up at the nearest window, and Alevtina Ivanovna the janitress was slowly sprinkling light-colored sawdust on the floor from a bucket.

"I don't know," she said when asked where the boy who had just been there had gone.

It got dark in the classroom all at once, too. Rodygin turned on the electricity and returned to his interrupted topic.

"So you see, children, in Singapore drunk drivers are treated in an even more original way than in Turkey. . . ."

5

Returning to the little market, Nadezhda Stepanovna asked loudly, "Did anyone find a wallet?"

The response to her was silence. The old women sat motionless on their crates, trying not to meet her eye. She understood perfectly well and moved between them, asking each of them individually. Walking alongside her was some old man wearing an officer's scarf. He was inquiring as to the prices for mushrooms, vociferating and praying to God—in the sense that it would do no harm to fear him a little at his pension age.

"But He's on vacation now," the old lady selling fly agaric said.

This boded no good, especially since Nadezhda Stepanovna had asked her, "You didn't happen to find a wallet, did you?"

"No," she'd replied, and she'd looked away.

At last that same old woman with the bird cherries spoke up.

"What's it like?"

"Black," Nadezhda Stepanovna said.

"And what's in it?"

"Ten rubles in bills. Receipts."

"And that's all?"

"And some change."

"What, isn't change money? How much was there?"

"I don't remember."

"She doesn't even know how much money she has," the old woman told another sitting on the next crate in front of a three-liter jar with colorless fall gladioli sticking out of it.

The other woman willingly expressed her solidarity, saying, "Everyone's so rich now, they don't count kopeks anymore."

"Then she's going to say I took it," the old woman with the bird cherries added along the same lines and only then turned back toward Nadezhda Stepanovna. "Come, dearie, try to remember. If you remember, I'll give it back. Lots of you come around here. Maybe it's not yours."

She was wearing a black plush jacket that had bald spots and men's boots. Her head was wrapped in a well-laundered scarf with a picture of Sacré Coeur and the Eiffel Tower.

"Their savings book has more in it than ours," said the old man in the officer's scarf, who was standing back a little, and he fell silent, biting his lip dolefully.

The city had quieted in anticipation of the storm. Passersby were glancing upward and picking up their pace. Nadezhda Stepanovna was about to give up and leave, not giving a damn about the stupid tenner, when suddenly she heard, "You just have to understand me right, young lady. I'm shaking all over now."

The old woman took out the wallet.

"Yours?"

Her eyes were shining.

"Why don't you say something? Cat got your tongue?"

"Yes," Nadezhda Stepanovna softly, feeling a shudder start to run through her as well.

She took the proffered wallet. The old woman didn't let it go immediately; their fingers touched for a moment, and Nadezhda Stepanovna felt the moment's solemnity with her whole heart.

"Ten rubles, eighty-four kopeks. Count it."

"What for?"

"Count it, I say, before witnesses!"

Meanwhile the witnesses were fewer and fewer. Concerned about the rain, the old ladies were hastily gathering their wares and leaving. The little market was being pulled down before her eyes. It was quickly growing dark, and the wind was bearing litter down the street. Small columns of dust were eddying up in the chilling air, like springs from a river bottom, and a line of torn newspapers and streetcar tickets was dancing around the empty crates.

Nadezhda Stepanovna obediently counted the change in the wallet, but she could not just take it and leave now, and she stood stupidly in front of this old woman in the men's boots not knowing how to redeem the shameful difference between her attitude toward her loss and the other woman's toward her find. Unable to think of anything better, she suggested, "Why don't I buy some more bird cherries from you."

"Go. No need," the old woman replied wearily, still trembling from the unbearable burden of responsibility that had rested on her shoulders.

After that she did let herself be persuaded, and Nadezhda Stepanovna paid for another two glasses' worth, but her sense of guilt would not go away. She watched the little black spheres roll into the paper cone and heard a distant, protracted howl rushing in from the northeast, from the direction of the dam, where a solid shroud drew heaven and earth together and gigantic waves rampaged on the reservoir's vast expanses. He who the old woman with the bird cherries had been talking about probably was in fact on vacation, otherwise it would be hard to explain a storm like this in late September.

The sky turned black, and they started turning on the lights at the school. The monitors were putting out pots of flowers on the ledges to give them a little rainwater. "I hope their stems don't snap," Nadezhda

Stepanovna thought. She took the second cone, and at that instant the skies split open with a crash, the gray shroud that had long clothed the northeast moved in rapidly, and the rain lashed with such force that the drops shattered as they hit the asphalt. There was a thunk and a watery spray spread over the ground. Then the thunk was replaced by a rustle—water falling into water. A river was coursing down the street and the opposite bank was fogged in, her paper cones were soaked through and Nadezhda Stepanovna's fingers had turned purple. She stepped back under the awning of the Soyuzpechat newsstand, and the old woman took cover with her pot under the ledge of the grocery, which was still closed for lunch.

Water was streaming from the ledge, and an undulating fringe of water was heaving in front of her. She thought she might not live till spring, which meant this storm would be the last of her life, but she had no fear of death. Her soul, weightless from her awareness of a duty fulfilled, longed for the heavens, longed to go where the electrical charges were bursting and glittering. When she died, her daughter would put a copper wire ring on her finger and thread the end of the wire out of her grave to the outside. That was what her neighbor had advised, to make it easier for her soul to quit her body. It would flow up the wire through the ground and go up to heaven. The more honestly you lived, the more electricity there was in your soul, and it was the same everywhere: on the earth, in the earth, and in the sky. So what was she to fear? Death?

6

Alevtina Ivanovna had scattered all the sawdust from the bucket, picked up the broom propped by the window, and started to sweep the second floor. In her pocket, two keys kept clinking against each other on the ring—one to the cloakroom and one to the fireproof box on the wall where the red plastic bell button was safely shut up, out of reach of children's fingers. It still wasn't time to press it. Alevtina Ivanovna was calmly sweeping the sawdust, which was darkening up from the dirt it was absorbing. She always did this during the break. Her inner voice still hadn't told her, It's time!

From the fourth floor, from his laboratory window, Vladimir Lvovich saw Nadezhda Stepanovna returning to the school carrying some kind of paper cone and then heading back across the street. With his mature, married man's natural, nonbinding interest in a mature unmarried woman, he couldn't help but notice the grace with which she balanced on the tottering boards thrown across the ditch dug next to the front steps. From behind, this made a special impression, and Vladimir Lvovich regretted having declined to go with her for the cake. He locked the laboratory, walked past the teacher's lounge, where they had already started drinking tea without cake, and went downstairs to greet Nadezhda Stepanovna on the front steps.

Outside, the pre-storm wind was gusting, and there was the smell of electricity such as you can never recreate in laboratory conditions. Around the corner from the school, three workers were sharing half a liter out of a single folding cup.

"What are we celebrating, *muzhiks*?" Vladimir Lvovich inquired in a false basso.

"The Day of the Virgin of Paris," was their surly response.

Vladimir Lvovich thought that they were probably the kind who hung a photograph of Stalin on their truck windshield.

He moved a little ways away and loitered on the steps for five minutes or so, feeling the heat of his fleeting temptation cool, and then headed for the teacher's lounge to drink tea. En route he stopped in at the bathroom and saw Filimonov sitting on the windowsill.

"Why are you here? Is your lesson over?" Vladimir Lvovich asked, stepping up to the urinal.

"I felt sick," Filimonov answered proudly.

This was the password that opened all doors and ensured sympathy and aid from adults, but Vladimir Lvovich did not treat it with the proper respect. He left in silence, and Filimonov was left alone in the bathroom once again.

Sitting on the windowsill, he looked at the stormy sky, which lay over the city like a coat. Occasionally, white scissors of lightning skimmed across it, ripping open its lining.

The window faced the street. Cars stopped at the light with a piercing squeal, jerking their rear ends around. The drivers were watching the road anxiously; they didn't know the rain was about to come down in torrents, increasing their braking distance on the wet asphalt.

The light turned green, and in the stream of vehicles Filimonov saw an ambulance, and right then, squeezing his left hand into a fist, he made a wish. He knew this trick from Vekshina. Today in the lunchroom she had taught him that if you saw an ambulance on the street you had to make a fist and not let go until three people wearing glasses walked by. Then you had to open your fist quickly, say your wish out loud, and it would come true.

Filimonov wished the public safety instructor would be struck dead by lightning.

Almost immediately after that, one bespectacled person walked by the window and a minute later a second—but the third never showed. There were fewer and fewer people out walking. His fingers, balled into a fist, were sweating and had started dripping.

Suddenly confident steps rang out in the corridor. They approached and stopped by the bathroom door. A second later the door flung open, banging its handle on the wall, but no one came in. Silence ensued, and then a familiar female voice ordered, "All right, come out!"

It was the head teacher, Kotova, who everyone was afraid of, even Nadezhda Stepanovna. Filimonov hid. Unexpectedly he had only just found a "mint pea" candy in his pocket and eaten it, and Kotova might think he had eaten it on purpose so that he wouldn't smell of tobacco. He took a few swallows of the remains of his saliva, which had dried up out of agitation, and breathed softly, airing out his mouth. He was afraid to come out.

No one emerged, so Kotova came in herself. She was famous for being the sole woman in the school who could boldly walk into a boy's bathroom full of upperclassmen when there was smoke drifting out. In cases like that, other teachers would call in the gym teacher or the military instructor.

It was empty in the bathroom now, and if it smelled of smoke, then it was old. Fifth grader Filimonov was standing all alone at the window.

"Why are you here? Why aren't you in class?" Kotova asked, getting her glasses out of their case to make sure there were no pornographic drawings or graffiti on the walls.

Filimonov explained the way he was by now used to explaining. He looked at her in hopes she would put on her glasses and become his third.

"What's that in your hand?" Kotova inquired.

"Nothing," Filimonov answered with just his lips.

"That's not true. I see you have something in your fist. Is it a cigarette?"

"No."

"What then?"

"Nothing."

"Show me," she demanded, and then finally she did what Filimonov had been waiting for her to do.

That moment he quickly opened the fingers of his left hand and whispered his wish. Kotova saw an empty palm but did not hear what he said. Everything was drowned out by a clap of thunder.

7

"Anyone who gets behind the wheel drunk in Singapore is arrested and put in jail for fifteen days." Rodygin cited that figure for clarity, though he had no idea what term was stipulated in that article of Singapore's criminal code. *Behind the Wheel* didn't say. "There wouldn't be anything particularly original about this if it weren't for one piquant detail: those drivers are put in jail with their wives."

"What about their children?" a transparent little girl at the second desk asked.

"The children are taken home by their grandmothers and grandfathers," Rodygin found the right thing to say.

"But what if they're dead?"

"Then some other relatives have to move home with them temporarily or take the children to their house."

"What if they don't have anyone?"

"Then they're put into a children's home for two weeks."

"And do they make them wear children's home clothes? Or do they let them wear their own?" Vekshina's neighbor asked.

"They let them wear their own," Rodygin reassured her.

"It's only here that they give everyone the same haircut," the boy with Jewish ears said sarcastically.

"Quiet," Rodygin ordered him.

He looked at Filimonov's empty chair again and continued.

"When the husband drinks, often the wife is to blame. It's the woman who creates the kind of family atmosphere where a man either takes to drink or doesn't. That means the wife has to answer to society for her husband. That's what they believe in Singapore. But what do you believe?"

In his talks he always presented the children with problematic situations. He taught by training and trained by teaching, the way the best pedagogues did.

"Well?" Rodygin asked with an inviting smile. "Are they right to put the wives in jail with their husbands?"

Buxom Vera said they were, that a husband and wife made a single Satan. The other girls were cautiously silent. One boy objected to Vera, saying that they were wrong in Singapore, but he couldn't explain why he thought so. Another boy came to his rescue and explained that the man wouldn't be as bored in jail with his wife.

"Aha." Rodygin nodded. "In your opinion a wife's presence eases his punishment, and you want it to be more severe. Is that right?"

"Yes," the boy agreed, and he added that it's bad being alone in a cell, but together, if you scratch the stone with something sharp, you can play Blockhead or Battleship.

"Or Tic-Tac-Toe," someone suggested from the last desk.

The list of entertainments available to prisoners began to get out of hand. Finally Vekshina's neighbor looked at the problem from the other side. She said that for people who loved each other the real punishment should be separation, and the class fell quiet, stunned by the profundity of this thought. The gusts of wind and the mournful ringing of the hollow metal basketball backstops were becoming more and more audible outside.

In the silence the lop-eared boy raised his hand.

"What now?" Rodygin asked him in a resigned voice.

The boy stood up and said that the children hadn't said that in jail the husband and wife could play chess made from bits of bread. Under the tsar, the revolutionaries always played chess like that in prison. He'd read about it in a book, *The Rook Is a Springtime Bird.*

"In Singapore they eat rice. Rice!" Vekshina shouted at him.

"What about breadfruit?" the boy parried.

"They have rice. Rice, rice, rice!" Vekshina, choking on tears now, said over and over, unable to stop.

Rodygin lay his hand on her head.

"What's the matter?"

Vekshina felt her neck stiffening. His hand felt like an ice cube on her head. That kind of cold could only come from a very big official. Even his chalk-marked trousers couldn't shake his soul-chilling grandeur. This person was perfectly capable of transferring the laws of Turkey and Singapore to their city.

"Her papa's an alcoholic and he was put in jail," Vekshina's neighbor told him.

Rodygin realized that in the whole class this one short-cropped little girl with the key around her neck was the only one capable of fully appreciating the monstrous efficacy of the Singapore punishment.

"Don't cry," he said. "Your papa will go through rehabilitation and he'll get behind the wheel again. And you could help him in that, by the way. Do you know how?"

Vekshina didn't answer. She was sitting with her face buried on her desk, and her shoulders were shaking from her sobs.

"Who knows how Vekshina could help her papa be cured of his alcoholism?" Rodygin asked.

The answer was so obvious that no one said it out loud. A few voices reported at once from several seats.

"She already is a good student."

Rodygin was a little embarrassed.

"That's not all I had in mind. I had in mind that children can affect the family atmosphere, too. Not just wives."

"But are there countries where they put children in jail with their parents?" Vekshina's neighbor asked.

"No," Rodygin answered.

Trying to suppress her sobs, Vekshina hiccuped loudly once, twice, three times. While everyone was listening to her hiccup, the big-eared boy offered to tell them about breadfruit in more detail.

"You can tell them in geography," Rodygin interrupted him.

He turned to Vekshina.

"Stand up now."

She stood up. An evil little imp was hiding in her throat. When he jerked his foot, an uncontrollable spasm squeezed her throat.

"Do this," Rodygin said, and he demonstrated.

He rose up on his toes, stood there a little, balancing his body, and then plopped down on his heels with the full weight of his body. This method, described in a book by the famous aviation designer Mikulin, helped rid the body quickly of harmful dross, the hidden wastes of our vital functions.

"It will pass quickly." Rodygin gave her a smile of encouragement and repeated the demonstration.

Vekshina didn't budge, and the same inquisitive boy announced, "I have a question."

Rodygin looked at him with hatred.

"Well?"

"Who lives in Singapore?" the boy asked.

"Singaporeans."

"But who are they?"

"People. Just like you and me."

What he said in reply had a Jewish categoricalness to it.

"No, not just like you and me. They're Muslims."

"What of it?"

"Muslims have lots of wives. Do they put all of them in jail with their husband, the whole harem? Or do they take turns?"

"Come see me after the bell and I'll answer your question," Rodygin promised.

He looked at Vekshina, who was stiff as a statue, and he shrugged.

"As you like. All the worse for you."

"I'll bring her some water. May I?" the smallest and most poorly dressed boy spoke up.

Rodygin nodded, thinking that it was in just such children that the ability to be compassionate was most strongly developed. The boy took his book bag and left. When the door shut behind him Rodygin was informed by someone in back with knowledge of the matter.

"He's not coming back."

Vekshina hiccuped again.

"Sit down," Rodygin told her.

She sat down, catching her book bag between her knees; it had fallen out of its cubby, and her textbooks and notebooks had scattered over the floor. The little glass slipper from last winter's vacation, which she kept in her bag always as a reminder that happiness was possible, flew off separately.

Rodygin picked it up and ran his finger thoughtfully over the cut above the heel, made to hold an unfinished cigarette.

"Why are you carrying this ashtray with you?" he asked.

"Give it back," Vekshina said, stuffing everything that had fallen out back into her bag.

The little imp in her throat jerked his foot one last time and jumped through the open pane and into the rain, which lashed at the windows for another five minutes or so, swathing the class in its steady, hypnotic drone.

"Is this your papa's ashtray?" Rodygin asked.

"My papa doesn't smoke," Vekshina answered.

"Don't lie. Someone who drinks, smokes," post-pubescent Vera with the green chin shared her life's experience.

Rodygin passed through the class holding the slipper on his palm, feeling Vekshina's eyes on him the whole time, even though she not only did not turn her head in his direction but did not even move her pupils. She was watching as if she'd been drawn on a propaganda poster. Rodygin felt like the victim of an optical illusion.

"I hope," he said, "there aren't any children in your class who already smoke."

"Filimonov smokes," the cheerful boy squealed as he climbed out from under his desk again.

"And he drinks," someone added from behind, and he snorted.

"Give it back, please," Vekshina asked again.

Rodygin hesitated. Fate had sent him a marvelous graphic aid for a story about the harm of smoking. He didn't want to part with it, but he still didn't know the right way to use it. His thoughts slid along the lines of the idea of the beauty of the slipper, with its feminine curves and sharp predatory nose being the beauty of sin, and you had to know how to tell it from genuine beauty, which makes a person better and doesn't arouse base desires in him. He had even started talking about this, choosing his words with difficulty, but he was interrupted by two well-dressed girls at the same desk.

"Please, give it back to her! Yes, please!" they whined, looking at Rodygin brazenly and lovingly at each other.

"Or I won't tell you about anything else!" the well-read boy threatened.

At that moment Rodygin suddenly realized that he still hadn't talked about the scariest thing, even scarier than smoking and even alcohol. You had to talk about drugs with extreme caution to an audience of children, but he was already off and running. Surprising himself, he plunged right in, asking,

"Who knows what *mulka* is?"

The room got quiet. Rodygin squinted.

"Does anyone know? Be honest."

"That's what we call our cat," the transparent little girl said timidly, doubting the correctness of her answer.

Everyone burst out laughing, and then she added, "We used to call her Murka, but we renamed her because of my sister."

"Whose?" someone asked from the far window.

"Mine. She's little still and can't say the letter 'r.'"

At this the lesson ended when the bell rang. Through the noise of the rain, the bell sounded weak and uncertain, like an alarm clock ringing under a pillow, not telling you to get up but delicately reminding you of that sad necessity.

The kids fidgeted with excitement. Calming them down, Rodygin raised his hand.

"Quiet! That signal is for me, not you."

He tried to end all his lessons like this, so that he left them with two contradictory feelings simultaneously—the completeness and incompleteness of what he'd said. It wasn't enough just to set out a topic and draw conclusions; you also had to instill in your listeners the notion of the subject's inexhaustibility. Rodygin was a virtuoso of this art, but right now the tropical downpour outside distracted him and kept him from concentrating. "Like in Singapore," he thought, and he saw Vekshina suddenly rush for the door.

She was holding her book bag, but she dropped it the moment Rodygin, who caught up with her in two bounds, grabbed the handle, and she whisked through the door. He felt like a little boy left holding the tail of a lizard that had slipped away. Rodygin tossed the bag on his desk and ran after her; the corridor rushed toward him in a din and shoving, and children's faces raced by, like lights in a tunnel. He ran after Vekshina to give her back her shoe, but she had already dived into the vestibule and flown onto the front steps.

Even here, under the roof, the air was saturated with a prickly drizzle, streams foamed down below, and clumps of clay plopped into the ditch like frogs. She heard the noise of the chase behind her; the heels of the man's heavy boots thundered over the tile.

In the vestibule, the smokers shied away from Rodygin, and in the corner a reedy voice said, "The water's run out."

It was the boy who had gone for water for Vekshina.

"The hot water," he clarified. "In the pot."

Rodygin strode by him and stopped in the doorway.

Vekshina was standing three paces away, at the very edge of the top step. It was as if she had run to the edge of a seaside cliff and was now prepared to throw herself into the water just to escape the person chasing her. The rain was whipping her little face, which was thrown back in infinite despair.

"Here, take it," Rodygin said in a whisper so as not to frighten her, holding the little slipper out to her on his palm.

Vekshina turned around, and then he gave her a companionable wink. She looked in horror at his contorted face and horribly screwed up eye and dashed down the stairs. Rodygin leapt after her, and cold streams ran down his collar. He took a running leap over the ditch, nearly sliding to the bottom on the slippery clay, jumped onto the lawn, and was gripped by a chilly presentiment of the irreparable. There was a red light and Vekshina was approaching the thoroughfare as fast as her legs would carry her. In front of her, splashing through the puddles, rushed a solid stream of cars.

Across the street, hiding under the kiosk awning, Nadezhda Stepanovna saw her and screamed "Stop! Stop!" and ran toward her. Her shoes, stockings, light coat, and under it the back and shoulders of her dress—everything was soaked through instantly; only under her belt was there still a thin layer of warmth. A broad stream seethed and twisted into tails along the edge of the sidewalk. Nadezhda Stepanovna stepped into the street, brakes squealed around her, time stopped, and she felt as if she'd been running in this rain her whole life.

All of a sudden something struck her hard from the side, an incredibly vivid but warm and soft light streamed before her eyes, and to the sound of leaves, not rain, a familiar two-story building with glass humps on the

     LEONID YUZEFOVICH

roof drifted out of the fog. Chrysanthemums were growing right above the ceiling of her small room, which she now saw as clearly and with the same detail as if she'd lived here for years. A narrow bed made up with pink or beige sheets, like on trains, a blanket, and a night table with a lace doily. The stove was hot. Pinned to the wall was a fan of get well cards with little roses and bear cubs from her former pupils. The dinner bell had rung. The doors of the neighboring rooms slammed, and she could hear unhurried steps and quiet laughter. She poked a few pins into the knot of gray hair at her nape and went down the wooden stairs scrubbed white to the dining room. Dinner was the pleasure of other people's company. The warmth of oatmeal and fresh milk and hot tea with jam, but also the warmth that came from understanding, so all the conversations here were about children, every night about children, always about them, the same as in the teacher's lounge of a real school such as she had never had occasion to work in. The abode of the righteous, an island of comfort and love, a heavenly corner extended by the garden that lapped calmly and joyfully out the window.

"Idiot! Where are you going, idiot!" hollered the *muzhik* in the leather cap after he jumped out of his Zhiguli.

Nadezhda Stepanovna stood there, leaning forward, both hands resting on the radiator, but at the same time she had managed not to let go of the two cones of bird cherries. How that had happened, she had no idea. By some miracle the berries were still in the cones, only a few little dark spheres had rolled over the hood and fallen on the asphalt.

Limping, Nadezhda Stepanovna continued across the street. Vekshina had disappeared somewhere, and the rain was pouring without letup. The city seemed to be rising slowly skyward from the waters' abyss. There had been the sensation of flight, but it had been lost, somewhere very close, barely, pushing the earth down, plunging it back into the deep, and lightning had struck.

Nadezhda Stepanovna was already stepping onto the safety of the sidewalk and Rodygin was running across the lawn when everything all around was illuminated by white, a brief and terrifying sizzle pierced the air, there was a sour smell, and steam was being thrown off by the grass, but he no longer saw or heard any of it. Even before, something had passed through him ponderously and soundlessly and plunged into the shuddering earth, knocking him off his feet.

Looking back, Vekshina saw Rodygin being snatched from the shroud of rain by a blindingly white burst, flapping his arms, and collapsing on the grass, where flames were darting. The rain quickly pounded down on them and they went out, hissing angrily, but one little flame lasted longer than the others. It made its way toward Rodygin, danced and bowed, and suddenly turned into that imp who had been sitting in Vekshina's throat five minutes before, jerking its little foot. She recognized him, as he clearly realized, because he immediately got busy and ran off, hiding under the acacia bushes.

8

"He's been killed," Filimonov shouted, staggering back from the window.

Kotova took fright.

"Who?"

Filimonov didn't answer. His whole body was shaking from horror and remorse and he wouldn't look out the window for fear of seeing his victim's charred corpse. Finally Kotova guessed she should go over to the window and see what had frightened him so. A second later she was racing for the phone to call an ambulance.

Thunder clapped mightily over the grocery and school and rolled on, toward the chimney that looked like the minaret of Kalyan. Nadezhda Stepanovna struggled over to the lawn, in the middle of which, like a bonfire site, there was an uneven black spot of burned grass covered with a dissolving little cloud of steam. A man lay on the line between the black and the green. Over him stood a thoroughly soaked Vekshina. She had already found her treasure and wiped it with her hem. The glass slipper was squeezed in her fist with its sharp nose pointing down, like a dagger.

"He was killed by lightning," Vekshina said with a murderous calm that frightened Nadezhda Stepanovna.

By this time the rain was letting up, the clouds were parting, their edges were brightening, and there was a rainbow. Directly in front of him Rodygin saw its steep, flickering, seven-hued bridge. The rainbow started somewhere behind him, but its other end was set precisely in the ditch. That meant a pot of gold was buried there. "They're digging in the right place," Rodygin thought.

The buildings and acacia bushes were spinning around him at 78 rpm. He recognized the familiar speed of the old records, which had been replaced long since by LPs, at 33 rpm. Gradually the spinning slowed and then he heard the click of a tumbler: Stop! He sat up. Vekshina's face appeared through the rainbow fog.

"Take it," Rodygin said, and he held out his empty hand.

Vekshina recoiled and then rushed to Nadezhda Stepanovna, put her arms around her, and sobbed into her belly, her whole skinny little body quaking. She didn't answer the questions about what had happened or where her coat was, she just held on tighter. The key hanging around her neck cut painfully into her belly. Over the child's little head, which smelled like mushrooms, Nadezhda Stepanovna saw the man who had been lying and then sitting on the grass stand up, staggering drunkenly, and head toward them. She recognized Rodygin and gasped.

"Lord! What happened to you?"

"I think I have a contusion. From the lightning," he said.

The next moment Kotova was bearing down on them, shouting that help was on the way, she had called, and the special brigade was en route, so someone should go out on the corner and show them the way.

"No need." Rodygin stopped her.

Vladimir Lvovich came up. Running behind him were the children, with Filimonov ahead of them all. His mouth was open in a soundless scream. When he ran up, Vekshina elbowed him away. She didn't want to share Nadezhda Stepanovna with anyone.

"Oh, Nadezhda Stepanovna!" Vekshina's neighbor tattled inspiredly. "You wouldn't believe what he told us! He told us how they cut off children's feet and they all get put in jail. With their wives."

"Wait a minute, wait. Who do they put in jail?"

"Everyone who, you know . . . Oh, like Vekshina's papa. And they make them walk thirty kilometers."

"With their wives, too?"

"No, with policemen on motorcycles."

"That's how they punish drunk drivers in Turkey," Rodygin hastened to explain himself. "And the wives, that's in Singapore."

"He said even worse things, he did!" a crafty childish voice rang out in the clearing air. "That in foreign countries they chop their heads off right away."

"Chop, chop," one of the children confirmed, "and take the corpse away."

"Filimonov!" someone else clarified.

"Because he's a bad judge of distance," a third added. "People like that don't live long."

"That's why he got feeling sick," Vera, mature beyond her years, summed up with feminine perspicacity.

"I see." Nadezhda Stepanovna nodded and looked questioningly at Rodygin.

He was silent.

"What do you have in your cones?" Filimonov asked.

Only now did Nadezhda Stepanovna remember her bird cherries, which were barely contained in the limp newspaper.

"It's bird cherries," she said. "Eat, children!"

When everyone had crowded around her, they heard the ambulance's high bleeping siren, and the white UAZ flew around the corner at full speed, went through the red light, braked, hopped the curb, and drove onto the lawn. Two men jumped out of the back doors and out of the cab, a woman. Kotova pointed to Rodygin.

"There he is!"

"I'm fine," Rodygin said, after briefly reporting what this was about.

One of the doctors squatted, ran his hand over the ashes, looked at his blackened fingers for a long time, rinsed them in a puddle, slapped Rodygin on the shoulder, and climbed back into the van. The special brigade left, Kotova left, and Rodygin watched from a distance as Nadezhda Stepanovna hand-fed bird cherries to her clamoring flock. Filimonov was grabbing fistfuls and Vekshina was pecking one berry at a time. Vladimir Lvovich, who had been standing off to the side, joined their feasting.

"Remember that crocodile in the museum?" he asked Nadezhda Stepanovna.

"Yes," and she marveled at how the same memories had flooded back to them on the same day.

"I think," Vladimir Lvovich said in a low voice, indicating Rodygin with his eyes, "there's quite a likeness."

"In what way?"

"He's a specimen, too," he answered in the same intimate half-whisper. "But that's all right, their rule will end soon. Mark my word."

Nadezhda Stepanovna said nothing, and Rodygin hadn't heard. Right then the boy who knew all about breadfruit popped up alongside him.

"You promised to answer my question after class," he reminded him.

"Go away," Rodygin said.

His head hurt, his bruised shoulder ached, and for some reason his feet had twinges of pain, as if the celestial electricity dissolved in the soil was shooting through his interstitial soles and heels. At the same time he couldn't shake the feeling that there hadn't been any lightning and that the ashen black spot under his feet had been burned by the heat of his soul, so misunderstood, slandered, and locked inside his old, freezing body.

"Come join us," Nadezhda Stepanovna called out.

Rodygin came over and took a few berries from the offered cone. The forgotten tartness spread over his palate and tears rose in his throat.

"You told us lots of very interesting stories," said the cheerful little boy who had sat under his desk for most of the lesson, and he spat out a pit making the sound of a bullet.

They ate the bird cherries until they were all gone. Their lips, teeth, and tongues turned black. Then they all went to the lunchroom to drink hot tea.

LEONID YUZEFOVICH

We wish to express our deep gratitude to all of the authors and translators who contributed their work to this unique effort. We encourage readers to use this collection as a launchpad to explore the authors' other works.

Special thanks is also due to Galina Dursthoff and Oleg Vavilov, whose tireless efforts spearheaded the original Russian volume, and who arranged the permissions for all the authors included in this special English edition. We also thank Erica Goodoff, who donated her time and effort to proofing this volume. Any errors that slipped through to publication are solely the responsibility of the publisher, who offers his regrets.

Contributors
AUTHORS

ANDREI GELASIMOV was born in 1966 in Irkutsk. In 1987 he graduated from the Foreign Languages Department of Yakutsk State University (YSU). In 1996-1997 he undertook a special course of study at the University of Hull (Great Britain). In 1997, he defended his candidate's (masters) dissertation ("Oriental Motifs in the Works of Oscar Wilde") in English literature at MPGU. In the early 1990s, his translation of Robin Cook's *Sphinx* was published in *Smena*. He was a docent in the department of English philology at YSU, and taught English stylistics; at the same time, he worked on his doctoral dissertation about the peculiarities of novel composition at the end of the 20th century. Since 2002, he has lived in Moscow. His book, *Fox Mulder Looks Like a Pig* (Фокс Малдер похож на свинью) was published in 2001, and the title story in that collection was short-listed for the Belkin prize in 2001. His story *Craving* (Жажда, 2002) was awarded the prestigious Apollon Grigoriev prize. In 2003, his novel, *The Year of Deceit* (Год обмана) was published. In 2009 he won the National Bestseller prize for his novel, *Gods of the Steppe* (Степные боги).

BORIS GREBENSHCHIKOV was born in Leningrad in 1952. In 1972 he and his classmate Anatoly Gunitsky founded the rock group Aquarium. Grebenshchikov first performed on stage in the spring of 1973, and Aquarium debuted in November 1974. The group attained popularity after their performance at a rock festival in Tbilisi in 1980. Yet the group was still forced to perform largely underground, in apartment parties, without official sanction. In the mid-1980s, with the arrival of *glasnost* and *perestroika*, Aquarium emerged from the underground and turned into one of Russia's most popular acts. They were allowed to play in large concert halls, appeared on state-owned television and recorded soundtracks for several films, most notably *ASSA*. Grebenshchikov played the role of a composer and actor in the film *Two Captains-2*

323

(Два капитана-2). Often compared to Bob Dylan for his linguistically rich style and his work across various musical genres, Grebenshchikov has written over 500 original songs.

YEVGENY GRISHKOVETS was born in 1967, in Kemerovo, and studied philology at Kemerovo State University. In 1985, he began three years of military service, serving in the Pacific Fleet. After his discharge, he returned to university and began to get involved in student theatrical productions and various theater festivals. In 1990 he founded the independent theater Lozha, which adhered to the principles of collective improvization, and which put on several plays based on his works. Eight years later, he moved to Kaliningrad. In 1998 he staged his first one-man show, *How I Ate a Dog* (Как я съел собаку), which received the Golden Mask Critics' Prize and Innovation prize. In 1999, he received the Anti-Booker prize for his plays *Notes of a Russian Traveler* (Записки русского путешественника) and *Winter* (Зима), and the following year he received the Triumph prize. He staged his self-authored plays *Simultaneously* (Одновременно), *The Planet* (Планета), *Dreadnoughts* (Дредноуты) and *The Seige* (Осада). Since 2003 he has collaborated with the music group Bigudi and with them recorded the album *Now* (Сейчас, 2003) and *Sing* (Петь, 2004). He has published several books, including *City* (Город, 2001), a collection of plays, *How I Ate a Dog and Other Plays* (2003), the novel *The Shirt* (Рубашка, 2004) and the prose memoir *Rivers* (Реки, 2005).

ALEXANDER KABAKOV was born in 1943. After the war, the Kabakov family (his father was an officer during the war) lived in Kapustny Yar, in Astrakhan oblast, site of the first Soviet rocket proving ground. Kabakov studied at Dnepropetrovsk University and served four years in the army in a rocket brigade. After his discharge he joined the staff of the newspaper *The Siren* (Гудок), where he worked until the advent of *perestroika*, when he moved to the newspaper *Moscow News* (Московские новости). Kabakov began publishing stories in the 1970s, in journals such as *Literary Gazette*, *Moscow Komsomolets* and *Krokodil*. He achieved notoriety with his anti-utopian novella *No Return* (Невозврашенец), which was published in the journal *Film Art* at the peak of *perestroika*. This was followed by *The Compiler* (Сочинитель), and *The Imposter (*Самозванец). Two films have been based on Kabakov's works: *Ten Years Without Right of Correspondence* (Десять лет без права переписки, Vladimir Naumov, 1990) and *No Return* (Sergei Snezhkin, 1991). His 2004 novel *Everything is Reparable* (Все поправимо) won the 2006 Great Book prize, and his 2004 work *Moscow Tales* (Московские сказки) won the 2006 Ivan Bunin prize.

ALEXANDER KHURGIN was born in 1952 in Moscow. In 1974 he graduated from the Dnepropetrovsk Mining Institute and worked for 19 years as a mining engineer. His literary debut was in 1977, as a writer-humorist. Since 1989, when *Ogonyok* published three of his stories, he has focused on what might be called "serious prose." His works have been published in the leading "thick journals" – *Znamya, Druzhba Narodov, Oktyabr, Novy Mir*. His books include *The Superfluous Dozen* (Лишняя десятка, 1991), *What Nonsense* (Какая-то ерунда, 1995), *The Country of Australia* (Страна Австралия, 1997), *Lawrence's Comet* (Комета Лоренца, 1999), *The Return of Desires* (Возвращение желаний, 2000), *Night Cowboy* (Ночной ковбой, 2001) and *Endless Chicken* (Бесконечная курица, 2002). *Lawrence's Comet* and *The Country of Australia* were both nominated for the Booker Prize, and *Lawrence's Comet* received the prize of the International Literary Fund. Literary critic Andrei Nemzer included *The Country of Australia* among the 30 best works of Russian literature of the 1990s. He now lives in Germany.

EDUARD LIMONOV (pen name for Eduard Veniaminovich Savenko) was born in Dzerzhinsk, in 1943, into the family of a military officer. In 1967 he moved to Moscow, where he became part of the literary group Konkret. In 1968 a *samizdat* collection of his poems, *Kropotkin and Other Poems* (Кропоткин и другие стихотворения), was published. In 1974, he emigrated to New York, worked in over a dozen jobs, including as a mover, a waiter and a servant. Beginning in 1979, he became a professional writer with the publication of his scandalous book, *It's Me, Eddie* (Это я – Эдичка), and a collection of poems *Russian* (Русское). In 1980, having ruined his relations with every sector of the Russian emigration, he left New York to live in Paris where, in 1987, he received French citizenship, joined the editorial board of the newspaper *L'Idiot International* and was published in the extreme right wing publication *Shock du Moi*. He moved back to Russia in 1992 and created the National Bolshevik Party, unifying leftist radicals. His provocative and largely autobiographical works include *The Executioner* (Палач, 1986) and *Murder of a Sentinel* (Убийство часового, 1993). His articles and essays are published regularly in the newspaper of the NBP, *Limonka*. Over time, the writer has moved away from literary work to spend most of his time in politics and journalism. In 2001 he was convicted of weapons possession and creation of illegal armed groups and sentenced to four years. While in prison, he wrote *Imprisoned by Dead Men* (В плену у мертвецов), *Russian Psycho* (Русское психо) and *The Holy Monsters* (Священные монстры). In June 2003, Limonov was granted early release and returned to politics and journalism.

DMITRY LIPSKEROV was born in Moscow in 1964. He graduated from the Shchukin Theater School in 1985. In 1989, Oleg Tabakov's Studio Theater performed Lipskerov's play, *River on Asphalt* (Река на асфальте). In 1990, Mark Zakharov's Lenkom staged his *School for Emigrants* (Школа для эмигрантов). In 1996, he published his first novel, *40 Years of Chanchghoe* (Сорок лет Чанчжоэ), in the journal *Novy Mir*. It was later published in book form by Vagrius and made it onto the shortlist for the Russian Booker prize (all of his eight subsequent publications have received nominations for the Russian Booker). In 1998, Lipskerov, together with State Duma Deputy Andrei Skoch, established the independent literary prize Debut. He lives in Moscow and also is a successful restaurant owner.

SERGEI LUKYANENKO was born in 1968, in Kazakhstan. One of Russia's leading science fiction writers of the 20th and early 21st century, he graduated from the Alma-Ata State Medical Institute and began working as a psychiatric doctor while working as deputy editor of the fantasy journal *Worlds* (Миры), published in Alma-Ata. His first published story, *The Violation* (Нарушение), appeared in in the journal *Zarya* (Alma-Ata, 1987). He became widely known with the 1992 publication of his novella *Knights of the 40 Islands* (Рыцари Сорока Островов) and has been a professional author since 1993. He has received numerous prizes for his work and has authored over two dozen books, many of them part of multi-volume tales. His most famous work is the *Nightwatch* series (five books), which has recently been turned into a film trilogy. Several of his other works have been adapted for film, but mainly just the *Nightwatch* books have been translated into English.

VLADIMIR MAKANIN was born in 1937, in Orsk. He graduated from Moscow State University with a mathematics degree and taught at the university level while also taking courses in screenwriting and directing. In 1965, he published his first novel, *Straight Line* (Прямая линия), and the second, *Fatherlessness* (Безотцовщина) followed in 1971. Over the two decades that followed, he produced a new novel almost every year, in many instances collections of new and previously published works. In 1985 he became a member of the Board of Directors of the USSR Union of Writers, and in 1987 joined the editorial board of the prestigious literary journal *Znamya*. Since the early 1980s, Makanin has increasingly employed folkloric and mystical motifs in his works, e.g. *Ancestor* (Предтеча, 1982) and *Loss* (Утрата, 1987). The author of over 20 books, he is a recipient of the Booker Prize (1992) for *Baize-Covered Table with Decanter* (Стол, покрытый сукном и с графином посередине), the Pushkin Prize, awards from the journals *Novy Mir* and *Znamya*, and the State Prize of the Russian Federation. One of his most famous recent novels is *Underground, or A Hero for Our Times* (Андеграунд, или Герой нашего времени, 1999).

MARINA MOSKVINA was born in 1954, in Moscow. After graduating from the journalism faculty at Moscow State University, she worked for *Moskovskaya Pravda* newspaper and in the Progress Publishing House. She began by writing books for children and then teens. Her novel *My Dog Loves Jazz* (Моя собака любит джаз, 1997) was awarded the Andersen International Gold Medal. She has also written several travelogues recounting her travels through the Himalayas, Japan and Nepal. Her first novel for adults was *The Genie of Unrequited Love* (Гений безответной любви, 2000). The novel extracted in this volume was published in 2005. For over a decade she has hosted a radio program *Together with Marina Moskvina* and has led master classes in developing one's creative potential and study of the art of letter writing at the Institute of Contemporary Art.

VICTOR PELEVIN was born in Moscow in 1962. He graduated from the Moscow Institute of Energetics with a specialty in electromechanics, served in the army and finished a course of study at the Literary Institute. For a few years, he worked at the journal *Science and Religion* (Наука и религия), preparing publications on eastern mysticism. His first published work was *The Sorcerer Ignat and People* (Колдун Игнат и люди, 1989), and his first novel was *Omon Ra* (1992). He has written some eight novels and dozens of stories and tales, and his works have been translated into every major world language. A French magazine included Pelevin in one of the world's 1000 most significant figures in world culture (the only other Russian included was film director Alexander Sokurov).

LUDMILA PETRUSHEVSKAYA was born in 1938 in Moscow, into the family of a Moscow State University (MGU) professor. She graduated from MGU and began writing stories in the mid-1960s. In 1972 she began to work as an editor at the Central Television Studio, and two of her short stories were published in the journal *Aurora*. In the mid-1970s, Petrushevskaya got her start as a dramatist. In 1977, Roman Viktyuk staged her play *Music Lessons* (Уроки музыки). In 1979, her one-act play, *Love* (Любовь), was published in the journal *Teatr* and, during the 1981-82 season, was included in a production of three short plays at Yuri Lyubimov's Taganka Theater. In 1983, her plays *A Glass of Water* (Стакан воды) and *Music Lessons* were staged in Moscow, and Mark Zakharov produced *Three Girls in Blue* (Три девушки в голубом) at Lenkom. Petrushevskaya gained wide notoriety with her play *The Columbine's Apartment* (Квартира Коломбины, 1985), staged at the Sovremmenik Theater. Petrushevskaya's first collection of prose, *Immortal Love* (Бессмертная любовь) was published in 1987. She was shortlisted for the first Russian Booker Prize and in 1991 received the German Pushkin Prize.

ZAHAR PRILEPIN (pen name for Yevgeny Lavlinsky) was born in 1975, in the village of Ilyinka, Ryazan oblast. He graduated from the philology department of Nizhegorodsky University, served in the OMON as a squad commander and saw action in Chechnya (1996 and 1999). His poetry began to be published in 2003. His novel *Pathology* (Патологии, 2004), about the war in Chechnya, received great critical and public acclaim, and was followed in 2006 by his second novel, *Sanka*, the story of a simple provincial boy who joins a young revolutionaries' party. His novel in stories *Sin* (Грех, 2007) received the National Bestseller prize and *Sanka* received the Yasnaya Polyana literary prize, in the category "21st Century." A member of the Nizhny Novgorod division of the National Bolshevik Party, he has taken part in dozens of leftist radical political demonstrations. He is presently editor of the regional analytical portal *Agency for Political News – Nizhny Novgorod*. He has been a recipient of the Boris Sokolov Prize (2004) and the prize of the newspaper *Literary Russia* (2004).

DINA RUBINA was born in Tashkent in 1953. She graduated from the Tashkent Conservatory and taught in the Institute of Culture in Tashkent. She lived for a time in Moscow before emigrating to Israel in 1990. Her first literary works were published in the journal *Youth* (Юность). A recipient of the Aryeh Dulchin literary prize (for her book *Duplicate Family*, Двойная фамилия, 1990) and the Israeli Union of Writers prize (for her book, *One Intellectual Sat Down in the Road*, Один интеллигент уселся на дороге, 1995). *Duplicate Family* was translated into French and published in 1996 by the ACTES SUD publishing house (Paris, Nice), and received a prestigious award from French booksellers as the best book of the season. Rubina's works have twice been nominated for the Booker Prize and she is a recipient (2007) of the Great Book prize, for her novel *On the Sunny Side of the Street* (На солнечной стороне улицы). She has a son from her first marriage and a daughter from her second.

DUNYA SMIRNOVA was born in 1969 in Moscow. She is the daughter of the famous film director and actor Andrei Smirnov, and the granddaughter of the Soviet writer Sergei Smirnov. She studied at Moscow State University, in the department of philology, and worked as a journalist at *Kommersant* and as a book reviewer for *Afisha*. She has written scripts for the documentaries *Butterfly Stroke* (Баттерфляй), *The Last Hero* (Последний герой) as well as for the fiction films *Giselle's Mania* (Мания Жизели, 1995), *His Wife's Diary* (Дневник его жены, 2000), *A Stroll* (Прогулка, 2003), all directed by Alexei Uchitel, whom she has collaborated with since 1995. Her screenplay for *His Wife's Diary* received second prize in the Harley-Merrill International Screening Competition. Together with Tatyana Tolstaya, Smirnova presents the Culture TV program *School for Scandal* (Школа злословия). She lives with her husband and son in St. Petersburg.

VLADIMIR SOROKIN was born in the town of Bykovo, near Moscow, in 1955. He graduated from the Moscow Institute of Oil and Gas and for several years earned his living drawing illustrations for books by other authors. He gained his first literary experiences in the early 1970s. His works are vivid examples of the underground culture and thus could not be published in his homeland during the Soviet era. In 1985 the Parisian journal *А–Я* published a collection of six of his stories. That same year his novel *The Queue* (Очередь) was also published. In 1989 *Russian Grandmother* (Русская бабушка) was published in Germany. That year, his works also began to be published in the USSR. Sorokin's works, in particular his novels – *The Queue, Marina's Thirtieth Love* (Тридцатая любовь Марины, 1987), *The Norm* (Норма, 1994) – are consistently countercultural in style and contain shocking naturalistic scenes that parody the literature of Socialist Realism. His books have been translated into at least 10 languages.

VLADIMIR VOINOVICH was born in Dushanbe. In May of 1941, he and his father moved to Zaporozhe, and then came the war, evacuation and continued relocations throughout the USSR. He worked as a shepherd, a carpenter, a fitter, an airline mechanic, a rural instructor, and a national radio editor. He served in the army from 1951-1955, during which time he began to write poems, then shifted to prose. In 1962 he was admitted to the USSR Union of Writers. Beginning in 1966, he participated in a human rights movement. Because of this, and because of his unfavorable portrayal of Soviet reality in his novel *The Life and Extraordinary Adventures of Private Ivan Chonkin* (Жизнь и необычайные приключения солдата Ивана Чонкина), he was subjected to persecution. In 1974 he was expelled from the Union of Writers, and in 1980, under pressure from the Powers that Be, was forced to emigrate. In 1981, by a decree of Leonid Brezhnev, he was stripped of his Soviet citizenship, only to have it returned 10 years later by the pen of Mikhail Gorbachev. While in emigration, he lived in Germany and the US, where, aside from *Chonkin*, he had several works published, including *By Means of Mutual Correspondence* (Путем взаимной переписки), *Ivankiada, Shapka, Moscow 2042, The Anti-Soviet Soviet Union* (Антисоветский Советский Союз), the plays *Tribunal* and *Fictitious Marriage* (Фиктивный брак), as well as numerous stories, poems and essays. His books have been translated into more than 30 languages.

VICTOR YEROFEYEV was born in Moscow, in 1947, into the family of a diplomat. During his childhood, he lived for a few years in Paris. In 1970, he graduated from the department of philology at Moscow State University, and in 1973 completed his graduate studies in world literature. He gained notoriety for his 1973 essay on the Marquis de Sade, published in the journal *Questions of Literature* (Вопросы литерартуры). In 1975, he defended his dissertation, *Dostoyevsky and French Existentialism*. In 1979 he was expelled from the Union of Writers for helping to organize the *samizdat* almanac *Metropol*, and was not published in the Soviet Union again until 1988. Since its publication in 1989, his essay *A Funeral Feast for Soviet Literature* (Поминки по советской литературе) has been the subject of sharp debate. In 1990, his novel *Russian Beauty* (Русская красавица) was published – an international bestseller which has been translated into more than 20 languages His story, *Life With an Idiot* (Жизнь с идиотом), was the basis for a 1992 opera by composer Alfred Shnitke and a 1993 film by director Alexander Rogozhkin. In addition to *Russian Beauty*, he has published (in Russia, Europe and the US, where he often travels to lecture) books of stories, a collection of literary-philosophical essays, *In the Labyrinth of Cursed Questions* (В лабиринте проклятых вопросов), and the novel *The Last Judgement* (Страшный суд, 1996). Other books include *Russian Flowers of Evil* (Русские цветы зла), *Men* (Мужчины) and *Five Rivers of Life* (Пять рек жизни). In 1994-1996, the Collected Works of Viktor Yerofeyev was published in three volumes.

LEONID YUZEFOVICH was born in 1947 in Moscow, into a family of white-collar workers. In 1970 he graduated from Perm University and worked as a middle school history teacher. He did scholarly research and became a Candidate in Historical Sciences. He began to be published in 1977, debuting with the story *Engaged with Liberty* (Обручение с вольностью), published in the journal *Ural*. He achieved fame as a writer with his novels about the head of the St. Petersburg investigative police, Ivan Dmitriyevich Putilin (1830-1893) – *The Harlequin's Costume* (Костюм Арлекина), *Meeting House* (Дом свиданий) and *Prince of the Wind* (Князь ветра), which received the 2001 National Bestseller prize. In 2002 he published the historical detective novel *Kazarova*, which concerns the 1920 investigation of the death of the eponymous singer and actress. The following year saw the release of *Sand Riders* (Песчаные всадники), based on one of the legends of the notorious Baron Ungern von Sternberg. A frequent writer for the journals *Znamya* and *Druzhba Narodov*, he also publishes reviews in the journal *Novy Mir*.

TRANSLATORS

ALEXEI BAYER was born in Russia but has lived in New York since 1974, where he is an independent economist and writer. Over the years, his fiction has appeared in various U.S. literary journals. His latest story will be published in September in *KR Online*, a *Kenyon Review* web project. He translated several of Andrei Gelasimov's stories into English. His own collection, *Eurotrash* (OGI, Moscow, 2004), was translated into Russian by Gelasimov.

MICHELE A. BERDY is a Moscow-based translator and writer. In addition to translating nonfiction, fiction and films, she writes a weekly column on language and translation for *The Moscow Times*. Her book reviews and articles on culture, current events and various aspects of intercultural communication have appeared in the Russian and English-language press. She has written or co-authored four guidebooks about Moscow, St. Petersburg and Russia, as well as a Russian-English dictionary.

LIV BLISS began her translation career in Moscow, with Progress Publishers and Novosti Press Agency, in the late 1970s and has been a happy freelance translator, editor, and language consultant ever since. She has an American Translators Association certification in Russian to English translation, and is on the editorial board of *SlavFile*, the ATA's Slavic Languages Division newsletter. She lives in the White Mountains of Arizona with her husband, Jim, and an assortment of far wilder creatures. Her translation of *Godsdoom; the Book of Hagen*, by Nick Perumov, was published by Zumaya Publications in 2007.

LISE BRODY has translated literature and critical works by Elena Makarova, Liudmila Petrushevskaya, Tatiana Mamonova and others. She is also a choreographer and interdisciplinary artist and taught high school for many years. She lives in Providence, RI.

NORA SELIGMAN FAVOROV has been struggling for decades to figure out the best way to express Russian thought in literate and natural English, a game she considers more entertaining than any crossword puzzle. Her most recent published translation is *Master of the House: Stalin and His Inner Circle* by Oleg Khlevniuk (Yale UP: 2008). She is associate editor of SlavFile, a newsletter for Slavic translators and interpreters. The name "Favorov" was acquired from her Russian husband, Oleg, whom she met in 1978 during a year-long stay in Moscow. They have two children and live in Chapel Hill, NC.

ANNE O. FISHER grew up in Oklahoma, got her Ph.D. in Michigan, and has taught in Michigan, Ohio, and Massachusetts. She has translated Ilf and Petrov's account of their 1935-36 road trip through the U.S. (*Ilf & Petrov's American Road Trip*, Cabinet Books and Princeton Architectural Press) as well as articles on Ilf and Petrov and artists' statements by contemporary Russian artists. She currently resides in Louisville, Kentucky, where she is working as a freelance court interpreter and juggling several translation projects, including new translations of Ilf and Petrov's two novels about Ostap Bender, a biography of Ilf and translation of Ilf's diaries (with the author's daughter Aleksandra Ilf), and the poetry of Maxim Amelin.

DEBORAH HOFFMAN is an attorney and freelance translator. She was the recipient of a 2005 PEN Translation Fund Grant for her translations from *Deti Gulaga*, to be published by Slavica in 2009. Her translations have appeared in the *Toronto Slavic Quarterly, The Literary Review*, and *Words Without Borders*. She was a Fellow for the American Literary Translators Association Conference in 2008. She lives in Ohio with her husband and three children.

MARCIA KARP has poems and translations in *Partisan Review, The Republic of Letters, Literary Imagination, The Guardian,Seneca Review, Agenda, Harvard Review, Ploughshares,* Penguin Books' *Catullus in English* and *Petrarch in English, Pusteblume,* the *Times Literary Supplement, The Warwick Review*, and forthcoming in WW Norton's *Contemporary Poets Translate Anglo-Saxon Poems*. She read her poems at Balliol College at the invitation of the Oxford Professor of Poetry, Christopher Ricks, during one of his residencies. She teaches at Boston University.

MICHAEL KATZ is C.V. Starr Professor of Russian and East European Studies at Middlebury College, where he served as Dean of Language Schools and Schools Abroad from 1998-2004. He previously taught at Williams College and at the University of Texas, Austin. He has written two monographs on Russian literature and translated numerous novels and short stories, including works by Herzen, Chernyshevsky, Dostoevsky, Turgenev, Artsybashev, and Jabotinsky. His latest translation, of *The Dacha Husband* by Ivan Shcheglov, will be published this fall published by Northwestern University Press..

DENIS KOMAROV is originally from Kaluga, Russia, where he attended the State Pedagogical University. In 2009, he received his degree in translation and interpretation from the Russian State University for the Humanities in Moscow. He is currently working as a translator at the Russian Ministry for Foreign Affairs.

PETER MORLEY is a London-based translator. A former arts editor of *The St. Petersburg Times*, he has also worked for *The Moscow Times, Russia Profile, Bloomberg News, St. Petersburg in Your Pocket*, and the OSCE. His translations range from reports on Russia's nuclear sector to academic papers on international development and a book on Marshal Mannerheim.

PAUL E. RICHARDSON is Publisher and Editor of *Russian Life,* and oversees all editorial, design, production and management out of the magazine's office in Montpelier, Vermont. Involved in US-Russian business for over 20 years, Richardson was deputy director of one of the first Soviet-Western joint ventures in Moscow in 1989 and 1990, and has a master's degree in Political Science and a Russian Area Studies Certificate from Indiana University, Bloomington. He has written numerous articles for *Russian Life* and frequently translates works for both *Russian Life* and *Chtenia*.

MARIAN SCHWARTZ is a prize-winning translator of Russian fiction, history, biography, criticism, and fine art, including works by classic authors Nina Berberova, Mikhail Bulgakov, Ivan Goncharov, and Mikhail Lermontov as well as contemporary authors such as Edvard Radzinsky and Olga Slavnikova. Schwartz is the recipient of two translation fellowships from the National Endowment for the Arts and is a past president of the American Literary Translators Association.

ANNA SELUYANOVA was born and raised in Moscow. Having earned her undergraduate degree in Philosophy, she is currently a doctoral student and teaching fellow at the Editorial Institute at Boston University, a graduate program that trains textual scholars. Anna lives in Cambridge, Massachusetts.

BELA SHAYEVICH is a writer and translator living in New York City. She is the Russian Editor-At-Large of *Calque*.

NINA SHEVCHUK-MURRAY was born and raised in the western Ukrainian city of L'viv. She holds degrees in English linguistics and Creative Writing. She translates both poetry and prose from the Russian and Ukrainian languages. Her translations and original poetry have been published in a number of literary magazines. With Ladette Randolph, she co-edited the anthology of Nebraska non-fiction *The Big Empty* (U of NE Press, 2007).